'TIS the
SEASON

Books By Jennifer Gracen

'Tis the Season

Someone Like You

More Than You Know

Published by Kensington Publishing Corporation

'TIS the SEASON

Jennifer Gracen

ZEBRA BOOKS
KENSINGTON PUBLISHING CORP.
http://www.kensingtonbooks.com

ZEBRA BOOKS are published by

Kensington Publishing Corp.
119 West 40th Street
New York, NY 10018

All Kensington titles, imprints, and distributed lines are available at special quantity discounts for bulk purchases for sales promotion, premiums, fund-raising, educational, or institutional use.

Special book excerpts or customized printings can also be created to fit specific needs. For details, write or phone the office of the Kensington Sales Manager: Attn.: Sales Department. Kensington Publishing Corp., 119 West 40th Street, New York, NY 10018. Phone: 1-800-221-2647.

Zebra and the Z logo Reg. U.S. Pat. & TM Off.

First Printing: October 2016
ISBN-13: 978-1-4201-3918-1
ISBN-10: 1-4201-3918-5

eISBN-13: 978-1-4201-3919-8
eISBN-10: 1-4201-3919-3

10 9 8 7 6 5 4 3 2 1

Printed in the United States of America

ACKNOWLEDGMENTS

To paraphrase Hillary Rodham Clinton, every book takes a village. With each new book, I'm only even more grateful to the people who make it happen.

Endless thanks to my editor, the talented and fabulous Esi Sogah. I gave you a bit of a run for it with this one. You were nothing but gracious and supportive, assuring me we'd get it on track. With your suggestions and feedback, I think I did. I hope I did! Thank you for all of it.

Thank you, Stephany Evans of FinePrint Literary, my wonderful agent. I'm always able to relax knowing you're in my corner and looking out for me.

Thank you to everyone at Kensington who has been involved with me and my books—my copy editor, the art department, publicity, marketing—and in particular, Jane Nutter, Lauren Jernigan, Ross Plotkin, and Vida Engstrand. I very much appreciate what you do. You guys all make me feel like a rock star.

Thanks and love to my immediate family: my mom, Linda; my dad, Rob; my brother, Jamie; Natasha, Kyle, Teri, and Stevie. The past year has been so full of challenges for me, and you stuck by me like an army of warriors. Thank you so much for your support, now and always. And to my vibrant, amazing sons, Josh and Danny—you're my reason for everything, and I'm so proud and lucky to be your mom.

To all of my friends, both in person and online, your unwavering support, enthusiasm, and kindness buoys and sustains me more than you know, and I'm beyond grateful for all of you. Thank you, thank you. Also, thanks to Team Gracen on FB and LIRW for your support.

Special hugs and shout-outs to: my local Long Island writing sisters, the Hive tribe, who can fill up a group thread with 50+ texts faster than I can blink. Love you all. And to my online writing group that's become something of an eclectic online family: the FB group The Phoenix Quill. I adore you all in this merry group; thanks for being out there.

And most of all, an endless thank you to my readers. That you carve some time out of your busy lives to read my books means the world to me, and I am deeply touched and grateful. Without you, there is no wonderful ride. Thanks for taking it with me.

Chapter One

The last thing in the world Charles Harrison III wanted was a big party for his fortieth birthday, but it wasn't like he'd had much choice in the matter. His sister Tess had told him that she wanted to have a little family get-together for his upcoming birthday, and he'd agreed to let her. But when he'd showed up at the Kingston Point Yacht Club, the "little family get-together" was actually a huge surprise party, with more than two hundred relatives, friends, and business associates crowded into the largest ballroom.

He truly appreciated Tess's efforts and intentions . . . but Jesus Christ, he did *not* want to celebrate his big milestone birthday. He'd been swatting away flashes of uneasy angst about it for weeks.

Even now, nursing the one scotch he allowed himself at public gatherings, he looked around the packed room and couldn't shake the feeling that had gripped him recently with a vengeance: the sense that something was missing.

"Tripp!" His father's steely voice boomed from a few feet away. Only his father and his father's old friends still called him that. Charles turned to see his father waving him over to where his father stood with four older men, all equally distinguished and polished. *A pack of sharks*,

Charles thought fleetingly as he made his way to them. His father, Charles Roger Harrison II, didn't have friends; he had business cronies. It was hard to keep friends when you were a multibillionaire in charge of an international conglomerate, and heir to a family legacy of four generations. Hard to trust anyone, and hard to know if you were genuinely liked. Charles knew that better than anyone, because it held true for him as well.

"Still can't believe my oldest is forty years old," Charles II said, giving his son a hearty slap on the back. "Especially when I'm still only thirty-nine."

The other men laughed as Charles commented, "Ah now, Dad, you don't look a day over thirty-eight."

"Atta boy." The patriarch tapped his glass of scotch to his son's. "Listen. We were just discussing the Benson Industries merger. I was thinking—"

"Do we have to discuss this now?" Charles asked, a stab of annoyance piercing him. "It's my birthday. Tonight, I'm off the clock."

"You're never off the clock, Tripp." Charles II's voice was light, but his gray eyes glinted like blades. "You're COO of Harrison Enterprises. Sun never sets on our empire. Want to keep it that way, you're never off the clock. God knows I've never been. Now"—he held his son's gaze for a long beat— "about the merger."

Charles bit back a sigh and let his father continue. At times like this, Charles wished he allowed himself more than one drink at a party. But the heir to the throne had to be in control and proficient at all times. Above reproach. There was no room to ever be even slightly drunk in public, or to be drunk enough to be gossiped about negatively, or to be off the clock, or to just . . . be.

His entire life, since childhood, Charles hadn't been able to think about much of anything but his place in the family company. As his father droned on about business in the middle of what was supposed to be a party, Charles longed for the ability to just walk away. Of course, he never would. He'd been too well trained. Groomed to be proper, reputable, capable, sophisticated, and most important, to be the shining example of the next generation of Harrisons. From the day he was born.

Charles took a long sip of his scotch as his father's associates launched into the pros and cons of the merger. He gazed at his father's face, the wrinkles and deep frown lines etched into his skin, and thought, *Forty years down . . . forty or so to go.*

Lisette Gardner sat quietly at the round table in the corner with the three kids, who were all completely consumed by their handheld electronic devices. Being the live-in nanny to Charles Harrison III's children was a full-time, arduous task, but she truly loved her job. She glanced at each of them, their dark heads bowed over their games. They were often difficult, but she understood why and had tried to be a source of warmth for them since her first day on the job.

The oldest was feisty Ava, nine going on nineteen, her tongue already as sharp as a teenager's; then sullen Thomas, who already at seven and a half barely swallowed his resentment every day; and little Myles, just turned six a few weeks before, who was rambunctious, but as sweet as they came. They were never boring, that was for sure. Myles was the friendliest of the children—probably because he had only been eighteen months old when his parents had divorced and his mother had moved across the country, so he'd never known a different life. The other two remembered what it was like to have their mother in their lives, and felt the absence more keenly.

Lisette reached over to run her hand over Myles's dark, wavy hair, and he looked up from his game for two seconds to flash a smile. She smiled back before his eyes went back down to the screen. He was the most affectionate, but really, she adored all three. In her almost two years with the kids, she'd watched them grow, and had grown to care for them so deeply she sometimes felt like they were hers. Which was understandable, since she was with them day in, day out, five or six days a week. Caring for the Harrison children was her whole life. And she was fine with that.

"I'm bored," Thomas grumbled without even looking up from his tablet.

"Me too," Ava said. "Why do we have to be here?" Her bright blue eyes, so like her father's, regarded Lisette with irritation. "It's not like Dad even cares we're here."

"Of course he does," Lisette said. "Don't say that."

"He hasn't come over to see us since we got here," Thomas said. "Not once."

"I want cookies," Myles said, and yawned.

Lisette glanced at her watch. It was almost nine, and even though it was a Saturday, it was the kids' bedtime. "It's too late for cookies, sweetheart," she said. If they were home, they'd be doing the nightly routine for bed right then. "You know what? Let me talk to your father. It is your bedtime . . ."

"I want to go home," Thomas said.

"Me too," Ava said. "This party's boring. It's for grownups. We're just . . . on display."

Lisette marveled at how astute the nine-year-old girl was. In this instance, it was sad. "I'll be right back," she said, rising to stand. "You guys stay here, okay? Be good."

"Okay, Set." Myles singsonged the nickname he used for her.

She smoothed out her dress and scanned the crowd, searching for her employer. Among the guests, she spotted the always charming middle Harrison brother, Dane, holding court near the bar with his arm around his sexy wife, Julia. Next to them were the youngest brother, Pierce, and his girlfriend, Abby. Lisette had gotten to know Pierce and Abby well, and she liked them. They came over once a week to see the kids, taking them out to the movies or the park, anywhere that was fun. The kids adored their lively uncle and always looked forward to his visits.

Ah. There was Charles, across the room by the large floor-to-ceiling windows, talking with a group of men that included the Harrison patriarch. Talking business no doubt, she thought, as she started to weave her way through the crowd in her boss's direction.

She found Charles fascinating. He always carried himself with such focus, attentive as a hawk to everything around him. For the most part he was a serious man, exuding intelligence, confidence, and quiet power. His manners were impeccable, and his poise and composure were renowned. But as Lisette had grown to know him, she'd seen glimpses of the humor and warmth he hid from the world and stuffed down inside. At home, alone with his children, was the only time she saw him smile freely or heard him laugh. And even then, it wasn't often enough.

Now, Charles smiled mildly at something his father said, but she could see the smile didn't reach his eyes. He wasn't enjoying himself, which was a shame, considering he was the guest of honor. And a very handsome guest of honor, at that. His face, all angles and strong lines, was a study in masculine beauty. At his temples there were already a few glints of silver in his wavy dark hair, proof of his stressful career. There was an urbane sophistication about him; he'd been born to that. Tall, lean, broad-shouldered, his build was flattered by the lines of his navy suit, and his pale blue shirt set off his bright blue eyes. Instead of his black-rimmed glasses, he'd opted for contact lenses tonight, showcasing those captivating eyes, which locked on her now as she approached. Her heart gave a tiny flutter, as it often did when he focused on her.

Before she could even speak, Charles's brow furrowed with concern. "Is everything all right with the kids?"

"Fine," she assured him quickly. Her voice always felt softer, smaller in her throat when she spoke to him, but especially in front of others. The other men, all in their sixties, were either ignoring her or studying her. She cleared her throat and said, "But they're getting tired. It *is* their usual bedtime. I was wondering if you'd mind if I took them home."

"Is it?" Charles flicked a quick glance at his Rolex. "Damn, you're right. Of course, take them home. They're probably bored anyway. I'll catch a ride with Tess."

She smiled demurely, grateful for his understanding.

"Hell no!" Charles's father said with disdain. "They're Harrisons. It's your birthday. They should be here. They have their video games; they'll be fine."

Biting the inside of her cheek to keep quiet, Lisette just stared. That man proved over and over that he was the coldest, most selfish bastard she'd ever met. How someone as wonderful as Charles had come from someone as horrid as his father, she'd never know.

Charles turned to glare at his father. "Dad. They're young children. They're bored, and they're tired. They've been here long enough. Now they're going home."

Charles II just snorted, rolled his eyes, and looked around at his cronies, his expression condescending as he shrugged. "Pandering to children. I thought you were smarter than that."

Feeling his blood pressure rise, Charles reined in his temper as he replied evenly, "I'm smart enough to know what young kids need and to respect that. Excuse us." He turned his back on the group of men, grasping Lisette gently by the elbow and walking away with her.

"He's such an ass," Charles muttered.

Lisette only nodded in response.

"Thank you for finding me on this," Charles continued. "I didn't realize what time it was. Also, you got me away from that pack of wolves. I owe you."

Lisette finally cracked a tiny grin. "Didn't know I was on a rescue mission."

"I should have sent up smoke signals." He grinned back and looked down at her, stopping a few feet from the kids' table. "I hope you got something to eat here? The food's pretty good."

"I did, thank you. The children did also."

"Good." Charles's eyes skimmed over Lisette briefly. All night, it had felt like his effort not to stare at her was an exercise in restraint. Because she didn't get dressed up and made up like this very often, and the problem was, she looked beautiful. Wearing a simple sheath dress of burgundy silk and matching heels that showed off her shapely calves, her thick dark hair up in an elegant twisty bun and her coffee-colored eyes set off by smoky makeup, she looked like one of the glamorous socialites who crammed the room. Actually, she was one of the prettiest women in the whole place.

Even in her usual attire—plain tops and yoga pants, hair in a braid or ponytail and little or no makeup—he'd always thought Lisette was attractive. But tonight, from the minute she'd come down from her room . . . Every time he looked at her, something hot and hungry hummed in his veins. It had taken him off guard, these new stirrings, and he wasn't comfortable with it. Nevertheless, he suddenly felt compelled to say some of what he was thinking out loud. "You look really lovely tonight, by the way. I'm not used to seeing you all dressed up like this."

A soft blush colored her cheeks, and her dark eyes rounded

before flickering away shyly. "Tess said to dress up, so . . ." Lisette shrugged. "Thank you," she murmured.

"You're welcome. That color is great on you." He realized he was staring and cleared his throat. Many times he'd cursed himself for hiring a nanny who was beautiful. Tonight was no exception. In fact, tonight he was cursing himself for it more than ever. It was more than a distraction, it was . . . What the hell was it? He walked over to his children, sitting at a table looking bored out of their minds. "Hey, guys."

"Hi, Daddy!" Myles smiled and shot out of his chair into his father's arms. "Are you having a fun birthday party?"

"It's fine," Charles said, hugging his youngest. "But you know what? Lisette said you guys are kind of bored. And it's past your bedtime. She's going to take you all home now, so I wanted to say good night."

Myles hugged his father tighter. "I love you, Daddy."

Charles's heart filled. He kissed the top of his son's head. "I love you too, little man." He looked over at his other two kids. "Anyone else have a hug for your dad?"

Ava put her tablet down and got up slowly, circling the table to give her father a weak hug. Thomas didn't even look up from his tablet; he kept playing his game with total concentration.

Charles hugged his daughter, then said to Thomas, "Didn't you hear me?"

"I heard you," Thomas grumbled, still not looking up. "Good night."

Charles felt the sting. His middle child was so full of anger; it worried him. Sometimes, Thomas reminded Charles of his youngest brother. As a kid, Pierce had been surly like that, full of simmering hostility all the time. He'd been miserable growing up, with no mother to nurture him and under constant attack from their father. But Charles never attacked Thomas. He made sure that Thomas felt cared for, didn't he? So why was Thomas still so angry all the time? Swallowing a sigh, Charles said, "Thomas. It's my birthday. A hug good night would be nice. Indulge me."

Thomas's eyes flickered up at his father, then down to his game again.

Before Charles could say a word, Lisette moved in behind the boy and whispered something in his ear, taking the tablet out of his hands as she did. Thomas gave a rebellious whine of annoyance, but pushed back from the table and got up. He hugged his father, quickly and with no warmth. "Happy Birthday." Then he went back to Lisette. "Can I have my tablet back now?"

"In the car," she said, her voice firm and quiet.

She was a magician; Charles was sure of it. She handled the kids, especially Thomas, with skills he simply didn't possess. Patience, warmth, understanding, yet firm with discipline when necessary . . . God, he was grateful for her. The three nannies he'd gone through before her combined hadn't connected with his kids like she had. Lisette was a jewel. She was wonderful with his children, and they responded to her better than they did to him. That was the truth.

She turned to the kids and said, "Come on, team. Time to go home."

"But I wanna say good-bye to Uncle Pierce and Abby," Myles protested.

At that, Thomas perked up. "Yeah, me too."

"And Aunt Tess," Ava added. "And Uncle Dane and Aunt Julia."

Charles stuffed his hands in his pockets. He'd had to all but beg for good-byes, but the kids adored his siblings. Yeah, that stung too. "Go ahead. Lisette and I will wait for you here. But come back in five minutes, no more than that."

The kids all ran off to find their uncles and aunts.

Watching them, he sighed and murmured, "They hate me, don't they?"

Lisette turned to him, wide-eyed. "Of course not!"

He arched a brow and stared her down. "Thomas?"

She couldn't hide the look in her eyes or the way she shifted how she stood. "He doesn't hate you."

"He doesn't like me, either."

She obviously didn't know what to say; her gaze fell to the floor. "He's got . . . a lot of unresolved anger," she said quietly. "That's all."

"That's all?" Charles snorted. "I'd say it's a little more than that."

Lisette said nothing, suddenly fascinated with smoothing out her dress.

Charles looked up again to see Pierce lift Thomas into his arms for a big hug. Ava and Myles had been surrounded by Abby, Dane, Julia, and Tess. Big smiles and warm good-byes were being exchanged all around. "Thomas likes his uncles more than his own father."

"Lots of kids are like that," Lisette said weakly.

"Yeah. In their teens. He's seven. Seven-year-old boys usually worship their fathers."

"Did you?" she asked.

"Sure. My father was larger than life." Charles shrugged. "When I was seven, I didn't realize what a hard-ass he was. He always treated me like gold. I thought I'd done the same for my kids, but . . ."

Lisette was quiet for a long moment, then said cautiously, "Have you considered that Thomas might benefit from therapy?"

It was as if she'd punched him in the stomach. He gaped at her. "Therapy? He's only seven years old!"

"So?" Lisette's eyes held his. "If he's this angry all the time, maybe he needs help."

God, she was right. Why did his nanny have to tell him how to handle his own child? Feeling foolish and uncomfortable, Charles ran a hand over the back of his neck and looked back out to the crowd. But he always admitted if he was in the wrong. Always. "I'll think about it," he said quietly.

The kids threaded their way through the crowd, back to where he and Lisette stood. "We're ready to go home now," Myles said with a smile, then yawned.

As Lisette went to retrieve the tablets from the tabletop, Charles leaned down to kiss each of his kids on the cheek. "I love you all," he said to the three of them. "See you in the morning."

"You don't have to go to work?" Myles asked.

"No, silly," Ava said to him. "Tomorrow's Sunday."

"So?" Thomas retorted. "Dad's at work *all* the time. Doesn't matter if it's a weekend. He goes in anyway."

Charles looked down at his middle child and said firmly, "I'll be home. I'm not going to work. Okay?"

Thomas shrugged. "Whatever."

Jesus, Charles thought. This is worse than I thought. "How about we all do something fun tomorrow?" he said. "It's October, we can go apple picking."

"Apple picking was September," Thomas snapped. "We did that with Uncle Pierce and Abby. You were away on a business trip."

Charles winced inside, but schooled his features into neutrality. "My mistake. How about pumpkin picking, then? Today's October twentieth. There's got to be a few left out there. We can drive out east, make a day of it. Do some fun fall stuff."

"Yes!" Myles bounced on his feet, his eyes lit up like stars. "Could we, Daddy?"

"Lisette was going to take us," Ava said.

"But we can *all* go tomorrow instead," Lisette replied.

"Tomorrow's your day off," Charles reminded her.

"I don't mind making an exception for a day of pumpkin picking," she said.

He gazed at her with appreciation. She was trying to help him bond with his kids, and he knew it.

Myles grasped his father's hand, looking up at him with excitement. "And you can come too? Really, Daddy?"

Charles nodded. "Of course. Tomorrow afternoon, all right?"

Ava smiled widely. Myles clapped with glee. Thomas stared at the floor.

"It'll be fun." Lisette placed the three tablets into her oversized tote bag and pulled out her ticket for the valet. "Okay. We're all set. Let's go, guys." She shot a quick smile at Charles. "Enjoy the rest of the party."

"Thank you." He smiled at her, hoping she could sense his genuine gratitude, then ran his hand over the shiny length of his daughter's dark hair. Ava gave him another hug, which he savored and returned. "Good night, all of you. Sleep well."

He watched Lisette usher the kids out of the ballroom. Something twinged in his chest, the same unhappy twinge he'd felt a lot recently. Then he caught sight of his father, a sour look on his face as he spoke to Tess. She was the only one of his siblings who still talked to the old man. Dane, Julia, Pierce, and Abby had moved clear to the other side of the room. Since the disaster at the family party last year, where Charles II had gotten vicious and verbally attacked Pierce and Abby, Dane barely spoke to him, and Pierce not at all. Yes, Pierce had moved back to Long Island, but the rift was as wide as it had ever been. The truth was, Charles had been so disgusted, he wished he didn't have to speak to his father regularly either. But working with him meant that just wasn't realistic.

His kids weren't as wild as they'd been before he'd hired Lisette, but there were still issues there. His siblings and his father were quietly at war. Charles felt like a benign peacekeeper at times . . . but it hadn't really done much good, had it?

The Harrison family was a lot messier than the public knew.

With a sigh, he headed to the bar. If there was any time he could break his one-drink rule, it was on his own birthday, dammit.

Chapter Two

The house was dark and silent when Charles entered it at one in the morning. The party had been nice, but way too long. And of course, as guest of honor, he'd had to stay until the end. Dropping his keys into the crystal bowl on the nearby table, he walked down the long main hall until he reached his study.

This was both his office and his haven. Spacious and elegant, warmed by lots of dark wood and different shades of brown, it had a large bay window that looked out onto the wide backyard and the Long Island Sound beyond. Not bothering to close the door behind him, Charles went right to the top shelf that held a few bottles of brandy and scotch. He reached for the Glenmorangie Signet, which he'd been saving for a special occasion. He thought his fortieth birthday qualified. He opened the bottle in the darkness, savoring the quiet.

Forty years old. As he poured himself half a glass, he thought about turning forty. He'd never really cared about birthdays, or numbers, or any of it. But this one bothered him, and had for months. Tonight, at the party, he'd finally realized precisely why.

There was a lot that wasn't right with his life. After months of mental inventory, he'd come up short. He was dissatisfied . . . and lonely.

With a long, slow exhale, he sank into the leather chair behind his impressive mahogany desk. Moonlight streamed in through the windows, bathing the room in a silvery blue. A full moon. Hell, maybe that was affecting his mood too. He took a sip of the scotch, savoring the taste. He took another swallow, feeling the burn of it down his throat. Too much was swirling in his head, and he needed to quiet it down somewhat.

"You're never off the clock," his father had said. And after fifteen years of it—hell, a lifetime, really—Charles was tired of it. Annoyed. Even . . . resentful.

He sipped some more as he stared absently out the window, alone in the dark. He'd been doing everything he was supposed to do to uphold the Harrison name since he was a toddler. He'd gone to the schools his father had wanted him to: the fancy private schools, then Harvard for both undergrad and business school. His father's choices, not really his. But Charles had just gone along with them. Like everything else in his life.

Feeling a buzz at last, he knocked back the rest of his glass and refilled it.

He was a powerful man, accustomed to getting what he wanted. But he'd never abused his power or thought it made him better than anyone else. It was just his nature. He tried to be decent, fair, and honorable in all things. But the one time he'd strayed off the straight and narrow Harrison path, the *one* time, he'd fallen for Vanessa Conti. Beautiful, fiery, exciting Vanessa, a model and a socialite. They'd met at a party on Martha's Vineyard. The affair had been quick and hot; he'd proposed; they'd married . . . and it had been a fucking disaster.

They were completely wrong for each other. While she loved the money, the settled married life was not for her. She was bored. She hated company functions and family expectations. Then the unexpected pregnancy, a honeymoon baby on the way. Vanessa hated being pregnant; she'd felt fat and her hormones had been out of whack . . . They had argued all the time. But she had Ava, then Thomas. By the third pregnancy, sex was all they had left, since they barely spoke. Myles wasn't even a year old when Vanessa had said she'd had enough. By the time Myles was eighteen months old, she'd taken her hefty settlement and moved across the country to California, leaving Charles alone with three tiny children and a severe case of wounded pride. Disaster.

Tonight, at the party, he'd seen Dane with Julia, laughing together and enjoying themselves. They seemed to always be laughing, always touching, and always having fun. Dane had already been that way, lighthearted and loving life, but since finding Julia, his glow had only magnified. Charles often thought that Dane was like the sun—a huge radiant presence, pulling whoever was near into his orbit of warmth and light. And his wife was a force to be reckoned with on her own. Combined, they were incredible. Loving Julia, and being loved by her, had only enriched Dane's already charmed, full life, and made him happier than Charles had ever seen him. Charles was glad for him . . . and secretly envied that just a little. Hell, more than a little.

Charles toasted his brother, lifting his glass before taking another sip.

And Pierce. The churlish black sheep of the family had returned home over a year ago to lick his wounds. The youngest had screwed up his life enough to force him to quit a successful soccer career in England. But his siblings had brought him back into the fold, trying to help him, make him feel supported. All their relationships with him had improved. However, it was Abby who'd made the biggest difference. The small-town, straight-talking teacher saw through his fronts, didn't put up with his bullshit, and adored him beyond measure. Pierce, in turn, was totally devoted to her. They were so different, but so right together. Charles wouldn't be surprised if they were engaged soon.

He'd even overheard Pierce just that night telling Tess how he wanted a bunch of kids who would all take after their smart, gorgeous mother, something Charles had never thought he'd hear from the formerly notorious womanizer. Pierce had bought into a New York professional soccer franchise, and coached local kids simply because he wanted to. It was heartening to see how Pierce had completely turned his life around, buoyed by the love of a good woman.

Charles raised another toast to another brother, then drank deeply.

Tess, his sister, was the best woman he'd ever known. And, sadly, was as alone as he was, also by choice. Burned by love, she'd pretty much sworn off men and buried herself in her work and her painting. Charles didn't even have a hobby like painting, no outlet for the steam he swallowed all the time. He supposed that was why he went to the gym and took boxing classes. Hitting the bag, and sparring with his coach, felt good. It let off some steam . . . but not nearly enough. Definitely not on nights like this.

Charles's head was a little woozy; he suspected if he stood, he might wobble. Who cared? He hadn't gone on a bender in a very long time. He was feeling lonesome, feeling sorry for himself, feeling angry, feeling . . . Dammit, he didn't want to feel anything. If he did, if he let himself indulge in all the things he choked back and repressed every day, it might all come to the surface and swallow him whole. His life had become a careful tightrope routine: doing what was needed for Harrison Enterprises, fulfilling the family's

heavy expectations, raising three children whose mother
visited them once a year, not dating because he didn't have
the time or inclination to be burned again . . .

Jesus Christ, he was turning into his father.

When Charles was younger, that had been an admirable
goal, maybe even what he thought he wanted. Now, it filled
him with icy dread. Charles Harrison II was a cold, stern
man who had always put the family legacy and company
first. He'd ignored his beautiful young wife, driving her to
have affairs before they had one of the ugliest divorces in
history. Embittered from that, he'd been alone for over
twenty years. The lack of love in his life and his drive to keep
the company thriving had sucked any warmth or light out
of him. In the past year, he'd all but alienated his grown
children. He had all the power and money in the world . . .
but very little love, and no joy.

Charles shuddered. So much in common . . . History re-
peating itself . . . Was that how he was going to turn out too?

He stared out at the full moon for a long time. *Happy
fucking birthday.*

A loud crash woke Lisette from her sleep with a start. Her
heart pounding, she sat up. What the hell was that noise?

She realized she was in the den; it was dark—she'd fallen
asleep reading. Often, after the kids were asleep, she went
there to curl into the oversized, plush loveseat by the
window and read for a while. Charles would work late at
the end of the long hall, in his study, and she'd read until she
started to doze off. They rarely interacted; he was a busy
man, no matter what time of day or night it was, so she kept
her distance.

Tonight, after the party, she'd been too wired to go to bed
right away and had done her usual routine of reading for

hours in the dark, with only the light of her e-reader . . . Now she grasped that she'd dozed off somewhere around midnight. She turned her dormant e-reader back on to check the time; it was past two in the morning. The house was quiet now, but that noise had woken her. It *had* happened.

Straining to listen, her breath held, she heard a *thump-thump,* then another thud, soft but audible, along with a loudly hissed curse. That was Charles's voice.

Rising from the loveseat, she tightened her long midnight-blue silk robe around her knee-length nightgown and slid her feet into her slippers before venturing out to the hallway.

The spectacular mansion had long hallways and spacious rooms. Charles had gutted the older mansion a decade before and remade it into something just for him and his new bride. All the bedrooms were on the second floor. There were the children's three rooms on one wing, the fourth bedroom that had been converted into a playroom for them, and a bathroom for them to share. Just around the corner, there were two large suites, bedrooms that had sitting rooms. One stayed empty for guests, and Lisette had been given the other. Along the third hall, there were three more guest rooms and another bathroom. The fourth corridor contained only one master suite, and that was Charles's bedroom.

With a mix of determination and unease, she made her way through the long main corridor of the ground floor. Until she was sure everything was fine, she wouldn't be able to go back to sleep.

Again a male voice uttered a curse somewhere down the hall, and she gathered it had definitely come from Charles's study. She went to the door of the study and tiptoed inside. It was dark, but she felt someone's presence there. "Hello?"

"Who's there?" Charles's voice came from the darkness. "Lisette, is that you?"

"Yes." Apprehension hummed through her whole body, making her heart rate take off. "Charles? Are you all right?"

"Before you come in," he said, "are you wearing shoes?"

What? Moonlight shone through the large windows, but her eyes hadn't fully adjusted to the darkness yet, and she couldn't see him. His voice had come from the far side of the spacious room. She peered harder and asked, "Excuse me?"

"Get shoes," he repeated. "There's broken glass on the floor. You'll cut yourself."

"I have slippers on; I'll be fine. Are you all right?" she asked again, more demanding this time.

"I'm fine too," he said. "Just a little drunk."

Lisette stopped in her tracks. Her eyes had adjusted to the darkness enough, and she could see him now. He was sitting on the wide leather couch, his arms crossed over his chest. Gesturing toward the floor by his desk with his chin, he explained, "I dropped the glass when I stood up."

"I heard it. It woke me up."

"You heard it upstairs?" he asked, confused.

"No, I fell asleep in the den. So . . ." She twisted the ends of her sash around her fingers, stalling, trying to process the scene. How drunk was he? "I'll get a broom."

"No. You're off the clock." He moved, sat, and patted the cushion beside him. "Come keep me company. Talk to me."

Lisette couldn't help but stare. What the hell was going on?

"Luckily, the glass was empty when I dropped it," he said jauntily. "No scotch lost. Just crystal." He patted the cushion again and slanted a grin at her. "Come on, sit down. We never really talk."

Apparently, her boss was a friendly drunk. But she didn't answer until she was sitting on the sofa, the leather creaking as she settled. "Should we turn on a light?"

"Nah. This darkness suits my mood."

Oh, boy. She turned to him, pulling her sash a little tighter, and asked, "Did you come home from the party drunk?"

"Nope," Charles said, shaking his head. "But I'm working on it." He scrubbed his hands over his face. "Can I get you a drink?"

"No, thank you," she said.

He grinned, making the corners of his eyes crinkle. "You're always so polite."

"Good manners were very important to my father," she found herself saying. "Army and all. So he drummed them into me early on."

Charles gave an approving nod. "Sounds like my kind of guy."

She merely quirked a return grin and folded her hands in her lap. This whole scene was unusual, to say the least, and she wasn't sure what to say or do just yet. So she let him lead, let him go on talking. Her father's words echoed in her mind: *Remember, honey. He who speaks first, loses. Always wait it out.*

Charles scrubbed his hands over his face as his eyes wandered around the room. "I can't be anything less than perfect, ya know. Perrrrrfect. Since I was a little boy. What a drag."

That gave her pause. He always held himself so carefully in check. Sympathy pinged through her, but concern flooded her. Something serious had to be going on. And the secret she swallowed every day—the feelings for him that were inappropriate for an employee to have for her boss—surfaced and took over. Because he was obviously not himself, and she cared about him. "Charles? What's bothering you? Are you okay?"

He peered at her from beneath his lashes, his gaze holding hers in the moonlight. "Not really," he murmured. "I . . . well . . . Can I confide in you, Lisette?"

"Of course," she said, her heart rate rising with a curious thrill.

"That party tonight . . ." He shook his head and sighed. "What a pain in the ass. I love Tess to death, but I didn't want a goddamn party. I don't feel like celebrating anything. I feel about a hundred years old today. Like a grumpy old bastard."

"You're not," she assured him in a gentle tone.

He shrugged, his gaze sliding back toward the window, and his shoulders slumped. "It's no joyride being me sometimes, Lisette. It really isn't."

She'd never seen him look so sad. It pierced her heart. This man had the world at his fingertips. And at the moment, he looked only sorrowful and lost.

She leaned in and touched his knee, the lightest, faintest press of her fingers. "Did something happen tonight, Charles? You wanted to talk. I'm here. Talk to me."

He shook his head no, but his eyes lingered on her hand that rested on his knee.

"You can trust me," she said. "I'm a vault. And it seems as if you really need to talk to someone right now."

"I do . . . But really, when it comes down to it, there's nothing to talk about," Charles murmured, his eyes lifting to her face. "My life is set in stone. Has been since before I was born. Nothing will change that, so no use in talking about it."

Lisette remained silent, apparently not knowing how to respond to that. Her hand withdrew from his knee back to her own lap.

Charles gazed at her. "You look different," he said, squinting as he tried to figure out why. Her hair. That was it. It was always up—in a French braid, or in other kinds of braids and ponytails, to keep it out of her face as she chased his kids around. Even at the party earlier, it'd been up in a sophisticated bun. But now, her shiny dark hair fell all around her face, tumbling over her shoulders and halfway down her back. "Your hair is down. You look so different this way . . ." He reached up to twirl a lock of it between his fingers. "I never knew it was so long," he said, fascinated. "Or so soft . . ."

He'd always thought her attractive, of course. But with her hair loose and flowing like this, illuminated only by moonlight . . . she looked softer, even prettier, and God help him, downright sexy. He was mesmerized. Her gorgeous dark eyes, her high cheekbones, her smooth olive skin, her lips that looked like they'd be so soft and warm if he tasted them . . . She was beautiful. A jolt of desire zipped through him, hot and quick, and something deep inside him groaned to life. His blood started pulsing through his veins, and the air around them seemed to get thicker, warmer.

Dropping the lock of her hair, he reached out to graze her cheek with the backs of his fingers. She stiffened beneath his touch, but something in her eyes . . . they darkened, widened, and a hint of color bloomed on her cheeks. Her tongue darted out to lick her lips, and his breath stuck in his chest. He felt drawn to her, hypnotized, as if an invisible electric charge was holding him in her power.

Heat and desire surged through his body as the feel of her soft skin woke dormant lusty demons. He hadn't been with a woman in way too long. Over a year. The last few times he'd had sex, they'd been meaningless and brief encounters, leaving him feeling empty. But at that moment all he could think was that he wanted Lisette, and he hadn't wanted any woman like this in a long, long time. Now, gazing at her, touching her, his body was betraying him with just how much he wanted her. "You're beautiful," he murmured thickly, trailing the backs of his fingers along her jaw. "You really are."

She shivered beneath his touch, but didn't back away from it. "You've been drinking. Your beer goggles are fogged up."

He laughed, but he couldn't stop staring at her mouth. Her full, soft, perfectly shaped lips. All he wanted, more than anything, was to taste that luscious mouth, just one time. He wanted to so badly . . . no, *needed* to. The urge was all consuming, and he gave in to it. His hand cupped around the back of her neck as he leaned in, pulling her to him as he pressed his lips to hers.

She jolted in surprise. He pulled back, but not much, still so close to her mouth that he was breathing her air. She didn't move. With a prick of embarrassment, he realized that the kiss likely wasn't something she wanted. That he was imposing. Obviously she didn't feel the same pull he did.

"I'm sorry," he whispered, moving back. "You just looked so beautiful, and I—"

Her hands flew up to hold his face, and she crushed her lips to his.

He gave a lusty groan, and his hands threaded through her long, thick hair, holding her close as his mouth consumed hers. Pure lust overtook his senses. Her mouth was as warm and soft as it looked and tasted sweet, like the spiced tea she often made at night.

Charles lost himself in that kiss. In how damn good she felt, and what kissing her awakened in him. In letting go for once, in living in the moment . . . in being like someone other than himself. The fire raged through him in a merciless flash, leveling him, leaving him mindless, but strangely galvanized. His tongue slipped into her mouth and found hers, sending a new rush through him, heady and intoxicating.

Their tongues tangled as the kisses intensified and his

greedy hands began roaming over her, learning the feel and shape of her tempting body. Her soft sighs and moans, the way she moved to get closer, only sharpened his desire. Her fingers ran through his hair, dropping to his shoulders and gripping tightly as his teeth scraped along her neck.

He shifted to pull her even tighter against him, but the sudden move put them off balance, bringing them both down. They fell back with a graceless thud and surprised grunts, still locked in an embrace.

"Oh my God, I'm so sorry," he said, rearing up on his elbows to look at her. "Are you okay?"

Her eyes were wide and round as she stared back up at him, trying to catch her breath. "I'm fine," she gasped, "but you're . . . well . . ."

Charles realized the full length of his body was aligned with hers. The feel of her lush body beneath his sent a new surge of desire rushing through him. And then she wiggled beneath him, and every nerve ending in his body flamed. His pelvis was pressed against hers, and if she kept that up . . . sweet Jesus. "Don't do that," he warned.

"Don't do what?" She blinked, confused, then moved again to try to relieve the pressure of his weight. Her breasts pressed against his chest, and her hips rolled under his. Blood surged to his groin; he was hard now, and his breath hitched.

"That," he half groaned. Holy hell, she felt so good. His eyes fell to her mouth. Want and need swamped him, his head dipped, and he took her mouth in a hungry, almost desperate kiss.

Her lips parted to welcome him. Moaning into her mouth, the taste of her warm, soft mouth and the feel of her warm, soft body made his mind reel, then go blank. A tiny whimper of surrender floated out of her, and her arms snaked around his neck. His tongue swept deeper into her mouth, tasting, savoring . . . and she kissed him back hard, her body melting against his.

Sweet Mother of God, she wanted him too. Threading his hands in her hair, cradling her head, he kissed her hungrily, devouring her. All that mattered at that moment was having her. Everything else in him fell away.

Chapter Three

This can't be happening.

That was the thought that kept going through Lisette's mind over and over . . . even as her hands swept over Charles's broad shoulders and strong back, even as he kissed her so passionately and commandingly that it stole her breath away, even as she kissed him back with just as much hunger and demand. It was as if she were drowning, and he was a lifeline. He'd brought her back to life in a bright, split second flash.

There were no words—only intense, consuming kisses; carnal, almost desperate groping; and the sound of their gasps, moans, and heavy breathing as they went at each other with unrestrained, reckless abandon.

She knew she should stop, but dammit, she just didn't want to. How could *any* woman resist him? He was movie-star handsome, smart and assured, sexy and sweet . . . but Charles Harrison III was an incredibly wealthy and power-ful man. Someone like her wouldn't ever appear on his radar. The fantasies she'd entertained on long, dark nights were just that: fantasies. She knew they could never actually come true.

But now Charles groaned from deep in his throat as his fingers dug into her hips, his pelvis grinding into hers, shocking her with the power of his obvious desire. His hot mouth, eager and wicked, kissed and bit and licked along her neck as his thick erection rubbed against her core, the delicious friction sending jolts of electricity through her. It had been so long since a man had touched her, much less like this. She'd forgotten what it was like to be desired—it was intoxicating, mind-erasing. Her body had taken over, working on pure instinct. She couldn't stop kissing him back, or letting her greedy hands roam over the smooth, masculine hardness of his body.

Between sumptuous kisses, his hands moved over her too, leaving trails of burning need in their wake. God, the way he kissed and touched her . . . Her whole body was tingling. One of his hands moved through her hair, again cradling her head, while the other reached for her sash, undid it, and pushed aside her robe. It was all happening so fast. She knew she should stop this, but she just didn't want to.

"Charles." Her voice was raspy, and she barely recognized it. He fondled her hip, then moved to her waist. Heat shimmered across her skin wherever his hands caressed her. "This is crazy . . ."

"I know," he whispered, his breath feathering her skin. "But God help me, I want you so much right now."

Her stomach flipped as a new rush of heady passion engulfed her. She wanted him too. She couldn't deny it. "I want you too."

His hand ran up along her ribcage to her breast, caressing it through her nightgown, giving it a gentle squeeze before he brushed his thumb across her nipple. She moaned into his mouth, and he kissed her even harder.

We shouldn't be doing this . . . for a million different reasons . . . but dammit he felt *so* good, and she hadn't been touched like this in years. *Years.* She felt like a starving woman who'd been given a long-awaited meal, delicious and forbidden, and she couldn't devour it—him—fast enough. Charles was gorgeous and sexy, and she'd never known he had this kind of passion in him, and he obviously wanted this too, and, ohhhh God, his mouth and hands were everywhere . . .

His hands fondling her breasts, Charles's head lowered, and his teeth gently scraped her nipples through her night-gown. She moaned and arched into him, seeking more of that dark, wicked pleasure. He was kissing her everywhere as his warm, sure hands slid down her body to push up the fabric of her nightgown, up past her thighs, and she let him. Her heart pounding, the throbbing between her legs filled her with desperate need, and something between a gasp and a moan ripped from her as she fisted her fingers in his wavy hair. His hot mouth trailed kisses along her belly as his fingers feathered up her thigh, making her tremble with lust and anticipation. She'd never been swept away by desire like this, never in her life.

And she was right there with him, panting and groping like he was, moaning and writhing beneath him like some porn star. His passion and need were mesmerizing and completely consumed her.

She was spiraling out of control, and, for once in her life, she didn't care about consequences, right or wrong, or anything but how she felt. About her own needs and her own desires, which she never considered, much less put first. He wanted her right then? Okay, fine. Yes, now, since he'd started it, she wanted him to take her, have his way with her, and she'd give back as good as he gave. Just this once, she wanted to feel like a sexy, desirable woman. And, more than anything, after years of feeling numb, she wanted to feel alive again, even if only for a few stolen minutes. And there was no one on earth she wanted to do this with—would have *let* herself do this with—other than Charles.

Charles was panting. Panting and clawing like an animal. He didn't care. He didn't recognize himself right then, and that was fantastic. He wanted to consume this sexy, gorgeous woman, to take her and to lose himself in her at the same time. To just throw himself over the cliff and let this sudden blaze of mindless, aching need and overwhelming desire burn through him, through both of them.

The fire was mutual. She grabbed at him and kissed him with the same ferocious lust that was turning him into some kind of senseless beast. Her wild passion was a shock to him, but made him want her that much more. She was so beautiful, all soft curves and velvety skin and warmth; he wanted to sink into her lush, enticing body, and nothing else mattered.

His fingers slid up her thigh to find the edge of her panties. "Jesus," he whispered roughly, blown away by the heat there, the dampness he could feel through the cotton. He pressed harder, rubbing her, and she cried out as her back arched, as she twisted beneath him.

But as he kissed and nuzzled her breast, he paused. Damn. Even in a mindless haze of lust, he had to make sure she really wanted this. He thought she did, but still . . . Barely able to speak over his heavy breaths, he lifted his head and looked into her eyes. "Lisette," he whispered raggedly, "are you okay?"

Panting just as heavily, she stared back at him, her dark eyes clouded with desire. "What?"

"Are you okay? I'm just making sure."

"Of course I'm okay."

"Good. But . . ." Even in his dazed, slightly drunken state, he would always respect the boundaries. "If you want me to stop—"

"No!" she whispered. "Please don't stop."

His heart felt as if it had jumped in his chest. The raw need of her words undid him. His gaze locked with hers.

"I don't want to stop," she said quickly. "I know that I should, but I don't."

"Thank God," he said. "Because I want you so much right now . . ."

"I want you too," she said. Her hands cradled his face. "So no more talking. Just . . . take me."

That did it. He crushed his mouth to hers, not holding back. He wasn't sure he could have held back then if his life depended on it, not after she'd said something so fucking hot. He wanted her, needed her, had to have her . . .

He took her mouth, wild with lust, and his fingers continued to explore her. She pressed her mouth to his neck to muffle her moans; her hips undulated against his hand, and it drove him insane. Her scent flooded his senses, from the trace of sweet vanilla on her skin to the musky smell of her arousal that made him reel with desire. His heart was pounding; he wondered if she felt it as her shaking hands undid the buttons on his shirt. She spread it open wide, then yanked it free from the waistband of his pants and ran her hands along his chest, his sides, everywhere she could reach.

Still kissing her, he pushed her panties to the side, then plunged two fingers into her soft folds, already so wet and warm. She cried out helplessly into his mouth, and her whole body arched, pressing closer. He broke away to kiss, lick, nibble, and suck on her neck, her throat, then back to her mouth as her hips moved in time with the primal rhythm his fingers set. She moaned and squirmed and grasped at him, and every sound, every movement, drove him closer to the brink. He couldn't hold back much longer. His mind had left the building long ago, and he was working on pure sensation.

"Touch me," he whispered gruffly against her ear. "I need you . . ."

She grabbed at the button at his waist, brushing against his erection as she lowered the zipper. He hissed at the contact and shifted to give her better access, his fingers inside her never stopping. She reached into his boxer briefs. When her fingers curled around him, hard and throbbing, his head fell forward and he groaned into her neck. He thought he might lose it right then. She stroked him; he stroked her; they panted and bucked and shuddered . . .

He didn't know how it happened . . . It all went so fast, like flashes of light. But he rolled enough for her to roughly push down his pants and briefs, and he tugged down her panties, and she dug her nails into his shoulders, and then he was inside her, thrusting deep into her liquid heat. Both of them groaned as he filled her, stretching her . . . Jesus, she was tight, but he pushed deeper . . .

With a gasp and a small cry, her legs came up to lock around his hips, and they rocked together, clawing to get closer to each other . . . Moving faster, panting, he thrust his hips harder, again, and again, and again . . . God, she felt so fucking good . . . It was desperate, frantic; the pleasure was too much; it felt too good. He moaned her name . . . then her legs tightened, and her nails dug into his back as she cried out, the climax overtaking her. Her throaty moans shattered him, and he went right over the edge with her, unable to hold back another second. His orgasm hit hard, the waves of sensation battering and flooding him. Finding release deep inside her, he gripped her hips, groaned, and buried his face in the curve of her neck and the soft tangles of her hair.

He couldn't catch his breath, and it sounded like she

couldn't either. They lay there panting, still holding each other.

Once the dark and stillness settled over them, Lisette's mind went into overdrive. Full-blown panic mode. "Oh, God," she whispered raggedly. "Oh, God, what did we—ohhh, my God!"

"Shhh," Charles whispered back, rearing up on his elbows to look at her. "It's fine. Everything's fine."

"Everything is so far from fine!" She squirmed beneath him. Good God, he was still inside her.

"Lisette," he began as he shifted. The couch was too narrow for him to roll off and lie beside her, so he withdrew from her body, then rose from the couch altogether. "Listen—"

"No, please." Alarm made bile rise in her throat. Now that the fog of lust had cleared, the severity of their actions hit her like a sledgehammer. Oh, God, she'd put everything that mattered in jeopardy. Had she gone temporarily insane? Apparently so. She needed to get out of there, needed to be alone to process what she'd done, and what might follow. Her nightgown had been pushed up above her breasts, and she yanked it down, then stood and pulled her robe around her. Where the hell were her panties? She'd never find them in the dark. Wonderful.

"Let's talk about this," Charles said quietly, watching her. "Don't just bolt."

"What should I say?" she asked, unable to keep the note of rising panic out of her tone. "Thanks, that was amazing, but I really hope you don't fire me tomorrow?"

"Whoa, wait." He stepped to her and put his hands on her shoulders, willing her to look at him. "That's not going to happen. We *both* did this."

She tied the sash of the robe around her waist with jerky

motions, her gaze sliding down. He was still naked, and even in her panic her eyes couldn't resist a quick final tour of his gorgeous body. With a soft gasp, she stepped back, putting distance between them as she averted her eyes. "Yes, we both did this. But we're not both on the same level here, Charles. Not by a mile. And I just broke every rule in the nanny book. Hell, the *employee* book. You're my *boss*. I live in your home. And everything that I—" She clamped her mouth shut. With a hard shake of her head, she headed for the door.

Charles watched her all but run from the room, her face still flushed, whispering an apology as she brushed past him. He reached for her arm, but she slipped from his grip. "Lisette, *wait!*" He wanted to talk to her, for her to hear him out, but he couldn't just follow her into the hallway naked.

Jesus fucking Christ. He was standing there naked, in the middle of his study, because he'd just had sex with his children's nanny on the goddamn couch.

Vehemently spitting a stream of curses, heart pounding, he grabbed his clothes from the floor and put them back on. For a minute, he paced the room, hands raking through his hair and over his face as his mind spun. What the hell had happened? Sure, he'd always found Lisette attractive, very much so, but this . . . The ramifications of his actions could be staggering.

He stopped in his tracks. One of the most incredible things was the truth: she'd wanted him too. More than willing, she'd been right there with him, practically from the first kiss. It'd been a passionate, hot romp, the sexiest encounter he'd had in years. The erotic sounds of her moans and sighs, of her whispered throaty pleas not to stop, all still echoed in his head, making his blood pulse through his veins. Lord help him, the whole thing had happened unbelievably fast, but it'd been so damn good.

Too good—and too fast. It hit him like a tidal wave: he hadn't used protection. Oh, for fuck's sake . . . A shiver ran over his skin as he winced.

He stormed to the standing bar and poured himself a new glass of scotch.

Chapter Four

Someone was knocking.

Lisette forced herself to consciousness, opening her eyes a crack as the knocking repeated. Someone was knocking on her door. She was in her bed. The sunshine that poured through her windows was bright, so it was morning. What day was it? Had she overslept?

"Set?" It was Myles's sweet helium voice. "Set, can I come in? You awake?"

She glanced at the clock. It was almost seven-thirty. Her mind was blurry. She hadn't overslept; it was okay; it was Sunday. And . . . *oh, God.*

Her heart skipped a beat before taking off with an anxious hammering as a chill skittered over her skin. Charles. Oh, God, oh no, oh noooo. They'd had wild, crazy, clawing animal sex on the couch in his study.

The anxiety forced nausea up into her throat, and she swallowed hard. Her life as she knew it was probably over.

"Lisette?" Myles knocked again. "Aren't we going to get pumpkins today?"

Shit. Her mind and heart racing, she threw back the covers and jumped out of bed, looking around nervously. She still wore her nightgown, the soft one with the red and hot-pink swirls, the one Charles had pushed up to under her armpits last night as he screwed her senseless. She wore no panties . . . He'd all but torn them off in the heat of the moment, in a lust-driven frenzy. Good God, where were they now?!?

"Lisette? Are you sleeping?"

She went to the door and flung it open, but forced her voice to stay calm as she looked down at Myles. "Hi, sweetie. Yes, I was still sleeping. Um . . . are you the only one awake?"

"Uh-huh." He smiled and nodded, his dark hair mussed, looking adorable in his light blue Olaf pajamas. "Ava and Thomas are still sleeping, and so's Daddy. But he's sleeping on the couch in his office. In his clothes. Isn't that funny?"

Lisette swallowed hard. "Yeah, it is kind of funny. He must've been really tired." Yeah, he'd likely been tired, all right. "Just let your daddy sleep, okay, sweetie?" she said, forcing lightness into her voice.

"Okay." Myles looked at her hair and giggled. "Your hair looks crazy!"

Her hand flew to her head, feeling the tangled mess; she could barely get her fingers through some of the knots. God, what she must look like. She probably looked like Medusa . . . or someone who'd gotten her brains screwed out by her hot boss on a couch in the middle of the night. She swallowed convulsively.

"I'm hungry," Myles said. "Can I have some breakfast?"

"S-sure." Poor baby was hungry. And why not start the day? It wasn't as if she was going to be able to fall back to sleep. Eileen would get there at eight, but she couldn't let Myles starve. "Just let me put my hair up, get my robe on, and I'll meet you in the kitchen in five minutes. Okay?"

"Okay! I'm gonna get some of my cars!" Happy and

blissfully clueless, the little boy shot down the hall to his room.

Lisette closed the door and leaned back against it. Anxiety welled, closing her throat and knotting her stomach. She started to tremble as she slid down the door, sinking to her knees. Her heart jackhammered wildly as she closed her eyes and tried to breathe. She had to own this. Because goddammit, she'd been just as responsible for what had happened as he was. She'd been a willing participant as they'd gone into forbidden territory together. But of the two of them, she was the one whose whole life was likely going to fall apart.

Would he be overly kind as he fired her, or cold and aloof? She didn't know which would be worse. Looking around her room, the place that she adored, sick misery filled her. This had become home to her. She loved her job, the kids, living here. And she'd blown everything sky-high for one insanely passionate encounter. Her eyes slipped closed as shame and regret flooded her.

Yes, she'd had something of a crush on Charles Harrison III from the day she started working for him. And yes, over time, that harmless crush had developed into some real feelings. But never in a million years had she dreamed something like *this* would happen. And deep down, she knew the dark truth of it: if she had it to do over again, she still wouldn't be able to resist him. The chemistry between them . . . it had ignited in seconds, like a brushfire in the desert. She was surprised that once they got started, they hadn't burned the house down with that scorching fire.

Her days as a nanny here were over; she was convinced of that. Now she just had to wait until he woke up and actually pulled the trigger. Shaking, she wrapped her arms around herself. Whatever happened, she was sure it was going to be hell on earth, but she'd deal with it. God knew she'd had enough practice with that.

* * *

Charles groaned, wishing he would just die already.

Lying on the tiled floor of one of the three bathrooms on the first floor, the one closest to his study, he cursed himself for the hundredth time for being a moron. How much scotch had he drunk after Lisette left the study? He had no idea, but he sure was paying the price now. Another wave of nausea rose up, and he stuck his head back in the toilet. When he was done retching, he flushed and flopped back down to lie on the floor. At least the black-and-white tiles were cool against his face.

He could see the headlines now: USUALLY DIGNIFIED COO OF HARRISON ENTERPRISES FOUND DEAD FROM HANGOVER ON BATHROOM FLOOR. Yeah, that'd be perfect. Just great. But at least he'd be dead, instead of puking his guts up with his head pounding and a clammy, sick feel to his skin.

There was a soft knock on the door, then Eileen O'Rourke's light Irish brogue. "Mr. Harrison? Can I come in? I want to check on you again."

"I'm alive," he called out feebly.

"Well, that's good," she said through the door. "I have some saltines and ginger ale for you. And some Gatorade. Whichever will stay down. Got to keep you hydrated, sir. Please, let me come in."

Charles closed his eyes and groaned. Eileen, the weekend housekeeper, had five children of her own, all grown now. Surely she'd seen worse than him in his present state. And he was getting light-headed; crackers and a drink could be good. "Come in."

He heard the door open, then close, and footsteps across the floor. "Oh, you poor dear." He opened his eyes to see Eileen set the tray on the sink as she looked him over and softly tsk-tsked.

"How long have I been in here?" he asked.

"About two hours now. Figure the worst must be behind you." She held out the glass of ginger ale. "Here."

He leaned up onto his elbows. "Jesus. I'm a little dizzy . . ."

"Then it's a good thing I'm here." She crouched down beside him and held the glass to his lips. "Drink this slowly," she instructed. He did as he was told. "There you go. Hopefully it'll stay down." She straightened again, and he watched her put down the glass and lift a washcloth from the tray. "You're a mess, mister."

"Can't deny that."

She ran the cloth under the faucet, wrung it out a bit, then came back to sit beside him. "Come here." With gentle care, she moved the cool, wet terry cloth over his forehead, then the rest of his face.

"God, that feels good," he murmured, his eyes slipping closed. "Thank you."

"You're welcome." She pressed it to the back of his neck.

"I don't think anyone's done this for me since I was a kid."

"I'd bet you didn't need anyone to do this for you."

"Probably." His eyes opened and focused. "What time is it, anyway?"

"Half-past two."

"Jesus. I've lost the day."

"Still have some of it left, and the evening. The sky won't fall without you." She smiled kindly. "Let's try a cracker now, shall we? And if you keep that down, we'll get you some ibuprofen for what I'm sure is a nasty headache."

Fifteen minutes later, Charles was sitting up against the wall, feeling more human. He'd kept down four crackers, a few sips of ginger ale, and some Gatorade. "I owe you for this, Eileen. Really, I'm very grateful."

"Nonsense," she said dismissively. "Though I don't mind telling you, you had me worried. I've never seen you like this."

"What, hungover? To the point of pathetic and massive vomiting? Because I don't think I have been since Vanessa left." He scrubbed his hands over his face, feeling the stubble across his jaw and chin, then froze. "Oh, God. The kids. Do they know?"

"Lisette told them you were very tired and weren't feeling well," Eileen said. "So that they'd leave you be. They just think you're a little sick. But they're fine. They're in the playroom, playing video games."

"Oh, good. Thank you." *Lisette.* His heart skipped a beat, then started pounding. *Holy fucking shit. Lisette.* Flashes went through his mind . . . her beneath him, him kissing her, running his hands all over her body . . . the feel of her lips against his neck, of her breath hot against his skin . . . of him thrusting deep inside her as her legs clamped around him. Her sexy moans rang in his ears. His eyes slipped closed as a deep chill ran through him.

But years of practice tamping down his emotions helped him swallow back the new surge of nausea and keep his voice neutral. He opened his eyes and cleared his throat. "Is Lisette with the kids, then?"

"No, sir. It's Sunday; you know it's her day off. She started breakfast for the children, but when I got here at eight, she went about her day. She was out the door by eight-thirty."

His eyes squeezed shut again. They were all supposed to go pumpkin picking together, but he didn't blame her for wanting to vanish. Who knew what she was thinking? He'd have to wait to find out. Lisette didn't usually come back to the house until late on Sunday nights, leaving him—or Eileen, if he was away on a business trip—to put the kids to bed. Which meant at least he had time to think and figure out what the hell to do next.

More flashes of his time with Lisette went through his mind . . . Her beneath him in the dark, soft and warm and smooth, her arms and legs wrapped around him . . . Her voice echoed in his head, raspy with desire: *"Take me."*

Something low in his groin heated at the memory. How the fuck had any of that happened?

He snorted at himself in derision. Getting slightly drunk and feeling lonely and sorry for himself, that's how. They'd toppled onto the couch . . . and the feel of her, the scent of her, the taste of her, had ripped all logic out of his head and replaced it with pure animal lust.

"Oh, my God," he moaned, raking his hands over his face. "What have I *done?*"

"You'll be all right, Mr. Harrison," Eileen assured him, patting his knee.

His head pounded along with his heart. He hoped so. Because this could be a mess of epic proportions. He'd slept with his children's nanny. How cliché could he get? What if she . . . Oh, God, would she quit? He'd never forgive himself if his kids lost her because of his recklessness.

"Eileen," he asked carefully, opening his eyes to look at the older woman, "how did Lisette seem this morning?"

Eileen's brows were as white as her hair, and they creased as she said, "Funny you ask that. She seemed off. Not at all right, actually. She seemed . . . anxious, maybe? I asked her if she was okay, but she insisted she was fine and went up to her room." She peered at her employer. "I hope she's not getting sick. Why do you ask?"

His eyes shut again, and he softly banged his throbbing skull back against the tile wall. Lisette was likely upset and probably even scared. He didn't know much about her personal life; she kept it to herself, and he'd always respected her privacy. In fact, she was very private. He didn't know much about her beyond what had been in her file when he hired her, and what he saw of her in his home. What he did know was that she was totally dedicated to her job, to his kids. That she was smart, refined, and disciplined, but warm and incredibly sweet . . .

He had to talk to her. He had to do something. He wasn't

sure what, but he'd figure it out. Holy hell, what a fiasco. God only knew what was going through *her* mind. If she was even half as thrown as he was by this bizarre turn of events . . . Dammit, he had to fix this.

"Help me up, please," he said to Eileen, grabbing a few crackers. "I have to get in a shower. I have to get myself together. Enough of this."

"That's the Charles Harrison I know," she said, reaching out to help him stand.

Lisette stayed away all day, as she usually did on her day off. She'd gone to the little coffee shop down by the water that she liked and had a bowl of seafood bisque, then took a long walk along the Sound. It was a gorgeous fall day, with a hint of crisp coolness in the air. She sat on a bench by the water and sketched in her spiral pad for a while. The feel of the pencil scratching against the heavy paper helped a little, but not enough. Her brain was a tangled mess, her chest felt tight, and her body prickled on and off with anxiety all day. Her mind kept spinning in chaotic circles as she overthought and analyzed every bit of the night before.

Finally, she'd gone to the movies, and that had helped, a brief escape. It was already dark by the time she got out of the theater, and cooler outside too. So she went to the bookstore, always a safe haven. Finding a novel she'd heard about, she settled into a cozy chair and started to read, lingering for two hours before her stomach rumbled. She got a muffin and some tea at the bookstore café, but was unable to swallow all of it down. She knew she was doing anything to avoid going back to the house. Really, all she wanted to do was crawl into her bed and pull the covers over her head.

But avoidance wasn't going to erase what had happened or make things any better. She had to face the consequences of what she'd done. Hell, what *they'd* done. If only she could get the images of Charles out of her head.

She still couldn't believe it. She kept closing her eyes and feeling his lean, hard body against hers . . . smelling the salty, masculine scent of his skin mixed with expensive scotch on his breath . . . oh, his *mouth*. The way he'd kissed her, his wicked, talented tongue, the feel of his warm breath as he'd panted and groaned with pleasure, and whispered her name when they . . . *oh, God*. Her belly did another wobbly flip.

She had to stop thinking about it. When she let herself remember how good he'd felt, how unbelievably raw and passionate it had been, she felt fresh stirrings of want and need unfurl low in her belly.

That's how it was when you had sex for the first time in too many years, she supposed. No matter how gorgeous and sexy the man was or wasn't, you weren't going to be able to stop thinking about it anytime soon.

She finished half of the book, not leaving until the store closed at ten and she had no choice. Her anxiety started to kick in again as she drove home—*home* . . . It wasn't her home. It was Charles Harrison's home, and she was merely hired help.

He paid her extremely well, better than most nannies, because he'd gone through three before he hired her and was desperate to keep someone. To him, a high salary and full benefits were incentives, and for most people, it absolutely would have been. She made $1,500 a week in salary and had free room and board. He had bought a BMW minivan solely for her to use for the kids and herself, covered her fully with medical insurance, gave her every Sunday off and Saturdays too if she asked, took her with him and the kids on his fancy vacations three times a year . . . She had a great life. And all she had to do in return was make his life much, much easier for him.

He paid her to be a mom. God knew she'd come to feel like his children's mom; she lived with them, took care of them, and knew them inside and out. But she wasn't their mother. She was just an employee. As comfortable as Lisette had become, as much as she genuinely loved those kids, none of it mattered. She was dispensable. And after last night, she had a feeling she would find out just how dispensable she was. As kind as he was, things would be awkward. Charles would likely feel he had no choice but to ask her to leave, and she'd have to find a new family to care for. If she even could. How would she possibly be able to explain why she had left the best job she'd ever had? What would she do?

As she pulled into the long driveway, her heart hammered, and she sniffed back threatening tears. Turning off the engine, she sat in the minivan for a few minutes. Deep breath in . . . deep breath out. Calling on every tactic her mother had ever taught her, she willed herself to calm down. She had to be calm when she went inside.

Opening the front door as quietly as possible, she listened. No sound. It was past ten-thirty; the children were asleep, and hopefully Charles was too. She hung her jacket in the front hall closet, slipped her keys into the crystal bowl, and tiptoed to the staircase.

"Lisette."

She froze at the sound of his deep voice behind her, then turned. Charles leaned against the high arch between the foyer and the living room, arms crossed over his broad chest, looking at her with a cool, unreadable expression. He was good at that. He never let what he felt show on his face. It was one of the many things that made him such a successful businessman. She envied that skill, now more than ever.

"I've been waiting for you," he said quietly.

"Why?" she asked, knowing how stupid the question was.

"We need to talk," he said. "About last night." He pushed off the arch and took a few steps toward her. His blue eyes pinned her from behind his black-rimmed glasses. As he got closer, she also noticed his eyes were bloodshot, the only evidence of his wildness the night before. Clean-shaven, dressed in jeans and a thin black sweater—even his casual look was devastatingly handsome. He looked like he'd stepped off the cover of a magazine. Did he have to look so damn good when she was trying to ignore how she felt about him and was possibly about to lose everything?

Her mouth went dry. She cleared her throat and licked her lips, noticing how his eyes went to her mouth when she did. Taking a deep, shaky breath, she said, "Are you going to fire me now? If you are, please just get it over with."

Chapter Five

"What?" Charles stared at Lisette, his face contorting with confusion and surprise. "No, I'm not going to fire you. Hell, all day I was hoping you weren't going to quit."

Her mouth fell open, and he caught the flash of shock in her eyes. "Seriously?"

"Yes! I don't want you to leave. God knows I'm not thinking of firing you. All day I just hoped you . . . that you were all right." He took another tentative step toward her, closing the gap. He wondered if she could tell how remorseful and repentant he felt. He hoped so. "But before anything else, I need to apologize." He shoved his hands in his pockets, steeled himself, and made himself look directly at her. "My behavior last night was inexcusable. It all happened so fast . . . Lisette, I'm so sorry."

To his surprise, she shook her head. "Don't do that. No apology necessary. There were *two* of us involved." She swallowed hard, but met his gaze. "I got carried away too. It was . . . intense. We got swept away in the moment. We're both human."

He peered closer at her, and her erotic whisper from last night resounded in his head: *"Please don't stop."* A shiver went through him as he remembered the primal need in her voice. Now, he studied her face. He saw fear there, a touch of resignation, but she stood straight and strong. Not shying away from what they'd done. He respected her even more for that, but no way would he let her shoulder the blame. "Yes, but I initiated it. I mean, you didn't . . . I just . . ." Not used to fumbling for words, he muttered a curse and raked his hands through his hair. Blowing out an exasperated breath, he crossed his arms over his chest. "Fuck, this is awkward, huh?"

A surprised laugh burst from her, and she clapped a hand over her mouth, her dark eyes flying wide.

He laughed softly at her reaction, the initial tension broken. Both of them seemed to relax a bit. "Why don't we go to the den and talk? Instead of here in the hallway."

She paused, then nodded. "Yes. Good idea. Do you want tea or something?"

"Lisette . . ." He shoved his hands into his pockets again. "You're off the clock. You don't have to get me anything or do anything. Just sit and talk with me." He watched her face, saw the surprise there. "I think in order to have this awkward conversation, we need to just be a man and a woman, not an employer and his employee. We need to be on equal ground."

Her dark eyes held his for a long beat before she murmured, "Thank you for that. For respecting me enough to suggest that."

"I've always respected you," he said quickly. "Last night doesn't change that. The only one I've lost respect for on this one is me. I'm disgusted with myself."

The look in her eyes changed, and he realized how that might have sounded.

"Wait, *you* don't disgust me. You understand?" he insisted, making sure he was clear. "I'm disgusted with *myself*, with my behavior, with my lack of decency and control. I honestly don't know what came over me last night. I wasn't myself. Damn, I've made such a mess of things." He sighed, shook his head, and admitted, "I don't want you to be uncomfortable here now. I want to make this right, if I can. Most of all, I don't want you to quit. I really, really don't want you to leave, okay?"

"Wow." Her long lashes fluttered as she gaped at him. "It's a relief to hear you say that. Because I really don't want to leave. I . . . I love this job."

"Good." He nodded a little too hard, but he didn't care. "That's good. You're so great with the kids—they've truly connected with you. I don't think they could bear it if you left. And I'd never forgive myself if you left because of one mistake, a mistake that was mostly my fault."

Her cheeks flushed, and he wasn't sure why. Then she simply said, in her usual soft, melodious voice, "Let's go talk in the den."

They walked together down the hall. He paused to let her enter the room first, watching her as she went in. The comfortable, open den was for when he wanted to entertain company in a more casual space than his extravagant living room. There were no toys there. The only electronic device was a flat-screen on one wall, taking up almost half of it. The curtains were drawn, hiding the floor-to-ceiling wide window that looked out on the back part of the property. In the corner was a wide, cushioned loveseat; Charles knew she often liked to read there at night. He'd been waiting there for two hours for Lisette to return home, reading himself while he listened for the front door and telltale tinkle of keys.

She stood in the middle of the den, looking at him uncertainly.

"Please, sit down." He gestured toward the long, curved couch. She sank down onto one end of it, almost curling away from him into the arm. He sat on the other end, giving her plenty of space, but turned to face her directly. He wouldn't shy away from her or any part of this conversation. It was too important.

He couldn't help but let his eyes roam over her. She looked tired, uneasy . . . and so damn pretty. Her thick, dark hair was pulled back in a ponytail; she had no makeup on, and was dressed simply in a long navy cowl-neck sweater and gray yoga pants. And she was lovely. He'd always found her attractive, but now something new was happening when he looked at her; something sinful and dangerous stirred deep in his core. When he watched her nervously lick her full lips, his blood began to heat and pulse through his limbs, rushing throughout his body. Those sweet, warm lips had driven him crazy last night . . .

Jesus, he had to stop thinking of her that way. He cleared his throat and shifted in his seat. "I don't know where to begin," he admitted.

She nodded in agreement, fidgeting with a thread on the end of her sweater. "Neither do I."

A long, awkward beat passed before he blurted out, "I basically threw myself at you. Or, more correctly, on top of you. I'm so embarrassed . . ."

Her eyes flickered down, glued to her fingertips as they played with the loose thread and made it longer.

"Will you forgive me?" he asked, his voice low and tight. "Can we get past this?"

When Charles said that, Lisette couldn't help but look up at him in shock. His features were taut with remorse. "There's nothing to forgive," she said.

"I took you on my *couch*," he choked out.

"We took each other," she retorted. "I didn't exactly lie there like a corpse."

He jolted at her words. "No, you didn't. That's . . . certainly true," he murmured, eyes blazing. "There are some blurry holes in my memory of last night, but not about that."

She felt her face heat and swallowed hard.

"I didn't mean that like . . . what I meant was . . ." Charles swore under his breath. "I'm not trying to demean you, or downplay what happened. But, well . . . it was pretty hot. It felt mutual. So I'm just trying to make sure you didn't feel . . . coerced. Or, God forbid, that I hurt you in any way. Those things are the most important here, Lisette."

"Hurt me? No, of course not. And no, you didn't force me," she said. "I never felt that way, not for a second."

"Good." He nodded and exhaled, visibly relieved. "Good, I'm so glad."

"You asked me if you should stop," she reminded him. "And I . . ." Her cheeks flamed. "I told you *not* to stop. It was mutual. Consensual. Okay?"

He stared at her, and she wished she knew what he was thinking. He looked so troubled.

"Charles," she ventured. "Last night, when I found you? You seemed very . . . unhappy. You wanted to talk, remember?"

"Yes," he admitted in a whisper, his gaze sliding away.

Something in his posture made her want to reach out and hug him. But she cleared her throat and went on. "So you were in a bad state of mind, I walked in, and then . . . we *both* got carried away. That's all." She tried to sound reasonable and calm, though her racing heart made it hard to speak. "It just . . . happened."

He nodded again, seeming to absorb her words. Then, suddenly, his face changed, and his eyes pinned her. "But I realized afterward . . . I didn't use any protection." His hands scrubbed over his face, then clenched into fists. "Totally fucking irresponsible. I'm so, so sorry."

Oh, God. He didn't know. Her heart thumped wildly in her chest as she reached out to grasp his knee. "It's all right."

"No, it isn't!" he cried. "What if you're pregnant, on top of everything else?"

"Charles. It's fine. Listen to me." She gripped his hands

hard, willing him to look right at her. "You didn't get me pregnant. I can't get pregnant; I can't have children."

He froze, staring back. She watched the wild horror in his eyes turn to confusion, and then . . . dammit, to the all-too-familiar pity. "I had no idea," he said gruffly. "I'm sorry."

"Don't be. I never mentioned it." She let go of his hands and drew back, balling her hands in the edges of her sweater. "It's not in my file, because it doesn't have to be."

"Of course it doesn't," he murmured, still staring.

Unable to bear the weight of his sympathetic gaze, she kept talking. "I'll never have children of my own. And I have no family anyway. So, being a live-in nanny, getting to help raise children for a few years and be part of someone else's family in a way . . . that's what I wanted."

He hadn't stopped staring at her, but now was doing so as if seeing her with new eyes. "I have to tell you . . . I always wondered why someone who graduated Boston College with honors and a degree in foreign languages ended up being a nanny," he admitted quietly. "I don't mean that to sound demeaning in any way. What you do is very important, and I appreciate what you do. It's just . . . Something didn't add up. But I didn't have any right or reason to ask, so—"

"Well, now you know," she said, rubbing her hands together. They were prickling like crazy, one of her least favorite anxiety symptoms.

He continued to study her in that deep, searching way before finally saying, "I get the feeling there's a lot about you I don't know. Haven't known. Things that maybe I should."

Her stomach flipped nauseously. "What? Why?"

"Because I'm interested," he said, low and quiet.

Oh, no. No, no, no. "I'm just your nanny," she blurted out, trying to breathe. "I'm not some intriguing woman of mystery. I have no earthshaking secrets that would affect you in any way. I take very good care of your children. That's all you need to know; that's all that matters."

"Of course it is. Please don't get upset." He reached out to touch her hand and frowned. "God, your skin is ice-cold. Are you really okay?"

"No, I'm not okay," she said sharply, her voice finally breaking. "I had sex with my boss; I barely slept last night or ate today; I'm afraid I'm going to lose my job and where I live, that it's going to blow up my career completely, and now you're prying into my life, asking personal questions that only make me more uncomfortable. I'm not even *close* to okay."

"Dammit, I'm so sorry . . ." Charles shifted in his seat, his face a mask of distress and his hands twisting frantically. "I'm making this worse. I don't mean to. This whole situation has my brain a little fried, I can't lie."

"That makes two of us," she said. Her stomach churned, her chest felt tight, and the numbness was creeping up from her hands into her arms. This wasn't going well at all. Tears of frustration sprang to her eyes.

"No, no, please don't cry," he said. He went to reach for her, as if to comfort her, then apparently thought better of it and pulled back. "Lisette, last night I was feeling sorry for myself. I was totally wallowing. You found me, you were kind, and . . . with a little liquid courage, I got reckless. You're a very beautiful woman. The world may think I'm made of stone, but I'm not." He sighed and rubbed the back of his neck, restless and frustrated. "I can't apologize enough. All I can do is hope we can get past this. I value you tremendously, more than I can express, and I'm sorry I didn't treat you that way last night. I don't want you to be upset, or fearful, or think you'll lose anything here. You won't, I promise."

He was saying lovely things, but she knew he didn't get what the real problem was: she couldn't stop being afraid of losing her job and her residence just because he said so. He was in the position of power, and she was at his mercy. No amount of kindness or lust or good intention could make that any less true. As much as he was coming at this as "just a man and a woman, not an employer and his employee," it just wasn't so. She was lucky he was such a decent person and was trying to make things better, but the balance of power was so skewed, nothing could set this right. No matter what, from now on, if she wanted to stay on, she'd have to walk on eggshells. And even if they never talked about it again, last night would always loom between them. God, she'd been so stupid.

Her heart squeezed, seizing with a real ache. She closed her eyes to try to stem the tears, but they slipped out and down her face. Before she could lift her numb hands to swipe them away, she felt his thumb sweep along her cheeks, wiping her tears. She flinched at his unexpected touch and bowed her head.

Her thoughts shamed her: what she wanted at that moment, more than anything, was to sink into his arms and let him hold her, comfort her. But she couldn't possibly do that. There was no one to go to for comfort. She was alone in this, like she was in everything. And she'd hadn't felt quite this alone in a long time.

Charles stared at Lisette, her head bowed as she cried without a sound. It made his heart twist in his chest. No matter what he said, it only seemed to make things worse.

And she seemed so . . . vulnerable. Sad. Fragile, suddenly. She was always composed, friendly, and light, even though she was quiet. Now he wanted nothing more than to pull her into his embrace, hold her, soothe her, and assure her everything was going to be all right. But was it? He had no idea.

"Lisette," he murmured. "I'm not trying to upset you or

hurt your feelings. I'm trying to tell you I want us to get past this, and I very much want you to stay on here. That's the bottom line. Your job is safe here . . . *You* are safe here."

She nodded, sniffling. "Thank you. I appreciate all that." Her head lifted, and she finally met his eyes again as she wiped her cheeks. "I think I'm exhausted, that's all. Dreading this conversation all day took a lot of energy."

"Well, that's honest. And I understand. I'm pretty exhausted myself." He sighed and slowly sat back, still watching her. "If it makes you feel any better, I was so hungover it was pathetic."

Her brow furrowed. "Really? I mean, you were a little tipsy, but not wasted. I didn't think you were . . ."

"Oh, I wasn't," he said wryly. "Not until after you left the study, and I realized what I'd done. I finished a bottle of scotch as I reprimanded myself."

Her eyes flew wide. "What?"

"Yeah. I made a bad move and followed it up with a flat-out stupid one." He snorted and shook his head in self-disgust. "Spent a few hours on the bathroom floor today with my head in the toilet. Know what? Served me right."

Her eyes went even wider at that. "Oh, no. You poor thing."

"I was a hot mess," he said, the corner of his mouth twitching up. "Eileen had to literally help me up off the floor. I wasn't human again until a few hours ago."

Lisette groaned in sympathy. It made him grin.

"And the kids were all totally pissed at me," he added. "I was sick; you were AWOL—we were all supposed to go pumpkin picking today, remember?"

She gasped, eyes rounding again. "Oh, no! I completely forgot!"

"Yeah, me too. They sure didn't, though. So I promised them we'd go tomorrow afternoon, after school. It's supposed to be a nice day, thank God." He pinned her with his eyes. "Will you please join us?"

She hesitated, taking the moment to sniffle again and wipe her cheeks dry with the wrist of her sweater. "Um . . ."

"Please. The kids want you to. And maybe . . ." One of his shoulders lifted in a half shrug. "Maybe it'll help us get back to a more comfortable place, you know? Just being in each other's presence, having a normal day. So join us. Please."

She hesitated again, then said quietly, "Of course."

"Great. Thank you. They'll be happy." He considered her for a few more seconds. "Are you okay now, I hope? Better, anyway?"

"I'm fine," she said.

"Good. And . . . are *we* okay?" he asked.

She smiled faintly. "We will be. We're both rational adults. We'll be fine."

He nodded at that. "Excellent." He prayed to God she was right. All he wanted was for everything to go back to normal. He was sure she did too. They could put this blip behind them and go on with their routine, back to their lives as before.

Now if he could just stop picturing her naked, remembering how sweet her mouth tasted, and thinking about how unbelievably sexy she was when she was swept away by passion . . . That would be really, really helpful.

Chapter Six

Charles ended the call and made a few notes about it on his laptop while the details were still fresh. Work had been insanely busy that day, more than usual, and the only reason he'd eaten a decent lunch was because it had been a business lunch. He glanced at the time on his monitor; was it really four-thirty already? One good thing about going nonstop was the day had flown by. Another was he hadn't had much chance to think about the weekend.

He stood, needing to stretch his legs, his back. Walking to the windows, he stuffed his hands in his suit pockets and gazed out to the Manhattan skyline. The view was magnificent from his office. He never tired of it. When business had boomed in the 1980s and the Harrison fortune had doubled itself, his father had moved Harrison Enterprises' home office to a grand, sleek, modern building near The New York Public Library. From the offices of the executive members of the company, the views of midtown skyscrapers offset by the splash of nature from Bryant Park were fantastic. A prime location, certainly; it was one thing his father had done that Charles was grateful for.

He mulled over the phone call he'd just had, going over

details his chief executive in the Los Angeles office had disclosed . . . but the images came crashing through, without warning, as they had sporadically for the past few days. Lisette beneath him in the dark. The sounds of heavy breathing, her sighs and deep moans . . . the two of them kissing and grabbing at each other like out-of-control teenagers. His dick twitched just thinking about it.

All he wanted was to forget it had happened. But he'd had a taste . . . and now he couldn't stop thinking about her.

Monday afternoon had been interesting. He'd promised the kids he'd take them pumpkin picking, so off they went. No chauffeur; Charles drove, piling his three children and their nanny into his Escalade to drive almost an hour east. The kids bickered at first, then grew silent in the backseat, heads down over their handheld video games. Lisette sat beside him, quiet in the passenger seat, her hands twisting in her lap as he and she both tried to act casual, as if the awkward tension wasn't as thick and suffocating as hell.

All things considered, it had gone nicely enough. Thomas had been surly to him, as usual, but softened a bit as the afternoon went on. They all traipsed through the fields, looking for decent pumpkins amongst what was left. They bought apple cider, apple butter, pumpkin pie, and pumpkin bread. The weather had cooperated, giving them blue skies and mild air. Lisette, as always, was focused on the kids, which gave Charles an opportunity to observe her.

For close to two years, this beautiful woman had lived quietly under his roof, and he'd never noticed many of the things he noticed that day. Like how her hips swayed when she walked. Or the way tendrils of her lustrous dark hair would slip free from her French braid, framing her face adorably. Or how graceful her hands were, even when doing work. Or how she handled his kids with such a perfect balance of discipline and warmth, or how her dark eyes lit with humor and warmth when the kids did things she liked . . .

Warmth. That was it. It hit him like a lightning bolt: it was her warmth that drew him to her so strongly. There had been such a lack of it in his life . . . Between Lisette's warmth and kindness, how good she was at her job, and how beautiful she was, he was suddenly consumed by her. Thinking of her all the time.

This was insanity.

He snatched his cell phone off the desk and hit speed dial. He needed to talk to his younger brother, who was also his best friend and most trusted confidant in the world. Because Charles did need to talk to someone about this, or his head would explode.

"Hey, Chuckles," came Dane's jovial voice. "How's it going?"

"Are you free tonight, by any chance?" Charles cut right to it. "I need to talk."

"Sure." Dane's tone changed from light to serious in a heartbeat. "What's going on? You okay?"

"I'm fine," Charles assured him, "but . . . I just need to talk to you. Some shit went down this weekend, and I need a trusted ear."

"Luckily for you, I have two of them," Dane said. "Why don't you come by the hotel? Get a drink or two, and we'll chat."

"I'm never drinking again," Charles said, shuddering. "But yes, I'll meet you there. Somewhere we can talk in private, though. Not the lounge."

"How about the billiards room?" Dane suggested.

"Perfect. See you at eight." Charles ended the call, then hit speed dial again.

Lisette answered her cell on the second ring. "Hello?"

Just her soft voice evoked a stirring in his chest. Jesus,

this was bad. "Hi, it's Charles. Just wanted to tell you I'll be getting home late tonight. Having a late dinner with my brother. So if you could let the kids know, and tell them I'll see them in the morning before they leave for school, I'd appreciate it."

"Of course. No problem. Have a nice time."

"Well, it's Dane, so I'm sure I will." He paced the office slowly. "Lisette . . . how are you doing? Everything . . . all right?"

"Yes, Charles." Her voice dipped a little. "I'm perfectly fine."

"Good. That's good. I'm glad." He closed his eyes and winced, hating himself for sounding like a babbling idiot. "Okay. See you."

Lisette put her phone back in her bag and sighed. Yeah, she was perfectly fine. Sure she was. She still had a job, despite having made a monumental mistake. She still had a place to live and security. She still had everything exactly how it'd been a few days before . . .

Except now that she'd had a sample of that raw passion and heat, gotten to see a glimpse of the real Charles Harrison III, she wanted more. She couldn't stop replaying the events of late Saturday night like a highlight reel in her head. The feel of his weight on top of her, so strong and solid . . . his mouth on hers, hot and hungry . . . the way his hands had slid over her body, greedy, almost frantically . . . the sound of his labored breathing against her ear as he moved inside her . . .

"Lisette?" Ava's voice cut through her reverie, making Lisette jump.

"Sorry, honey. Daydreaming." She smiled down at the girl. "Did you say something?"

"I can't figure this out," Ava whined. She sat slumped

over the small kitchen table, her science homework spread out before her. Lisette knew Ava liked to do her homework in there to be with her and Tina. Tina Rodriguez was the housekeeper and cook in the mansion from Monday through Friday; Eileen O'Rourke was the weekend shift. In Tina, Lisette had found something rare in her isolated world: a friend. The short, older brunette shot Lisette a glance and a wink now as she stirred sauce in the pot on the stove, knowing the kid's routine.

"Did you *really* try to figure it out on your own first?" Lisette asked, her usual question to make sure Ava wasn't just being lazy and looking for Lisette to do her homework for her.

The girl nodded emphatically. "I tried; I did. But can you help me with this one thing? I just don't see where they talk about photosynthesis in this article other than giving the definition. How am I supposed to 'impart my thoughts' on that?!"

"Okay, okay. Let me see." Lisette scooted her chair a little closer to look over the papers Ava thrust at her in frustration.

A few hours later, after Lisette had picked Thomas and Myles up from soccer practice, and all three kids were playing up in their playroom, Lisette and Tina stole a little time to have a cup of tea together and chat. They sat at the same table where Ava liked to do her homework, tucked into the corner of the large, modern kitchen.

"So spill it," Tina demanded, munching on one of the chocolate chip cookies she'd made that afternoon.

Lisette's brow furrowed. "Spill what?"

"I'm older, wiser, and I know you," Tina said, her dark eyes dancing. "You're not yourself today. What's up? I'm here for you, you know."

Lisette stared at her friend, so grateful to have her in her quiet, lonely life. She darted a glance over her shoulder toward the door, making sure none of the children were nearby. Then, for extra safety, she started to speak in a low tone, slipping into Spanish. She and Tina were both fluent, so they used it when they didn't want any of the Harrisons to know what they were saying.

"I did something so stupid," Lisette began. "And I can't stop beating myself up for it, even though it's supposed to be okay now."

"What happened?" Tina set down her cup in its saucer and reached for Lisette's hand.

Lisette's eyes welled up at the small show of support. Her throat thickened, and all she could do was shake her head.

"Shhh, shh, shh. Come here, mama." Tina reached over to hug her friend.

Lisette gratefully accepted the embrace, clinging to Tina for a minute as tears slipped out of her eyes. Then she pulled back, wiped her cheeks and sniffled hard, and sat up straight. "I'll be fine. Honest."

"Well, when you're ready to talk about whatever happened, you know I'm here for you." Tina squeezed Lisette's hands for emphasis. "In the meantime, if you fixed it, and it's behind you, leave it there. Pick up and move on; just keep moving. That's all you can do. Right?"

Lisette nodded and sniffed once more, then pulled her hands from Tina's to cradle her mug. It was nice and warm against her palms, and she lifted it to her mouth for a sip. "Thank you."

"Maybe you just needed a hug." Tina smiled kindly.

"Maybe I did." Lisette smiled back, gratitude welling in her chest.

"I always have a hug for you if you need it. And stop beating yourself up, whatever happened. Let it go. Okay?"

"Okay."

"Set?" Myles's voice rang out. "Liseeeeeette . . ." A few

seconds later, he appeared in the kitchen doorway. "Can I have a snack?"

Lisette glanced at her watch. "Now?" Tina pushed the plate of cookies out of Myles's line of vision. "It's a little late, sweetie. You're going to bed soon."

"But I want to wait up for Daddy," Myles said.

"You can't tonight," Lisette said. "He's not going to be home until later, way after the three of you are asleep. I told you that when I picked you up from soccer, remember?"

The boy's mouth folded into a dramatic pout. His big blue eyes, so like his father's, crinkled with added sadness. "But I wanna wait up."

"But you can't, little man." Lisette took another sip of tea. "Go on and finish your game, or your TV show, because bedtime is in half an hour."

"Aww, c'mooooon," Myles needled.

"This is not up for debate, Myles," Lisette said, her voice quiet but firm. "Say good night to Tina and go back up now."

The little boy huffed and kicked his foot against the floor, but said, "Good night, Tina," and did as he was told.

Tina shook her head, speaking in Spanish. "And he's the easy one. He's a good boy. Always was. But those other two were turning into bratty little shits 'til you came to this house. Amazing what you've done with those kids. Seriously. I see it every day."

"They're great kids," Lisette murmured, also slipping back into Spanish. She reached for a cookie and bit into it, then moaned. "Oh my God, this is so good. You're a magician, Tina."

"So are you," Tina remarked. "I may work magic with food, but you've worked magic with those kids. I hope Charles Harrison really knows what a treasure he found in you."

At the mention of his name, Lisette's eyes fell to her teacup. "I actually think he does," she murmured. She recalled the look of relief on his face when he learned she wasn't going to leave; he truly did appreciate what she did here. Everything would go back to normal eventually, as time passed.

Tina was right. Lisette had to stop dwelling on this and somehow move forward.

Charles leaned over the table, carefully lining up his shot. He narrowed his eyes, taking his time, then slid the cue through his fingers to make the break. The cue ball smacked the group of balls hard, sending them scattering across the green cloth.

"Nice," Dane said, eyeing where the balls stopped rolling. He lifted his bottle of dark beer to his lips and stole a sip before moving around to the other side of the table. "So? Talk. You're wound up tight. Worse than usual. I could see it as soon as you walked in."

Charles just nodded, his gaze canvasing the room. Dane's upscale hotel had a wide, extravagant billiards room with eight tables for guests, but a smaller private room in the back with only one table. Taken by reservation only, it was used for everything from covert meetings of businessmen to private trysts for lovers. Dane had reserved it tonight so they could speak freely.

Charles took a deep breath as he watched Dane take his shot, then blurted out, "I went home after the party on Saturday night, was feeling sorry for myself, and went into my study to have a drink and brood. Lisette found me there. She was just being nice to me; we were talking . . . Next thing I know, I'm on top of her on the couch, and I . . . we . . . Christ, Dane, I fucked her right there, on the couch in my study. I slept with my goddamn kids' nanny. I'm a walking cliché, and a pathetic moron to boot."

Dane slowly straightened to his full height, his shell-shocked gaze glued to his older brother. "Are you serious?"

"No, I'm making up a horrible story like that," Charles snapped sarcastically. He ran a hand over his face, scrubbing at his jaw as a muscle below his eye twitched.

"Holy shit." Dane blew out a long, slow breath. "Um . . . you're sure you don't want a drink?"

"I don't ever want to drink again. After she left the study—fled the scene, to be more accurate—and I realized what we'd done, I drowned myself in a bottle of scotch. I was sick as a dog most of the next day."

"I'll bet." Dane set his cue against the wall and turned back again, intently scanning his brother's features. "Are you okay?"

"No, I'm not okay!" Charles spat. "I'm a fucking mess. I can't believe what I did."

"What you *both* did," Dane corrected him. His eyes widened a fraction. "Unless . . . you're telling me you forced her . . . ?"

"*What?* God, no. It wasn't like that!" Charles raked his hands through his hair and glared back. "I can't believe you think I'd—"

"I don't!" Dane cut him off. "That's why the thought of it horrified me. Because that's *not* you."

"Dane," Charles growled, "I'm an idiot, but I'm not a rapist."

"I know that. Calm down." Dane's voice softened, and he reached for his cue again. "So clarify it for me." He gestured to the table. "Take your next shot and tell me what happened, starting at the beginning."

As the brothers played, Charles told his story, glad to have the game as a distraction. It was easier to get out the words with his eyes glued to the colored balls, the ornate light fixture over the table, the soothing green of the cloth. Dane didn't interrupt, just let him keep talking until he grew silent.

Finally, Dane eyed the last ball on the table. He called it, shot hard, and sent it sailing into the corner pocket.

"Well done." Charles reached for his wallet, pulled a hundred-dollar bill from it, and handed it to his brother. It was their usual wager. As Dane pocketed the money, Charles reached for the triangle to set up a new match.

Danc watched him, hip leaning against the table. "What's really going on with you?" he finally asked.

Charles reached beneath the table for the balls, placing them two by two back on the table. "What do you mean?"

"This whole thing. It's not like you." Dane pinned him with a knowing stare. "What happened with Lisette . . . it's a symptom of a bigger problem, not the disease." He twirled the cue between his fingers. "Something bigger is going on."

Charles froze at the accuracy of his brother's words. "What makes you say that?"

"Because someone as reserved and tightly wound as you doing your kids' nanny on a couch? That's an act of rebellion, if I ever heard one. Or a cry for help." Dane reached for the small blue cube and chalked the end of his stick. "You know, Charles . . . a lot of people tend to start reassessing their lives when they hit milestone birthdays. And forty is supposed to be the worst of all. Coincidence? I don't think so." Casually, Dane put the chalk back and glanced at his brother again. "You never *had* a rebellious phase. You were too well disciplined, and you weren't allowed to do anything crazy even if you wanted to. Not as a kid, not in your teens . . . The most—the *only*—rebellious thing you've ever done was marrying Vanessa."

"And we all know how well that turned out," Charles grumbled. Feeling his throat tighten, he finally reached up to the knot of his tie and loosened it, then popped open the top button of his shirt.

"That's beside the point, Chuckles. Look. You just told

me the play-by-play of what happened with Lisette. But what you didn't tell me is why you went home feeling sorry for yourself in the first place. You'd just been to a big party, for *you*, with everyone who knows you there. That's, like, supposed to be a happy thing." Dane's eyes narrowed, crinkling at the sides. "Talk to me, man."

"I'm fine," Charles growled.

"The hell you are."

"I didn't come here for you to play psychoanalyst."

"Yeah, actually, you did. You just can't admit it, because you never ask anyone for help. You're too proud."

Charles glared at his brother. Unfazed, Dane added, "You trust me more than anyone in the world. And you should. No one on this planet knows you better than I do, or cares more about you, other than Tess." His voice and expression softened. "I'm worried about you."

"I just . . ." Charles started to say. He tore off his glasses with one hand and scrubbed a hand over his face with the other. "I'm tired. Tired of . . ."

"Of what?"

After a long pause, Charles sighed and put his glasses back on. "Everything."

Dane put the cue stick in its notch on the wall. Turning back, he splayed his hands on the table, and demanded, "Talk to me, goddammit. *Talk*."

"Well, how about we start with how Thomas hates me," Charles said. "He's just like Pierce was as a kid, and that scares me. I saw it at the party, how fucking pissed he is at me. But then I watched him happily go to his uncles for hugs . . . and it hit me. He's turning into Pierce, and I'm turning into Dad. And that's not a good thing."

"It's a fucking horrible thing," Dane agreed. "If it were true. Which it's *not*."

"Isn't it?" Charles started to pace the small room, hands

running through his thick hair, tousling it. "Just like Dad, I have no love life, but a bitch ex-wife who took me for my money, had a few kids, and split the scene without a look back. I also have children who are angry and hurting, and I don't see them enough because I'm working all the time. *All the time*, to secure a future for them like Dad did for us . . ." Charles stopped and looked up at Dane to murmur, ". . . and, just like him, I'm alone. With kids that resent me a little more each month, and no partner at my side."

Charles's shoulders slumped, and he exhaled a forlorn breath. "I'm forty years old, half my life's gone by, and on Saturday night, I realized I'm just like him. When I was a kid, that was all I wanted. Now . . . no. God, no. He's bitter, he's ruthless, he's . . ." Shaking his head, Charles moved to the one long window and stared balefully down at the people who walked along the bustling Manhattan streets. "The truth is, I'm getting tired of the whole thing. Being the 'heir to the throne,' as you've always called it." Rubbing a hand across the back of his neck, he looked out at the sparkling lights of Manhattan. "So, yeah, Dane, I don't know what to do with all that."

Dane went to stand next to him. "You listen to me," he said, his voice low and determined. "All your life, you've done the right thing. You've been a dutiful son, a dutiful corporate leader, doing all the right things without complaint." Dane sighed in sympathy. "That's got to be exhausting."

Charles flicked a glance at his brother and murmured, "You have no idea."

"I don't. You're right. I was lucky. I was born second. Very little pressure on me. It was all about you." Dane moved to one of the couches, motioning for Charles to join him. "I've always admired how you took the mantle with dignity and grace, even when we were kids. I was also grateful as hell that since Dad pinned all his expectations on you,

I had much more freedom to do what I wanted. You never did. He controlled every bit of your life."

"Yup." Sitting across from Dane, Charles leaned his elbows on his knees and sighed.

"It's really no wonder you married Vanessa. Hell, she was fucking stunning. A fireball, a rebel, not a blueblood. Exactly what Dad didn't want for you." Dane grinned mischievously. "I was kind of proud of you for going through with it, truth be told. I wasn't sure you would, once Dad really started throwing threats around."

Charles shrugged, sitting back against the leather cushions. "He needed me too much. He'd spent my whole life grooming me; he couldn't afford to lose me. You were off doing your own thing; he'd never let a woman run the company, so Tess was out; and Pierce . . . was Pierce." They both grinned at that. "Of course, later, after Vanessa tore me apart, I wished I'd listened, but whatever. It's history now."

"Yup." Dane stretched out his legs. "As for the kids . . . yeah, they're a handful. But that solution is not only simple, but doable. You want to see them more? Make the time. You want them not to resent you? Spend some quality time with them."

"You make it sound so easy," Charles mumbled.

"Because it is." Dane snorted. "I don't have kids, but I understand human beings. They all need attention, to feel wanted and important. I'm not telling you how to be a father to your kids, Charles. I'm just telling you how easy it is to not be like Dad."

Charles nodded in slow agreement.

"So, let me guess." Dane sat back, crossing one long leg over the other. "You turned forty, you looked around, and you didn't like a lot of what you saw. Yes?"

"Yes." Charles felt the tension ebb a little from his shoulders. Dane knew him so well, it was uncanny. He and Tess were the only people who knew the *real* him. And right then, looking at his brother and best friend, Charles was so damn grateful for that.

"So you're all 'woe is me,' get a little drunk," Dane added with an amused smirk, "and the mishap with Lisette isn't surprising, really. She was just in the wrong place at the wrong time."

"I suppose." Charles studied his hands as he admitted in a husky murmur, "But the other problem is . . . I can't stop thinking about her." He didn't look up. He couldn't. "It was like wildfire. Once we started, I don't think either of us could've stopped. She was so . . . God, she was gorgeous. And *hot*. Passionate. After that night . . . knowing now what she's like . . . I can't look at her the same way. I don't think of her the same way. And worse . . ." He swallowed hard. The truth was turning his insides into knots. "I want more of her. And I shouldn't. I *can't*."

Dane snorted, making Charles raise his head. "Gee," Dane taunted lightly, "you have the hots for someone who works for you? Can't get them out of your head, think about them all the time, have to have them, even though you know on paper it's totally wrong? Tell me, what's that like? Because I have *no* idea."

Charles had to laugh wryly at the parallel Dane presented. When Dane and Julia had first gotten involved, she had been the singer he'd hired for his new hotel lounge. Several times, Charles had warned Dane about the perils of getting involved with someone who worked for him; and, even though Dane had known he should, he hadn't listened. The similarity of the situations was more than ironic. It would have been kind of funny if it weren't so serious.

"I was drawn to Julia like no other woman in my entire

life," Dane reminded his brother. "I couldn't stay away from her."

"But Lisette isn't an unattached woman I see a few nights a week at work," Charles pointed out. "If this blows up, the ripple effects . . . She lives in my *home*. I see her every morning and every night. She takes care of my children." He huffed out a breath. "Hell, she spends much more time with them than I do. She knows them better than I do." The admission pained him, but he knew it was the truth. "I can't ever go near her again like that, for a hundred reasons. But most of all for my kids' sake, if nothing else. If she ever felt like she had to quit . . . I'd never forgive myself. They need her."

"They need you more. You're their father," Dane said. "Look, you're being noble, as always. But just admit it to yourself: you want her again, and you want her bad. If you didn't, we wouldn't even be having this part of the conversation."

Charles scowled and ran his hand across the back of his neck. "Well, shit."

"Sorry to break it to you, Chuckles, but you're a flawed human being after all. And merely a man, at that. With some women, once you've had a taste . . ." Dane shrugged and shot him a crooked grin. "Good luck with that."

"Thanks a lot," Charles muttered.

"Hey, big brother?" Dane's brows arched. "From what I've seen, Lisette is caring, bright, and just plain nice. She's quiet and sweet, but capable of taking care of your three little whirlwinds day in and day out. Which, let's face it, must be an exhausting job, but she does it well. Add to all that the fact that she happens to be really easy on the eyes?" Dane shrugged again. "You could do a lot worse, you know. Just sayin'."

Charles blinked, stunned at the implication. "She's. The. *Nanny*," he ground out.

"Ohhhh. Okay." Dane's eyes narrowed, his stare piercing. "So really it's about her being below you in social stature. That's the issue?"

"Hell no!" Charles snapped. "That's not the problem at all."

"Isn't it, though? One of the bigger problems, anyway. Of course it is." Dane arched a brow haughtily and continued, "I mean . . . what would people *say?* Right? You're the COO of a powerful, well-known international conglomerate, and she's your kids' nanny. It's so fucking cliché, it's gauche. The gossip would be epic."

"Shut the hell up," Charles hissed. "For the record, just hypothetically—if I ever did get involved with her, I don't care about what people would say. Let them gossip. I don't give a rat's ass."

"Sure about that?" Dane asked.

"Yes! She happens to be a fantastic woman," Charles said, suddenly all fired up. "It's more than just her being kind and taking excellent care of my kids. She's a real sweetheart. She makes me smile, a lot. She's smart, and she's educated. And she—"

"Whoa, there!" Dane cut him off. "You don't have to defend her assets to me." He held up his hands in mock surrender. "She's lovely and down-to-earth. She *is* great with your kids. And she's gorgeous." His brows lifted as he summed up, "You're right, Chuckles; she's a pretty fantastic woman. And you haven't dated in *how* long?"

"All right, enough." Charles couldn't help but think about her warm, chocolate-colored eyes. The feel of her soft olive skin. Her long, thick hair, out of its usual braid, loose and smooth as silk between his fingers. And her hot, sensual mouth—how it tasted, how it felt when she kissed him back with raw hunger . . .

He shot to his feet and strode to where his cue stick stood.

"This topic is closed," he said. "It was a mistake, a fluke. I'll get her out of my head. Things will go back to normal. There won't be a repeat."

"If you say so," Dane said lightly.

"I say so," Charles repeated with firm resolve. And felt something go strangely hollow inside as he said it.

Chapter Seven

Lisette grabbed her keys from the tiny crystal bowl on the front table beside the matching one that usually held Charles's keys. She did a quick last check of her tote bag: plastic bags to hold extra candy, wipes, cell phone, sunglasses, lip balm . . . The other tote with extra clothes was already in the minivan.

"Okay, you guys," she called. "Everyone ready to go?"

"Yeeeeesssss!!" Myles cried as he flew down the stairs. "Time for trick or treat!"

Ava and Thomas were right behind him, giggling with excitement.

"It's gonna be so fun trick or treating with Uncle Pierce," Thomas said.

"And Abby and Dylan," Myles reminded his big brother.

"We'll be a big traveling party," Lisette said, leaning down to tie Myles's sneaker. "You all look fantastic." She straightened to survey them in their Halloween costumes. Thomas was a ninja, dressed all in black; Myles was a red Power Ranger; and Ava was the heroine Merida from the movie *Brave*, complete with a long, red curly wig and a plastic bow and arrow. Lisette pulled her phone out of her bag and said, "Let's get a few pictures of you out front by the pumpkins and flowers. I know your dad will want to see how awesome you all look."

The front door opened, and as if on cue Charles stepped into the foyer.

"Daddy!" Myles and Ava yelped, throwing themselves at him for hugs. Thomas stood and watched. Lisette saw the conflict in the boy's dark eyes: part happy to see his father, part wanting to stay angry at him for all his perceived sins. She touched Thomas's shoulder and smiled down at him, meaning to comfort. Thomas gave her a hint of a grin.

"Hello, Charles," she said to her employer. She ignored the low burn starting in her belly at the sight of him. Dressed in a navy suit, crisp shirt, and striped tie, Charles looked every bit the urbane COO that he was. He also looked like a cover model, confident, handsome, and sexy . . . *Damn*. She had to stop thinking those thoughts. Clearing her throat, she put on a bright smile. "This is a surprise."

"A good surprise, I hope?" Charles said, an arm around each child. He looked down at them.

"Yes, yes!" Myles shrieked, bouncing on his toes. "Look at me, Daddy, I'm a Power Ranger!" He struck a pose, intending to be fierce.

"So cool!" Charles said, smiling. "Hey, has anyone seen my daughter? She's got dark brown hair. I don't know who this redheaded warrior princess is . . ."

"Merida," Ava said proudly. "I'm Merida from *Brave*. I can shoot arrows, and I'm strong, and I'm better than all the boys."

"That's definitely awesome," Charles said, fingering one of the long fake curls. "I've always said you're a force to be reckoned with."

"Why are you here?" Thomas said. Curiosity and annoyance mixed in his tone.

Charles blinked, his smile faltering a bit. "It's Halloween.

I wanted to go trick or treating with you all. I thought it'd be fun."

"We were about to leave," Thomas said, more surly this time.

"Then I'm glad I caught you," Charles said, flicking a glance at Lisette. "Where are you going?"

"To Pierce's," she said. "Their neighborhood has a lot more kids; they said it would be fun. We're meeting him, Abby, and her nephew Dylan at Pierce's place."

"We'd better get going, then, huh?" Charles said, tweaking Ava's nose playfully.

"You never come trick or treating with us," Thomas said. "Don't you have work? You *always* have work."

"I left early." Charles's eyes narrowed, studying his elder son's face as he stepped to him, and said carefully, "Thomas. Does it bother you that I'm here?"

Thomas didn't answer, but his stare stayed petulant.

Charles sighed as he thought, *Well, at least he didn't say yes.* "I left work early," he said, "because Halloween is fun, and I wanted to be with my children." He shoved his hands in the pockets of his slacks and looked around at all three of his kids. "I don't see you guys as much as I should. That's *my* fault. So I . . . well, I'm going to make an effort to see you all more. And not to miss things like your concerts and your soccer games . . . and trick or treating on Halloween. Okay?"

Myles banded his arms around his father's leg and hugged tight. "Okay!"

"That would be really nice," Ava admitted softly.

Charles's heart squeezed, and he reached for her, pulling her into his side and hugging her with his free arm. "I love you," he said. "All of you. I'm sorry I've been gone so much . . . I'm going to try to be better about that."

Thomas looked wary, but he nodded. Charles exhaled; maybe he'd gotten through to him a little. It was a start.

Then he looked at Lisette, whose big brown eyes were warm and . . . approving. Well, that was a nice bonus. His gaze quickly traveled over her, drinking her in. Her curves were hidden by a long orange sweater, black yoga pants, and multicolored sneakers. Small, simple gold hoops hung from her ears, the only jewelry she wore besides a thin gold watch. As usual, her dark hair was pulled back in a long French braid and her face was devoid of makeup, except for what looked to be tinted lip balm on her luscious mouth. She didn't need any makeup. Her long lashes were black as night, her smooth olive skin glowed, and that kissable mouth . . . She really was, as Dane had said, a natural beauty.

And Charles enjoyed looking at her, much more than he should. In fact, just looking at her made his heart beat a little faster, made his blood pulse a little hotter, and made him want things that he shouldn't.

He tore his gaze from her and said to the kids, "Give me two minutes to change out of this suit. You all go ahead to the car; I'll be right there."

It was almost ten o'clock by the time the kids fell asleep. An afternoon of walking around Edgewater should have worn them out, but the excitement of Halloween—and the sugar rush from the candy they gobbled—had them buzzing way past their normal bedtime.

When the hallway was soundless, and Lisette was sure they were all sleeping, she went down to the kitchen to fix herself a cup of tea. A hot cup of orange spice tea, along with the new book waiting on her e-reader, after the frenetic noise and energy of the afternoon and evening, was all she wanted. That and quiet, to sit and read until she fell asleep.

The spacious kitchen was dark and empty. She flipped on the lights and hummed to herself as she filled the white teakettle with water. The last song that had been playing in the minivan on the way home was stuck in her head.

"I can't get that damn song out of my head either."

"Oh!" She whirled around in surprise, sloshing water from the open kettle onto the tiled floor. Charles stood a few feet behind her. Wide-eyed, she clutched a hand to her chest.

"I'm sorry!" he said. "Wow, I didn't mean to scare you."

"I—I didn't hear you come in." She turned off the faucet and glanced at the puddle on the floor.

"Here, give me that." Charles strode to her and took the kettle from her, his fingers brushing hers as he moved away to place it on the stove. "Enough water in here for me to join you? I assume you're making tea."

"Yes. I mean, yes, there's enough water, and yes, I am." Still flustered, she hurried to the paper-towel rack, tore off a few, and went back to the puddle, dropping to her knees to wipe it up.

After setting the kettle on the stove and flicking on the gas, Charles watched her, casually leaning against the marble counter of the center island. "You couldn't sleep either, huh?"

"Not yet," she said, throwing the sopping pile of paper towels into the trash.

"Me either. But it was a nice evening." Charles smiled warmly and crossed his arms over his chest. "The kids had fun, and it was good to be out with them. Thanks for letting me tag along."

"Tag along?" Lisette frowned at him, puzzled. "They're *your* children."

"Well, you didn't expect me to show up. I infringed on your plans."

"What? Charles . . ." She wiped her damp hands on a cloth kitchen towel. "This is your home, your family. You don't ever infringe on plans. You do whatever you want."

"I know all that. But I know if *I* made a plan and someone popped in at the last minute, it might throw me off a little."

She waved a dismissive hand. "Nothing throws you off. You run a billion-dollar international company. Unflappable, solid as a rock, that's you. Everyone knows that."

His lips pursed, his jaw tightened, and his gaze intensified. It almost made her squirm. She'd intended it as an offhand compliment, but he looked almost . . . agitated. What had she said wrong? She turned to go to the pantry, then stopped, realizing he intended to stay. "Um . . . what kind of tea would you like?"

To her relief, his features softened. "What are you having?"

"Orange spice. Decaffeinated."

"Sounds good. I'll have the same."

As she ducked into the large pantry, she placed a hand to her still pounding heart, closed her eyes, and tried to take a deep breath. God, he'd startled her. And God, he looked gorgeous. She loved how he looked in his expensive custom-tailored suits; that was a given. Few men were as downright dashing in a suit as Charles Harrison III, and the man practically lived in his suits. When he got home from the office, he usually discarded the jacket and pulled off the tie, but stayed in his clothes until he went to his bedroom for the night. Even living in his house, the too-rare glimpses of a casual Charles were delightful.

So, seeing him like he was now—in a tight navy pullover sweater and jeans, hair a little rumpled, and his glasses on, not his contacts—he was deliciously adorable, appealing, and just . . . normal. Well, if movie-star kind of handsome men were normal, other than the whole mega rich, smart, and powerful thing.

She found the box of tea bags and left the pantry. Charles now sat at the small table in the nook, where she usually did

homework with Ava or talked with Tina. He flashed her a
smile and gestured to the center island. "Got out some mugs."

She dropped a tea bag in each cup, feeling as though she
were being watched. She snuck a glance at Charles from beneath her lashes. He *was* watching her, and when caught, his
eyes held, and the grin stayed on his face.

Jesus, was he actually smoldering at her? Or was she just
wishing he were? Either way, the warm, wobbly feeling she
lately got whenever she looked at him took merciless hold
of her insides.

This new dynamic between them had thrown her way off
course. She'd never been intimidated by Charles, and she
knew some people were, simply because of the immense
power he had. Yes, he had a commanding presence and was
incredibly smart, but he was not arrogant or condescending.
He was reserved in nature, but always extremely courteous,
genial, and respectful, to her and to everyone around him.
He didn't micromanage her, obviously trusting her abilities
enough to hang back and let her do her job. And yes, she'd
harbored some feelings for him, but nothing that kept her
from doing her job, being around him, or talking to him. It'd
just been a crush, really.

But since the night of . . . well, *that night*, it was a whole
new ball game. For almost two years, they'd shared an easy
coexistence, but that mellow calm in his presence had van-
ished. Now, the thought of him, the sight of him, even the
smell of him got her all worked up and flustered. She'd
always thought he was gorgeous, sure; but now she also
thought of him as sexy, and amazing in bed—well, on the
couch—and tempting, and quietly charismatic, and . . . and
she was in big trouble, that's what she was.

The shrill whistle of the teakettle snapped her out of her
thoughts. He rose from his seat and went to the stove.
"Allow me."

Biting down on her lip as he took the kettle and poured

the boiling water into the cups, she fought to appear calm and collected, as she'd always been before. Now, it was taking everything she had to appear that way. Her skin felt warm, her stomach felt swirly, and she was sure her cheeks were flushed because she felt as if they were burning. She felt like a silly teenager with a secret forbidden crush— and it was *not* okay. Not if she wanted any sort of peace and sanity as she continued to live with him and do her job each day.

Steeling herself, she smiled demurely and thanked him as she took one of the mugs. He wrapped his large hands around his mug as they sat at the table in the kitchen nook. An awkward silence settled over them. Suddenly the kitchen felt too big for just two people sitting in the corner, which made that simple act feel somehow intimate. She stared down into her mug and chewed on her bottom lip.

"Today was nice," he said amiably. "I think you enjoyed it. I hope?"

His deep, warm voice made her heart twinge. Or maybe something a little lower twinged. Or maybe both. His voice was so sensual, like everything else about him . . . Oh, yeah, this was very, very bad. She cleared her dry throat.

"Yes, I did," she managed to say. "It was a fun day, and I know the kids loved having you with them." She lifted her steaming mug to her lips to take a tentative sip. "That was a wonderful surprise for them. You made their day."

He grinned. "I don't know why I didn't go last year." Then he frowned slightly as he turned his mug in his hands. "Must have been working, of course . . ."

"Last year, you were on a business trip," she reminded him. "Tokyo, I think."

His brow furrowed harder as he tried to recall. "I think you may be right. Probably. Damn. And the year before that? And the year before *that?*" With a shake of his head, now it was he who stared into his cup. "I've missed too many things. It's not fair to them. It isn't right. I'm the only real parent they have. I have to start being around more."

"Then you will," she murmured. It wasn't her place to offer opinions. She sipped her tea.

"Don't worry, I still need you," he kidded. "You're not out of a job, not by a long shot. I just need to start being around a little more, and I'm very aware of that."

She only nodded. They were his children; she had no say in whatever he did or didn't do in regard to them. If he wanted to spend more time with them, good for the kids. They already didn't have a mother around, and their father was barely home when they were actually awake. All she said was, "I'm sure they'd love that."

Charles looked down into his cup, then back up at her. "When we were kids, our father was always working. We felt his absence. My mother felt it too, and she . . . started seeking attention elsewhere."

Lisette had heard plenty of stories about the infamous Laura, of her multiple affairs and the ugly divorce that followed.

Charles stretched his arms over his head and yawned. "My father threw my mother out when I was fourteen. I was away at boarding school, so it didn't affect me as much as it did Pierce. He was only six years old." Charles took another sip of tea, and Lisette did too. "Pierce quickly turned into a surly, angry, hell-raiser of a kid. He felt ignored, unwanted, which was awful. He and my father have always resented each other. Knocked heads for years, and now they don't speak unless forced to. It's tense and uncomfortable . . . and my God, I don't want that for Thomas and me. I can already see the parallels, and it worries me."

His marine blue eyes narrowed, making the corners crinkle as he steadily held her gaze. "I know you know what I mean. Hell, you're the one who suggested he might need therapy. He's only *seven*." Charles shook his head in frustration, huffing out a breath. "He deserves better. All three of them do. So I have to fix it somehow, while I still can. I need to be a better father. I thought I was doing okay, but I've come to realize and admit that's not the case. Thomas wouldn't even hug me willingly on my birthday. That's on me."

Lisette realized her mouth had dropped open, and she quickly closed her lips tight. He was revealing such private information to her; it was astonishing. They'd always talked, but it was insignificant chatter—typically about the kids, their schoolwork, their activities, maybe even the weather. This was so . . . personal.

"You're shocked that I'm telling you all this," he said, studying her shrewdly.

She had to laugh. "Did you read my mind or something?"

"Didn't have to. It's all over your face." He gave her a lop-sided grin. "You're not often easy to read, but you sure are right now."

She was surprised by his words. "You don't think I'm easy to read? Really?"

"Nope. You're very quiet; you keep to yourself. Kind of . . ." He searched for the right word. "Guarded. That's fine; don't get me wrong! But yes, it makes you hard to read sometimes. And I'm pretty good at reading people. In my position, I have to be. So the fact that you aren't . . ." His brows arched as he added, "I have to admit, it's intriguing. I find you interesting."

She stilled at his assessment. It unnerved her. Maybe because it implied he'd paid more attention to her than she'd ever thought he would.

"So, shifting the topic a bit, what was your childhood like?" he asked in a lighter tone. "Hopefully better than mine."

She peered at him cautiously. "I thought when you hired me, you did a full background check on me. You know my history already, don't you?"

"Sure, I know the basics," he said. "But I want to hear a little more, right from you. Something a bit more personal."

She blinked, and a wave of alarm washed over her. She schooled her features into neutrality and managed, "Why?"

Charles crossed his forearms on the table and leaned in a bit. His posture was casual, but the look in his eyes wasn't. "Because I'm curious. I mean, I've known you for a while now. You've lived in my home for almost two years; you're with my kids day in and day out . . . but really, I don't know you at all." His eyes were piercing, commanding, and she felt held in place by his gaze.

Her heart pounded erratically in her chest, but she looked right back at him as she said, "Why the sudden deeper interest? Just because we slept together?"

He stared at her for a long, heavy beat. It made a rush of heat whoosh through her. Then the side of his mouth quirked up. "I suppose so. Yes. Is that wrong?"

"N-no," she stammered. "It's not wrong, but it's just . . . strange, I guess."

"Everything about this situation is a little strange," he murmured. "But I do like you. So I want to know more about you. That's all."

Her heart beat even faster, and her chest felt tight. "We have defined roles, Charles. As it is, some people look at me funny because I call you by your first name instead of 'Mr. Harrison.'"

He blew out a dismissive breath and smirked. "Let them. Who cares? You live in my home. We're both adults. There's no reason you shouldn't use my first name."

Even something as simple as that, he didn't grasp how it crossed what most people considered to be unspoken boundaries. She wasn't sure if it was just his way because he was nice, or if it was his way because a man as powerful as him rarely had to adhere to boundaries, so he didn't care about them.

"We've always gotten along fine," he pressed on. "From the beginning."

"Yes, we have," she agreed. "We get along quite well. But . . . in our defined roles, Charles." Her gaze held his. "We aren't friends or even peers. I work for you."

"I know. But—"

"But nothing. That's all there is to it." Lisette swallowed hard. "I love my job, and you've always been more than generous. I don't want anything to jeopardize that."

"I don't either, Lisette. And I thought I'd made it clear your position here isn't in jeopardy." His voice was a little rough. "But if I've made you uncomfortable—"

"Well, yeah, it's awkward now; of course it is. I mean, we . . ." Blood rushed to her face, and she had to look away.

"That's why I'm trying to make simple conversation," he said softly. "We need to find a way to be able to talk to each other again without this . . . tension. The awkwardness. It's been hanging over us since that night, and it's painful. I don't want that to continue, and I'm sure you don't either. We've always gotten along well. I want to get back to that somehow, if we can. I'm trying here."

She hadn't been prepared for such direct words. But Charles wasn't only the COO of Harrison Enterprises because of his name; he was a born leader. He was brilliant and sharp, bold and upfront. She knew this, and she admired those qualities. They had just never been focused like a laser on *her* before, not since her first of three interviews for the job. It was unnerving, especially because at the moment, he was right.

"Let's talk about something else. Tell me about your family," he coaxed in a gentle voice. "You never talk about them."

"Because I don't have one," she said simply. She rubbed the handle of her mug with her thumb, up and down, up and down. "There's nothing to talk about."

His brow furrowed. "I know you have no siblings, and your mother passed away when you were a teenager, right?"

Lisette nodded. "She had breast cancer. I was sixteen."

"I'm so sorry." He paused. "But still you have your father, don't you?"

"Not exactly."

"I'm sorry, but what does that mean?"

She sighed, knowing the whole story would likely make him feel sorry for her, and she didn't want that. But she'd given that ambiguous answer; it was her own fault if she'd made him curious. So she lifted her chin and launched into it, wanting to get it over with. "Okay. My father joined the army when he was twenty. He met my mother while he was stationed overseas; she grew up in France. She was half French, half Portuguese, which is why I speak both of those languages fluently. Because she did. They came back to America while my mother was pregnant with me so I'd be born an American citizen. It was important to my dad."

Charles nodded and sat back, his riveted expression urging her to continue.

"I was an army brat. We moved a couple of times. I was born in upstate New York, near Rochester. Then we moved to"—she ticked off the states on her fingers—"Texas, Hawaii, South Carolina, Maryland, Virginia, then back to New York when I was fifteen. Because my mom was sick. I had an aunt in New York, my father's younger sister, and she helped . . ." Lisette spoke quickly and quietly, mentally editing as she went. "My mother died two weeks after I turned sixteen."

"I'm so sorry," Charles said, his voice warm and gentle. "I can't imagine . . . That must have been horrible for you."

"Yes, it was." Lisette stole a swallow of tea to wet her suddenly dry mouth. "Anyway, because we moved so often, and my mother was also an only child, we didn't really have roots or a big family. My mother's parents lived in France,

I rarely saw them, and they're both gone now. My father's parents lived upstate, but died when I was little; I don't really remember them. My one aunt moved to Vegas after my mother died. So really, it was just the three of us. And then, just the two of us." Memories battered her, and she licked her dry lips. "My mom and I were very close. It was devastating. I . . . I still miss her all the time."

"I'm sure you do." Charles regarded her with sympathy. She knew that look. She hated that look. But at least from him, it didn't seem pandering or disingenuous. His compassion was sincere. Then he said, "Well, now I know what made you so resourceful and resilient. Army training. You needed it to handle *my* kids."

She couldn't help but smile, and a giggle slipped out. "Yeah, well . . . my dad got a leave from the army when she died because I was a minor. He had to take care of me. But when I turned eighteen, he went back to serve, and I went away to college."

"Where you studied languages," Charles said. "What was the plan? What did you want to become? A translator, I think you said?"

She drew a long, deep breath as her mind flashed through more memories, good and bad. "Yes, I planned to be a translator," she finally said. "Possibly for the United Nations, or a foreign embassy, or something like that. I was used to traveling, and I thought it'd be interesting."

"It likely would have been." Charles leaned in, still studying her. "So what changed your plans?"

She felt the telltale flush travel up her chest, then up her neck, before creeping into her cheeks. "Do you really need to know?"

"*Need* to know?" His brow furrowed, and his gaze held. "No. I'm not trying to pry or anything. I'm just trying to get to know you better."

"I think you already know me better than I'd ever planned," she muttered.

Surprised, he snorted out a laugh. "You have a point. For the record, I hadn't planned that. Like, *at all.*"

"I know." She couldn't look at him. She fidgeted with the string of her tea bag.

"But since we're exchanging such personal details, I'll tell you the truth about something . . ." His voice trailed off. It was a long enough pause to make her look up. He was staring intently at his hands as they cupped his mug, a strange expression on his face. "It wasn't planned, and I know it was a huge mistake . . . but I can't stop thinking about it. About that night. About you."

Chapter Eight

Jesus, what the hell had possessed him to tell her *that*? Was he insane? Charles plowed a hand through his hair and made himself look into Lisette's eyes.

Judging from the look on her face, she was as surprised as he was.

Might as well go the distance. "And now I'm more curious about you; I admit it. I just want to know you a little better," he said. "That's why I'm asking questions. I didn't mean for all this to feel like an interrogation. I'm sorry if I've made you uncomfortable. Again."

"I think I passed 'uncomfortable' the morning after we slept together," she quipped. "Curved around stunned, then went straight into flabbergasted."

He smiled. She had a dry sense of humor that she often kept under wraps. He liked when it burst through.

They stared at each other, the air heavy with awkward tension. Then he realized *no* . . . It was also sexual tension. He could feel it coming off her in waves. "You're thinking about it now," he said in a low voice. "Aren't you?"

She shivered, and her face flushed anew. "Well, yeah, since you brought it up . . . How can I not?" She gulped down a swallow of tea, too much too fast—her eyes watered as she gasped and choked.

"Went down the wrong pipe?" he asked.

She could only nod as she kept wheezing and coughing. He got up and went around the table, grasped her arms by her wrists, and held them straight up over her head. "Deep breaths," he told her. "Just try to take deep breaths through your nose."

She did as he commanded, and after a few seconds, the coughing lessened. Still sputtering, she pulled her arms from his grip and wrapped them around her middle until she was breathing normally again. "Well, that was charming, huh?" she said, her voice raspy and rough.

He brushed a tendril of dark hair back from her eyes and murmured, "Happens to all of us." Damn, she was so pretty, even all flushed and with watery eyes. He sat down again, next to her this time, noting how she watched his every move. "You still need to explain how you 'don't exactly' have a father, please."

"What? Seriously?" Her eyes rounded.

"If you're willing to explain," he said, gentling his voice to a velvety tone, "I'd really like to know."

"He has early stages of dementia," she bit out. "And PTSD. He's a mess. He did a few more tours after Mom died. Iraq, Afghanistan. Suicide missions, if you ask me. God knows what he saw, what happened to him there. Long story short, he lives in a VA facility now. Sometimes he has violent outbursts. Things trigger him without warning. Most times he knows who I am, but sometimes he doesn't. A couple of times, he thought I was my mother. We look very much alike."

Lisette's voice was steely, but her dark eyes betrayed her; the pain and sadness there were unmistakable. It made Charles want to hold her hand as she kept talking, but he didn't dare. "Two years ago, on a visit when he was lucid, he demanded that I stay away. To go have my own life. That he didn't want to be a danger to me, or a burden, or for me to watch him deteriorate. He's . . . a very proud man. Stubborn as hell. But I have respected his wishes." She twisted the edge of her sweater between her fingertips, staring down at them. "You gave me a place to live, and you pay me well, and I'm very grateful for that. I send some of it to the VA for extra care. Extra therapy, or new clothes, whatever he needs. I call once a week to check on him and get updates, but there's not much to tell. He's . . . not really there. Not the dad I knew. Not anymore."

Charles felt a twisting pang that was more than just sympathy. So strong and heartrending, it was something like anguish. She reached for her cup and took a few swallows of tea. "So . . ." he said softly, "you really have no family at all?"

"No. Okay?"

He sat back in his chair, scanning her face. For a young woman—he knew she was thirty-four—she'd suffered so much loss. She'd told him she couldn't get pregnant, so she wouldn't have children of her own. But if she had no parents, no siblings, no extended family . . . The loneliness of the life she revealed pierced his heart. Even when being a Harrison was hard, and he felt no one in the world would understand, he had his three siblings, he had his kids, and he even had his father if he really needed him. Lisette was alone in the truest sense of the word. It was gut-wrenching to contemplate.

And he'd never known. All he'd known was she was always available, which had made her an even better nanny for the kids. She barely asked for days off, much less holidays. Now that he thought back, she'd been there for every holiday, even Christmas, but he'd never . . . shit, he'd never cared enough to ask why or find out; that was the truth of it. He'd been appreciative that she was always there, and had taken it for granted. Now his heart squeezed as he looked at her, actually ached for her. She was so kind, so nurturing . . . God, why hadn't he known any of this before? "Lisette, I—"

"I need to go to bed." She shot to her feet, clearly indicating the conversation was over. "You wanted to know more about me; now you do. Okay? Good night, Charles."

"Lisette, wait. I didn't mean to upset you." He rose along with her.

"I don't need you feeling sorry for me," she asserted. "I'm fine on my own."

Whoa. He'd never heard her voice get tough like that. Or seen that glint in her eyes. This sweet woman had a hidden spine of steel, and it intrigued him. "I'm trying not to feel sorry for you, but to be honest, it's hard not to. I mean, when I think about what you—"

"Then don't think about it. It's why I don't talk about it. There's nothing to say. Now that I'm grown and situated and can take care of myself, I'm fine." She tried to move around him, but he blocked her. He felt even worse now, for bringing up painful memories and for upsetting her. He couldn't let her leave on this note.

But momentum made her slam into him, gasping as her breasts rammed hard against his chest, and on pure instinct his hands flew to her waist to steady her.

Their faces only inches apart, he stared down at her. He watched her eyes widen, her pupils dilate, the spots of color that bloomed on her cheeks. He affected her, that was clear, and seeing that made his blood start to heat. She felt good under his hands, and she was so gorgeous. And the way she looked back at him . . . They had chemistry, all right, and it was crackling in the air right then, like electric shocks around them.

With both hands she pushed back on his chest, putting space between them. But her eyes stayed locked with his. "What—what's going on here?" she asked breathlessly.

"I don't know," he answered. His heart pumped in thick, hard beats. "But there's definitely something going on. It's called chemistry, plain and simple. We have it. Can't deny it anymore, can we?"

"We have to," she whispered.

In his head, he knew that. But he couldn't take his eyes off her, and he was dying to put his hands and mouth on her again.

For Christ's sake, he had to remember who he was, and who she was to him. She was right: he was her boss; she was his employee. One time was a fluke, but if something happened a second time, it would be deliberate. As much as he found himself drawn to her, he couldn't do this; she might construe it as sexual harassment and leave, or worse . . .

"You're right." He cleared his throat and straightened, assuming the same broad, proper stance he would in a boardroom meeting. He locked his arms across his chest. "I apologize, Lisette. I overstepped, yet again. Chemistry or not, it's completely unacceptable. I don't want you to be uncomfortable, and I want you to stay on here. So from now on, I'll keep my distance." With a curt nod, he added, "Good night," and strode out of the kitchen without a look back. He went straight up the grand spiral staircase to his bedroom and locked the door behind him. But his heart thumped against his ribs, his blood raced through his veins, and his erection still throbbed in his now-too-tight jeans.

This was crazy. Why did he suddenly want her so much? Why did she have to be so tempting and vulnerable and beautiful and likable and fucking off-limits?

Swearing under his breath, he blindly grabbed the nearest thing and hurled it across the bedroom with all his might. The sound of it shattering gave him only a split second of satisfaction. Breathing hard, he raked his hands through his hair and over his face. He had to stop thinking about her, stop wanting her, just swallow it and shut it all down. His sense of reason seemed to evaporate whenever he was close to her. He'd just have to stop entertaining fantasies about her, stay away from temptation, not be alone with her . . . and pretend he wasn't affected by her that way. Business as usual. For everyone's sake, it was the right thing to do.

Leaning back against the wall, he closed his eyes and took deep breaths. Forcing his feelings down, swallowing them back, was something he'd done millions of times in his controlled life. He'd had to, from an early age. As a preschooler, he'd grasped that Daddy didn't like it when he acted out or lost his temper; he had the Harrison name to represent. He had to be the picture of refinement, strength, and control. After four decades, Charles was a goddamn pro at swallowing back his emotions and desires.

He stayed very still for a minute, waiting until he was calmer. Then, with a heavy sigh, he crossed the room to see what he'd shattered in his fit of pique. He didn't even know what he'd grabbed off the low shelf. Pieces of broken glass and an upside down picture frame lay scattered on the carpet beside his bed. He couldn't help but snort out a laugh—it'd been the framed photo of his father and him, on Charles's first official day at work at Harrison Enterprises.

Instead of catching up on e-mails and work on Saturday morning, as he usually did, Charles decided to go to Edgewater Park to watch all three kids' soccer games, one after the other, giving Lisette most of the day to herself. As soon as she got Charles and the kids and all their stuff into his Escalade, she called Tina and asked if she wanted to do something together. Being a good friend, knowing how rare a free Saturday afternoon was for Lisette, Tina jumped at it. "Yes! Cleaning my own house can wait. A girls' day out, woo hoo! I'll come pick you up."

They did some shopping at the outlets, then went to lunch

at a small bistro and caught a movie, a rom-com they'd both been dying to see. By the time Tina pulled back through the gates and up the long driveway to Charles's estate to drop Lisette off, the sky was beginning to darken.

Lisette entered the house wondering what she'd find. Chaos? Mayhem? Had Charles survived a whole day, three soccer games, and two meals with his kids? As she dropped her keys into their crystal bowl, she realized she heard some sound, like a TV show or a movie, but no wild kids. Huh.

Realizing the sound was coming from the den, she walked to it and stopped in the doorway. Charles sat in the middle of the U-shaped couch, handsome in jeans and a white turtleneck sweater, his socked feet up on the coffee table. Ava was curled into one of his sides, Myles into the other, and Thomas sat beside Myles. Each of them had a bag of microwaved popcorn in his or her lap as they watched a movie.

It was such a picturesque domestic scene, it made her heart give a tiny ping. "Well, this is lovely," she said, making all four heads turn her way.

"Hi." Charles smiled brightly at her. "How was your day?"

"It was great," she said.

"Good, I'm glad." He gestured with a flick of his chin in the direction of the kitchen. "Eileen made pizza tonight. There's plenty left if you haven't eaten."

"If Eileen made it, I'm likely to steal a slice or two," Lisette grinned. She looked at the kids, then back to him. "Did they take baths yet?"

"When we got home from soccer," he said.

"We won our game," Thomas told her proudly.

"So did my team," Ava piped in.

Myles frowned and pouted.

"Aww, Myles," Lisette said. "Your team didn't win today, I guess?"

"No," he said. "But there's always next week. Right, Daddy?"

"That's right," Charles said.

"Only two weeks left in the season," Lisette said. "We'll discuss if you plan to take them to those games too?"

"Absolutely," Charles said. "I'll be here next weekend, but I have a trip coming up midmonth. West Coast offices. So yes, we'll work that out."

"Okay." Lisette watched the four of them for a minute. They looked very much a content family, which both warmed her heart and released a whisper of melancholy at the same time. Suddenly, she felt like an intruder on the scene. "I'll go get that pizza now," she said. "Enjoy the rest of the movie."

"Why don't you bring it back in here?" Charles asked. "You don't have to sit in the kitchen by yourself."

She forced a smile. "Thanks, but you should have your time together." Before he could say anything more, she walked away.

In the kitchen, she found Eileen cleaning up. "Ah, hello there. Just finished the dishes," she said. "I'm leaving in a few minutes. You need anything, sweetie?"

"No, you go," Lisette insisted. "I'm just going to help myself to dinner. Heard you made some pizza."

"I sure did." A broad grin spread on the older woman's face. "One plain, one with mushrooms, onions, and pepperoni. Just finished wrapping them up; they haven't been in the fridge for more than a few minutes. Might still be a bit warm."

"Thanks. Now go home, lady." She and Eileen exchanged good-byes, and Lisette went to the wide steel refrigerator. Finding the wrapped slices, she took out two and put one in the toaster to warm up.

"Lisette."

She turned at Charles's low, commanding voice. "Yes?"

He cocked his head to the side, studying her. "You don't have to banish yourself to the kitchen. I hate the thought of you eating in here all alone when we're all home. It . . ." He shoved his hands in the pockets of his jeans. "It doesn't feel right."

She looked at him blankly. "I eat alone often. It doesn't bother me."

"Well, tonight, it bothers me," he said.

"Charles." She looked into his eyes. Framed by the black-rimmed glasses, their brilliant blue beauty seemed even more pronounced to her. "This is the weekend, and you're home. It's family time. Go be with your family. I'm not part of it."

He gazed at her for a minute, assessing long enough for her to feel uneasy from his stare. Her arms slid around her middle.

"I know all that," he said quietly. "I'm merely saying you don't have to isolate yourself from the kids whenever I'm home. Especially if I'm going to start being home more often."

"But that's exactly what I've always done," she pointed out. "I don't infringe on your time with them. You never even blinked at that before."

He nodded, considering that. "I suppose that's true. But Lisette . . . at this point, they're just as comfortable with you as with me. Maybe even more so, in a way. You make them feel genuinely cared for—which I'm very grateful for, by the way, if I don't tell you that enough."

She held herself tight and acknowledged the compliment with a demure smile.

"So you don't have to disappear when I'm around," he said.

"Just three nights ago, you said you wanted to keep your distance from me," she reminded him in a murmur. "And you have. I'm doing the same."

His eyes narrowed. "Playing tit for tat?" he asked. "I didn't think you were like that."

"I'm not. Not at all. I'm just following your lead." She met his intense gaze directly.

He didn't move, but a muscle jumped in his jaw, and his lips flattened in a thin line of frustration.

"I'm an employee," she said, her tone sharper. "Like anyone else on your household staff."

"You're not like the other staff members," he said. His voice and gaze took on a steelier edge.

"Why? Because we slept together?" she whispered hotly.

"*No*. Because you're—you're like—you're kind of a mother figure to them," he sputtered. "They adore you. They love you."

"That's nice to say, but—"

"But nothing. It's the truth. They're not attached to any other staff members like they are to you, so it's totally different."

"You're being purposely obtuse," she said, her self-control starting to fray. "You don't ask Eileen or Tina to come hang out with you and the kids. You *are* treating me differently."

"Solely because you have a different relationship with the kids!" he said, voice rising. His mouth twitched. "And did you just call me obtuse?"

"Oh my God, I did." Her face bloomed with color. "I'm sorry."

"Don't be. It'd be funny if we both weren't getting frustrated."

"Still, you're my boss. That was disrespectful."

He stepped to her, standing so close that his hot breath fanned her cheek as he said, "You don't have to defer to me like that. You think I'm being obtuse, fine, tell me so. It's not like you called me an asshole or something."

She wanted to laugh, but her breath was stuck in her chest.

His blues blazed as he said, "Don't ever act as if I should

treat you like a second-class citizen because you work for me. I never have, I never would, and I resent the implication."

"But I am, Charles," she said quietly. "In this house, I am."

"Bullshit!" he spat, eyes flashing.

"It's not bullshit!" she cried in response. "You can't make facts obsolete just because you want them to be. We are on different levels, Charles. That's a fact."

He muttered a curse before insisting, "The only one who'd ever make you feel that way is *you*. I treat everyone in this house with nothing but respect and appreciation."

"You do. And that's wonderful," she said. "And no, you've never made me feel beneath you. But it doesn't change the fact that *I work for you*." She turned away, pacing for a few seconds. What could she say to get through to him? "This isn't my home; it's yours. That's not my car; you own it. The money I make all comes from you. Don't you understand? My livelihood—everything in my life—is dependent on you. No matter what kind of chemistry we have, no matter what happened the other night, no matter what you're choosing to willfully ignore, that is the bottom line. Please . . . *hear me*."

He looked stunned. She almost felt bad for him. "I hear you," he finally said. "Doesn't mean I have to like it."

She nodded, not knowing what to say.

With a heavy sigh, Charles leaned back against the marble-topped island in the middle of the kitchen and gazed at her balefully. "My kids love you," he said. "Therefore, I think of you as special in this house. I always have."

"Not like you do now." She also took a long, deep breath. "Just admit that."

"Fine, you're right, not like I do now," he ground out. "All right?"

She turned away, unable to look at him, and opened the toaster. Without thinking, she pulled the slice of pizza out to put it on the plate, but it was too hot. A gasp and a hiss escaped her as she dropped it onto the plate.

"Did you burn yourself?" he asked with concern.

She rushed to the sink and ran her fingertips under the cold water, furious with herself.

"Lisette," he said sternly. "Are you all right?"

"No, I'm not all right!" she cried, feeling the last frayed threads of her control unravel and snap. "Up until two weeks ago, I was fine. I'm good at my job; I'm capable and strong; everything was fine. Now, every time I see you, I'm off-kilter. I'm bumping into things, or choking on water, or saying things I shouldn't, or burning my fingers to hell . . ." Hot tears of frustration sprang to her eyes.

He moved to her side and took her hand from under the stream of water. "Let me see." With tender care, he examined her fingertips. She saw how gently he attended to her, and it made her heart flutter. His eyes lifted to hers. "You'll be fine. Your somewhat burned fingers, and the rest of you too."

"Of course I will," she whispered. With her free hand, she turned off the faucet. He was still holding her hand and staring at her intently.

"I've been off-kilter too," he said, his voice low. "You're not the only one."

She licked her dry lips and saw his eyes travel with the motion, glued to her mouth for a few seconds before looking back up to her eyes again. She saw hunger flare in his blazing blues, and searing heat. Her heart started to thump in heavier beats. Oh, God, what was happening? He was attracted to her; it was obvious. And she'd always been attracted to him too. It was as if the heated discussion they'd just had had never happened, and sizzling lust had taken them both over. This was disastrous. He edged a bit closer, his eyes focused on her mouth, and she couldn't move. She wanted him to kiss her, and if he did, she knew she wouldn't push him away. She could barely breathe.

"Daddy?" Myles padded into the kitchen, holding an empty popcorn bag. "Are you coming back? We're waiting for you. And I'm thirsty."

Lisette yanked her hand from Charles's, whirled to face the little boy, and said, "Of course he's coming back, sweetheart. And he'll get you a drink, okay?" She swept her plate from the counter and grabbed a napkin. "I'm just taking this up to my room. You all have fun." She tousled Myles's hair as she passed him and practically ran from the kitchen without a look back.

Chapter Nine

Charles scribbled on a pad beside his keyboard, then went back to looking over the itinerary of his trip to the West Coast offices in less than two weeks. He'd be away from home for ten days. Some of the plans were golf outings, meals, the social aspects. If he cut out some of the superfluous things, he'd only be away for seven or eight days, not ten. His kids needed him. He'd simply have to disappoint some of his investors and break a few plans. They'd get over it.

His private line rang, and he picked it up without hesitation. Only a few select people had that number: his father, his siblings, his closest colleagues, and his kids' nanny. He hit the SPEAKER button. "Charles Harrison."

"Funny, that's my name too." His father made the same joke every time. "How's it going, Tripp?"

"Fine, just busy as usual." Charles hadn't minded that nickname when he was younger, but he almost hated it now. It was one of the reasons he hadn't named either of his sons Charles and made them a fourth. He'd adamantly wanted to let them have their own names, their own identities, free of all the preconceived notions that moniker would have brought.

"I want to further discuss the Benson Industries deal," his

father said. "Come to my office for breakfast tomorrow so we can discuss it."

"Can't," Charles said, even as he tapped on his keyboard. "Have a meeting at nine, a meeting at eleven, and my afternoon is pretty booked too."

Charles II snorted. "Shit, you'd think you were running a company or something with that kind of schedule."

"Indeed."

"Well, come earlier, then."

"No. I'm—"

"You putting me off, son?" A steely edge crept into the patriarch's tone.

Charles bristled at it. "Yeah, I am. Tomorrow's not good for me."

"Make it good for you."

A dry laugh escaped him. "No. I'm busy. Running a company, remember? I can see you on Thursday. How about lunch?"

"I said I want you to—"

"I heard what you said." Charles kept his tone even but firm. The fact was, even though Charles II still held the CEO position, it was Charles III who was more hands-on with all aspects, even as number two. "If you're that concerned, call Collins or Bosworth. If you want to discuss anything with me, we'll go over it on Thursday."

Charles II grunted, but said, "Fine. Noon. Meet me at the steak house; I'll have Patty make a reservation. Don't be late." He ended the call with a click.

Charles clicked off his phone, turned back to the monitor, and rubbed his temples. His father's arrogant demands and surly tone had brought on the start of a headache. He wanted to get out of there in time for dinner. Soon, he'd call his driver to make sure he'd be ready to go. But when the private line rang again, this time he jabbed at the CALL button and bit out, "Charles Harrison."

"Wow. Whatever it was, I didn't do it." His sister's voice floated from the speaker.

He snorted out a laugh, instantly relaxing a bit. "No, you didn't. Dad just . . . irked me a little."

"Ah. Shocking," Tess said sarcastically.

"Yeah, right. Anyway. How are you, sister dear? What can I do for you?"

"I'm fine, thanks. And what you can do for me is tell me which works best for you: Friday, Saturday, or Sunday. I haven't had any quality sibling time in a while. I miss my guys. So I'm inviting you to my house—you, Dane, and Pierce, sans their women. Just us four."

"That sounds nice," Charles admitted. "Um . . . hold on . . ." He pulled up his Outlook and checked, but then remembered Lisette had Sundays off. "Saturday would be better."

"Then Saturday it shall be," Tess said. "How about lunch? One o'clock work for you?"

"Kids all have soccer on Saturdays, goes past one o'clock. How about dinner?"

"Okay," Tess said. "Six o'clock?"

"I'll make it work." Charles rose from his leather chair to stretch his arms and legs. "What brought this on?"

"It's like I said. We haven't had any quality time in a while, and I thought it'd be nice to get together before the holiday craziness kicks in."

"Does sound nice," Charles said. "I'll bring something sweet and decadent."

"Your brothers will love you for it."

"I know my audience. Speaking of holiday craziness, how's work going for you? You must be up to your eyeballs in preparations."

"I am," Tess said. "But the Holiday Ball is my favorite event of the year. I don't mind the insanity that goes along with it."

"If you say so."

Tess ran the Harrison Foundation, the family's nonprofit organization that worked with charities. Since she had taken over, the roster of charities they worked with had doubled, and the annual Holiday Ball the foundation threw had turned from a lovely black-tie affair at the Harrison estate to a tremendous social event at the Waldorf Astoria. One of the year's biggest parties, it always boasted an elite guest list of celebrities, socialites, activists, artists, and business people from all walks of life.

"How many are invited this year?" Charles asked.

"Five hundred and twenty-three."

"People?" he shrieked. "Jesus."

"This will be our biggest ball yet," she said, unable to keep the pride from her voice. "Make sure your tux is ready."

"When is it again? I know I have the invite somewhere, but remind me."

"December eighteenth."

"Okay. Got it." He scribbled it on the pad. "Ava is pissed that it's adults only. She's dying to go."

"I know," Tess sighed. "When she's thirteen, I might break the rules for her."

"I'll tell her that. Maybe it'll appease her . . . for at least three minutes."

Tess laughed softly. "Give all the kids hugs for me. Gotta run. See you on Saturday. Six o'clock, don't forget."

"I won't. See you then." Charles removed his glasses, set them on the desktop, and rubbed his eyes. He was tired. A glance at the clock showed it was only three-thirty. He wondered what the kids were doing now . . . and what Lisette was doing now. She'd been avoiding him since Saturday night, when she'd all but run out of the kitchen and up to her room.

He huffed out a breath of frustration. The whole thing was nuts. He was drawn to her; he couldn't deny it. The night before, he'd watched her from the doorway as she sat on

Myles's bed and read him a bedtime story. She was so . . . nurturing. It was obvious that she truly loved the kids.

Her inside was as beautiful as her outside, and he just didn't know many people like that anymore. Something deep inside him wanted that warmth and gentleness to be lavished on him too.

He moved to the wide windows and looked out again at the impressive view. The tall buildings of Manhattan lay before him, with Bryant Park visible a few blocks away. The trees were changing, more yellow and rust in the leaves than green now. Fall had always made him a bit melancholy—the disappearing daylight, the longer nights, the knowledge that the long, cold winter was just ahead . . . At times, it made him feel even more lonely.

He leaned against the window ledge and dug his hands into his pockets. He was tired of being lonely. He hadn't even realized how much until that one encounter with Lisette. It made him grasp how much he missed simple human touch, some intimacy, and yes, passionate sex. He was only human, after all.

With a soft grunt, he dropped his forehead against the glass. If people knew that the COO of Harrison Enterprises was dissolving into a lonely sap of a guy, they'd never believe it. He was known for his strength and for staying unruffled. But the past few months, there had been times when he wasn't 100 percent sure who he was anymore.

He gazed down at the street far below. When he had his moves planned for him in his youth, he hadn't minded so much. He'd been proud and honored to take his place in the family legacy. This year, something had shifted. It wasn't the tryst with Lisette; that was a symptom of the problem, as Dane had said. Things had been changing in his head long before that. Maybe it had been watching his father clash with Pierce last year, when Pierce moved back to New York. That had turned ugly, downright vicious, and Charles had been more than disgusted; he'd been horrified. But had stayed silent ever since.

He didn't feel right about that.

Charles had spent his whole life rationalizing his father's sometimes malicious behavior toward the youngest Harrison. When they were younger, Charles had believed Pierce's wild behavior, the way he always snubbed his nose at the family like an ungrateful brat, had warranted such strong words from their father. But after that party last year, there was no rationalizing it, no goddamn justification for the way Charles II had gone after Pierce and Abby. It'd been way over the top. Only now did Charles realize that since that night, he hadn't felt the same about his father, or Pierce . . . or his own place in everything.

He spun away from the window. Who did he want to become? A copy of his father, or his own man? God knew he'd taken the company to new heights in the past decade, and he was proud of his accomplishments. But he was . . . tired. He shouldn't be so tired at forty. His father's words echoed through his mind: *You're never off the clock, Tripp*. Dammit, his life wasn't his own. What good were insane amounts of money and power if you never had time to enjoy the benefits of them? To know his own children, who were growing up before his eyes, and without getting to know and be with him like they should?

The sticky truth welled inside him. He wanted something else out of life . . . something for himself, as selfish as that sounded.

Was it any wonder he'd grabbed at Lisette that night as if she were a damn life raft? He was just lucky his spectacular fall from grace had been with someone as kind as she was. His explosive actions with her that night, wrong though they might have been, had made him feel alive for the first time in forever.

Of course he hadn't been able to get Lisette off his mind

since that night, and he felt the chemistry crackle around them whenever she was close. But he had to stop this nonsense and get his head out of the clouds where she was concerned. Stop with this . . . infatuation, or whatever the hell this was.

Then he could focus on the other things. Like finding a way to balance his work with being a better father, and feeling more alive again in some other way. Because with each passing day, the Harrison legacy, the COO title, and everything that went with it were feeling less like a privilege and more like a cage.

Lisette always brought her e-reader with her wherever she went. That way, she could read one of her many books or play Trivia Crack while she waited in between kid pickups. Between Ava's being in one place and the boys in another, Lisette found it wasn't worth going all the way home to go back out again to get them. She'd sit in the car and make use of her time.

During the day, when the kids were in school, she helped Tina with the kids' laundry and cleaning their rooms. She took a yoga class in town two mornings a week, and an art class once a week. These were the hobbies she allowed herself to indulge in.

Now, Lisette left the minivan and entered the lobby of the gymnastics center just as Ava walked through the other door, her duffel bag slung over her shoulder.

"Perfect timing," Lisette smiled. "Ready to go?"

After that, it was off to the Sandy Point Pools, where they picked up the boys from their swimming lessons.

"I don't want to do swimming anymore," Thomas said as soon as they pulled out of the parking lot. "It's boring."

"It is not!" Myles cried. "I love it!"

"I think it's boring," Thomas repeated emphatically. "I wanna do hockey."

"Well," Lisette said, glancing into the rearview mirror to meet Thomas's eyes for a moment, "you'll have to discuss that with your father."

"He won't let me," Thomas grumbled. "He never lets us quit anything once we've started. *You made a commitment; you have to see it through. Harrisons aren't quitters.*" His stuffy impression of Charles was amusing, but Lisette managed to press her lips together hard to hide the smile that threatened.

"Well, we aren't!" Myles said, pride in his little voice. "We're tough! We're strong!"

"You're six," Thomas sniffed. "Real tough guy, you are."

"Neither one of you are tough guys," Lisette said calmly. "And no one wants you to be."

"Uncle Pierce is tough," Thomas said. "He has tattoos and everything."

"Well, Uncle Pierce is cool," Ava put in. "Daddy isn't. Daddy is . . . a boss. In a good way. Like a leader. Daddy's a leader."

"He's boring," Thomas said, "just like swimming."

Lisette concentrated on the traffic. Since the time change a few weeks before, they always came home from activities in the dark now. By the time she pulled through the gate at the edge of Charles's property, the kids were bickering over who was cooler, Uncle Pierce or Uncle Dane. Pierce seemed to be in the lead by virtue of his former pro-athlete status and tattoos. She drove up the long, winding driveway to the front of the house, tripping the sensor for the bright security light that went on. The kids piled out of the minivan; she wrapped her scarf around her neck to ward off the chilly evening air and wondered if Charles would indeed be home for dinner as he'd said he would.

She opened the front door, the kids all went inside, and

before she could even turn around, she heard Myles cry happily, "Daddy! Daddy, you're home!"

She turned to see Charles, still in his black suit, gray dress shirt, and striped tie, crouching down to hug his kids. Smiling brightly, looking from one child to the next as they all babbled at him at the same time, Charles laughed and tried to make sense of the commotion.

Something pinged in Lisette's heart at the sight. He was always so handsome. It wasn't fair. The only thing more attractive than a gorgeous man in a gorgeous suit was said gorgeousness being openly affectionate with his kids.

Charles looked up at her from his crouch, flashing a friendly grin as he straightened up. "Good evening, Lisette. How were things today?"

His deep, smooth voice set off butterflies in her belly. Between that sexy tone and his blue, blue eyes boring into her, her insides went all liquid and wobbly. "Fine," she said, licking her suddenly dry lips. "Nothing unusual to report. School, gymnastics, swimming." She glanced at the kids and said, "All three of you need to go upstairs for quick showers. Take turns; go fast. You can do it."

All three of them whined and moaned in protest.

"Come on now," Charles said. He ruffled Myles's hair. "Ick. Chlorine hair. You need a shower, and you know it!"

"But I'm starving!" Myles whined.

"I know you're all hungry," she said to them. "But make them fast showers, get dressed even faster, and dinner will be ready and on the table when you come down, I promise. You know the routine. Go on."

"Last one up's a rotten egg!" Thomas yelled, taking off like a shot. Myles and Ava shrieked and ran after him, the three of them racing up the stairs and down their hallway.

Charles turned to Lisette, chuckling. It made the corners of his eyes crinkle in a way she adored. "Dinner is actually ready now, but I didn't want to step on your routine. And they really needed showers. His hair felt disgusting!"

Lisette only smiled and went to hang up her coat and scarf, and the kids' coats, in the front closet. Just being near Charles had her hormones soaring. She had to stop this. She had to control this somehow.

With a deep breath, she went back down the hall and saw Charles was waiting for her. "Is there something else?" she asked.

He said quietly, "You're talking to me. Even looking at me. You barely have in three days. This is progress."

She felt the blush rise in her face. "I—I hadn't thought about it."

"Good. That's how it *should* be." He shot her a lopsided grin. It made the corners of his eyes crinkle, and it made her heart flutter. "Tina made tilapia with a pecan crust for dinner. Steamed broccoli, red potatoes. It all looks delicious. I think I'm going to open a bottle of wine to go with it. Would you like a glass?"

She blinked, the question surprising her. "Um, no. No, thank you. I never drink when I'm with the children."

He nodded slowly, his eyes on her face. "And I appreciate that. But surely half a glass here at home wouldn't be a problem, if you wanted? I'm here, after all. You don't have to handle them all by yourself."

"I'd rather not," she said. "Not while I'm working. But thank you anyway."

"Sure." Shoving his hands into his pockets, he said, "Come, let's have dinner." His brows lifted as he leaned in and said pointedly, "*All* of us, together, in the dining room. Don't you dare take your plate to the kitchen to eat by yourself again. It's not acceptable."

"But Charles—"

"Stop. Every night, you eat with the kids. Right?"

"Yes. But that's because you're rarely here. When you are, I shouldn't be—"

"Stop." He took a step closer, his stare pinning her. "I'm asking you to join us. Just have dinner with us. That's all."

Her throat felt thick, and her chest got tight. His presence engulfed her, overwhelmed her. He was so close, she could feel the heat radiating from his body, and it made her want to melt into him. But she said firmly, "Charles. I work for you."

"I'm well aware of that. I hired you."

"But I'm not . . . It's like . . ." She groped for the right words, wanting to make her point, but not offend him. "Charles, it's like you're acting as if we're all like a—a *family*. All having meals together, doing things together . . . I just don't know that it's appropriate. Or that it sends the right message to the kids." She shook her head and stared back, lifting her hands, then dropping them in resignation.

"Lisette," Charles said, "you started here when Myles had just turned four. He was so young, and his mother was gone, and several other nannies had come and gone. He absolutely adores you. All the kids have become attached to you. And you're a lovely person, so I'm okay with that." His head cocked sideways as he studied her. "Didn't you tell me that you became a nanny in the first place to experience something akin to family life?"

Her breath caught. "That's . . . that's not . . ." Her heart raced. "You've hired me to play a mother, but I'm not their mother."

A muscle in his jaw twitched. "I didn't say you were."

"It sounds like it. It feels like it." Her hands fluttered at her sides as she pressed, "I'm not family. I'm hired help. And we'd all do better to remember that and not cross any lines that shouldn't be crossed. I wouldn't ever want them to be confused or hurt."

"Me neither," he agreed. "Of course not. But I can tell

that you love them. And Lisette, they love you. I can see it. And you're allowed to have feelings!"

She didn't know what to say. Her breath felt stuck in her lungs.

"I'm trying to tell you . . ." He scrubbed his hands over his jaw. She'd rarely seen him fumble for words. "I'm saying that your place in their life matters, and I respect it. I respect *you*."

It felt hard to breathe. She rubbed her sternum in tiny circles. God, did he have any idea what he was saying? How it all affected her? She doubted it.

"More important," he continued, taking another step closer, "I don't think anyone who works for me is beneath me somehow. Not my house staff, not my office staff, no one. Why do you?" His tone turned inquisitive, almost pleading. "Have I ever done anything to make you feel that way? If I have, I'm sorry, because I don't."

"You haven't. But you're not getting it," she whispered miserably, her gaze falling away.

He gripped her chin with his fingertips, soft but insistent, making her look into his eyes again and her breath catch and stick in her throat. In a low murmur, his face only inches from hers, he said, "I understand what you're trying to get across. But I don't agree. I think you're . . . maybe over-reacting a bit, because of what happened between us."

"Really?" she whispered, not breaking their gaze. "You ever talk to Tina or Eileen this way? Insist that they share meals with you? Touch them, at all, much less like you're touching me right now? Look at them like you want to take them to bed?"

As if jolted by a slap, he released her and stepped back, eyes wide.

"Then added to the fact that you're my boss how very wealthy and powerful you are," she choked out. "We are *not* on the same level. Totally different worlds. You do have power over me."

"I don't want to have power over you."

"That's nice. But it doesn't make it any less true."

His blue gaze intensified. "Lisette. I'm just a man. A human being. That's all."

Her heart panged for him. His earnestness was palpable. But she said, "You just turned forty, you're feeling your mortality, and you're lonely. And I'm right here, in the house. How convenient."

His eyes flashed. "This is not about convenience," he insisted, but his voice lowered to a hot whisper. "It's not about that at all. It's . . . more than that."

"Is it?" Her heart pounded in her chest. "Since when have you thought of me as anything but the nanny? Tell the truth."

"I've always thought of you fondly . . ."

She stared at him. "*Fondly?* Charles, for once, don't talk and act like the damned crown prince. Just *talk* to me."

He blinked, apparently stunned, then huffed out a frustrated breath. "Fine. Okay. I've always liked you. Always thought you were really pretty, but didn't let it take over or anything. We're both adults, both professionals. But, yes, since that night . . ." His stare heated to an all-out smolder, making her knees wobble and her stomach flutter. "Yes, okay, now I think of you differently. And what's more, I think of you often. And it's not platonic. All my money and power doesn't change the fact that I'm just a normal man who's lusting like hell after you. When you're on my mind, I'm not thinking about my billions, or your assets . . . only your God-given assets."

Alarms tripped off in her head. The way he was looking at her . . . God, it was absolutely carnal. And hell yes, she wanted him again too. But if she went down this road with him, it couldn't possibly end well. He stepped closer again, and her mouth went dry as her blood raced through her veins.

"I want to kiss you again, touch you again, and I can't,"

he whispered. "I want to get you out of my head . . . and I can't."

"You have to try harder," she said, even as her heart pounded against her ribs.

"Believe me, I've been trying."

He was so close now that if she leaned in only a few inches, they'd be kissing.

"Dinner," she said. "The kids are waiting. It's dinnertime."

He just stared at her, and the air around them crackled with electricity.

"That one night can't change everything here," she insisted in a desperate whisper. "It *can't*, Charles."

His eyes bore into hers, blazing with heat. "But it already has. And we both know it."

Chapter Ten

Later that night, Lisette glided soundlessly down the grand staircase. Tina had gone home at seven, the kids had all fallen asleep by ten, and the house was quiet. There was something about the stillness that settled over the mansion at night that Lisette loved. It was such a large and magnificent home; yet with the lights off, somehow the silence wasn't cold or intimidating to her, but peaceful.

Clutching her e-reader to her chest, she headed toward the den. The wide, soft loveseat by the window was a perfect spot to curl up and read, legs wrapped under the chenille throw, with only the light from her e-reader for illumination.

And tonight, she needed that distraction. Her brain had been spinning wildly since Charles had told her he thought of her often, staring at her as if the world were on fire . . . only to have the conversation cut short by the shrieks of the kids as they came thundering down the stairs, ready for dinner. She'd jumped and pulled away from him quick as a flash, busying herself with the children.

She'd had dinner with them, but had been barely able to look Charles in the eye. She'd helped the kids with their homework while Charles disappeared into his study to respond to a few calls and e-mails, then she had brought them up to their rooms. By the time they were in bed, Charles was upstairs too, helping her to tuck each of them in and kiss them good night. He was trying to be a better father, he really was, and it warmed her heart. But the truth was, he didn't have to try very hard. He was sweet with them, attentive and present. His love for them was obvious. All they wanted from him was more of his time.

She paused at the door of the den, peering further down the hallway. The door to the study was open, light pouring out into the corridor. Something in her wanted to tell him that he was doing well at this new stab at fatherhood. Like he'd said earlier, he was just a man, and all men needed assurance once in a while, didn't they? A pat on the back, a "you got this!" affirmation? She chewed on her lip, debating, pulling the sash of her robe tighter around her waist.

Don't lie to yourself, a voice admonished in her head. *You want more than to talk to him. You want to see him, be near him. You want to just be in his presence.*

Yes. Yes, she did. After what he'd admitted to her openly, she could admit that much to herself. Drawing a long, deep breath, she walked to the study.

Charles leaned back in his leather chair, pulled off his glasses, and rubbed his tired eyes. He'd put out the fires for the evening and wanted nothing more than to have a few sips of scotch and go to bed. He yawned and set his glasses down on the desk.

A soft knock on the doorframe instantly drew his attention, and then his heart skipped a beat. Lisette stood there, wrapped in a dark purple robe. Her hair was still up in its braid, and her dark eyes and olive skin were luminous in the low light. She was so effortlessly beautiful.

With a hesitant smile, she cleared her throat and said, "Hi."

"Hi." He smiled and sat up straighter in his chair. This was a nice surprise. "Come on in."

She did, stopping in the middle of the room. He watched as her eyes flicked to the infamous couch before coming back to his face, then as she clutched her e-reader to her chest, fingertips skimming along the edges in an endearingly nervous gesture. The plush robe looked soft and flowed down past her knees, but from beneath revealed the bottoms of blue fleece pajama pants and . . . feet tucked into fluffy white slippers that looked like sheep.

He couldn't help but grin. "I like your slippers."

She glanced down at them as if she'd forgotten what they looked like, and her face flushed deeper. "Oh. Um. Thanks. Eileen got them for me last Christmas. They're silly looking, but they're really warm and cozy, so sometimes . . ."

"They're adorable." He rose from the chair and moved slowly around the desk, noting how her eyes followed his every move. He'd discarded his jacket and tie before dinner, but still wore his slacks and dress shirt, the top two buttons open and the sleeves rolled up to his elbows. "So what's up? What brings you here?"

"I, um . . ." She licked her luscious lips before her gaze rose to his, unleashing a warm pull low in his belly. "I came downstairs to read for a while, but I saw the light on and the door open, so I thought I'd . . . Well, I wanted to tell you something."

He nodded, encouraging her to continue, and stuffed his hands into his pockets.

"I know you said you wanted to be a better father, spend more time with the kids and all." Her fingertips kept sliding along the edge of her e-reader, slow but steady. "And I just wanted to say—I mean, I really hope this isn't out of line, and I don't mean it to be—but I think you're doing a good job at it. They've seemed happier lately. I mean it. You're great with them, and I think they're really appreciative of it, even if they don't always show it. Even Thomas. *Especially* Thomas." She flashed a tiny grin. "So, I just wanted to tell you that. Just to affirm that what you're doing is working, if you were unsure. For what it's worth."

"It's worth a lot, actually." A warm feeling spread through his chest, and he smiled. "Thank you. That means a lot to me. Especially coming from you. Because you know them better than anyone, so you'd see any subtle nuances or changes."

"Oh, I don't know about that," she hedged.

"You're too modest," he said, leaning back casually against his desk. He sat on top and crossed his arms against his chest. "I appreciate your observation, and that you wanted to tell me. I hope you're right."

She smiled, but said nothing, fidgeting endlessly with the cover of her e-reader.

"I was about to pour myself a glass of scotch," he said. He held up two fingers, barely an inch apart. "Only about this much, I swear."

A giggle escaped her lips, and she clamped them together.

"Kids aren't here now." His eyes met hers and held. "Join me for one drink?"

Her smile fell away. "I don't know if that's appropriate . . ."

"We keep dancing around what's appropriate, don't we?" He pushed off the desk and walked around her to the small wet bar. "I took you right there on that couch, and there was nothing remotely appropriate about it. I don't think having a few sips of scotch with me will push any untoward boundaries that we haven't already smashed."

As he opened the bottle of Laphroaig 18, he glanced up to gauge her reaction. The blush was quick, spreading from her chest, up her neck, darkening her face right up to her hairline. But she gave a tiny nod and said, "You have a point." She cleared her throat, and her chin lifted a notch. "Okay. Fine. But just a little."

"Excellent." Adrenaline rushed through his limbs. He strove for nonchalance as he poured the scotch into two short, round glasses, but something stirred in him. The last time she'd wandered into his study wearing a robe . . .

"Please, sit down." He gestured toward the couch with his glass as he handed her the other. She placed her e-reader on the mahogany coffee table before joining him. They sat on the leather sofa, at opposite ends, as much space as possible between them.

He raised his glass to her. "Cheers."

"Cheers," she murmured back, lifting hers in return before taking a sip. "Whoa."

"Yeah. It's good stuff." He grinned before taking a swallow of it, then swirled it around slowly in the glass, watching the dark gold liquid catch the light. She shifted slightly, and he caught a peek of a V-neck top, the same blue as the pajama pants. His fingers itched to touch it, to slide his hands inside the robe and skim them over that top and over her full breasts. He took another slow sip.

"I'm going to ask you a strange, kind of forward question," he said, "but I'm seriously curious, and I hope you'll be honest with me."

She stared back. "All right."

He paused, wondering how to phrase what he wanted to say. After torturing himself with the question countless times in his own mind, suddenly it was hard as hell to verbalize it to her. He ran his free hand across his jaw, feeling the late-day stubble. "When we . . . had sex." He saw her brow pucker, knowing she was already trying to figure out where he was going with this. Shit, why was this so hard to say out loud? Her dark eyes were locked on him, waiting. "It was really *hot*. For me, anyway. It was intense. And I was kind of wondering if, even though it was crazy and spontaneous and all that . . . if you liked it too. Or am I building this up in my head and it wasn't like that." He raked his free hand through his hair and hissed out a breath. "Jesus, this is so awkward. Am I making any sense?"

She nodded, gnawing on her bottom lip for a few seconds. Then she said, so quietly he almost couldn't hear her, "It was like that for me too. We were like . . . It was so . . ." Hot pink stained her cheeks, and her eyes fell to her drink as she tried to hide a smile. "I liked it too. You're not imagining it."

His breath stuck in his chest. "Wow. Okay."

She laughed softly, then peeked up at him from beneath her lashes. "Yeah, it was wow all right. Why do you think it's been so hard to go back to the way things were? For both of us. If the sex had been bad, we'd both be able to forget what happened. Hell, we'd be dying to, right?" She pressed her lips together to suppress a giggle.

Amused and charmed, he sat back a little to gulp down a swallow of scotch. "Yeah, probably. So . . . thank you. For being brave enough to admit that."

"Well, you did it first, so . . ." She shrugged and bit down on her lip. The gesture sent blood rushing to his groin.

"We do seem to have some chemistry," he said. "Don't we?"

She nodded, gazing back at him in wonder. "I thought it was just me."

"No. No way." His heart started thumping in heavier beats.

The weight of the mutual admission hung in the air as they stared into each other's eyes, wondering what to say next.

"Well, while we're making bold declarations," he said, "I need to tell you something else. I think it needs to be addressed. Just once, and that'll be the end of it."

Her eyes widened a bit, but she only nodded.

"When we . . ." He motioned to the couch, then between them, with the hand that held the glass. "I didn't use any protection. I know you said pregnancy wasn't an issue, but if you were worried about . . . anything else . . . I just wanted to assure you it's not an issue either. That you don't have to worry."

Her brows puckered in obvious confusion. "I'm sorry. I'm not following you."

"Diseases," he said flatly. "I'm clean."

Her mouth dropped open as the telltale blush flooded her face. "I . . . I never even thought of that. I mean, you're . . . I wouldn't . . . Wow." Her dark gaze slid away, and she took another sip, a bigger one this time.

"Before that night, I hadn't been with a woman in over a year." He kept his voice mild and businesslike. "I'd been tested before that, as part of my annual physical. I get a full screening for just about everything. Insurance and all that . . ." He eyed her with a touch of remorse. "I didn't mean to be so blunt. But it had to be said. I didn't want you to have any lingering concerns, if you had any."

"I hadn't. But thank you," she murmured. Suddenly her eyes widened again as they lifted to his. "Wait. Are you also wondering if I . . . ?"

He shrugged as casually as possible. "It crossed my mind."

"Huh. Well." She lifted the glass to her lips and stole yet another sip before saying, "I'm clean too. Trust me."

"Because you've been tested?"

"No . . . Because it'd been a very long time. For me. Before that night." Her voice now sounded strangled in her throat. "And I'd been tested back then, so . . ."

"I'm not trying to embarrass you," he said quietly. "I'm sorry about this."

She shrugged and stared down into her glass. She moved as if to take another sip, but apparently thought better of it and lowered the glass back into her lap. One hand gripped the glass, while a fingertip of the other traced slow circles around the rim.

"I'm afraid I have to ask," he said, trying to make his voice as gentle as possible. "If you haven't been tested recently, how do I know . . . I mean, what do you consider a 'long time'? A year? Two?"

He'd never seen her face the way it was now. A deep red flush, her eyes wide, her lips pressed into a thin line. She was horrified. Christ, he felt awful for making her feel so uncomfortable. When he'd realized they hadn't used protection and all the other implications, he'd known sooner or later he'd have to ask. But hell, thinking it and actually asking her were much different things, weren't they? "Look, you can tell me. Anything you ever say to me stays between us, Lisette. You have to know that."

Her gaze lifted to meet his, and her whole body went still. Rigid.

"Three years?" he guessed, trying to help her along.

She snorted out the tiniest laugh and said, "No. More than that."

Surprise rippled through him. Wow. "Okay. Um . . . five?"

Softly biting down on her bottom lip, she shook her head, then finally whispered, "Eleven."

Charles's heart stopped in his chest. Hell no. Surely he hadn't heard her right. "Excuse me?"

"Eleven," she said, her voice soft but sure. She looked directly into his eyes. "Before that night with you, I hadn't slept with a man in about eleven years."

Chapter Eleven

Lisette watched as Charles froze where he sat, his eyes rounded and glued to her face. She wondered if he'd actually fall off the couch. Then he leaned over, set his drink down on the table, shifted his position slightly, and said, "I can't believe that."

"Ohhh, believe it." She took another sip of scotch, welcoming the burn of it down her throat and the soft buzz that was starting to take hold. If they were actually going to talk about this, she'd need half the bottle to get her through it. "So yeah. No worries. I'm clean too."

All the emotions she'd expected to see in his face—horror, shock, pity—weren't there. Surprise, sure, of course, but not that aghast surprise she'd predicted. More like . . . stunned curiosity. Okay. As long as it wasn't pity, she was all right with that. "I suppose now you want to hear why."

"I do, yes, I admit it." He cleared his throat and added, "But only if you want to tell me. I mean . . . it's a sensitive subject . . ."

"Charles. Please. I'm not made of glass." She looked down at her hands, then at the intricate pattern of the glass she held. "I've never told anyone. Because I didn't have to. The only people who know the story are my father and

Karen, my best friend from college. Because they were there." She stole a glance at Charles, then looked back down to her lap. "It's not in my file because it doesn't need to be. My personal history has nothing to do with my ability to do my job. I've never been arrested; I've never done anything wrong. It was just . . . extremely painful." A lump formed in her throat, and she swallowed it back.

"Lisette." Charles's voice was like a caress. He leaned in slightly. "You don't have to tell me any more. I believe you, and also, I don't want to bring up painful memories for you. But just know that if you want to talk about it . . . you can trust me."

She looked up. He was gazing at her with such softness. He was so good-natured, so kind. The COO of Harrison Enterprises, one of the most powerful men in the country, her usually stoic boss, was being downright tender with her. It was stunning. "I was engaged," she said quietly. "I was with Brandon for my last two years of college. My first serious boyfriend ever. A few months after we graduated, I realized I was pregnant. We got engaged." Long-repressed memories trickled through her mind. Taking the third and final pregnancy test . . . then the next night, when Brandon took her out to dinner and ended it with an engagement ring on top of her chocolate cake . . .

"Go on," Charles nudged gently. "I'm listening."

"A baby wasn't part of the plan," she said. "As you know, I graduated with honors in linguistics, and I was going to be a translator. I had an internship at the United Nations, and then a position. You can look it up if you don't believe me."

"Why wouldn't I believe you?" His voice was so soft. She swallowed hard. She hadn't spoken of these things out loud in such a long time. She'd locked them all away. Now that she was . . . She had had no idea it'd be so hard. "I didn't want to give up that dream, but I didn't think I'd *have* to. I thought I'd have it all." A dry wisp of a laugh floated out of her. "I was going to have everything I'd ever wanted. The awesome career, the loving husband, the baby . . . just a little sooner than I'd planned, that's all." Brandon's face appeared in her mind. His lazy smile, his short, dark blond hair that she used to run her fingers through, the glint of his gray eyes . . . then the cold emptiness in them the last time he'd looked at her, standing at the door of their apartment as he left.

"What happened?" Charles asked, bringing her back to the present.

"I got in an accident." Lisette took a breath and cleared her dry throat again. "I was in the city, in the back of a cab, on my way to a meeting for work. A truck pulled out too fast and slammed into the cab. I wasn't wearing a seat belt."

Charles winced, but said, "Few passengers do. I know I don't. We feel as if we're somehow safe in the back of a cab; people don't even think about it."

"I never did," she said plainly. "And at twenty-three, you never think something like that will happen to you." Her throat felt tight, her breaths were shallow, and her skin felt clammy all of a sudden. The usual physical reactions when she thought about the accident. It didn't alarm her much; she was used to that.

But Charles must have picked up on it. With the gentlest touch, he lifted the glass from her hands to set it on the table, then took both of her hands in his. "Jesus, your hands have turned to ice." He rubbed hers between his. The kind gesture made her heart stutter in her chest. Her eyes slipped closed.

"Obviously, you were okay," he offered. "I mean, you're here, and you're fine."

"Not 100 percent." She made herself open her eyes to look right into his as she told him the truth. "I had a concussion, three broken ribs, broken left arm, sprained left ankle . . . and I lost the baby. I was five months along."

"Damn. I'm so sorry," he murmured, genuine empathy in his voice and his gaze.

"Long story short, when I woke up, the doctors told me there was scarring; there was too much damage . . . that I'd never get pregnant or, if I did, never carry a baby to term." She drew a long breath and pulled one hand free to rub at her tight chest, making small circles in the center of her sternum. After all this time, she had thought it'd be easier to tell this story.

Charles kept rubbing her other hand, still clasped in his. "That's horrible. And you were so young. I just . . . Lisette, I'm so sorry that happened to you."

She nodded, her eyes drifting down, away, looking anywhere but at his face. His sweetness and caring were palpable, and as good as it felt, it lanced her heart. She'd always thought Charles was deeply kind underneath all the assured poise and polish. But this show of tenderness and empathy, when she felt raw and vulnerable, was overwhelming. Half of her wanted to bathe in it, and half of her wanted to turn away. It was as though he was looking *into* her with those blazing blue eyes.

"So . . ." Charles asked carefully, "what happened with Brandon?"

Her stomach clenched. "Brandon."

"Yes, you said that was your fiancé's name, right? But your file said you've never been married. So . . ."

Her chin lifted, almost in defiance, but her voice came out all gravelly. "He dumped me, as soon as he found out. Said he was young and wanted a family of his own, so if I could never have kids, what was the point of our staying together?"

Charles hissed a curse under his breath.

"He told me that I was basically useless if I couldn't have children." She swallowed, hating the tremor in her voice. "That what guy would want to *marry* me? Maybe a much older man who already had kids and wanted some pretty young thing on his arm, but no man our own age would ever seriously consider me. Damaged goods and all that."

"And you believed that garbage?" Charles ground out.

"I didn't want to. But I . . . I was a mess." Her shoulders lifted and sagged dejectedly. "You have to understand, I was in the hospital for ten days. Between the concussion and the broken bones and the blood loss, I was *very* weak . . . and by the time I got home, he'd thought it all over and made up his mind." She saw it all in her mind, as clearly as if it'd happened yesterday. "He took me home from the hospital . . . I was so weak I literally couldn't make it to the bedroom; I collapsed onto the living room couch. And that was where I got the 'welcome home, we're over' speech. For him, it was already done, and I just had to understand and catch up with the program."

"Despicable bastard," Charles spit. He raked his hands through his hair, looking as if he wanted to hit something. "I can't imagine how you felt. That's cruel! I . . . God. What did you do? Did he leave, like, that *day?*"

"No. The next day." Lisette shut her eyes for a moment, wishing she could shut out remembering the devastation, the sense of abandonment, the disbelief that had taken hold of her. How he had locked himself in the bedroom while she cried on the couch for hours, too weak to do anything . . . "I took too many hits in too short a time. I was completely broken. Inside and out." She pulled her hand from Charles's and wrapped her arms around her middle. "I didn't care about anything anymore. I felt like my life had ended. Melodramatic, I know, but I was young."

"No," Charles cut in. "You were dealing with so much pain, and more loss, and a bad breakup, and . . . Lisette, *anyone* would've shut down from all that. Come on."

"Yeah, well . . . I called Karen, and she came and stayed with me for two weeks. I quit my job. I didn't want to stay in the apartment, and I couldn't have afforded it on my own even if I had wanted to stay. Karen insisted I move in with her, and she's in upstate New York, near Rochester. So I went. She and her family took care of me for almost three months while I healed. Well, physically healed. The blood loss and the concussion took a lot out of me . . ."

The large bay window appeared in her mind, clear as could be. She'd spent that winter lying in bed a lot, staring out the window beside her bed at the snowy ground outside, thinking, hurting, thinking . . . "And in the spring, when I was stronger, and I was functional and could be independent again, I started a different path. Forged a new life." Her voice dropped to a whisper. "I just wanted to be left alone. So yes, I guess you could say I hid in other people's families, since I figured I'd never have one of my own."

Charles's jaw clenched so hard, a muscle jumped. "I want to find this bastard and kill him. I swear to God. How could anyone . . . when you needed . . . when you'd just . . . I mean . . ." He shook his head and huffed furiously. "I can't wrap my head around it! Lisette . . ." He reached for her hands, pulling them into his. "He was dead wrong. He just hit you when you were at your most vulnerable."

Her eyes filled with tears. "Thank you. But back then, I had nothing, Charles. No one but Karen, really . . . In less than two weeks, I lost everything I had. I was devastated. And so I . . . saw myself the way he did."

Shaking his head, Charles's hand lifted to hold her cheek. "He was so wrong. Jesus, I want to find him. I want to hunt him down like the animal he is and—"

"No!" she said quickly. "Don't even say that. Because I know very well you could if you wanted to, with the power you have. I don't ever want to see him again. I don't care where he is now or what he's doing." She sniffed hard, trying to stem the tears, trying to compose herself. "So. Now you know everything. I know it's a horrible sob story, but it was a long time ago, and like you said, I'm fine now."

"You're not fine, sweetheart." His eyes scanned her face, searching. "If talking about it still brings you to tears, it still hurts. And of course it would. Horrible things happened. And that man . . . He's not a man. He's scum."

"You're right. But I didn't even date after him," she said, again sniffing back the unwanted tears. "I didn't want to get hurt like that ever again. Besides, I didn't think any man my age would want me. If he wanted a family, I could never give that to him. So I . . . yeah." She hiccupped out a watery laugh. "Basically, I've been a nun. Eleven years, give or take."

Charles shook his head, then dropped his gaze to his glass. "I'm disgusted with myself right now, even more than before. God, if I'd known—"

"Stop it," she said. "I could've said no. But I didn't."

At that his head lifted, and he peered into her eyes. "Why didn't you?"

Oh, God. *Because I'm crazy about you.* But she could tell him most of the truth and still withhold the one crucial piece. "Because you felt so good," she whispered. "Because of the chemistry we've admitted we have. It was instant; it was like wildfire. I got swept away by it." She couldn't believe she was saying these things, but they were pouring out. "Because no one had touched me like that in forever, and because I . . . at that moment, I was just so happy to *feel* something again. I'd been numb for so long. And I . . ." She shook her head, not able to say the rest. *I wanted you. I've had a thing for you since I met you. You're beautiful and sexy and a good, decent man, and for that one moment in time, I wanted to be with you.* She shot to her feet. "I've said too much. *Way* too much. Oh my God . . ." She looked around wildly, pulling her robe tighter around herself, needing to escape.

He was at her side in a second. "Don't run away. Come here." He tried to pull her into his arms, but she resisted.

"Lisette . . ." His eyes radiated kindness. "Goddammit, you just need a hug. Let me."

The velvety yet insistent tone of his voice melted what was left of her reserve. He drew her in, nudged her head to rest on his chest, and wrapped her in his embrace. "Shhhh," he whispered. "It's all right." The delicate tenderness of it all brought the tears back and made them spill over. As if her strings had been cut, she melted into him.

"That's it," he whispered, holding her close. "Shhhh."

Her mind went blank, and she welcomed it. For a few seconds, the incredible feeling of being held and soothed was like a lifeline, and she let herself take it.

"That's all in the past now," he murmured against her hair, rubbing her back in slow circles. "You made it through all that, and you're standing tall. You made a good life for your-self. Don't you know how strong you are?"

"Army training," she whispered hoarsely. The tears leaked from her eyes; her boss was holding her, and she was too raw and drained to care.

He chuckled gently and rested his chin on top of her head. "Maybe so. But you're also one of the sweetest women I've ever known. You have such kindness, such warmth." His hand swept up and down her back. "That bastard couldn't kill that in you. No one can. Because you have a beautiful heart, Lisette."

Stop saying such wonderful things, dammit. How am I supposed to keep myself steeled against you when you're so sweet? She went to pull away.

"Shhhh. Relax," he murmured, not releasing her. "Every-one needs some comfort sometimes. We're all only human." His large, warm hand swept up and down her back again, gentle and assuring, as the other encircled her waist. "Know what I think? That night, with you? I needed comfort. It's the truth. I was feeling pretty damn sorry for myself that night." He snorted and added, "It was the absolute wrong way to seek out comfort, of course. But ultimately, you were there for me." He smoothed his hand down her hair, down her back. "I know you're not feeling sorry for yourself, and I'm not feeling sorry for you. But your pain . . . it's palpable. So lean on me. I'm not your boss right now, I'm . . . tonight, I'm just a friend. Okay?"

His words rocked her to the core. She'd never thought she'd meet a man capable of such kindness, such generosity of spirit—and she hadn't expected it from him, not like this. Without really being aware of it, her arms squeezed him tighter, welcoming his embrace and returning it. God, he felt so good. Strong, and sure, and good.

"As for your past," he continued, still stroking her back, "and everything that happened . . . Honestly, other than how sorry I am, I don't even know what to say."

"You don't have to say anything," she said. Suddenly her mind reeled. She'd told him the truth, all of it, and he was *holding* her. Trying to soothe her. It felt so good to let herself talk about her demons and not be shunned, but to receive comfort from someone like this . . . She couldn't even remember the last time she'd really been held. It felt wonderful. It was heavenly.

He's your boss, a voice hissed in her head. *What the hell are you thinking?* Her stomach roiled and clenched. Jesus, what was she doing? Hugging her boss, crying all over him, spilling her deepest secrets? Showing him herself at her most fragile? Humiliation washed over her, cold and cruel. She jerked back, untwisting herself from his embrace.

"What's wrong?" he asked, brow furrowed.

"You're never going to look at me the same way again," she choked out, anxiety kicking in. "I should just resign right now."

"Whoa, stop." His hands lifted to hold her face and make her look into his eyes. "I'd never judge you based on any of this."

"You say that now," she said. "Until you think about it some more. Poor Lisette and her sob story—"

"Stop that!" he ordered. "I *care*. I'm not looking at you like some broken china doll. Do you think so little of me?"

"No," she whispered. "That's the problem. I think the world of you. So I—"

Still cradling her face, he pressed his lips to hers, stopping her words with a fiercely tender kiss. He sipped from her lips, slow and savoring, before he whispered against them, "I think the world of you too."

His mouth consumed hers, and her mind went hazy. These weren't the hard, consuming, hungry kisses from that first night. These kisses were long and sweet and sumptuous. Heat flooded her, making her senses reel. He kissed her once more before pulling back to look into her eyes. "I'm so sorry for what you went through. And you're right, I don't look at you the same way. But not in the way you implied. Now that I know what you've gone through, I have more respect for you than ever. I admire your resilience. Your strength. Your incredible sweetness, in spite of all that happened." He dropped the gentlest kiss on the top of her head.

She shook her head, wanting to believe him, but unable to let herself. She was trembling. "Let me go. I should go."

"Look at me," he commanded. Again he held her face, to still her.

She did as he asked, and her breath caught in her lungs at what she saw in his eyes. The adoration, the sincerity, were unmistakable.

"I think you're amazing," he murmured. "Amazing and warm and wonderful. And so beautiful that sometimes it hurts to look at you, because I want you, and I know I shouldn't."

A startled gasp flew out of her. He leaned in slowly . . . and cradling her head in his hands, pressed his lips to her forehead. Her eyes slipped closed as he lingered there; she was stunned into stillness by the exquisite tenderness of his gesture.

"But we'll talk about that another time. Right now, you must be exhausted," he said against her skin. His hands lowered to rub her arms. "Let me walk you up to your room. Help get you into bed."

She startled, looking up at him in shock.

"Not like that!" he exclaimed. "No! I just . . ." He gently grasped her shoulders. "I just want to get you into your bed and make sure you get some sleep."

"Why are you being like this with me?" she whispered in consternation.

"Because your sadness makes me want to comfort you. It's really that simple." Something flickered in his eyes. "Also, because I truly care, which isn't as simple. You aren't the only one who'd felt numb for a long time, and now . . ." He cleared his throat. "But most of all, because right now, you need me to be here, and I'm here." The corner of his mouth quirked. "You were there for me when I needed you. Reciprocation is more than fair play, don't you think?"

"I'm too tired to argue that line of thought," she said. "Actually, all of a sudden, I'm too tired to do much of anything."

He wrapped an arm around her shoulders and led her from the study. By the time they reached the stairs, she felt the adrenaline begin to ebb and drain from her limbs. By the time they reached her bedroom, the exhaustion had overwhelmed her, and it was hard to even untie the sash of her robe. She managed to slip it off and lay it over the chair, then went right to her bed and slid beneath the covers. The pillows felt like heaven beneath her achy head.

Charles was right there, pulling the covers up to her chin. He leaned over her, sweeping loose tendrils of her hair back from her face. "Feels good to lie down after all that, I bet."

"Mmmm." She felt hazy, half-asleep already. She had nothing left.

He bent to kiss her forehead, again so gently it made her heart smile. "Good night, Lisette. Sleep well. In fact, sleep late tomorrow. That's an order."

"But the kids . . ." She yawned. "School in the morning."

"I'll get them there," he said. "You sleep as long as you need to, okay? I mean it. I'll make sure no one disturbs you. It's totally an order."

"If you insist," she murmured, her eyelids drooping.

"I insist."

"Oh, all right. Charles, wait . . ." With great effort, she opened her eyes enough to meet his. "Thank you for everything tonight."

"You're welcome." He smiled sweetly. "Good night."

She felt cool air, the lack of his presence beside her. Then she heard the flick of the light switch, and the room went dark. From heavy-lidded eyes, she saw him in shadow, standing in her doorway . . .

He stood there, leaning against the frame, arms crossed over his chest, watching over her as she quickly fell into a deep sleep.

Chapter Twelve

Lisette woke up with a start. Tears leaked from her eyes, and she swiped them away. Her dreams had been so visceral, especially the last one . . . She could smell her mother's perfume; her mother had felt so real, it was as if she'd visited. It'd been a long time since Lisette had dreamed about her mother looking healthy and vital, not emaciated and sick as the cancer had ravaged her at the end of her life. And seeing her healthy for the first time in a long time was a comfort. Maybe her mom *had* visited her in her dreams, just to reassure her after such an emotional night.

Oh, God. Last night she'd told Charles everything. And, *holy shit*, the kids! She had to get the kids to school and—oh, *no*, it was nine-thirty. While she looked wildly around the room, she noticed a folded paper taped to her inside doorknob. She flung back the covers and all but jumped across the room to grab it and read it.

Good morning, Lisette.

I took the liberty of turning off your cell phone and turning off the alarm on your clock, so you would sleep as long as you needed to. Don't worry, I managed to get my own kids to school, and on time.

I also asked Tina not to disturb you under any circumstances because you hadn't felt well last night (told her you had a terrible headache, just so we have the same story) and you needed to sleep. Everything's fine.

I'm going to be home late tonight. Have a meeting up in Connecticut and likely won't be home until after 9:00.

I hope you're okay. Hope a good night's sleep recharged you.

Go get something to eat and have a good day. Call me if you need anything.

Charles

Lisette sank onto her mattress and read the note again twice before reaching for her cell phone on the nightstand. She turned it back on, curled up in a more comfortable position, and stared out the window. It was one of those overcast autumn days, but the sun behind the clouds added a silvery glare. She could see the maples and oaks beyond, lining the perimeter of the property, stunning in their peak crimson and gold glory.

Charles had taken care of everything. Last night, he'd taken care of *her*. Today, he'd covered for her, and had even done a part of her job for her, and had left her a sweet note on top of it all . . .

With a deep sigh, she clutched her pillow and held it close. God help her, she loved that man. She couldn't deny it: she'd fallen in love with him last night, helplessly and deeply. She could almost pinpoint the exact moment she'd felt it hit and swallow up her heart. When he'd held her and leaned in and kissed her forehead, lingering with such tenderness, such earnest sweetness . . . After that, her poor heart never had a chance.

And even though a part of her wanted to leave while she

still could, before she spent the rest of her life loving a man she could never have, she was so grateful that he wanted her to stay. She loved the kids, and she was in love with him, and even just being part of their lives and in their presence would be enough for her. That was her sad truth, and it would stay her most guarded secret. If she could just keep her head on straight and continue to do her job well, she'd be able to stay with them all for a few more years, and at least she'd have that much.

Charles felt himself start to relax the instant Tess opened her door and hugged him. His siblings were the only people in the world he trusted completely, could let down his guard with, could laugh and just be himself with, with no worry over how he was being perceived, if what he said or did was on or off the record. More than just his brothers and sister, they were his closest friends and confidants; they were the only ones who truly understood what it was to be a Harrison. The pressures had been heavier on him than on the others, but they all understood that and gave him that extra measure of support and respect for it. Even Pierce; Charles and Pierce had forged a new relationship since Pierce had returned to New York, and Charles was glad for it.

As Charles entered the living room, Dane got up to embrace him, and Pierce crossed the room for a quick but genuine handshake. Pierce lacked Dane's natural amiability and warmth, but after years of angry self-isolation, he'd finally edged his way back into the fold. Not with their father, hell no, but with his siblings. Charles's heart lifted at the sight of Pierce relaxing with them, something that would have been unthinkable only a year ago.

"I heard you were bringing something sweet," Dane said. "Give it up."

Charles lifted the bakery box in his hand for all to see. "Rainbow cookies from Roberto's."

"Yesssss," Dane said, taking the box with greedy hands. "Gimme gimme."

Laughing, Tess took the box from him. "Give me that. We let you have this, there won't be any left within the hour."

"I'll be good," Dane said, batting his eyes coquettishly.

Tess snorted and walked toward the kitchen. "What are you drinking, Charles?" she asked over her shoulder.

He glanced at the bottles of IPA on the coffee table and said, "Whatever they are, looks fine."

"It's good stuff; you'll like it," Dane assured him. He grinned, gave Charles another slap on the back, and sat in one of the three lushly cushioned armchairs.

"Drinking beer from a bottle, Tripp?" Pierce teased. "How very bourgeois of you. Awesome." He flopped down on the couch, reaching for his bottle before stretching his legs out. He rested his socked feet on the table and crossed one ankle over the other. "How goes it, biggest brother?"

"Fine, thanks. You're awfully chipper tonight," Charles remarked as he sat in one of the other chairs. Clad in a long-sleeved T-shirt and track pants, Pierce still looked like the professional athlete he'd once been.

"I'm feeling really good," Pierce said. "I don't know about 'chipper,' but yeah, things are good."

"Tell us more," Tess said as she reentered, holding a glass of white wine in one hand and a bottle of beer in the other, which she handed to Charles before sitting on the couch with Pierce. The living room felt warm and inviting, nothing like the home they'd all grown up in. Tess had decorated with earthy colors, deep rust and tan and wheat. The furniture was plush and cozy, the furnishings elegant but not ostentatious, and the artwork complemented it all perfectly. With a fire blazing in the stone fireplace and old R&B songs playing softly, Tess had created such a welcoming atmosphere that

Charles felt himself melt into the chair and the stresses of his daily life ebb away as his siblings talked and bantered.

Pierce told them how his soccer teams were doing, both the Edgewater youth league and the New York professional team he'd personally invested his time, energy, and money into. When Tess asked about Abby, the mere mention of his girlfriend lit Pierce's face with such a glow that Charles was momentarily taken aback. He'd never seen Pierce look like that over a woman . . . or anyone, ever.

"Why are you looking at me like that?" Pierce asked.

"Like what?" Charles retorted.

"Like I suddenly grew two heads or something," Pierce said.

"Um . . ." Charles took a sip from his bottle, using the time to choose his words carefully before speaking. "I'm a little stunned, frankly. At the look on your face when Abby's name was mentioned. Your whole demeanor changed, do you know that?"

Pierce made a face, something between a scowl and a look of disbelief. "Get out."

"He's right," Dane piped up. He ran a hand through his curly hair as his eyes sparked with mischief. "It's nice. But boy, are you a smitten little kitten."

"A what?" Pierce laughed, shooting Dane a look. "You're bonkers."

"We've never seen you like this, is all," Charles said. "You look . . . content. Happy. It's kind of amazing, and I'm glad for you."

Pierce fixed his brother with a long look, before saying quietly, "I was going to say something smartass, but you know what? You're right. I *am* content and happy. Abby's made it that way. She's everything to me." He looked down at his bottle for a few seconds, taking his legs off the coffee table and shifting position. Leaning forward, elbows on his knees, he looked around at his three older siblings and said, "I bought a ring. Last week."

Tess gasped, practically bouncing in her seat. "Omigod! Oh, honey!"

"You serious?" Dane said, grinning.

Pierce nodded, unable to keep the almost shy but pleased smile off his face. "Dead serious. We've been together for a year. We live together. It's time. And I know she's it for me. I've known from the start, so . . . yeah. I'm going to ask her to marry me. Holy shit, huh?"

"Holy shit indeed," Charles said with a chuckle. "And good for you. She's a fantastic woman."

"Hey, anyone who puts up with your crap is a damn saint," Dane teased.

"Wish I could deny that," Pierce said, "but I won't. She's the best thing that's ever happened to me. Time to make it official."

"When?" Tess squeaked, her smile wide and bright.

"I'm surprising her with a quick trip," Pierce said. "Day after Thanksgiving, that three-day weekend, I'm flying her out to Sedona. She loves it there; she's been there twice, and she keeps saying she wants to go there with me, so . . ."

"So you'll take her on a hike up to one of those red mountaintops and propose," Dane concluded. "Very nice. Good luck, brother."

Tess vaulted across the couch to hug him. "Oh, Pierce. God, I'm so happy for you. I adore her. She *is* the best thing that's ever happened to you. I wish you two all the luck and happiness in the world."

"She'll be a wonderful addition to the family," Charles said.

Pierce snorted at that as Tess released him. "Yeah, I'm sure Dad will be thrilled to hear about this. Maybe he'll give me a bottle of arsenic as an engagement gift."

All three of them quieted at that.

"I'll tell you all something right now." Pierce's voice got low and steely as he looked from one face to the next. "Whatever kind of wedding Abby wants, I'm going to give her. And I want it to be everything she's ever dreamed of. So I don't want him there. I won't let him give her even a moment's worry that he might say or do something to ruin the day. He's not invited."

"Sounds reasonable to me," Dane said, and took a swig of beer.

Tess nodded and reached for her glass of wine. "We understand."

Pierce looked to Charles. "Well?"

Charles shrugged and pushed his glasses up on his nose. "It's your day. Your rules. It should be whatever you want it to be. You don't want him there, done deal."

"How about actually proposing to Abby first?" Dane said. "Making sure she'll say yes to a troublemaker like you."

"Shut up," Pierce said on a laugh.

"Dane's right, though," Tess said. "Let's concentrate on the good parts, okay?"

"Excellent idea." Charles lifted his bottle to his mouth and stole another swallow of the dark beer. Mentally, he was already strategizing. If anyone would have to run interference between their father and the wedding, it would be him. Pierce was obviously counting on the three of them to have his back; no way would Charles let him down.

"I can feel you thinking from here," Dane said, breaking him from his thoughts.

"Oh, really." Charles crossed one leg over the other. "What am I thinking about?"

"A certain dark-haired beauty, perhaps?" Dane's mouth quirked at the corners.

Tess's head whipped to Charles. "You're seeing someone?"

Irritation prickled over Charles's skin. "You bastard," he growled at Dane. "You absolute bastard."

"You need help," Dane asserted. "I can only do so much. You need a Team Harrison powwow, and we're all here."

"Getting together wasn't my idea," Tess admitted softly. "It was Dane's. He was worried about you."

Charles swore under his breath, set down the bottle on the table, and raked both hands through his hair. "I don't fucking believe this."

"Charles," Tess tried to begin.

But Charles pointed a finger at Dane and snapped, "I trusted you with all that. How dare you open it to the floor as if it's a subject up for discussion! It isn't."

Unfazed by Charles's anger, Dane leaned in and met his glare. "It's about more than what happened with her, Charles. It's about all of it. You need to talk about it, and you need to with us, because you know we're the only three people on the planet that you can talk to. I'm not afraid of you. Go ahead and be furious at me. I'm trying to help you."

Charles grunted, but sat back in his seat, letting out a heavy sigh. "I came here to have a good night, not to be dissected and analyzed, dammit."

"Don't think of it as a dissection," Dane said. "Think of it as more of an intervention."

"Fuck you," Charles ground out.

"What's going on?" Tess asked tersely, looking from Charles to Dane and back again. "Because you're worrying *me* now. Dane was right; you're not okay."

Pierce watched them intently without a word, waiting.

"Charles." Dane's voice was soft, coaxing. "Tell them. We're here for you."

Charles glared at his brother and blew out another frustrated breath, rubbing his hands over his face. "Jesus, Dane."

"Someone start, please," Tess practically begged. She looked to Charles, her blue eyes wide with concern. "Honey?"

The gentleness of her voice broke him. He took off his glasses, rubbed his eyes, put them back on, and heaved a sigh of surrender. "For a few months before I turned forty, that milestone birthday had me doing a lot of . . . introspection. And I realized a lot of things."

"Like what?" Tess asked.

With one last sigh, Charles gave in. He talked about how resentful he'd grown about being groomed for the COO position since birth, how his life hadn't been his own . . . everything he'd said to Dane already, everything he'd been holding inside. "And most of all, I'm worried that I'm turning into *him*. Into Dad."

The fire crackled in the fireplace, the popping sounds of the shifting logs filling the silence. Tess's eyes had flown wide. Dane took a sip of beer. But Pierce leaned forward, put his bottle on the table, and stared at his eldest brother.

"I can't speak to most of that," he said. "It must be hard on you. I can't imagine the constant pressure of it. I've always been grateful as hell that it all fell on you. But you always seemed to be born to the throne. Like you really were made for leading the company, and one day, the family. All these years, I thought you *liked* it."

"For a long time, I did," Charles said. "Until I looked around a few months ago and realized my life was all about work. I barely see my kids; my son, Thomas, is starting to hate me and he's still in single digits; and after a disastrous marriage and ugly divorce when the mother of my kids took off, I'm alone." He looked around at his siblings. "Don't you see all the parallels? I'm becoming just like him. That used to thrill me. Now, seeing how bitter he's become . . . it terrifies me."

"No. You'll never be like him," Pierce said earnestly. "You

have a heart. You care about those things. That alone means you're a much better man than he's ever been."

Charles sucked in a breath. He and Pierce had butted heads throughout the years. With an eight-year gap between them, and Pierce's shitty attitude and determination to be wild, Charles had had little patience for his youngest brother. Until last year, when Pierce had returned to New York, and as grown men they were able to forge a new kind of relationship. Now, Pierce's soft but strong words had the same effect on Charles as a sucker punch and a hug combined. "Thank you for that," he murmured.

"It's the truth," Pierce said. "Look. You realized you weren't spending time with your kids and they were starting to resent it. You fixed it. You changed it. The old man never even thought about that, much less did anything about it."

"Point to the jock," Dane said.

"But Charles," Tess said. "If you're that unhappy about working so much, do something about it. We'll all back you. Call a meeting; give some of the other board members more responsibility. Because one day, you'll be CEO, and you can step back and do less, like Dad does now. And he can only do that because as COO, *you're* the one who's really doing all the work."

"You're already in charge," Pierce said. "Everyone knows it. It's just not said out loud."

"He's right," Dane added. "The board knows it. Dad does too. The company would take a major, major hit without you at the helm. Use that power and change some things for your benefit. Don't let the power use you, you know?"

Charles nodded and picked up his bottle again, taking a few long swallows. "I'll think about it. Okay?"

"Okay. Let's change the subject and let him breathe on this a bit," Tess said. She tapped her manicured nails against her glass. "Soooo . . . who's the dark-haired beauty?"

Charles winced. "I was hoping you had forgotten about that."

"Not a chance in hell," Tess proclaimed with a wide smile. "Spill it."

Charles shot a glare at Dane, then looked back to Tess and Pierce. "If I do . . . it can't leave this room. I'm dead serious."

"Charles." Tess leaned in, causing her long dark curls to spill over her shoulders. "You know whatever you tell us stays with us. That's a given."

"This is . . . It could be really unfortunate if any of it got out at this juncture," Charles said.

"Stop with the fancy talk and just say what you need to," Pierce demanded.

"I slept with Lisette the night of my party," Charles said quietly. "I got a little drunk, she wandered in, and I basically threw myself at her." He noted the way Tess's lips parted in shock, the way Pierce's eyes rounded, but made himself say the rest. The part he hadn't even told Dane . . . that he hadn't even admitted to himself until now. "And that's not even the worst of it. Because since that night, I can't stop thinking about her. I think I'm falling for her."

Chapter Thirteen

"Whoa," Pierce breathed. "The *nanny?*"

"Watch it," Charles warned with an edge.

"Don't get me wrong, I like her," Pierce said. "She's really nice. Great with the kids. She's made them . . . uhh . . ."

"Easier to handle," Dane offered tactfully. Tess flattened her lips to suppress a grin.

"Yes," Pierce said. "That. Hey, Abby likes her a lot. Lisette's so quiet, kind of shy, and I'm usually playing with the kids, so she and I don't talk very much when I see her. But Abby draws her out, and they've talked. Abs thinks she's really sweet."

"She is," Charles murmured, reaching for his bottle. He stared at the label and tried to ignore the way his heart was thumping around in his chest.

"She's lovely," Tess agreed. "Kind. Patient. Caring. I've seen it."

"She's also gorgeous," Dane said, "which is a nice bonus."

"Yeah, she is," Pierce said. "I'll admit it, I always wondered if you hired her because she was so pretty. You couldn't know how she'd be with the kids, so . . ."

"That's not why I hired her," Charles snapped. "I hired

her because she was qualified for the position. And because I could tell right away that she was a warm, kind person, so she'd bring that to the kids. Her looks had nothing to do with it."

"Touchy," Pierce noted, and it was almost a taunt. "Yeah, I'm not the only smitten little kitten in this room."

Charles raised the bottle to his lips and knocked back a few swallows of beer.

"So . . ." Tess ventured. "Had anything ever gone on between you two before that night?"

"No!" Charles said firmly. "Never."

"Okay. So how . . . ?" Tess asked.

"I told you, I was drinking. I was in the study, and I broke a glass. She heard a noise and came to check it out, and it just . . . happened." He shook his head as if he still couldn't quite believe it himself.

They were all quiet for a minute.

"Hey, I'm glad you got laid," Pierce said, trying to lighten the moment. "If anyone ever needed to—"

"Shut up," Charles snapped.

"Charles." Tess swept her long hair back over her shoulders. "What about since then? How's it been between you two?"

"Since then? It was fucking awkward at first, of course. But I kept trying to get her to talk to me, to break that ice, so we could be at ease around each other again." Charles thought back to the night after, the anxious look in Lisette's eyes when she got back to the house. "I think she was plain scared. She loves her job, and she thought I was going to get rid of her. Which was ludicrous, since it was my fault, really."

"Um, hold on," Pierce said, pinning him with his gaze. "Why is it ludicrous? Of course she was scared—you hold her life in your hands."

"What?" Charles stared in confusion. "No, I don't."

"Yeah, you do," Pierce shot back. "Think about it. Everything in her life depends on you. Her job, her income, even where she lives. You have total power over her life. Hellooo?"

"He's got a point," Tess murmured.

Charles scowled as Lisette's words echoed in his head. *This isn't my home; it's yours. That's not my car; you own it. The money I make all comes from you. Don't you understand? My livelihood—everything in my life—is dependent on you . . . Hear me."* He swore under his breath.

"What are you getting at?" Dane asked Pierce.

"Well . . . someone has to say it." Pierce eyed Charles and asked quietly, "Did she sleep with you because she was scared to say no? Have you even considered that?"

Charles swore viciously under his breath and slammed his bottle down on the coffee table. "You've got some set. I'd never abuse my power that way," he seethed. "And I can't believe you'd imply that I would, or that I did."

"You're not hearing me," Pierce said. He took a swig of beer.

"What I just heard," Charles said, blood pulsing at his temples, "is you implying Lisette slept with me out of fear, that I used her in a power play or something much worse. That's a hell of a thing to say."

"Charles. I know you didn't, and you wouldn't. But did *she?* I'm trying to make you see it from her point of view." Pierce scrubbed the back of his neck. "You've had insane wealth and power your entire life. You're a great guy, but you're not getting this: you have *a lot* of power over her," Pierce said. "That puts her at your mercy. Whether you would use that power or not is irrelevant. That imbalance still exists. If you're falling for her, you have to acknowledge that."

Charles took a swallow of his beer as his mind worked. "Perhaps."

"You know . . . Julia got supremely fucked over by her ex-husband," Dane said. His tone had turned somber, and they all turned to look at him. "He was rich, powerful, and treated her like a toy. And then like dirt. He used all the power his wealth and connections gave him to bury her when he decided he was done with her. He was ruthless. People like that exist, Charles. You're not one of them, but regular people are wary of people like us."

"People like us?" Charles echoed.

"Yeah. Insanely rich and privileged, which makes us powerful. We *are* different, Charles. To most of the world, we are." Dane shrugged. "You have no idea what it took to get Julia to see me as just a guy who wanted her. To trust me. To trust that I wasn't going to use my power over her, in any way, ever." His brows arched to punctuate his last point as he said, "And she didn't live under my roof. She had her own life."

"Not to mention," Pierce added, "word gets out you're doing the nanny, and she'll be tabloid fodder in the blink of an eye. Remember how it was when it first got out Abby and I were a couple? Her face was on gossip websites, all that shit." His eyes narrowed. "Remember when that sleazy photographer followed her to work one day, and I called you, asked for a bodyguard for a few weeks?"

"I remember," Charles grumbled.

"Abby's a first-grade teacher," Pierce reminded him. "She works with children. She could have lost her job. Luckily, the paparazzi got bored with us pretty fast, and besides, I'm not a COO. If you and Lisette don't work out . . . you think she'll find another nanny job again so easily?"

"Okay, fine! Goddammit! I hear you." Charles rubbed the back of his neck. "I didn't think of those things. But *she* does. She's the one who's concerned about the difference in social status, not me." He took off his glasses and pinched the bridge of his nose. Then he huffed out a frustrated breath and said, "I don't think about the power balance; I just think of her. So it's what *she* thinks. And I hate it."

"Then show her she's wrong," Dane said. "That's what I did, and I have the most incredible woman in the world. You want Lisette? Then go after her. And show her, and the whole world, that you don't care about any of that stuff. Show her she's wrong."

"Very romantic," Pierce said. "But she's *not* wrong; that's the problem."

"Since when are you the voice of reason?" Charles snarled.

"Since I'm the only one here who's endured a public smearing and paparazzi following my very normal, small-town girlfriend to her job and to her house," Pierce said, a hard edge to his voice. His eyes flashed as he fixed his brother with an unflinching stare. "Nothing touches you, Charles, you're like fucking Teflon. But I've seen firsthand what happens. I felt awful bringing Abby into my circus of a life. You ready to do that to Lisette?"

"So that's it?" Charles said, feeling a wave of anger and hopelessness batter his insides. "Just give up on the idea of pursuing something meaningful with her because of power issues and class wars?"

"If you just want to sleep with someone," Dane said quietly, "maybe find someone else."

"That's not —I want something with *her*," Charles admitted. "And I haven't wanted anything real with anyone in a long time. She's different. She's special, and I . . ." He swore, shook his head, and stared at the floor. Why had he finally found someone he found interesting enough to pursue, and it had to be tangled up in class bullshit? Couldn't he do anything the easy way?

"Oh, honey," Tess whispered. She leaned in and grasped his hands. He looked up at her, and she squeezed his hands tightly. "You're a good man. You can find a way to make it work if you really want to try. Nothing's impossible. Difficult, but not impossible."

"You really care about her," Pierce said.

Charles nodded. "More than I realized." His voice had grown low and gruff, and he cleared his throat. "She's a wonderful woman. She's got this steely inner strength, surrounded by unbelievable softness and beauty and warmth. Her warmth . . . I want that in my life. I need that; I'm craving it. I want *her*." He looked up at his siblings. He had their full attention. "I'm what, too good for her because I come from big money? That's bullshit. We're just two people, goddammit. I'm not royalty; she's not from the gutter; this isn't some fairy tale. We're just *people*."

"Hey. Charles." Pierce stared intently at him. "Right there. You just proved you're not like Dad. Because no way would he ever lower himself to date someone from a lower social class, much less his kids' nanny. He would totally care what people would think or say. He'd never take it public. He *does* think he's royalty. So congratulations. You hearing me?"

"Yeah. I hear you," Charles took his brother's words on board. "Thanks."

Pierce nodded and winked before taking a swig of beer.

"If something actually happened between us," Charles said slowly, "I'd . . . I'd shield her from the spotlight and the bullshit as much as I could. The gossip, and anything or anyone nasty. You know, use my powers for good, not evil?"

They all smiled, the tension in the air dissipating like mist.

"You're already thinking in terms of trying to be together, more than a fling," Tess pointed out softly. Her smile spread and lit her eyes. "So you just need to find out if she has feelings for you too. Do you think she does?"

"I don't know." Charles uncrossed his legs and shifted in his seat. "I know we're attracted to each other, and we're both fighting it like hell, but I don't know if she has actual *feelings* for me."

"Ask her," Dane said, as if it were the most obvious thing in the world.

"Jesus, dude," Pierce said, sitting back and stretching out his long legs. "For one of the most powerful businessmen in the country, you're being a total candy-ass about this."

"I am not," Charles insisted. "I'm trying to be careful with someone who, according to you, feels powerless and vulnerable in comparison to me. Not to mention that I'm still trying to wrap my head around the fact that I have feelings for her at all, much less deal with all the difficulties and obstacles that come along with it. It's a mess." With a heavy sigh, he reached for his beer bottle. "You've all given me a lot to think about today."

Chapter Fourteen

On Sunday evening, when Lisette got home from her day out, the house was oddly quiet. It was six o'clock, dinnertime . . . but there were none of the typical sounds of the children or television or . . . or anything. Putting her coat in the closet, she called out, "Hello?"

"Hello," came Charles's voice, from deeper in the house. "I'm in the dining room. Come on back."

Still frowning with confusion, Lisette headed for the dining room. Lights were on in some of the rooms, but the unusual silence in the house made her uneasy.

"Charles, where are the—?" she began as she entered the large arched doorway of the dining room. The words died in her mouth. The large, elegant dining room had been transformed . . . and the scene was clearly a dinner for two. A huge crystal vase was filled with colorful flowers. Long white candles flickered in the dimmed light. The best china on the table, set for two. Across the room, Charles sat at the head of the polished mahogany table, so handsome in a black pullover sweater, no glasses—and those intense blue eyes were locked on her. Music played softly, a bluesy Eric Clapton. Gripping the back of the chair in front of her, Lisette tried to process what she'd walked into. Finally she blurted out in consternation, "What *is* all this?"

"I was hoping you'd have dinner with me," he said.

Her heart started to thump harder. "Where are the children?"

"Their Aunt Tess took them to her house for a sleepover party."

"On a Sunday night? But they have school tomorrow."

"Tess will get them to school." He rose from his chair, smiling, and approached Lisette slowly. "You have nothing to worry about. You have the night off."

"But I had all day off," she said, almost stammering. The closer he came, the more her heart pounded. "I don't understand."

"I wanted to have some time alone with you," he said quietly. "To talk, uninterrupted. So Tess has the kids, and I sent Eileen home early. We're the only ones in the house tonight."

She could only stare. Words failed her.

"I mean, I'd take you out to dinner, but I didn't think you'd be comfortable with that. So I tried to bring some special ambience here to the house." The side of his mouth curved.

"Like . . . a date?" she whispered, barely able to get out the words.

"Um . . . if you want," he said. "I'd love that, but I'm not pushing. I really did just want to talk."

She stared at him in astonishment, torn. Half of her was afraid for everything she had and didn't want to lose. The other half was swooning. Charles was making an openly romantic move for *her*? He wanted to have her alone, to have dinner together like a couple on a date? The two sides warred in her head, making it hard to think.

Charles stepped right up to her and stared down at her, his beautiful blue eyes smoldering. "Lisette . . . we keep trying to go back to the way things were before." He shook his head as a wry grin spread on his face. "But it's not going to happen. It can't. It won't."

With a soft groan of resignation, she whispered, "I know."

Charles nodded slowly, his features softening. "What we shared was unplanned. But the chemistry between us is real. We both keep trying to ignore it, and it's only getting stronger. I've tried to stay away from you, but I don't want to. I think you feel the same way . . . ?"

Before she could answer, he held up a hand. "You know what, wait. I need to make something clear here." He drew a deep breath, still watching her. "I'm not trying to assert any power over you. This is *not* a boss and employee situation. If you don't want to have dinner with me, that's fine. If you don't want to talk with me, that's fine too. If you want to leave the room right now and we pretend this never happened, okay. Your job isn't in jeopardy. You want to tell me to go to hell, I will *not* hold it against you." His gaze turned earnest. "I just . . . I don't know how to reach out to you without it seeming as if whatever I ask is a command of some sort. It's not, I swear." He heaved a deep sigh, a mixture of frustration and melancholy. "It's so damn complicated."

She nodded, unable to speak. Her breath was stuck in her lungs, and her head was reeling. Had what she'd been trying to tell him finally sunk in? And was he ignoring it all simply because he wanted her anyway?

The side of his mouth curved in the lopsided grin she adored. "So, bottom line: I'd like you to have dinner with me. I'd like to talk for a while. But it's not an order, and if you don't want to, that's 100 percent okay. All right?"

"All right," she whispered. She met his searching gaze directly, looking deep into those brilliant blues.

He edged closer. "I've been trying to figure out what

to do about this . . . and finally what I came up with this afternoon was, instead of trying so hard to resist the change . . . what if we tried to embrace it?"

Her stomach rolled in a total free fall of emotion.

"I have everything a man could want, Lisette," he said softly. "And yes, a lot more. I'm very lucky. I've made a mark with my career; I've traveled; I've got great kids; I've got more money than I'll ever be able to spend. The only thing I don't have is someone special to share it all with. And I want that. I'm ready for that. And you . . ." He took a deep breath. "Turns out you're everything I've wanted in a woman . . . and you've been right here the whole time."

She could barely breathe. She swallowed hard, trying to open her suddenly thickened throat.

"I want you, Lisette. And I think maybe you want me too. I'm tired of dancing around it, trying to ignore it." His eyes pinned her. "Aren't you?"

She could only stare back into his eyes, spellbound. He had no idea how deep her feelings were for him. No idea how much the things he'd just said meant to her. No idea how much she wanted to just lean into him and feel his arms around her.

"Say something," he coaxed.

"I want to believe you, to trust this, but I'm afraid," she said. "I trust *you*, Charles. But it's everything around us. And what I could lose. I'm afraid of all of it."

"Don't be. Please." He reached out and took her hand. His skin felt so warm, so good. "Let's change things tonight. Stop fighting it, and start giving this a chance."

"Giving what a chance?" she asked, her voice wobbly. She realized her hands had started trembling. "My losing everything? You're not the one in danger here. I am."

He frowned hard. "I'm not dangerous, in any way."

"Yes, you are," she whispered hotly, pulling her hand from his.

He stared harder, and she thought he was trying to look right into her head to figure her out. "You *do* want me too."

She closed her eyes and wrapped her arms around her middle. It wasn't just her hands that were trembling now.

"I'd never fire you or throw you out; I've told you that," he said, his tone growing fierce. "Dammit, Lisette . . . if we want each other, why can't we try to make something work?" He raked his hands through his wavy hair, and his eyes flashed with frustration. "Just for tonight, can we not be boss and employee? Can I not be Charles Harrison III, and all the crap that comes with it? Can we just be a man and a woman who like each other, who are attracted to each other, and just . . . goddammit, can't we just be that?"

"*You* can," she said. "You have nothing to lose. I'd lose my job, where I live—people would talk. Everyone. You'd be ridiculed, and I'd be destroyed."

He gently gripped her arms, the rising heat coming off him in waves. "I don't care what anyone would have to say about our dating, if that happened. I just care about *you*. And I do care. More than you realize . . ." His hands dropped to his sides, and he gazed at her with a mixture of longing and vexation.

Her blood rushed through her body as a wave of shock rippled over her skin. He cared about her, had real feelings for her? Stunned beyond measure, she could only stare back at him.

"Do you want me?" he asked directly. The penetrating look on his face left no room for her to hedge. "Just say it, this once. Yes or no, just tell me the truth. If you don't want me like this, I swear I'll never do or say anything about it again."

"Of course I want you!" she cried, finally breaking. "But

I'm kind of terrified, Charles! There are so many reasons why we shouldn't—"

He grasped her face between his hands and pressed his mouth to hers. It was the most passionate kiss she'd ever experienced, filled with commanding heat and palpable longing. Lost to him, she kissed him back, melting in his arms as they wrapped around her to pull her closer. His lips were warm, and she could taste a hint of scotch on his tongue as it swept into her mouth, sliding against hers. She could smell a hint of musky cologne and the heady male scent that was just Charles. Need burned through her, scorching hot as they kissed. Her hands plowed through his wavy hair, holding his head, as she arched to get even closer. He moaned into her mouth and grabbed her at the waist, pressing her harder against him. She whimpered softly as the last bits of rational thought fled from her mind. No one had ever kissed her like this. His desire for her was unmistakable, a tangible thing. Her legs felt weak, and she held on to him.

Slowly he pulled back, breathing hard, and leaned his forehead against hers. She felt a bit woozy, dazed, as if he'd put her under a spell. "There's something real between us," he panted. "If those kisses didn't just prove it, nothing could."

"Are you kidding?" she managed. "The only reason I'm standing is because you're holding me up. My limbs are like jelly. Oh my God."

She swallowed hard, trying to catch her breath and what was left of her mind. Once they started this, there'd be no going back. He wasn't pulling a power play; he wasn't playing her; he was sincere. She knew him well enough to know that. All he wanted from her, it seemed, was her.

But if things went wrong and the fallout affected the kids in any way . . . She knew their well-being would always come before hers. She had a serious choice to make. Was

giving things a shot with him worth losing her job if it all
blew up?

His fingers pushed back the free tendrils of hair from her
face, and he looked into her eyes with such gentleness it
made her heart clench. "Give me a chance," he whispered.
"Give *us* a chance. I think we could have something real. I
swear you won't regret it."

Ohhhh, it was nearly impossible to think only with her
head and not with her heart. She loved her life here . . . but
yes, she could find another place to live. Hopefully, she
could find another job. She'd rebuilt from scratch before. If
she were forced to, she could do it again. But would she find
another man like Charles? No. He was one of a kind.

And the truth was, she already loved him. She'd never tell
him that, but she did. Her eyes slipped closed as her breathing calmed and she desperately tried to think. He held her
close, wordlessly, waiting.

"I'm so scared of this," she finally whispered. Her eyes
opened, and she met his gaze. "I'm scared of how much I
have to lose here. But . . ." *Just say it. He has. Just say it!*
"I'm even more scared of losing the chance to be with you.
Because I want you too. I care about you too." She felt her
face heat, even as his eyes warmed at her confession. "I just
can't believe . . . you really want to *date* me?"

"More than you can imagine," he murmured, caressing
her cheek with careful, tender strokes of his fingers. "This
isn't just me trying to sleep with you. I can sleep with
anyone, without jeopardizing so much. This is more. I hope
you believe that."

She bit down on her bottom lip and sighed. "I want to
believe that."

"I'll *make* you believe that," he swore. "I'll show you." He
kissed her lips softly, then released her and pulled back,
taking her hands in his. "Let's take a little breather here. I

don't want to overwhelm you. Let's have dinner, and we'll talk. We'll discuss whatever you want to. All right?"

"All right." She drew a shaky breath. Was this real? Still in a daze, she let him lead her to her seat.

Charles couldn't stop staring at her as they sat together, sharing a meal like any normal couple on a date. The candlelight made her luminous, her dark eyes shining as they met his. And there was so much going on in her gaze—he caught moments of surprise, caution, delight . . . but most of all, she was enjoying herself. She *wanted* to be there with him, and the more she relaxed, the more obvious that became.

He'd spent his life studying others, a sure way to always stay a step ahead. He thought he'd had a handle on Lisette Gardner after almost two years of her living in his home. But this woman sitting with him now . . . she was like a different person. Still gentle and lovely, of course; but once she loosened up some, she made him laugh. He found himself chuckling as she told him stories about the kids he hadn't heard before, and he enjoyed her animated storytelling. She also warmed his heart with the obvious affection she had for them.

And yes, she was attracted to him. He caught it in the almost shy glances she stole. Those deep, dark, gorgeous eyes . . . everything showed there, if he paid attention. She'd been hiding her true self all this time. Now, he was getting to know the real her, and the more he did, the more he wanted to know.

The food he'd ordered from Chez Antoinette—the most upscale, renowned, and expensive French restaurant on Long Island—was marvelous, and he was happy to bring it out himself from the kitchen to the dining room table.

"I can't believe *you're* serving *me* dinner," she murmured.

"I do know how, you know," he joked. "If my staff all quit tomorrow, I'd be able to fend for myself."

They started with butternut squash bisque, and followed with traditional Boeuf Bourguignon. Lisette *mmmm*'d several times with varying degrees of ecstasy. "If you're trying to win me over with top-notch French cuisine," she said with a light smile after the first bite of the beef, "I'll admit, it's working. This food is incredible."

"I'm so glad you like it," he said, making a mental note to take her to the restaurant sometime. "I wasn't as sure about Portuguese cuisine, so . . ."

For the first time, her smile was teasing, almost cocky. "I'll tell you where to get great Portuguese food if you really want."

"Oh, I do." He met her flirty gaze. "But only if we go there together."

Her dark eyes took on a sparkle, and she bit down on her lush bottom lip. "Deal."

Elation rushed through him. He cut into the meat and took another bite. It really was fantastic. "So you think this is authentic French cooking, then?" Charles knew damn well the chef had been trained in Paris, had been wildly successful there before moving to New York. It didn't get more authentic than him.

"Absolutely," she nodded. "My goodness, it's wonderful. That bisque alone was sublime. Reminds me of when I was a little girl, and we'd visit my grandparents in Paris. My mom and I would go, just the two of us, once a year. My grandmother used to make a bisque kind of like this . . ." Her voice trailed off, and she beamed at him with pleasure. "Thank you, Charles. I appreciate all this. You obviously put thought into it, and I'm touched."

His insides warmed, and he smiled softly. She hadn't fled when she saw the dining room set for a romantic dinner, or when he'd made his heartfelt overture to her, and now she was delighted with the food he'd carefully chosen with her in mind. So far, the night was going better than he'd hoped.

She refused to drink any wine at first, sticking to water. But halfway through dinner, when he offered again, she agreed to half a glass. He matched her with his own. The only thing intoxicating him tonight was her presence.

"This really was so delicious," Lisette said as she set her fork down. "What a treat. Thank you again."

"My pleasure," he said. He wiped the corner of his mouth with his linen napkin, then reached for his wineglass and drained it. "Ready for dessert?"

"Oh, no thank you," she said. "I couldn't eat another bite right now."

"You sure?" he taunted. "Wow. You can say no to crème brûlée, chocolate soufflé, and apple tart?"

She gasped softly, and her eyes widened. "Ohhh, you don't play fair."

"Not where sweets are concerned."

"You got *all* those things? For just the two of us?"

He smiled and nodded. The enchanted look on her face was priceless. "I wasn't sure which you'd prefer, so I got all three, figuring you'd like at least one of them."

"I love *all* of them," she moaned with a grin. "I'm a sugar junkie; I love desserts, did you know that? But especially baked pastries . . . I have a serious weakness for them." She sat back in her chair and giggled ruefully. The sound made his heart lift. "Ohhh, I want them all, but I'm really too full right now!" She reached for her wine and sipped.

"Tell you what." Charles dropped his napkin on the table, beside his empty plate. "It's a nice night. Why don't we go for a walk outside, and then afterward, maybe you'll be ready for dessert. Dessert, a glass of brandy . . ."

She considered him over the rim of her wineglass, the candlelight flickering on her face. At that moment, she was so beautiful, she seemed almost unearthly.

"You're really pulling out all the stops tonight," she murmured.

He grinned. "I'm trying."

"Charles . . . I'm flattered. I really am. And I've very much enjoyed both the food and your company." She put down her glass and faced him directly. "Tell me what you want. When you planned all this . . . What are you hoping for tonight?"

He set down his glass too. "Merely for us to come to a decision, together, about what we want. To decide if we're willing to take this risk together." He leaned in on his elbows, holding her gaze. "I'm not playing a game. I'm romancing you tonight because I like you and I wanted you to see that. It's really that simple."

"Nothing about this is simple," she countered. "Not one thing."

"Yes, that's true." His heart beat more heavily as he realized she still might be too scared to believe in him, or to try. "I want it anyway. I want *you* anyway. I just wish you could trust me."

"I do trust you," she said quickly. "As much as I can at this point, anyway."

He rose and slowly moved around the table to stand before her. "But do you trust me enough to give this a shot?"

She stood to face him. "If I didn't, I wouldn't be here right now, and I never would've slept with you that night." Her hand rose to touch his face, and he realized she was trembling as she looked into his eyes. "Charles, you're one of the best men I've ever met. I don't want this all to go to hell. You mean something to me."

Something in him melted, like liquid heat, filling him entirely. Maybe it was hope. Maybe it was pure affection. Maybe both. He cupped her face in his hands and said, "Then keep trusting me. Let's get to know each other better, spend some time together . . ." He brushed his lips against hers, a hint of what could be. "Some people say there are no accidents. This all got started off in a very . . . well, unorthodox way, yes. But all I know is I haven't been able to stop thinking of you since that night. That I'm drawn to you a little more each day. I want to try this. I want you."

"Oh, God," she whispered, slightly swaying on her feet, and his hands moved to her arms to hold her steady. She looked away, and he pulled her in close. As if in sweet surrender, her head dropped lightly to rest against his chest. He could feel her exhale, and his eyes slipped closed from the incredible feel of her in his arms. His hand lifted to run over her thick, soft hair, still secured in its ponytail, and he kissed her temple.

She pulled back and looked deep into his eyes. What she was thinking, he had no idea. He could feel her body trembling, and he braced himself for her to pull away from him, go to her room, and shut him out. But her gaze instead turned into something . . . wanting. He saw the longing there, and hope flickered through him.

"It all sounds like a dream," she finally whispered. "But I'm scared as hell."

"I know." His heart started beating a little faster. Reflexively, his arms tightened around her. "Sweetheart . . . take a chance with me, and I promise you won't regret it." He leaned in and kissed her mouth with all the tenderness he possessed. "I promise."

Chapter Fifteen

After the intensity of their conversation, Lisette was glad Charles had pulled back and suggested that walk outside. Bundled in their coats and scarves against the cool night and gusty breezes coming off the nearby Long Island Sound, they strolled along the perimeter of his tremendous property side by side. With the quiet stillness around them and blanket of stars overhead, she could almost pretend they were walking through the countryside instead of his eight-acre backyard.

They kept the conversation light, as if they both needed a breather from the heavier vibe before. He asked for some stories from her childhood, some good ones, and she told him. Things like how her dad would take her fishing in lakes and ponds, or how she'd bake cookies and pastries with her mom, or the hours she spent sketching while staring out of windows or sitting in faraway fields. He listened attentively and seemed truly interested. That, along with everything else he'd said and done that night, surprised her. If he was putting on a show just to get her into bed, it was beyond elaborate.

She swatted that thought away. He was sincere; she just couldn't believe that he was pursuing her this way. She wasn't some socialite or celebrity, someone who traveled in the powerful circles that he did. Yet he claimed he was drawn to her. Wanted not just her body, but all of her. To try to be together, like any normal couple. Could that be possible for them?

"I can feel you thinking," he said.

She glanced at him. His features were carefully schooled, as always. Sometimes he was impossible to read. The moonlight bathed his profile in a cool glow, making him so handsome it stole her breath away. She stopped in her tracks, and he stopped beside her. "Charles, I need you to know something. To understand."

He gazed down at her, kindness in his eyes. "I'm listening."

"I've been alone for a long time," she said. "I know how to take care of myself, and I almost always have. And I've always cared for others, both because I had to, and because it comes naturally to me."

"You're a nurturer," he said with soft conviction. "I sensed that from the moment I met you. It was one of the main reasons I hired you."

"You're right, I am," she said. "But I'm not used to anyone's wanting to do anything *for me*. Or being demonstrative, or doing something incredibly lovely like you did with dinner tonight." She swallowed hard, hoping she was making any sense at all. "It may seem as if I'm unaffected by it, or as if I'm still holding you off, but that's just how I'm wired. It's my way."

"It's your army training," he offered, trying to diffuse her growing angst with humor.

"Heh. You're not totally wrong. That's part of it, I guess. My father always tried to teach me to be as self-sufficient as possible. And like him, I'm not very good at accepting things—gifts or unforeseen kindness . . . or affection . . . graciously. Lack of experience." She huffed out a breath of frustration and shoved her hands into the deep pockets of her coat. "What I'm trying to say is that everything you've said and done tonight mean something to me, and that I appreciate all of it. It's been romantic, and sweet, and I'm moved. And God help me, I care about you too, and I'm sorry if that hasn't been clear."

He grasped her face and pressed his lips to hers, silencing her. His warmth enveloped her in the crisp night air. They held each other close and kissed under the stars . . . It was the most romantic handful of minutes she'd ever had. For those few minutes, there was nothing in the world but them, and she let herself melt into him and enjoy that feeling.

And his cell phone rang in his coat pocket, vibrating against her belly.

"Ignore it," he whispered between sweet and sultry kisses.

"What if it's important?"

"Nothing's more important than this right now."

The phone stopped ringing and vibrating. He smiled against her lips for a second, then took her mouth with deeper, more demanding kisses. She savored the feel of his tongue tangling with hers, the taste of him, the feel of his hands on her body, the warmth of his breath—

The phone rang again, vibrating against her through his coat once more.

"Dammit," he muttered.

"What if it's Tess?" she asked. "Something about the kids?"

At that, he released her. He reached into his pocket, pulled out the phone, looked at the caller ID, and swore under his breath. "Tess? Is everything okay?" She watched his eyes shut as he winced and listened to whatever Tess said. "God, I'm so sorry . . . I'll pay to clean that, first thing tomorrow . . . No, I insist. How is he now?" He looked at Lisette and shook his head. "No, stop. Stop apologizing! My kid is sick; that's not your fault. I'll be there soon; I'm on my way. Lisette will be with me. We'll take all three of them home. No, you don't have to—they're both asleep? Well . . . okay. We'll just come get Myles, then. If you're sure . . . Thanks. Okay, see you soon." He ended the call and groaned.

"What happened with Myles?" Lisette asked, concerned.

"He's sick." Charles took Lisette's hand, pulling her gently with him to walk back to the house. "Tess said they all were fine all night, but Myles seemed a little quiet. She figured he was tired, and he actually fell asleep on the couch while they were watching a movie." Charles's breath came out in visible puffs against the chilly air, white clouds against the darkness. "She got Ava and Thomas to bed, then went back to the den to try to wake Myles enough to shuffle him off to bed. He woke up, stood up, and threw up all over her floor."

"Oh, nooo," Lisette moaned. "Aww, poor baby."

"Yeah. I'll have her carpet cleaned tomorrow. She said he feels warm to her. He must have a bug." Charles put a hand at the small of Lisette's back as he ushered her through the side door.

"What about Ava and Thomas?" Lisette asked.

"She said they were fine and sound asleep, so why bother them. She'll take them to school in the morning, as planned. So we just have to get Myles." Charles sighed. "You'll come with me?"

"Of course," Lisette said. "That's my job." Just like that, a crack had appeared in their romantic bubble, and they stared at each other. Her face flushed as she headed for the stairs. "I just want to get a pair of clean pajamas for him," she said over her shoulder. "Give me a minute."

He watched her as she quickly flew up the grand spiral staircase. She was a true gem; her concern for his children was endearing. But their romantic evening had come to a disappointingly abrupt end. *"That's my job."* Damn, damn, double damn.

* * *

As he drove home from his sister's house, Charles snuck a few glances in the rearview mirror. Lisette was in the wide backseat of the Escalade, Myles bundled in her lap. She had a plastic bag next to her in case he vomited again, but both her arms were wrapped around his little boy, her fingertips smoothing his hair back from his forehead. She and Myles had chatted quietly for the first few minutes, then had gotten quiet.

"How's he doing?" Charles asked. "Fell asleep already?"

"Yeah. And he definitely has a fever," Lisette said.

"Damn." Charles turned into his long driveway. "Well, we're home. I'll carry him straight up to his room, if you could take his things."

"Of course."

As a team, they got Myles in and up to his bed easily. As Charles pulled the covers up to his son's chin, he turned and realized Lisette had shed her coat somewhere along the way and was already in action. She hadn't stopped since the minute they'd reached Tess's house.

Now, he watched as she knelt by Myles's bedside, holding a tiny plastic cup of purple liquid. "C'mon, sweetie, sit up just a bit . . ." she cooed as she slid her free arm under his shoulders to raise him.

Charles leapt forward to help, holding Myles up enough for her to get him, even though the boy was mostly asleep, to swallow the Tylenol. Then he eased his son back down to the pillows, dropping a kiss on his forehead. Yup, he was warm, all right, poor little guy.

"Thanks for the help there," Lisette said as she rose to her feet. "Might be a long night, though. You should go to bed."

Charles stared at her. In the past, that was exactly what he'd always done when the kids got sick—he'd let Lisette take care of them, barely going near them, not wanting to catch whatever they had. He couldn't afford to get sick; he had a company to run. Now, guilt and self-reproach washed over him. "No. He's my son, I'm not going to just push him off on you. We'll take shifts."

"But you're leaving for your trip on Wednesday," she said. "You can't get sick now, and we don't know yet what he's got."

"Well, I've been exposed already, haven't I?" Charles reasoned.

"Yes, but I can do this. You have work tomorrow." She looked into his eyes. "This is my work. This is exactly what you hired me to do."

Dammit, again she was right, and again he didn't like it. The lines seemed so blurry all of a sudden . . . He sighed, glancing down at his son where he slept. "He seems okay for now. Shouldn't you get your sleep too?"

"I suppose," she conceded. "Not that I'll sleep well, knowing he's sick. I'll be up to check on him a few times; I can't help it."

Charles smiled and stepped closer to her. "You're the best, you know that?"

"Thank you," she said. "But isn't that why you hired me?"

He paused, peered at her closely. "You don't have to keep reminding me you work for me."

"I don't know . . ." she murmured, looking away. "Maybe I do."

"No, you don't." Only an hour before, they'd been kissing outside like lovestruck teenagers, wild and frantic. Now she was trying to put up her wall again. "Maybe I should remind you that there are some incredible desserts in the kitchen waiting. Don't want them to go to waste, do we?"

"Unfortunately, I don't have much of an appetite right now. Vomit tends to have that effect on me. Speaking of which . . ." She crossed the room and grasped a large blue plastic bowl, setting it down beside Myles's bed. "In case there's more."

Charles shuddered and made a face. "Yuck."

A giggle flew out of her, a deliciously light sound. He couldn't help but grin.

"I'll wrap the desserts up," he said, "and you can have them for breakfast."

"That sounds decadent," she said. "But really good, too. Thank you."

He put a hand to the small of her back to usher her out. She left with him, turning off the light and closing the door behind her, leaving it open a bit so she could hear Myles if he called for her. In the hallway, Charles spun her around, pressing her back to the wall and his mouth to hers. Her muffled gasp of surprise disappeared into his mouth as he kissed her firmly. His tongue swept inside, tasting her, teasing her. When he pulled back, he stared into her eyes. "You're already trying to act as if earlier tonight didn't happen. Why?"

"I-I'm not."

"Yes, you are. Sweetheart, I know you're scared. I am too."

"Charles . . . I think we're scared of very different things," she whispered.

He didn't move, didn't look away. "Like?"

"Like you're scared you won't have what you want with me," she murmured. "I'm scared I'll have absolutely nothing left if this all blows sky high. An affair versus an everyday life . . . quite different things, don't you think?"

His jaw tightened, along with his gut. She saw things more clearly than he did; it was true. He *was* used to getting what he wanted. Maybe he was pushing too hard. But . . . "I hear you," he said. "I do. But please don't shut me out." He leaned his forehead to hers. "We *both* feel this."

"Yes, we do," she whispered, her warm breath fanning his face. "That's no longer in question."

"I want this." He brushed his lips against hers. "We'll take it one step at a time; we can do it together. Just take that leap of faith with me." He saw the emotions warring in her eyes, the battle between her mind and her heart, and kissed her lips lightly. "Trust in me. Try. Because I'm just a man, Lisette. A man who wants a shot with you. Okay?"

She stared at him for a long beat. He stared back, their eyes locked as his heart pounded. Then she leaned forward and kissed him, long and sweet, in unspoken accord.

Lisette and Myles holed up in his room on Monday. The poor kid had a nasty stomach bug and couldn't keep anything down. Tina had to go pick up Ava and Thomas from school; Lisette couldn't leave Myles. Charles checked in every two hours via text to see how they were doing—both Myles *and* her.

She had a lot of time to think, sitting with Myles all day while he napped, puked, or played games. Sunday night seemed like a surreal dream. Charles wanted her. He'd made that abundantly clear, in every way he knew how. Maybe that first night hadn't been a total accident after all, but him reaching out to her in a way he'd subconsciously wanted to but hadn't even been aware of? In any case, something had taken hold of both of them that night and hadn't let go, that was for sure.

He didn't care that she was his kids' nanny. He didn't care if people would talk about them if it ever went public. He didn't want her to leave, and had agreed to be careful around the kids as they attempted to start something. He wanted to be with her. Why couldn't she wrap her head around that? Exhausted from the long night and day, when Myles fell asleep around five o'clock, she lay on the floor beside his bed. She was so weary, it actually felt good. She grabbed the extra pillow she'd brought into the room and fluffed it behind her head.

She didn't realize she'd fallen asleep until she heard

Myles retching, waking her with a start. Even half-asleep, on instinct she rolled away from the bed to grab the big plastic bowl, but it wasn't there. She opened her eyes and looked up from the floor to see Charles sitting next to Myles, holding the bowl in the boy's lap as he vomited into it.

"Charles." She sat up and got to her knees. "When did you get home?"

"About fifteen minutes ago." He rubbed Myles's back with his free hand as the boy heaved twice more. Then Myles wiped his mouth and burst into tears. "I'm sick of being sick!" he wailed.

"Ohh, honey, I know," Lisette said as she stood.

"It stinks being sick," Charles said, holding his son close as he cried. "It sure does, buddy."

"Poor baby," she said as she took the bowl from his lap. "It's been a rough day. But I'm sure it'll be better tomorrow." She handed Charles a few tissues. "Have him sip some water," she told Charles gently, gesturing to the glass on the nightstand before leaving the room to clean out the bowl.

When she returned five minutes later, Charles was still sitting with his son, an arm around him as they stared down together at the tablet in Myles's hands. Her heart squeezed at the sight of this tall, powerful man, dressed in a costly dark gray suit and tie, cuddling his little boy. Charles glanced up at her as she entered the room, shooting her a wry grin as he pushed his black frames up on his nose. "Long day, huh?"

"Yeah. But he's such a good boy." She ruffled Myles's hair before she sat in the one cushioned chair in the corner. Usually, it had a few of Myles's toys on it, but she'd spent a good part of the day there. "How was your day?"

"Better than yours, I'll bet." He peered at her, studying her. "You must be wiped out. When I came in, you were out cold on the floor."

"Why didn't you wake me?"

"Because I knew you must have needed the sleep."

She lifted her wrist and glanced at the delicate gold watch that had once belonged to her mother. "It's 6:15? Oh my God, I must've been out for about an hour! I'm so sorry."

"Sorry? You were so exhausted you were sleeping on the floor. I should be apologizing to you, for not having someone else here to help you."

"Tina did help me," she asserted. "She made our meals and brought them up here, and she picked the other kids up from school today so I wouldn't have to leave Myles." She looked down at herself. At her rumpled Boston College pullover sweatshirt and black yoga pants with unidentifiable stains. Her hands flew to her hair; the braid felt loose and lopsided. "I must look frightening," she said ruefully.

"Not at all. You look like a woman who's been taking care of a sick child all day," he said. "You're not supposed to look glamorous."

"Glamorous?" She laughed as she quickly undid her braid. "That's not a word that's ever applied to me."

Charles smiled at her and opened his mouth to answer, but Myles piped up, "What's 'glamorous' mean?"

Lisette grinned as she ran her fingers through her hair to loosen it. Charles's eyes were glued to her, watching as she separated parts of it and began to braid her hair again. He seemed entranced by the process.

"Well?" Myles asked, louder.

Charles looked down at his six-year-old. "Um . . . well, it's kind of like being really fancy and pretty at the same time."

"Like all dressed up with lots of makeup and stuff?" Myles asked, his eyes never leaving the tablet as his fingers continued to play.

"Yes, kind of like that," Charles said.

"Then nope, Lisette's not glamorous," Myles said. "'Cause she's not fancy." Then he looked up and gave her a huge smile. "But she *is* pretty, and that's better. Right?"

Her heart warmed as she smiled back at him. His earnest, innocent compliment made her feel like a queen. With practiced fingers she finished the braid, and as she wrapped the elastic around the end of it, she realized Charles was gazing at her in appreciation. His bright blue eyes, framed by his black-rimmed glasses, seemed to sparkle.

"You're right, Myles," he said in a low, reverent tone. "She sure is pretty."

Lisette felt the blush bloom on her cheeks in an instant. She bit down shyly on her lip as she met Charles's eyes. The look on his face and the timbre of his voice sent a shiver over her skin and made her stomach do a wobbly flip. Good God, the effect he had on her. She was in deep trouble, no doubt about it.

Chapter Sixteen

Charles made a point of tucking each of his children into bed Tuesday night, spending a few minutes with each of them. He'd gone on business trips before, all the time. But his ritual was to spend at least ten minutes with each kid at bedtime, so they'd feel his love before he left for a while. He went to Myles last, since Lisette would be with him. By the time he got to his room, the boy was half-asleep.

"I only throwed up three times today, Daddy," Myles said. "Lisette says maybe tomorrow I won't throw up anymore."

Charles grinned and hugged his son. "I sure hope so, buddy. I really do. I want you to feel better already."

"Lisette said the teacher said half of my class is out sick," Myles said, wide-eyed. "We all caught the same bug!"

"That tends to happen," Lisette said from the chair in the corner. She didn't seem as rumpled as the day before. A long pink sweater hid her shape, but her gray leggings at least showed off the bottom half of her legs. The sheep slippers were on, and her hair had stayed in its long braid, with only a few tendrils loose. But she did look tired; the hint of dark circles beneath her dark eyes gave her away.

Charles leaned down and kissed Myles's forehead, which was still a little warm. "I'm leaving very early, so I'll be gone when you wake up. But I'll be back a week from tomorrow, okay? The day before Thanksgiving. You can call me or text me whenever you want; Lisette will show you how."

"I will. I'll miss you, Daddy," Myles said, curling into his blankets with a yawn. "I love you."

"I love you too, sweetheart." Charles ran a hand over his son's hair, then his back. "Feel better really soon. Lisette will take good care of you while I'm gone."

"Yup. She's awesome . . ." The boy yawned again and closed his eyes. "Good night, Set," he mumbled.

Lisette smiled from her seat. "Good night, honey. Sleep well."

Myles was asleep in about thirty seconds. Charles rose from the bed and held a hand out to her. "You. Come here."

She slanted a sideways look at him, but got to her feet and crossed the room.

He took her hand and pulled her in, holding her close. With gentle affection, he wrapped her in his embrace and said against her temple, "Thank you."

"For what?" she asked against his neck. "Doing my job?"

"You go above and beyond just doing your job," he said. "Every day. And I know it. Thank you for taking such good care of him while he's been sick."

"You're welcome," she said. She moved to pull back. "Um . . ."

"I kinda wasn't done hugging you," he told her, still holding tight. "You feel really good. If that's okay."

A staggered laugh flew out of her. "Yeah, it's okay." After a few seconds, she leaned into him more. He felt her body ease and relax against his, felt her let go and let herself be held. They stood that way for a few minutes, quiet and close.

"I think I'm going to miss you when I'm away," he murmured.

She pulled back enough to look into his face. He saw

the glints of surprise and delight in her eyes as she asked, "You are?"

He nodded and pressed his lips to hers. "When I get back, I'd like to spend some time with you. Just you and me. I'll work it out somehow, if you'd like that too . . . ?"

"I can't believe this is happening," she whispered.

"I want this," he whispered back. "You said you did too."

"I do," she admitted. "Still scared, though."

"That's fine." He kissed her again, soft and tender. "As long as it doesn't stop you from trying."

She stared into his eyes and nodded, almost timidly.

He kissed her once more, then, still holding her hand, led her out of Myles's room. The house was quiet; Tina had gone home; the children were all asleep. He led her down the hallway.

"Where are we going?" she asked.

"Follow me. You need something . . ." The side of his mouth curved up as he brought her to his bedroom. She paused at the doorway.

"It's not what you think," he said with a grin. "I'm not going to just throw you down on my bed, though the thought of that is tempting as hell." He led her through his enormous bedroom, past his king-sized bed, past the loveseat, armchair, desk, and flat-screen TV, into the adjoining master bathroom. By now, she was looking at him as if he'd gone insane.

"What are you doing?" she asked, watching him.

"Giving you something you need." He leaned over and turned the faucets in his huge tub, then started the jets. "Think of this as a quickie spa experience. You need some time in here."

"Because I didn't shower today?" she asked wryly. "Do I stink?"

He laughed. "No, but that just affirms your need to sink into a tub and relax." He stepped to her, took her face in his hands, and kissed her soundly. "I'm here. If Myles wakes up, I'll go to him. Take a long soak in here, as long as you want. I bet you'll feel like a new woman when you come out."

She stared at him in wonder. "That's very thoughtful of you, Charles."

"You deserve it." He pointed to his navy terry cloth robe hanging from a silver hook on the wall. "Wrap up in that when you're done." Bending to a low cabinet, he pulled out a plush navy bath towel and set it on a small table beside the tub. Then he went to a different cabinet, rummaged around, and pulled out a glass jar of bath salts, two fat white candles, one smaller blue one, and a lighter. "I thought these were still in here," he murmured as he set them along the far edge of the tub, where her feet would be. He tossed some of the bath salts into the water. As the candles flickered to life, he went to the switch and dimmed the lights. He'd transformed the room, creating a soothing, tranquil atmosphere in under a minute. "Okay. All yours. Enjoy."

She flung herself at him, wrapped her arms around his neck, and kissed him passionately. Happy and surprised, he kissed her back, drinking in her sudden show of affection as he held her close.

"You're so sweet," she whispered against his lips. "Thank you for this."

"You're very welcome." He kissed her again for a minute, tasting her, losing himself in her. "If we don't stop now," he said, his voice husky, "you won't make it into that tub. I'll do what I told you I wouldn't instead."

She held his gaze for a long beat. Good Lord, she was mulling that over. He'd wanted her to relax, to have some downtime, knowing once he left she'd have even less of it. But she was so damn tempting . . . He kissed her quickly and said, "You need this. I'll see you when you come out." Walking away from her, he stopped at the doorway to turn back and look at her. "And you will only be wearing my robe, so . . ."

She smiled, and a mixture of mischief and lust sparked in her warm brown eyes. "That's true. Okay. See you soon."

Before he changed his mind, he closed the door to let her be.

Half an hour later, Lisette opened the bathroom door and peeked out. Charles was lying on his bed, wearing a long-sleeved navy T-shirt and pajama bottoms with varying stripes of blue. His glasses were on, his brow furrowed in concentration as he typed on his laptop. Propped up on the pillows, legs crossed at the ankles, and barefoot, he seemed like a regular guy, not the imposing COO of a billion-dollar company. Appealing, handsome, and solid. Everything she wanted in a man . . . and God help her, she wanted this man. More than she'd ever wanted anyone in her life.

And though she found him irresistibly sexy, right now she wanted to just curl up next to him and sleep for a week. She'd been so tired before the relaxing soak in the tub, and that had felt like heaven. It had been so relaxing that she almost fell asleep, prompting her to end the bath. But she knew he was likely hoping for more than just a snuggle. He looked up as she stepped into the large room, and his eyes lit up. That look sparked a warm pull, low in her belly. God, he was gorgeous. It wasn't right, him just lying there all sexy and dazzling like that. She wasn't making it out of here without action, nope, no way. She wanted him too much.

"How do you feel?" he asked, smiling. "Was it good?"

"It was wonderful," she said softly. "I did need that. Thank you."

"I've wanted to do something for you since I found you asleep on the floor yesterday." He put the laptop aside.

"You've been up 'round the clock with Myles. I know you're more tired than you let on. You've got to be."

"I'll be fine. I'll sleep well when he's better."

He took off his glasses and let his eyes rake over her. Standing there in nothing but his robe, she suddenly felt self-conscious. She reached for the end of her braid and played with it, curling the damp lock of hair around her fingers.

"You're beautiful," he said, his voice pitched low and his eyes blazing.

She smiled softly. "Thank you, but I don't feel beautiful right now. I likely look as wrung out as I feel."

"Nope." He got up from the bed and went to her. Her heart beat more rapidly as he approached. "No makeup," he murmured. "Hair up in a braid, pieces coming loose . . ." His thumb lifted to caress the skin beneath her eyes. "Dark circles, the sign of devotion." He leaned down to kiss her forehead. "Absolutely beautiful."

She thought she might swoon right there, if women actually swooned anymore.

His nose trailed softly along the side of her face, down to her neck. "You look good . . . You smell good . . ." His mouth landed on the fleshy spot behind her ear, his teeth gently nipping her skin before his warm lips kissed her there, sending a jolt of electricity right to all her sensitive spots. "Mmmm . . . you taste good too."

She giggled, but when he started kissing, nibbling, and licking her neck, her breath hitched and turned into sighs of pleasure. Her head dropped back, her fingers dug into his hair, and he continued his sensuous ravaging of her neck as his arms slipped around her.

Her body arched to press against his, aching for contact. She whispered his name, and he raised his head to take her mouth in a searing, heady kiss.

"I want you so much," he said, his voice husky. Her heart

pounded as he kissed her again. "But if you're not ready, I understand."

"My brain is saying, 'what are you, crazy?'" she admitted. "But my body isn't listening. Charles, I want you too."

Their mouths met in a consuming kiss as their arms wound tightly around each other. His tongue swept into her mouth as his hands slid down her back, squeezing her bottom before pressing her harder against him. Her fingers dug into his shoulders, and a soft whimper escaped her mouth.

The cell phone started ringing on his nightstand.

"No," he spat, kissing her fiercely.

She pulled back, her hands on his chest. "But you're leaving in the morning," she said, trying to catch her breath. "What if it's important?"

He closed his eyes for a second and swore harshly under his breath, then stalked across the room to answer the phone. "Harrison," he bit out. His erection was obvious in the cotton pajama pants, and she couldn't help but stare at it. He caught her and quirked a grin. With his free hand he gestured at it, then to her as if to say, "Ta dah!" She snorted a giggle as he said into the phone, "I don't care. The merger is still moving forward."

"No, it's not," she said, and put on an exaggerated pout.

A laugh ripped out of him at her joke, and he slapped his finger over the phone to block the sound. His eyes bright, he shook his head and whispered, "I know, and it's a damn shame." Back into the phone, he said, "No, I'm here. Could you repeat that, please?"

She waited patiently, looking him over, her blood still racing and the throbbing between her legs wreaking havoc. But after a minute that felt like ten, it was clear he couldn't get off the phone.

"I'll be in my room," she whispered, moving toward the door.

He shook his head no, mouthed "Wait!" and held up a

finger, still listening to whomever was speaking on the other end. "I don't care about that," he said. "You're not hearing me. It's not enough of a concern to hold this up . . . no. No!"

She sighed, gave him an apologetic smile, and waved good-bye.

He scowled and held the phone away. "I'm so sorry," he whispered to her. "I'll come to you as soon as I'm off this call."

While he argued with whomever was on the phone, she went back to the bathroom, grabbed her clothes, and quietly left. She could barely think; she was flustered and filled with aching need. When she got to her room, she left the door open the tiniest crack, shed his robe, and went searching through her dresser. Toward the back of a drawer, under her winter pajamas, she found the satiny hot-pink nightshirt Tina had given her last year as a birthday gift. It was the only pretty item she had. She didn't own anything remotely sexy, no lingerie, nothing like that. The satin was smooth and the cut of the long shirt was flattering. It would have to do.

Do I put on panties? she wondered. Maybe not, since he would want . . . ? Or should she put them on anyway? She rolled her eyes at herself. *I can't even believe I'm thinking these things.* Making the decision to go without, she slipped into her bed, excitement rushing through her. She took some deep breaths to try to calm herself down. Five minutes passed. Her racing blood had slowed, and she kept up the deep breaths . . .

From what seemed like deep in a fog, Lisette felt soft, warm lips kissing her forehead. "I'll miss you," the voice whispered. She was so tired; her eyes felt weighted shut, and she couldn't even speak. Was she dreaming?

The alarm went off, and she slammed her hand down to silence it. With a yawn, she opened her eyes. It was 6 A.M., her daily wakeup time. The room was still dark; the fall patterns wouldn't bring sunlight for another hour. As she sat up, it all came back to her in a rush. Charles. Oh, God, she'd fallen asleep waiting for him. She groaned and dropped her head into her hands. Why didn't he wake her up? A whisper came back to her: *I'll miss you . . .* His warm mouth on her forehead. Oh, dammit, he'd likely tried to wake her. She'd been dead to the world.

Her cell phone light was blinking, and she checked her text messages.

You look beautiful when you're sleeping, Charles had written only fifteen minutes before. I'm so sorry the call took longer than I thought it would. When I got to your room, you were out cold. Knowing how tired you were, I didn't have the heart to wake you. Hope you slept well; you needed it. Will text you later today.

Her lips lifted in a besotted little smile. God, he was sweet. And he—

There was a quick knock on the door, and Ava stumbled in. She looked pale. "I just threw up all over my bed," she said.

Wonderful, Lisette thought, but put her phone down to go to the girl. Ava's head felt warm. "I bet you have whatever Myles had."

Ava started to cry. "I don't want to be sick like him!"

Lisette sighed and rubbed Ava's back. "I know, honey. I know."

Chapter Seventeen

Charles's trip was packed. Three days in Los Angeles, four days in San Francisco, scheduled from the time he woke to when he slept with barely a moment to breathe. But every day and night, when he could sneak time for himself, he texted the beautiful brunette back home. He called the kids each night to say hello, but he texted her two or three times a day. He was way past smitten; he was downright hooked. Their text exchanges were good in that she was more relaxed; he could sense it in her playful banter. Talking with her that way, without the immediate temptation or need of physical contact whenever they were alone and near each other, was a little gift.

But while he was out in LaLaLand, she had her hands full at home. Apparently Ava had caught the bug the morning he left, while Myles was on the last day of his being sick. Just like Myles, Ava puked for two days, then stayed home on the third day, as well, until the fever broke. Lisette sounded as if she had it all under control, but he felt bad for her.

Friday night, in the limo on his way to dinner, he texted: When I get home, I'm getting you a full weekend at a first-class spa, with every bell and whistle.

That's very generous of you, she wrote back, but you don't have to do that.

You're going to let me do that for you, he texted, and you won't argue with me.

I am, huh?

Yeah, that's right, you are. And you'll like it. Got it, gorgeous?

Yes, sir, Mr. Harrison, sir, she responded. You sure are bossy sometimes ...

He chuckled and wrote, Look, you've been up to your elbows in puke for days. I'm totally pulling rank on this one. You're going to the spa, & soon.

Fiiiine, she wrote with a winky face. I'll let you pull rank. On one condition.

His brows lifted at that. Intrigued, he wrote, What condition?

You come with me.

An enamored smile crept across his face. You drive a hard bargain. Terms accepted. Happily. We'll make a long weekend of it. How does 3 days at a spa sound?

Like paradise.

Saturday morning, he woke at seven and rolled to reach for his phone before his eyes were even open. He planned to catch a quick workout in the hotel gym, then shower, eat something, pack up, and check out at ten. A car would be waiting to take him to the airport; today he'd fly from L.A.

to San Francisco. But he saw Lisette had texted him two hours before: We have a hat trick. Third kid down. Nice of Ava to stop throwing up yesterday so when Thomas started this morning, my hands were free. ;) Just letting you know he's sick. Same bug as other 2. He'll be fine in a few days. Don't worry.

Charles groaned. Jesus, those poor kids, and poor Lisette! She hadn't had a break from a sick child in a week, and it looked as though she wouldn't for another few days. He called her cell.

"Hi," she answered on the second ring, sounding both happy to hear from him and a little ragged.

"I'm so sorry," he said immediately. "God, three for three, huh?"

"Yup. Be very glad you're not here. It's been some week."

"Actually, I feel terrible that I'm not there. What a shit-show."

"Oh, we have plenty of that," she joked dryly. "And puke, and snot, and every other gross body fluid you can think of."

"Your Christmas bonus this year will be *huge*," he said. "Do you want me to buy you a Ferrari? A plane? A small, secluded tropical island?"

She laughed, then said, "You'd actually do one of those things if I asked, wouldn't you?"

"Damn right." He grinned at her voice sounding a bit lighter. "Are you getting any sleep at all? Do you have backup?"

"Don't worry, Tina helped me all this week, and Eileen's here now; she'll help me all weekend. They both deserve heftier bonuses too."

"Consider it done."

"Abby even offered to come over and help, but I wouldn't let her."

"I'm sure Pierce appreciated that. And so do I. If Abby

got sick, I'm sure he'd blame me somehow. He can still be a surly bastard sometimes."

She chuckled softly. "It's good to hear your voice."

"Good to hear yours too," he said. "I miss you, you know."

Her pause was weighted. Then she said shyly, "I miss you too."

He smiled and rolled onto his side to stretch out a little. "I'm in a big, big bed, in a fantastic suite at the Beverly Hills Hotel, all by myself. What a waste. We should be having top-notch hotel sex here."

She giggled, the sound warming him. "I've never had any hotel sex, much less top-notch hotel sex."

"Oh, Jesus, we're going to have to do something about that."

Now her laugh was full. "Oh, really?"

"Hell yes. You know, an eleven-year dry spell is a lot to make up for," he said. "But I'm up to the challenge. You can count on me, Ms. Gardner. I won't let you down."

She laughed again, pure delight.

He threw the covers aside and got out of bed. "Talking with you like this makes me happy," he said. He crossed the room and leaned against the wall to stare out the window. Stretched out beyond was a view of palm trees, mountains in the distance, and bright morning sky.

"Me too," she said. "Why is it easier for me to talk to you through texts and over the phone?" She sighed. "You get in front of me, all handsome and intense with those piercing blue eyes of yours, and I turn into mush. It's pathetic."

"That's not pathetic; that's adorable. And one of the sweetest things anyone's said to me in a long time."

"It's the truth," she said. "But I'm sure . . . if we spend time together, real time, I'll get over that, no problem." She paused, and he waited. Finally she murmured, "I've just been alone for such a long time that I feel like I don't know what to do, how to act. I know that must sound ridiculous for a thirty-four-year-old woman to say. But I really . . . I'm like a fish out of water here."

"Don't worry, and don't think so much," he said. "You don't need to do anything or act a certain way. Just be yourself. That's who I've fallen for."

"Okay," she whispered, so softly he almost didn't hear it.

He scrubbed his free hand over his face. The stubble on his jaw needed shaving. Sunlight rippled off the walls as a soft breeze blew outside. He wished she was there, standing in front of him. "We can make this work, you know. I believe that. I wish you did a little more too. I know you're nervous, but . . ." The California landscape was so different from that of New York. It felt good to be far away from the norm, but again he wished she was there, with a pang that made his heart squeeze. "Lisette? You still there?"

"I'm here."

He heard her draw a long breath and anxiety pricked him. "Did I say something wrong?"

"No, not at all," she said. "Quite the opposite. You keep saying all the *right* things. Lovely things. Things that make me feel like . . . like I haven't in forever."

"I mean all of them," he said quietly. "Because you do the same for me."

"Oh, Charles," she whispered. "It's still overwhelming. All of this."

"Yeah, it is," he agreed. "But it'll be worth it. It already is."

Charles walked out of the terminal, Bruck following with his bags. The cold air of New York was like a slap back to reality after a week in sunny California. Sliding into the backseat of the car, Charles scowled as he looked at his watch. It was ten-thirty already. Dammit! He'd planned to be home by dinnertime, so he could spend time with the kids—who were all finally well again—and then have some quality time at last with Lisette. All day, he'd been operating at a low simmer, thinking about seeing her. Every night, thoughts of her had filled his head and taken hold. Sultry, wicked thoughts . . . He was ready to have a damn orgasm with her along for the ride; there was only so much masturbation a man could take before he needed more. Especially when he finally had someone to be with.

But Wednesday morning, it had rained in San Francisco. It fucking rained long and hard, with high winds, and the plane couldn't be cleared for takeoff. By the time it was cleared, they'd been delayed more than four hours.

The next day was Thanksgiving; at least he wouldn't have to go back to the office until Monday. But there would be no real downtime. His kids would all want a piece of him; the big family dinner at his father's estate for the holiday would include fifty people; he had tickets for Saturday afternoon to surprise the kids with the Radio City Christmas show; he'd have to keep checking in with the office, even if he wasn't physically there . . . His time was never his own.

You're never off the clock, Tripp. His father's voice echoed in his head as Bruck got back in the car and pulled away from the curb at Kennedy. With a frown, Charles let his head fall back against the seat and closed his eyes.

"Good trip, sir?" Bruck asked.

"Fine, thanks," Charles replied. "Sorry about the delay. I hope it didn't screw up your evening."

"No worries," Bruck assured him. "I'm just going to my sister's tomorrow for the holiday; I didn't have any plans tonight."

"That's good; I'm glad. Thank you."

"California was nice, though?" Bruck merged onto the parkway.

"It was fine. But I'll be glad to get home."

"Have you there in half an hour, sir."

Charles pulled out his phone and scrolled through e-mail

while they drove. Tonight, once he got home, he didn't want to think about work at all. Before he knew it, they were in Sandy Point, and the car had turned into the private road that led to his long driveway. At the house, Bruck unloaded Charles's suitcases from the trunk. "I'll bring these inside, sir. You go on, go get some sleep in your own bed."

"Thank you." Charles turned to Bruck and held out a hand. "Have a happy Thanksgiving."

"Thanks." Bruck smiled as he shook it. "You too."

"You're taking the weekend off, right?" Charles asked. "It's a holiday."

"Just tomorrow. I figured—"

"Nope. I don't want to see you back here until I have to go into work Monday morning," Charles said firmly. "Have a great weekend, Bruck."

Bruck's nod was begrudging, but his steely eyes glinted with appreciation. "Thank you, sir. You too. Happy Thanksgiving."

Carrying only his briefcase, Charles made his way up the grand front stairs and through the wide front doors of the mansion. He checked his watch—11:05. The house was quiet, all the lights out. A trickle of disappointment ran through him. Lisette must have gone to bed, and he'd have to wait to see her until morning. No, wait . . . Down the hall, it looked like the light was on in the den. Had she waited up for him? He made his way down the corridor.

Lisette heard a noise—the front door? Had Charles finally gotten home? She paused in her reading, cradling her e-reader in her lap. She pulled her soft, spa-like robe tighter around her and burrowed into the plush loveseat. A few seconds later, there were footsteps in the hall; then, there stood Charles in the doorway. He wore a dark gray suit and striped tie, and his eyes looked tired behind his glasses, but he was handsome and magnificent and *ohhh*, the way he smiled at her. It made her stomach flip and a spark ignite in her chest, warm and wonderful. "Hi."

"Hi."

"You're back."

"I am. Finally." He stepped into the room, gazing at her as if he were drinking her in. "It's good to see you."

"It's good to see you too." She smiled.

"I'm glad you're still up."

"I . . ." She felt her cheeks heat up. "I was waiting for you. I was a little concerned."

"Concerned? The flight was fine, once we finally took off. Nothing to be concerned about." He shoved his hands into the pockets of his trousers as his blue eyes captured hers. "Is that the only reason you waited up for me?" His voice had turned into a low, seductive rumble that made her insides go all gooey. He was so sexy he stole her breath away.

Do it, demanded the voice in her head. *He wants you. You want him. Do it.*

"No." She put her e-reader down and got to her feet. "No, that's not the only reason I waited up for you." She adjusted the sash on her robe as they met in the middle of the room, gazes locked. Her heartbeat roared in her ears. She could barely breathe. "I couldn't wait to see you. And I was hoping for a kiss hello."

He grinned. "Good. But I'm not kissing you in here, now, because once I start, I'm not going to want to stop."

"I won't want you to stop either," she said quietly.

His eyes blazed with carnal desire, and a muscle jumped in his strong jaw. "You're sure? Absolutely sure?"

"Yes."

He held out his hand and murmured, "Come upstairs with me."

With a soft, sweet smile, she took a deep breath and slipped her hand into his.

Chapter Eighteen

With Lisette's small, soft hand in his, Charles wanted to run up the stairs and pull her down the hall to his bedroom. But he went leisurely, willing the adrenaline rushing through him to slow down. There was too much at stake.

His mind spun as he escorted her upstairs. First of all, her past . . . Before their encounter in the study, it had been, more or less, *eleven years* for her. Jesus. Second, the last time they'd been together, the only time, it had been a rush of animalistic alcohol-fueled groping. And while it'd been hot as hell, she deserved better than that. Tonight, he wanted it to be a little special for her.

Because he knew damn well this meant something. She was placing her trust in him, willingly putting aside her fears to take this step. This night had weight, and he wanted to make it count. For both of them.

"Kids are all asleep, right?" he asked as they got to his bedroom door.

She nodded. He saw the high color in her cheeks, the mixture of excitement and nervousness in her warm brown eyes.

"You're sure about this?" he murmured. "You can still stop this if you want to."

In answer, she stood on her tiptoes, placed her hands on

his shoulders, and brushed her lips against his. "I'm sure," she whispered, looking up at him. "Take me inside."

He all but threw the door open, ushering her into the dark room before locking the door behind him. He turned on the small lamp on the side table, opting for dim, softer light instead of the brightness of the overhead fixture. Lisette stood nearby, looking at him as she fidgeted with the edge of the sash around her waist.

He kicked off his shoes, then reached up to unknot his tie.

"No, wait," she said, stepping to him. Her hands lifted to cover his, she licked her lips, and his heart started pounding. God, he wanted her. "I have a confession to make," she said, her voice low. His brows arched in curiosity. "You always wear your suits and ties . . . your crisp button-down shirts . . ." She glanced up at him coyly. "Do you have any idea how handsome you are when you're dressed like this?"

He stared down at her, the corner of his mouth curving. "No. Tell me?"

"It's devastating," she murmured. "You're so handsome it should be illegal." Her slender fingers worked at undoing the knot of his tie. "You have no idea how many times I've fantasized about undressing you. Taking off layer by elegant layer of your suits . . ." His breath felt stuck in his chest. She pulled the tie loose and dropped it to the floor. "Sliding your jacket off . . ." Her hands slipped under the blazer and swept it off him, dropping that to the floor too. "Unbuttoning your shirt . . . oh, yeah, mostly this . . ." She started to do just that, and as he watched her, his blood rushed hot through his body, slamming him with desire.

Her dark eyes rounded with what seemed like appreciation as she got the last button undone and spread his shirt open. Her eyes on his body, her hands ran over the planes of his broad chest. "Oh, are you gorgeous," she whispered.

"Who's seducing who here?" he asked with soft but amused astonishment. "You're killing me."

A look of surprise flickered across her face. "Really?"

"Are you kidding me?" He cupped her face with his hands and brought her mouth to his, kissing her deep and hot. He let his hands glide down her back. Her chenille robe was soft, but he wanted her skin. "But I need to touch you. Time to get rid of this robe."

She shivered as his mouth trailed down her neck. He helped her get his shirt off, still feasting on her skin as he reached between them to untie the sash of her robe. When his fingers brushed smooth silk, he pulled back to see what she wore. His breath caught as his eyes widened. "You . . . wow." He drank in the sight of her luscious curves in a wine-colored lace-and-silk nightie that stopped just below her knees.

"I bought it yesterday," she whispered, blushing. She smiled, but bit down on her lip as she admitted, "I didn't own anything . . . well, sexy. And I thought you and I might, uh . . . so I . . ."

He silenced her with a long, consuming kiss. "You look incredible. So beautiful I don't know where to start . . ." With gentle hands, he slipped her robe off her shoulders, letting it pool at her feet. His hands moved slowly up her bare arms, bringing goosebumps to her soft skin and making him smile. "You said you often fantasize about getting me out of my suits?" His smile turned into a playful grin. "Well, I often fantasize about doing this . . ." He reached around to the back of her head and pulled out the elastic that held her long hair in its ponytail.

"Your idea of foreplay is a little kooky," she joked, unable to hide her smile.

He laughed. With both hands, he ran his fingers through her long, dark locks. "When your hair is down and loose like this"—he let it slide from his hands, and it swished before stilling—"you look different. Your hair is free; your whole body is free. And tonight, you look like a seductive goddess . . ."

His hands ran up her sides, luxuriating in the feel of her body beneath the silk. Desire heated his blood and sent it searing through his limbs. "You are so, so beautiful. I love to look at you, you know."

Her eyes filled with pleasure. "That's very sweet," she whispered.

"It's very true." He lowered his mouth to hers, kissing her gently at first. His hands stayed at her waist, but pulled her in closer. Her mouth opened to welcome his kisses and deepen them as her arms snaked around his neck. Their tongues met and circled, their bodies pressed together, and Charles let himself just enjoy the feel of her. The kisses burned hotter, and he eased her backwards toward the bed, laying her gently on the mattress, covering her body with his. As their greedy mouths gave and took, he loved the feel of her hands roaming over his shoulders, his chest, along his back. She was exploring him tentatively, and he wanted her to, but he wanted to explore her even more.

His hands roamed over her body, learning every delicious curve. She made sounds that let him know what she liked, and what she loved—little whimpers and moans and gasps that had his whole body tense with need. Still kissing her, he ground his erection against her hip, needing the contact, and her hands slid down to his ass to grab it, pressing him closer to her. A lusty groan fell from his lips.

"You still have your pants on," she whispered between kisses. "That's not right."

He chuckled and rolled onto his back, undoing the belt and yanking it free of the loops. Before he tossed it away, her hands were already at the waistband of his pants, pulling down his zipper over his throbbing erection. Her fingers stroked the length of him over his boxers, and he sucked in a breath.

He stood up and let his boxer briefs and pants drop to his ankles, kicking them away. He watched her dark eyes travel over his body; she'd never seen him fully naked before, and now she was quiet. He hadn't slept with a woman in long enough that a twinge of self-doubt lanced him. Did Lisette like what she saw? After all, he was forty now, and he stayed in good shape, but she was only thirty-four and maybe she—

"You're a stunning man," she said. "Beautiful, really."

He relaxed instantly, relief washing through him. "Very glad you think so."

"I always have. But seeing you like this . . ." She leaned up on one elbow to study him, so he stood still and let her. When her eyes dropped to and lingered on his erection, it twitched under her attentive gaze. "It's a new thrill. A delicious one."

He smiled, his body simmering with anticipation, and he lowered himself to the bed again. He hovered over her, leaning on his forearms, and brushed back a lock of dark satiny hair from her forehead. The sight of her in that deep burgundy negligee, so flattering against her olive skin, her nipples hard through the silk and her long, dark hair fanned out beneath her . . .

"You take my breath away," he murmured with reverence. He kissed her mouth, long and sweet. He trailed kisses along her jaw, down her neck, down to her shoulder as his hands glided over her silk-clad body. Her warm skin smelled faintly of vanilla, and he breathed in her scent, letting it feed his senses. Still kissing along her skin, he cupped her breast and squeezed gently, drawing a shuddery sigh from her, loving how the soft weight felt in his hand. Nipping at her shoulder, he tugged down the thin strap with his teeth as he fondled her breast and tweaked her nipple. It pebbled beneath his fingertips as she moaned and writhed beneath him. She reached for his cock, and he stopped her.

"Not yet," he murmured. "Right now, I want to focus on you. Let me."

"But—"

"Shhhh." He silenced her with a commanding kiss as his hands went to her waist. Not breaking the kiss, he slid the nightie up her body. He reared up to pull the silk over her head and toss it over his shoulder. "My turn to look at you."

Her face flamed, and she bit her lip, almost shy. "No one's seen me totally naked in a very long time. I'm a little self-conscious; I admit it."

"You shouldn't be," he said. "Because you're gorgeous." His hands ran over her velvety skin, the feel and sight of her making his blood race. "I want every inch of you."

Lisette was so on fire, she could barely speak, much less think straight. And for once in her life, she was fine with that. She'd crossed a line, and there was no turning back now, even if she wanted to. Being with Charles like this was everything she'd dreamed of, and she was going to let herself enjoy every moment.

Charles was all over her, hands and lips and tongue and teeth everywhere he could reach, slowly driving her to heights of passion she'd never before reached. He kissed his way down her body, nipping and licking, claiming her inch by inch, leaving trails of fire in his wake. Her head fell back against the pillows, and her eyes slipped closed as the sensations battered and washed over her. His warm, ravenous mouth took possession of her as he moved lower, lower . . . She panted and sifted her fingers through his wavy hair, mindless with desire.

But he teased her, moving torturously slowly along her inner thighs, kissing, nuzzling, skimming his lips back up until she wanted to beg for mercy. Just when she thought she couldn't take anymore, his mouth sealed over her warm core, his tongue pushing through the folds. She gave a low cry, and her hips bucked and her fingers twisted in his hair, holding him to her as the incredible waves of pleasure crashed over her. He spread her legs wider, then slid his hands under her bottom to pull her closer, the assertive move making her moan and shudder. Then his tongue flicked her clit and she cried out, nearly arching right off the bed. He held her hips; she held his head.

Burying his face between her legs, he feasted on her, his hot, masterful mouth taking complete control over her. Her mind went wonderfully, blissfully blank. His hand moved up to squeeze her breast as his mouth worked magic, and she lost all sense of time, any coherent thought. There was only Charles, and what he was doing to her, how he was making her feel. She writhed and squirmed and moaned, not recognizing herself . . . It was so good . . . so incredibly good . . . The sensations overtook her quickly, and she shattered under him, crying out his name. His fingers dug into her skin, holding her to his mouth as her hips rocked and she rode out the waves of intense pleasure.

She was still floating, panting and dazed, when he moved up and entered her with one easy thrust. "Oh, Christ," he gasped. "God, you feel so good."

Her hands went to his shoulders as she wrapped her legs around his hips, silently urging him on. "I'm already close," he said, his voice strangled.

"Good," she breathed, and kissed his chest. "Let yourself go."

He began to move inside her, staring into her eyes. "I've wanted this," he whispered, swiveling his hips. "Wanted you. So much."

"I've wanted you too," she whispered back. "You feel so good inside me."

"Made for each other," he gasped out, his breath hitching.

With another groan, he thrust hard and fast, and her hips met his, matching his pace. She felt his body begin to tense and watched his eyes slip closed, felt his warm breath against her skin as his breathing quickened and staggered, watched the muscles in his neck and shoulders tighten from his efforts. "Christ, I'm gonna come," he panted. "Lisette . . ."

She kissed his neck, grabbed his ass and pushed him deeper as she whispered his name into his ear, only one thought in her mind: *I love you.*

A long, fierce groan ripped from his throat as his body tensed and shuddered. She held him tight, wrapped around him, and felt his warm release deep inside her. He collapsed on top of her, panting hard for a few seconds. Still trying to catch his breath, he sealed his mouth to hers, kissing her deeply before burying his face in her neck. They held each other close, a sweaty tangle of arms and legs and kisses that didn't stop.

"That was amazing," he finally murmured, a lazy, sated grin on his face.

She grinned back. "For me, too."

He sipped from her lips, playful and languid kisses. "I wanted it to be good for you. It'd been so long for you . . . and since the last time was—"

"Hot and quick and intense," she said. "No more apologies for that night. It was hot and I loved it and now here we are."

He laughed. "Yes, ma'am." He was so at ease now, downright relaxed and casual . . . She'd never seen him this way. It made her heart happy. His fingers swept her hair back from her face, and he shifted slightly. "Am I crushing you?"

"No. Stay there. You feel wonderful."

"So do you." He kissed her, long and sultry and affirming, until there was nothing but tenderness. "Stay with me tonight."

"I can't," she said. Reality creeping in, she sighed. "What if the kids—"

"I know, I know. Dammit." He sighed too, still caressing her face. "Stay a little while longer, though? Don't just run back to your room now. I want you here."

She smiled, the affection in his eyes and voice intoxicating her. The sparse dark hair on his chest tickled her breasts, and she shifted slightly beneath him. "I'll stay a little longer. Believe me, after what we just did, I'd love nothing more than to fall asleep in your arms, and wake up there too. We just can't."

His gaze sobered. "Lisette . . . I don't do casual very well. I go all-in. I do relationships, or it's not worth my time and energy."

You have no idea how I feel about you. How much I want this too. "Same here," she managed. Her voice felt small in her throat.

"On everything? Everything I just said?" His lips grazed hers with such aching sweetness, a little wave of adoration squeezed her heart. Good Lord, the man was like a heady, universe-expanding drug, and she was already helplessly addicted. "Tell me exactly what you want, Lisette. Please."

"I want what you want," she whispered. "Yes, everything you just said. I've never done casual in my life; I don't know how. And I certainly wouldn't jeopardize everything I have here for a meaningless fling. I've thought about it a lot . . . and what I keep coming back to is, I want to really be with you too."

His smile showered light on her. "Then that's what we'll do." He kissed her soundly, passionately. "I haven't had a girlfriend in a looong time. This'll be fun."

"We have to take it slow, Charles," she said, even as her heart fluttered in her chest. "Have to be careful. Hide it for now. I don't want to confuse or upset the kids."

"Agreed, absolutely. As long as you understand I don't think of you as some dirty secret." He rose up on his elbows so he could better hold her gaze. "I'd take you out, show you off to the world. I don't want to have to hide. But yes, because of the kids, we have to be careful at first."

She had to look away; did he know she was already in love with him? He was so smart, so intuitive, she couldn't imagine it wasn't all over her face. "It's scary, how good this feels. Is this too much too soon?"

He snorted out a laugh. "Maybe. Probably. But it's exactly what I want." He kissed her forehead. "*You're* exactly what I want." He kissed the tip of her nose, then her lips, then finally withdrew from her and rolled onto his side, pulling her with him. She curled into his side, savoring the warmth and feel of his strong body. A light sheen of sweat still coated their skin, and she traced her fingers along his chest, tantalized.

He tipped her chin up with a fingertip and pressed his mouth to hers. His kiss was tender, but compelling and softly possessive, as was his gaze. "Make no mistake, sweetheart. You're mine now." He kissed her again, soft, sweet, and lingering. "And I'm yours."

Her head swam, and her heart expanded with light and wonder. All the affection and connection she felt with him tonight was tangible. The way he looked at her . . . the tenderness in his caresses . . . what was flowing between them now as they held each other felt true and pure and real.

An hour later, as she tiptoed back to her room, she felt as if she were floating. She slipped into her bed, content and exhausted, a besotted smile on her face. The whole night with Charles had been like a dream. Her eyes closed, and she could see him, recall how he looked as he hovered above her, how his hot, labored breathing felt against her skin, how his hard shaft had filled and stretched her, felt like he was made to fit perfectly inside her . . . then how they'd lain together, kissing and caressing as they talked for more than an hour. When his eyes had grown heavy, she had kissed him good night, slipped out of bed, and gotten dressed.

In the two minutes it took her to dress, he had fallen asleep. She stared down at him, all mussed up in his tangled sheets, handsome and appealing as could be. All night, he had been nothing less than perfect.

Now, as she lay alone in her own bed, her body was exhausted, but her mind wouldn't stop. God, she hoped they could somehow make it work. He seemed so sure that they could. But she knew the obstacles facing them hadn't simply disappeared while they were in each other's arms. There would be trouble ahead; she wasn't naïve. But if they were in it together . . . maybe they actually had a chance. She was already in so deep; she would fight like hell to keep it. To keep *him*.

For the moment, she allowed herself to bask in the glow of happiness, post-sex satisfaction, and hope. No matter what happened now, she'd always have the memory of this perfect night. Nothing and no one could take that from her. She just had to believe, like Charles did.

And think of some backup plans for herself, like her nomadic parents had always taught her to do.

Chapter Nineteen

"Happy Thanksgiving!" Tess greeted Charles with open arms, hugging him before leaning down to hug the children. "Oh, all three of you look great. I'm so glad none of you are sick anymore!"

"So am I," Lisette murmured.

Charles glanced at her and grinned. "I bet you are." He said to Tess, "She was amazing, taking care of them all week. She deserves a Medal of Honor."

"I'm sure," Tess said. "I'm glad you could join us today, Lisette. No one should be alone on a holiday."

"Thank you all for having me," she said. "But I'm on duty today so Charles can relax and enjoy."

He turned to her with a frown. "Nonsense. You're a guest here."

She looked back at him, her expression giving nothing away.

"Why don't I bring the kids inside so you two can talk," Tess said. Charles met her eyes and gave the faintest nod, grateful for her intuition.

"Is Uncle Pierce here?" Thomas asked her hopefully.

"No, honey," Tess said, taking Myles by the hand. "He and

Abby are with her family today. But Uncle Dane and Aunt Julia are here. And there are already really yummy appetizers out; you'll like them. Come on." She ushered the three kids down the long, wide hall of the original Harrison mansion. "We're all in the back den," she said over her shoulder.

"We'll be right there," Charles said, then turned to Lisette, jaw set. He lowered his voice. "When I invited you to come with us for Thanksgiving, it wasn't just so you could watch the kids."

"Initially it was," she pointed out, equally quiet so no one could hear.

"Well, that was more than a month ago. That was before . . . You're not on the clock today. You're here *with* me."

"I appreciate that," she replied. "I really do. But Charles . . . how will it look if I don't act like I always do?" She stepped closer and whispered, "I have a role to play here. Every holiday, you've invited me along graciously, and I've watched the children so you were free to mingle. That's how it's always been. I can't go in there and suddenly start acting like anything other than the nanny. Don't you realize that?"

He held her eyes as her words sank in. She was right, of course. *Shit.* "Okay, I know you're right. But I want you to enjoy yourself."

"I will," she said. Her dark eyes took on a playful sparkle. "I get to look at you all day, and you look very handsome. We're here together. I'm more than fine."

He gazed down at her, this dark, sweet beauty who'd stolen his heart. The sides of her hair were pulled up, but the rest flowed freely down her back. Her outfit, a simple chocolate-brown dress and matching knee-high leather boots, was lovely on her. She was so damn pretty. He looked at her and smiled. Yes, they had roles to play today. But having her there . . . it felt good. And it felt right. "I wish I could kiss you right now," he whispered.

"Hopefully later," she whispered back.

"Definitely."

She smiled as a hint of color bloomed on her cheeks. Dusting something off his shoulder that likely wasn't there, she straightened his navy blazer and whispered, "Maybe we could do a lot more than kissing?"

"Oh, God." A rush of heat flushed his face and zipped through his veins, pure scorching lust. "Don't make me hard now; I won't be able to walk in there. And there's got to be fifty people here. Dad doesn't do anything small."

She stepped back from him with a smirk. "Then I'll be very glad to stay on the sidelines with the kids. I don't like crowds."

"I've noticed."

"I also . . ." Apparently thinking better of what she was going to say, she shook her head and took a step forward. "Forget it. Let's go."

"No. Tell me." He blocked her way and stared down at her. "Please."

She huffed out a breath. "I don't like being around your father. He's . . . not a nice person."

"Unfortunately, I know that very well." Something in Charles simmered . . . anger, disdain, and protectiveness. "Wait. Has he ever done anything to you that—"

"No, no! Not at all. He likes to put the hired help in their place; that's all. He looks at me like I'm . . . Well, *he's* aware of the class differences, even if you aren't. Let's leave it at that." She shrugged. "I just stay out of his way. Everything's fine. I shouldn't have said anything. I'm sorry."

"Don't be. I'm glad you told me how you feel." Charles sighed, and something gnawed at him. She was right to stay out of his father's way. His father could be ruthless, and Charles knew it better than anyone.

God only knew what the patriarch would do if he found

out Charles and Lisette were together now. The old man had nearly managed to wedge Pierce and Abby apart with one attack, and they'd been on more solid ground at that stage than Charles and Lisette were now. Sudden concern laced with anxiety flooded him, and he gripped her elbow. "Listen to me. If he ever, *ever* does anything to upset you, you have to tell me. Right away. I'm serious. All right?"

She frowned at him in consternation, but murmured, "All right."

"I mean it. Promise me."

"Of course. I promise."

With a firm nod, Charles placed his hand at the small of her back. "Let's go."

Later that night, Lisette lay back on her bed and closed her eyes. The kids were on the phone, talking to their mother for the first time in a while. Lisette would put them to bed as soon as they were done. It wasn't as if they had school the next day anyway . . .

There was a soft knock on her half-open door. Lisette opened her eyes to see Charles standing there. Fresh from a shower, his dark hair was still damp, his glasses had replaced his contacts, and he wore simple navy pajamas. He looked adorable, and she smiled as she yawned. "Hi."

"Were you sleeping?" he asked. "Kids are ready for bedtime. Myles said he came in to get you and you were asleep, so he came to get me to tuck him in."

With great effort, Lisette sat up. She felt a little woozy. "I'm just exhausted. I'll go and—"

"Are you all right?" Charles peered harder at her.

"I've been really tired for days," she said as she stood. "I think I'm just rundown from this past week, maybe even got a touch of what the kids all had."

He nodded. "Makes sense. You had a long, rough week

with them. It's no wonder you're still tired. I can put the kids to bed just fine, you know."

"No, I'll do it." She swept her hair back over her shoulders.

"We'll do it together." He raised his hand to caress her cheek. "This weekend, you can catch up on some sleep. You need to take care of yourself, too."

"I'm fine," she assured him. "But yes, some extra sleep this weekend would be great." She squeezed his free hand, then brushed past him to move into the hallway.

He followed her until they reached the kids' rooms. "I'll take Thomas first."

"I've got Myles," she said.

"Um, Lisette?" He moved closer to whisper in her ear. "After the kids are all asleep, can I interest you in a glass of wine?"

"Only if you take me to bed right after it," she whispered back.

His eyes lit with seductive pleasure. "That was the plan."

Forty-five minutes later, Charles and Lisette sat in the den enjoying a glass of Cabernet and each other's company.

"It was a nice Thanksgiving," Lisette said from her end of the couch.

"It was," Charles agreed. "I was glad you were there."

"That's sweet." She took a sip of her wine. "I got to talk a little with Tess and Julia. They're both lovely. I'm finally getting more comfortable around them."

"Really?" He cocked his head, studying her. "I never realized you were *un*comfortable around them."

"A little bit. Um, in case you never noticed, sometimes I'm painfully shy," Lisette said with a wry grin.

"I noticed," he said, chuckling.

She smiled and took another sip from her glass.

His eyes glided over her, taking her in. Her hair was down

and loose, her body clad in a black top and leggings, her legs tucked beneath her. She was adorable and sensual at the same time. Best of all, she seemed at ease, relaxed, and her eyes . . . they were sparkling. She was happy to be there with him. No power play at work here. She wasn't there because she felt coerced; she liked him.

He held out his hand. "You're too far away. Come closer."

She couldn't hold back the smile that spread as she scooted over to him. He slid his arm around her shoulders and pulled her into his side. "That's better," he murmured. He lowered his lips to hers, sipping from them languidly. "Mmmm . . . I wanted to do this all day," he whispered between kisses.

"Me too," she said. "But I should put this glass down before I spill wine everywhere."

"I have a better idea," he said. "Why don't we take this up to my room? I like to be able to lock the door when I have you in my arms. Shut out the whole damn world."

"That sounds wonderful."

He kissed her, lingering on her lips. "It will be. I promise."

Charles locked the bedroom door behind them, took her wineglass from her hand and set it down, then pulled her into his embrace and kissed her. "I might have lied," he said, kissing her again as his hands ran down her back. "I might not let you drink that wine right away."

"Oh, really . . ." Her head fell back as he trailed his open mouth against her skin, hot and demanding. "I might not be too upset about that . . ."

"I knew you were a reasonable woman." He fisted his hand in her hair and took her mouth with his, crushing her against him.

They quickly undressed each other between kisses as they made their way to the bed in a flurry of mouths and hands and gasps and sighs. There were no words; their kisses became frantic and consuming, their hands greedy as they roamed over each other's bodies. When she reached down in between them to grasp his cock, it was already rock hard. A rough groan escaped him at her touch.

"I love how you feel," she whispered as she stroked him.

"Holy hell, that's so good," he breathed, his hips rocking with the rhythm her hand set. He kissed her deeply, his tongue plundering as his hands lifted to squeeze her breasts. She gasped into his mouth, but kept stroking him, driving him insane with need as the incredible sensations shimmered through him. They kissed wildly, her pace increased, and he almost lost control right then.

"Stop, wait," he gasped. "I want to be inside you when I come."

Without a word, she pushed him onto his back and straddled him. He looked up at her, delightfully surprised by her aggressive move, then watched as she positioned herself and slid down slowly onto his cock. She was already slick and ready for him, her wet heat taking him in deep. A long, low groan rumbled out of him as his fingers dug into her hips; she set her hands on his chest, and she began to ride him.

Watching her move, her eyes closed and lips parted, her cheeks rosy and her hair falling around her face, her breasts softly bouncing as she rocked on top of him . . . she was mesmerizing. He thrust up into her, guiding her as she moved, pushing deeper inside her.

"You are so beautiful," he rasped. "So damn beautiful."

She smiled down at him and rolled her hips, grinding into him hard. They both moaned from the intense pleasure of it. Her head fell back as she found her rhythm, grinding into him and moaning as she rocked.

"Christ," he whispered. "That's so good. Too good . . . ah hell . . ."

He moved a hand over to find her clit and rub it with his thumb. She cried out and bucked; her passionate response made him almost come right then. He kept moving his thumb in circles, pressing into her, her soft moans now wild cries. They moved faster, grinding, rocking, until she called out his name and the orgasm hit her hard, making her shudder and moan as her hands gripped his torso. He thrust twice more and followed her over the edge with a long groan, burying himself as deep inside her as he could as he took his release. They rode out the waves together before she collapsed on him in a quivering heap.

The only sound was their hard, labored breathing. His hands ran down the long curtain of her hair, smoothing it back from her face as she panted on his chest, spent.

He brought her face to his to cover it in tiny kisses before sealing his mouth to hers. They kissed until their racing hearts slowed, until their breath came easily again.

"I could get used to this," he said.

She snuggled into his side. "You think so, huh?"

"I know so." His arms banded around her, holding her close. "How about you? Think you could get used to this?"

"All too easily," she admitted. "It just . . . still doesn't seem real."

"It's real," he whispered, and kissed her soundly.

Chapter Twenty

The long holiday weekend was busy with activities and filled with holiday cheer. On Friday, Charles took the kids, Lisette, and Tess to get their Christmas trees. They dropped Tess's tree at her house, but she came back to Charles's home with them. Charles called Dane and Julia to come join them, and within an hour, most of the Harrisons had filled Charles's house and made it a small party.

Lisette watched from the corner as the two brothers put up the huge tree the kids had chosen. They all—the adults and the kids—were happier together that day than she could remember seeing them in some time, and she could not help noting that the Harrison patriarch wasn't there. The air felt lighter when that man wasn't around.

Charles's staff would decorate the rest of the mansion's interior later, as well as the massive façade and grounds, but the living room was the kids' domain. As they all decorated the tree and the room, Christmas music played, and Lisette brought out hot cocoa and the chocolate chip cookies she'd baked that morning. When she tried to return to the kitchen, Charles gently grasped her wrist and asked her to stay. She looked into his eyes, wanting so much to say yes, but shook her head.

"I want you here with us," he whispered fiercely.

"It would give us away in a heartbeat," she whispered back. "The kids . . ."

He sighed and released her wrist. "Right now, I hate our secret." He stared down at her, mixed frustration and affection radiating from him.

"Enjoy all of this," she said. "It's a wonderful day. Be with your family."

Obviously conflicted, he just kept staring at her until she finally turned away. She went to the kitchen, wanting to be nearby in case any of them needed anything . . . wanting to be nearby, even though her heart was aching a tiny bit. Her e-reader was at the table in the corner, where she'd left it earlier, and she sat there to read with a cup of cinnamon apple tea.

Ten minutes later, Dane sauntered into the kitchen. "Hey there," he said jovially. "Reading?"

"Um, yes," she said, looking up at him. "Do you need something?"

"Yeah," Dane said. "I need not to see you all alone in here while we're all having fun in the living room. That just sucks."

She blinked at him, not knowing how to respond.

"Please come join us," he said. He leaned his hip against the table, stuffing his hands in the pockets of his jeans as he flashed one of his renowned charming smiles. "Come onnnn. Come and play with the rest of us kids."

She set her e-reader down on the table. "Did someone put you up to this?" she asked quietly.

"Nope. No one puts me up to anything. Except maybe my wife on occasion." He arched a brow, his bright blue eyes fixed on her. His tone was casual, but his stare wasn't. "Miss Gardner. It's the holidays. No one should be alone. Come enjoy the afternoon with us. Pretty please?"

He knows, she thought. Dane was more than Charles's

brother; he was his most trusted confidant. If Charles would tell anyone about them, it'd be Dane.

He quirked another blinding grin and gestured with his head toward the doorway. "Come on, lovely Lisette. Let's go. Off your seat, on your feet."

"It seems you're insisting," she murmured.

"I am. And if you know anything about me, it's that I'm known to be pretty damn persuasive." The crooked grin that had broken many hearts was aimed right at her. "I'll wear you down, darlin'."

She had to laugh. Dane's charm was legendary; right then, she could see why. The man's smile and easy, good humor were infectious. "Fine," she said with mock resignation, and rose from her chair.

"Atta girl," he said. He gave her a meaningful look and added, "You won't be sorry."

When Lisette entered the living room with Dane, Charles gazed at her with such adoration it made her knees weak. Oh, she loved him. She even adored his family, God help her. They were all such good people, welcoming her into the fold so warmly that within minutes she felt as if she was not just the nanny, but one of them.

On Saturday, Charles had a stretch limo take them into the city; it was a car-service agency used by his office. His surprise—front-row seats to the Radio City Christmas show—had the kids bouncing and squealing with glee. Lisette had to admit she was pretty thrilled herself; she'd never seen the famous spectacle. At the show, which was indeed spectacular, she and Charles sat apart with the kids between them. But when they all went out to an early dinner afterward, he made sure she sat beside him. He held her hand under the table whenever he could. Then they all walked around the city to see some of the famous holiday window displays . . . At seven the limo took them home, everyone happy and exhausted.

Sunday was Lisette's day off. After breakfasting with Charles and the kids, she went out with Tina for the afternoon to do some Christmas shopping and have lunch. When they parted ways, Lisette took a walk by the Sound, thinking of everything that had happened in the past few weeks, wondering how and why her life had changed . . . wondering how long it would last. When she returned home that night, Charles and the kids welcomed her as if she'd been gone for days instead of hours. And as was now becoming their delicious routine, once the kids were asleep, she and Charles locked themselves in his room, made love, and talked until their eyes grew heavy and she returned to her own room.

Before Lisette knew it, Monday had come, the kids went back to school, and Charles went back to work. Time always seemed to speed up around the holidays, and as they entered December, the excitement and higher energy were almost tangible. The week flew by, and Lisette had never been happier in her entire life.

The only thing that bothered her was how tired she was all the time. She'd never really bounced back from that week when the kids were sick, and sometimes a wave of nausea would clobber her out of nowhere. She'd choke down some crackers or a piece of bread, drink some peppermint tea, and feel better, but she wondered if she'd ever shake the remnants of the kids' virus. She thought it might even be an iron deficiency, or even . . . perish the thought . . . she was just getting older. She'd turn thirty-five in April; maybe she simply didn't have the energy she'd had before.

She thought she was doing a good job of keeping her concerns to herself, until on a Friday night, she felt herself being gently shaken. "Lisette. Lisette, wake up."

Charles's voice was clear, but it felt as if it were coming to her through a fog, from miles away. Her eyes fluttered open to see him standing over her, handsome as always in a slate gray suit and patterned tie, staring down at her with concern. "Hi," she said.

"Hi." His brow furrowed harder. "I'm worried about you."

"Why?" She struggled to sit up, realizing she was on the couch in the den. "I . . ." It hit her in a flash that she'd been watching a movie with the kids. They weren't there now, the TV was off, and the windows showed it was dark outside. Oh, boy. "I fell asleep, I guess?"

"I just got home from work five minutes ago. The kids were all in their rooms, playing video games. They were fine," he added quickly, dropping down to sit next to her, "but they said you fell asleep during the movie. More than an hour ago. That you were so deep asleep, they didn't want to wake you, because they figured you were really tired." His blues narrowed as he studied her. "Because you fell asleep the other day after school too, for a little while."

Lisette felt the blood rise in her face. "I'm so sorry," she whispered. "I understand if you're angry with me."

"Angry? I'm not angry," he said, taking her hand. "I'm concerned. You haven't been 100 percent since the kids were sick. When's the last time you had just a basic physical?"

She shrugged. "Honestly, I don't know. Two years? Could be three . . ."

"I want you to get checked out," he said in an authoritative tone. "You'll make an appointment on Monday."

Something in her bristled at that tone. "That sounds like a command, not a request. Are you pulling rank, ordering me as my employer?"

"No," he said. "But I will if that's what it takes to make you go."

Was she overreacting? She brushed it aside. "I'll make an appointment," she murmured.

He leaned in and pressed a kiss to her forehead, lingering there before he said, "Thank you."

"I'm not used to people being concerned for my welfare," she said softly. "I didn't mean to sound snippy."

He grinned and said, "You were only a tiny bit snippy. And it's fine." He touched her chin, forcing her to look into his eyes. "As for people being concerned for you, get used to it. Because I care about you, so that means I'm going to be looking out for you. It's really that simple."

"Nothing about you is simple, Charles," she said.

He cupped her cheek, his hand warm against her skin. "One thing is. I'm head over heels for you."

Her breath caught. The look in his eyes was so sweet it was almost too much. "If you are, that's the most complicated thing of all," she said.

"No, it isn't. Not really." He rubbed her jaw with the pad of his thumb. "Right now, you're the best, brightest part of my days. Other than the kids, of course."

"Of course," she murmured back in wonder.

He leaned in to steal another kiss and said, "Let's go find something to eat."

On Saturday morning, after breakfast, Lisette had just gotten out of the shower when there was a knock on her bedroom door. "Hold on a minute," she called out. She quickly finished toweling off, put on her robe, and wrapped her long, wet hair in a turban-like towel. She sprinted from her adjoining bathroom through her bedroom and flung open her door. Charles stood there, leaning against the doorframe, looking gorgeous in a blue-gray sweater and jeans.

"Good morning," he said with a smile.

"Good morning," she echoed, her insides warming at the sight of him.

"Sorry I wasn't here five minutes ago." His voice dropped to a whisper. "I wish I could toss you down on the bed right now and have the pleasure of stripping you out of that robe. You know that, right?"

She tried to hold back her smile by biting down on her bottom lip, but it didn't work. "Didn't you get enough of me last night?" she whispered flirtatiously.

"I never get enough of you," he whispered back. Behind his glasses, his eyes sparkled with enchantment. "So anyway . . ." He cleared his throat and spoke at normal volume. "Can you pack a bag for a three-day trip?"

She blinked. "Um. I guess so. Why? Am I going somewhere?"

"You are." He glanced at his watch. "In about six hours."

"What?"

"You'll be back on Tuesday evening. So that's three days, because we have a flight that leaves at seven tonight. It'll be cold, so pack warm clothes. Sweaters, jeans, those yoga pants that always make me want to grab your ass and bite it . . . Boots would be good. Snow boots too." The amused look on his face showed he was clearly enjoying himself. "And you can bring the sheep slippers, but no pajamas necessary." He winked.

"What on earth are you talking about?" she asked. "We're going somewhere? Together?"

"Yes."

"Without the children?" She felt foolish standing there with her hair wrapped in a turban and in her robe while they had this conversation, and yanked the small towel from her head. Her damp hair came tumbling down over her shoulders.

"God, you're gorgeous." He glanced over his shoulder to make sure no one was near, then looked back at her and said, "We need time alone. I want you all to myself. I want, for once, for us to be able to fall asleep in each other's arms after we've been together. I want to wake up with you next to me, kiss you awake, and make love to you first thing in the morning." He leaned in closer, reached out, and twisted a long lock of her damp hair around his forefinger. "I want to spend time with you. Just the two of us. So we need to get away, and I've arranged for that to happen."

She gaped at him in astonishment. Her brain wasn't processing all of it fast enough. Then she stammered, "B-but the kids—"

"Will be fine," he said, cutting her off. "I've made every arrangement. They'll be taken care of while you and I are gone. They'll spend some time with their favorite Auntie Tess. Pierce and Abby are even going to lend her a hand."

She could only shake her head and murmur, "You've gone crazy."

"Yes, yes, I have. Crazy about *you*."

"You're just going to whisk me away somewhere? The two of us will vanish?"

"That's the idea, yes."

"And how are you going to explain my absence?" she whispered. "Especially since it happens to be while you're away too? Gee, what a coincidence."

"Leave that to me," he said. His eyes glinted with determination and assurance.

"People will put two and two together in a hot minute," she said anxiously.

"Lisette. Sweetheart." He lifted her hand to his lips and kissed her knuckles, continuing to hold her eyes. "Leave everything to me. You have nothing to worry about. This is one of those times when you can say it's a good thing that your new boyfriend is a powerful billionaire executive."

"I can't even believe those words were strung together in that sentence."

"Get used to it."

Chapter Twenty-One

Twelve hours later, Lisette couldn't believe she was sitting in the ski house Charles owned in Aspen. As he'd promised her, he'd swept her out of the house covertly, into a waiting limo driven by Bruck. The Harrison Enterprises private jet had been waiting at Islip's MacArthur Airport; it was only there that Charles had finally revealed where he was taking her.

She had been to Aspen twice since coming to work for Charles. It was a magnificent home on more than six acres of land—on Red Mountain, famous for its mega-wealthy residents. Charles, Dane, and Tess had bought the property together, each having an equal share, with the intention of making it a family compound independent of their father. Pierce, in England at the time, had not been in on the deal.

In her past visits, she'd been completely focused on the kids, but there'd been some downtime when they were skiing and after the children were asleep. During the day, when the Harrisons were on the mountain, she'd walk into the nearby downtown, buy a cup of hot cocoa, and window browse the boutiques and shops. She and Charles hadn't spoken much on those two trips once the kids were sleeping; Charles had been busy catching up on work he'd missed during the day, and she was only the nanny. But he had always been friendly and considerate, making sure she was comfortable and had whatever she needed.

Now . . . he'd brought her there in a spontaneous romantic gesture, and her sole concern for the next seventy-two hours would be him, and she would be his. It was both unnerving and exciting.

Everything between them had changed in such a short time. In the bubble of his mansion, she'd managed to adjust to their new dynamic. But they'd never gone out in public together, like a new couple, much less away together. If he wanted to continue to keep their budding relationship a secret and they never left the ski house this whole weekend, she'd be fine with that. Being here was a wonderful getaway.

As Charles escorted her through the house, she felt slightly off-kilter. She'd always been his employee here. Now she was his . . . exclusive guest.

Charles was in high spirits. He'd obviously enjoyed sweeping her away on a surprise trip and was still enjoying it. "You've been here before," he said, "so you know where everything is, right?"

"Sure," she said, looking around as so many different emotions washed over her. Elation, shock, delight, anticipation, confusion, unease . . . She looked over to the huge wall of glass in the middle of the house, in the great room. During the day, she knew that offered an incredible view of the mountain and surrounding trees. But now the blackness outside made the large window a mirror. She saw the two of them reflected, standing side by side, the first time she'd ever really *seen* them together that way, and she couldn't help but stare.

"You all right, sweetheart?" he asked, stopping to look down into her face.

"I'm fine," she said.

His blue eyes narrowed, scrutinizing her. "When a woman says she's fine, she's anything but fine. What's up?"

"Nothing!" she said, too quickly to be convincing. "Just . . . taking this all in."

"You're not upset that I brought you here, are you?"

"Of course not. I'm touched, flattered, shocked . . . a lot of things."

He nodded, seeming to consider that, then took her hand and continued walking. "I believe when you were here last time, you had one of the guest rooms. That isn't where you'll be sleeping on this trip, obviously. Have you ever been in the master suite?"

"No," she said. "Why would I have?"

"Just wondering. Come, I'll show it to you." He put his hand to the small of her back and led her up the stairs.

At the end of the hall, the master suite was a large, open space, decorated like the rest of the house, with the same color scheme and patterns but on a slightly grander scale. The king-sized sleigh bed was an exquisite piece, facing a fireplace and two cushioned armchairs. A fire had already been set, and flames licked at the logs. As in the great room below, one wall was all glass and looked out on the same killer views.

"This is so beautiful," she said on a dreamy sigh. "My goodness."

"I'm glad you like it." Charles smiled. "I had the house manager come and ready everything for our arrival," he said. He gestured to the door across the room. "Master bathroom. European steam shower, deep tub, the works." He stepped closer, watching her. "And you're not comfortable. Your body language is screaming it. Talk to me."

She tried to smile, but her eyes went to the fire, and she turned her whole body toward it. Wrapping her arms around her midriff, she said quietly, "I can't believe you brought me here. Like this. I'm just . . . I'm a little overwhelmed, that's all."

He came up behind her, sliding his arms around hers to press her back to his chest and hold her close. "I told you I wanted some time with you. For us to just be together, like any other new couple." His chin rested on top of her head. "Why are you still so scared? What are you afraid of, honey?"

Her heartbeat felt erratic. The warmth from the fire in front of her and the warmth of him at her back enveloped her in a soothing glow as she tried to find a response to his gentle questions. They stood together, watching the fire blaze in the hearth.

"Why do you want me?" she asked. It was easier to ask that when she wasn't looking at him. "Sometimes I really don't know. At first I wondered if it was because . . . I was so available. You know, I'm always there, at the house. And, well . . ."

"I can't believe you'd say that," he rumbled against her temple. "Jesus, Lisette, give me more credit than that. Give *yourself* more credit than that."

Her body stiffened from his soft rebuke. "I don't think that anymore. I admit I did at first, a little bit. But . . . if easy sex was all you wanted, you wouldn't have bothered with everything you've done so far, much less with a trip like this. You didn't have to go out of your way or do anything; I'm already sleeping with you. So this is just . . ." She closed her eyes and drew a shaky breath. "You made an effort. You put thought into this, made arrangements. For me. For us. And I'm floored. No one's ever done anything like this for me before."

"You need to learn how to accept nice words, nice gestures. That's first of all." He turned her around to face him. The stormy look in his eyes and the way he grasped her shoulders let her know she'd disturbed him. "Why can't you let yourself believe I just want you for you, plain and simple?"

"Because there is nothing plain and simple about this whole situation," she said hotly, "and you know it."

"What I know," he said, "is that I feel more alive with you than I have in years. That when I touch you, hold you, even just talk to you, I feel . . . whole. At peace, but at the same time, full of life again. What I know is that we're connected, Lisette." He reached up to caress her cheek with the backs of his fingers. "I feel that connection every time we make love, every time we're close, every time you look at me and your eyes light up. Our connection is strong." He cupped her face with both hands and pinned her with his gaze. "I thought you felt it too. Was I wrong?"

"No." Her heart pounded in her chest, and her eyes welled. "I do feel it too, Charles. I do."

"Then why are you still afraid to be with me? Because of gossip?" He shook his head dismissively. "I don't care about that bullshit. Because of how the kids might react? *That's* why we're being discreet for now, until we both feel this is rock solid. So what is it? Because other than those things, I don't know, and I wish I did."

"Because I'm—" *Because I'm in love with you.* Her whole body started trembling. "Because I've had feelings for you for so long . . . and everyone I've ever cared about, one way or another, has ended up leaving."

"Wait a minute." His eyes flew wide behind his glasses, and his lips parted in shock. The only sound was the crackling of the fire. "You had feelings for me before we started any of this?"

She nodded, wishing her body would stop shaking.

"Oh my God," he whispered, his stare so piercing she felt as if it would slice through her. "You sweet, beautiful woman. I had no idea. I . . ." His hands held her face as he pressed his lips to hers, kissing her so tenderly she thought her heart would burst. Then he leaned his forehead to hers and said, "You're not going to lose me. I'm not going to leave, I promise."

"People leave, Charles," she whispered. A sharper tremor ran through her. "Or, what if you decide you want *me* to leave?"

"Not going to happen," he said. "I'm falling for you a little more each day, and you're all I think about. Do you really not know that? I thought I was so transparent!"

She shook her head and drew a deep breath, trying to calm her racing heart.

"Lisette, I'm not Brandon." He said it so fervently that she could only gaze back at him. "Don't punish me for his sins."

The unexpected words struck her like a physical blow. She drew back, still trembling. "I'm not doing that."

"You are; you just don't realize it. The thing is, you're punishing yourself too. A thousand times more." His hands were on her upper arms now, not letting her out of his grasp. "You've punished yourself for trusting and believing in him. You've punished yourself for loving someone who turned out to be a selfish bastard. You've punished yourself"—his voice dropped to a whisper—"for losing the baby. I know you have. Because I know you now."

She felt the blood drain from her face, and a violent shiver ran over her skin.

"Jesus, you're shaking like a leaf," he said. "Come here." He pulled her against him, holding her close and rubbing her back, her arms. "Shhhh. It's all right."

"N-no, it's not," she said. "I put everything at risk when I chose this path, and if it all blows up in my face, I have no one to blame but myself. I guess I'm just trying to steel myself for that."

"Christ, you're so hard on yourself." He kissed her temple and continued to rub her back. "Why do you have to live like a monk because some bad things happened? You put yourself in isolation; no one did that to you. It's time to come out."

She couldn't speak, her throat thick with emotion. She just shook her head.

"Lisette. Sweetheart . . ." He kissed the top of her head and spoke to her in a velvety tone. "You're a young, beautiful woman with a tremendous heart. So much to give. You have a man in front of you right now who's crazy about you, who's doing everything he can to convince you his feelings are true and his intentions are good. I know it's scary. I'm taking a leap here too. So take the chance. You're already halfway there. Stop blocking your own path, and be happy." He squeezed her, a hug filled with affection. "Hopefully, be happy with *me*, but either way, be happy again. Find a way; let yourself. You deserve that."

Something inside her broke apart. She closed her eyes and buried her face in his chest, the tears sliding down her face as she clung to him. He understood her better than she'd imagined, and cared more than she'd allowed herself to acknowledge. Even now, as she trembled and cried, his hands swept up and down her back, meant to soothe and comfort. It felt so good. It felt like a lifeline. No one had held her like this since . . . God, she couldn't remember when. She cried quietly, the tears falling as she tried to take deep breaths.

"I'm not going to leave," he whispered. "I don't *want* to leave you. I'm in this as deep as you are."

"God, Charles, I'm scared; I admit it. I've made a safe little bubble around myself, and you're trying to breach it."

"Damn right I am," he said, running his hand over her hair. "Just take the leap. I'll catch you; I swear."

Her arms tightened around him as the tears kept falling. "You're wonderful."

"Thanks." He dropped a kiss on her forehead. "You are too."

"Then why can't I stop crying?" she sobbed.

"Because maybe you're finally hearing me," he said,

"and you don't want to be numb anymore. So cry all you need to. I'm here." He held her close as she cried; he soothed her, caressed her, kissed her. "I know we can make each other happy, Lisette."

"You already make me happy," she said, sniffling.

"And to think I've barely tried," he said. She had to grin at the teasing note in his voice. "Imagine once I start really pulling out all the stops. I'll sweep you off your feet."

"You've already swept me off my feet," she whispered. She pulled back to look up at him. "Just by being you."

He wiped the tears from her cheeks, then lowered his mouth to take hers.

Chapter Twenty-Two

Tuesday morning, Charles woke slowly, feeling the heated naked body beside him and reaching to pull her closer before even opening his eyes. Lisette made the tiniest happy noise and snuggled into his side. They wrapped their arms around each other, a tight cocoon of warmth and affection in the tremendous bed.

He let himself lie still, not fully awake yet, and just savor the moment. Their time at the ski house had been perfection, everything he'd wanted. Since they'd arrived on Saturday night, he and Lisette had spent their time making love, holding each other, and talking, eating, or sleeping. They'd ventured out each day for a walk outside, breathing in the crisp mountain air and admiring the views around them. On Monday afternoon, they'd gone downtown and done some Christmas shopping. But the rest of the time, they had been in the house, in front of one fireplace or another, exploring each other's bodies, minds, and hearts.

She finally trusted him and their feelings for each other. At least, he thought she did.

He didn't want to fly back home that evening. He wanted to stay there with her like this forever. Feeling her in his arms, feeling her soft warm breath against his chest as she slept peacefully . . . When they returned home, it would be back to secret trysts in his room after the kids were asleep. Now that he knew how fantastic it felt to watch her sleep and to wake up with her, he hated to have to give that up.

It wouldn't be forever; he knew that. As they got more solid, eventually they would get to the point when they could tell the kids—and the world—that they were truly together. It would happen, and sooner rather than later. Because if he had thought he might be falling in love with her before this trip, he now knew with total certainty that he had. It didn't scare him to admit that. He wanted to shout it from the rooftops: *I'm in love, people! I never thought I'd fall in love again, and I'm in love, dammit! And she's amazing.* He just wasn't sure when to admit it to *her*.

This weekend Lisette had finally really let him in. He'd seen her grow more comfortable with him every day, and the bond they shared had strengthened. It was powerful, and so sweet it made him ache.

He'd even started thinking ahead. He could see Lisette at his side, in his life . . . and yes, being a real mother to his children. Hell, in a lot of ways, she already was, but once she was free to openly shower them with her love instead of holding it back to be professional? My God, they'd all thrive from that. The kids, her, and even him.

He wanted a future with her. He wanted it all.

But he still had three children to think about, and their welfare came first, even before his happiness. He'd have to tread with caution.

"Mmmm . . ." Lisette groaned as she stirred.

His hand slid along her arm as he kissed her mouth lightly. "Good morning," he whispered.

"Good morning," she whispered back, snuggling even closer.

He trailed soft kisses along her face, her jaw, her neck.

Her fingers ran through his hair as he nibbled at the soft spot at her nape. "I'm going to make you breakfast."

She chuckled, a raspy sound. "As in, make *me* breakfast? Or make food for us?"

"Both," he said with a wicked grin. Continuing to devour her neck, his hands glided over her warm, smooth skin, stopping to cup and squeeze her breasts before traveling lower.

"I'm not even awake yet," she breathed as his fingers feathered along her thighs.

"I know," he said. "Which is why I'm waking you up properly."

"Mmmm, you are." She smiled, then her breath hitched as his fingers brushed over her most sensitive spot. "Ohh . . ."

Her ragged sigh fired his blood, heating it in his veins. He began to stroke her slowly as he kissed her mouth, then slid a finger into her wet folds, loving how she squirmed and gasped with pleasure. The little mewling sounds she made sent shimmers of electricity racing over his skin. "You like that?" he whispered in her ear, husky and low.

"Yes," she gasped as her hips moved with the rhythm his fingers set. "Oh, God, yes. Don't stop . . ."

"Not until you scream for me," he whispered, nipping at her lobe. A low moan fluttered out of her, and her arms snaked around him, her nails biting into his shoulders as she crushed her mouth to his. Their tongues tangled, and her hands roamed over his back, then down in between to reach for him. When her fingers closed around his hard shaft, he groaned, grinding into her hand. "You feel how hard I am for you?"

"Yes," she breathed, kissing him. "I love feeling you . . ."

He rolled to position himself at her opening, teasing along her slickness with his hard cock and drawing a long, shuddering moan out of her.

"I need you now," she said urgently. "Now, Charles . . . please, now."

He grabbed her hips and thrust into her hard, burying himself to the hilt. Her cry of ecstasy filled him with electric pleasure as her legs closed around him, and he pushed deep inside her, claiming her. He thrust again, and again, possessing her, loving her erotic gasps and sounds. "Oh, Lisette . . ." Another hard thrust, then another, another, and he was rewarded with her low moans of sweet surrender. "Tell me you're mine," he rasped.

"I'm yours," she whispered against his lips. "All yours."

"Yeah, you are." His hips rolled as he pumped inside her, over and over, and her nails dug into his skin as she cried out. Her eyes slipped closed in bliss. He sucked in a breath as he stared down at her, her beautiful face flushed from passion. "Christ, sweetheart, you feel so good."

"So do you . . ." Her head fell back as she lost herself to him, and he devoured the soft skin at her throat. Then his hands swept her hair back and cradled her face.

"Look at me," he commanded.

She looked into his eyes as they moved together.

"You're mine," he panted, straining over her. A light sheen of sweat coated their skin. "And I'm yours."

"Yes, Charles, oh, God, yes . . ." Her hands clutched at him, moving down his back to grab his ass and push him even deeper inside her.

He thrust harder, faster, driven by high emotion and the powerful sensations rippling through him. The air around them felt electric. As he whispered her name like a fervent prayer, their bodies rocked together, the pace growing more urgent, frantic, until they climaxed together, moaning and gasping and shuddering as the waves of intense pleasure swept them away.

When their breathing slowed, they lay together kissing and caressing for a long time, whispering words of affection and devotion.

"I don't ever want to get out of this bed," he finally said, "but I'm starving."

"I'll make breakfast," she said.

"We can do it together," he said. "Faster that way." He grinned and kissed her once more before rolling away to rise from the bed.

She sat up, then stopped. He was already in his robe at the door when he turned back. She was still sitting in bed where he'd left her. "You coming?"

"In a minute," she whispered, her eyes closed.

He realized her face was pale, and she was holding herself still. A lick of concern washed through him. "You okay, honey?"

"I . . . I just sat up too fast," she whispered. "I'm a little dizzy."

He swore under his breath and crossed back. "You probably need to eat," he said as he sat on the bed. His weight made the mattress shift slightly.

"Don't move," she gasped, and swallowed hard.

"Sweetheart," he said, the concern sharpening in his gut. "What's wrong?"

She threw the covers back, bolted from the bed, and ran to the bathroom. By the time he was on his feet, he could hear her retching. He went to her, crouching behind her to pull back her thick hair as she vomited into the toilet. It passed quickly; she was done in a minute, reaching up with a shaky hand to flush. He grabbed a tissue as she leaned back against him, and he wiped her mouth.

"I'm so sorry," she mumbled. "And embarrassed. Really romantic, huh?"

"Stop it," he reprimanded softly. "You need to eat something. Toast, some tea."

She nodded and moved to stand. He helped her to her feet, staring with concern as he watched her go to the sink.

His jaw felt tight, and he consciously unclenched it. She rinsed her mouth before turning back to him.

"Stop looking so worried," she said, trying to break the tension. "I just sat up too fast. It happens sometimes in the mornings. Low blood sugar, low blood pressure . . ."

"This happens to you?" he asked.

"Sure. You just didn't know because you don't wake up with me."

He continued to watch her like a hawk as she brushed her teeth. When she finished, she turned to him with a smile. The color had returned to her face.

"See?" she said cheerfully. "I'm fine now."

He slanted a sideways look. "You sure?"

"Yes. You're right; I just need to eat. Toast to start. Come on." She went to him, slid her arms around his waist, and kissed his neck. "You really are a true gentleman. Holding my hair back while I puked, sitting naked on your bathroom floor. I'm embarrassed, but I have to admit I'm touched at the same time. Thanks for that."

He still stared at her. Something was off. He felt it in his gut.

"Charles, I'm fine!" she insisted. "I sat up too fast; that's all. It happens more often than I like to admit. I just need to eat now." She stepped back and moved to the closet. Pulling out the plush rust-colored robe she'd used all weekend, she slipped it on and pulled the sash tight around her waist. "Stop looking at me like that!"

"I'm concerned for you," he said. "If you get sick like that from sitting up too fast, due to low blood pressure or whatever, have you ever seen a doctor about it?"

"Um, no," she said, fidgeting with the end of the sash.

"Then you're going to when we get home," he demanded.

She tilted her head, and her gaze sharpened. "Excuse me?"

"Lisette," he began.

"No. Stop. Charles . . . when I'm the nanny, on the job, you can tell me what to do," she said curtly. "When I'm your lover, off the clock, you can't. Ever. You can't pull rank. I know you're used to people doing whatever you say. But when we're like this, I have to be your equal, or this will never work."

His jaw clenched. "I wasn't trying to tell you what to do. I didn't mean it like a command."

"Did you even hear me?" Her stare held. "If this has any chance, you have to treat me like an equal when we're together. When the kids are around, yes, you're the boss. When we're like this . . . you aren't. I'm serious."

"I hear you." He paused, then nodded and sighed. "You're right, of course. I apologize. Really, I'm sorry."

"Thank you." She still watched him, her posture tense.

"I didn't mean to be dictatorial . . . I just want to know you're okay." His eyes traveled over her as his mind worked. "It might just be a blood pressure thing. Or low blood sugar. Or it could even be an equilibrium issue, or—"

"Let's discuss it over breakfast," she said. "Okay, Dr. Harrison? Come on." She turned away and exited the bathroom, effectively ending the discussion.

Frowning, he scrubbed a hand over his face before following her to the kitchen.

By Thursday evening, Lisette felt as if her weekend away with Charles had been a long time ago. Everything had gone back to the regular routine—she, busy with the kids; he, busy running an empire. That afternoon, he'd called to tell her something had come up and he had to fly to the Atlanta office for a quick overnight. He wouldn't be back in the house until late Friday night. She missed him already.

Their time together in Aspen had been so romantic and wonderful; it felt like recalling a dream when she thought of it. Their quality time alone had sealed them together in a way nothing had before.

They still had to be discreet. They were in total agreement on that. And she had a few ideas on how to be less vulnerable should things . . . not work out. Things she needed to put in place for herself. But the possibilities for Charles and her, in the long run . . . the thought of them made her absolutely giddy.

"Your head's in the clouds," Tina teased on Thursday night as they cleaned up dinner together. "Where are you?"

"What do you mean?" Lisette asked, unable to look her friend in the eye.

"I know Mr. Harrison said you went upstate to visit your friend Karen," Tina said. "But since you got back from that, you've been floating around with this weird little smile on your face." Tina's eyes narrowed. "Did you meet somebody up there?"

"What? No!" Lisette said, even as she blushed.

"Ha, right, that's why you just turned red." Tina laughed. "Okay, keep secrets from me, fiiiiine."

Lisette brought the last of the dishes to the wide double sink and put them in the left basin; Tina was working on a huge pot in the right basin. "I just . . . I'll tell you as soon as I can, I promise."

Tina's eyes flew wide. "You did meet someone!"

"Kind of," Lisette mumbled, hating having to lie to her friend. "I swear I'll tell you everything eventually. Just please don't ask me anymore right now."

Tina cursed a long streak in Spanish, making Lisette laugh. "Whatever it is," Tina said, "I'm happy if you're happy."

"I am happy," Lisette said quietly. "It scares the hell out of me, but I am."

"Don't be scared. You deserve to be happy. Enjoy it." Tina went to put the pot in the dish rack, and a fork fell to the floor with a noisy clang.

"I got it." Lisette bent over to get the fork . . . and the room spun around her. She tried to grab onto the counter, but there was a roaring in her ears and her vision dimmed. She heard Tina say her name . . . then everything went black.

"C'mon." Tina's voice. She sounded worried. "Open your eyes, mama."

Slowly Lisette opened her eyes. She was lying on the kitchen floor, her head in Tina's lap. "What . . ."

"Okay, good, you're with me." Tina stared down at her, then switched to Spanish. "*Dios mio,* Lisette—you scared the shit out of me!"

"What happened?" Lisette murmured, continuing with Tina in Spanish.

"I don't know," Tina said. "You leaned over to grab the fork and just went down like a bag of rocks. Passed out cold."

A chill ran over Lisette's skin. She'd never fainted in her life. She moved to sit up.

"Easy, now. Slowly." Tina helped push her up to a sitting position, her eyes never leaving Lisette's face. "You okay?"

"Yeah. I think so."

"Thank God I caught you, or you could've hit your head. What the hell happened?"

"I have no idea." Lisette's stomach roiled. She usually had an amazingly strong immune system; she rarely got sick. The vomiting episode with Charles had been mortifying. And she'd blatantly lied to him to cover. That hadn't ever happened before—none of this had. "I've been off since the kids were sick. I thought maybe I'd caught their bug. But that was weeks ago now . . ."

"You should go to the doctor," Tina said. "You hear me? Just to get checked out."

Lisette nodded and promised, "I will." Anxiety made her skin go clammy. Her mother had been strong and healthy all her life . . . until she wasn't. She had gotten sick out of nowhere, and then she had died. Lisette's breath felt stuck in her lungs. What if . . .

No. *No*. Dammit, she refused to speculate like that until she had some answers.

"You're probably right, and it's nothing," Tina said. "But better to get it checked."

"I'll call in the morning to make an appointment. I promise." Lisette sat up slowly, grateful that she felt fine. "Now let's get up off the floor, how about that?"

On Friday morning, Lisette called the doctor. Luckily, the medical insurance Charles provided her with ensured that she had access to a top-notch physician. And when the doctor's office realized she worked directly for Charles Harrison III, an appointment was made for her within two hours, while the kids were at school. The doctor fully examined her, drew blood, talked with her at length. He assured her he didn't think it was cancer—probably a virus. But he promised to follow up once he got the blood work back, and she went home feeling somewhat better. A virus was a drag, but nothing life-threatening.

Her anxiety ebbed as she drove home. Now that she'd been given some kind of answer, she was relaxed. Drained, actually. She was ready to take a nap before she picked up the kids from school.

As she lay down on her bed, her phone pinged with a text from Charles. Hi beautiful.

She smiled, flooded with warm delight. Hi yourself. How are you?

Fine, Charles wrote. In between meetings now. Last one should be over around 3. Hoping to be home by 8. Let the kids know, please?

Of course. Safe travels.

Thanks. So . . . have any plans tonight?

She giggled to herself. Like she'd have anywhere to be. Yes. Huge plans. Mahjong tournament at the yacht club, then dinner with the secretary of state.

Sounds like an interesting evening! Charles texted. She could almost hear the note of amusement in his tone. Maybe you could find a few minutes for your man after? Try to pencil him in? He misses you terribly.

I think I can do that. Her smile bloomed from ear to ear. Tell him I miss him too.

Fantastic. See you tonight.

Lisette sighed happily, put her phone down, snuggled into her pillows, and fell asleep within five minutes.

Later that afternoon, Lisette sliced some apples, setting the slices into three bowls for the kids. They all sat around the table in the kitchen nook, doing their homework. The boys had decided that maybe Ava was on to something by choosing to always do her homework there, and wanted in on it.

"You guys are doing a great job," Lisette said as she placed a bowl in front of each child.

"I hate homework," Thomas grumbled. "And apples aren't a good snack."

"You hate everything," Ava said, not even looking up from her notebook as she wrote out her spelling words.

"I do not," Thomas retorted. "I do hate you, though. You're a pain."

"Stop," Lisette chided gently.

"Can I have some more milk?" Myles asked. He gave Lisette a big smile, all the more endearing with his bottom front tooth gone. "Pleeeease?"

"Of course," Lisette said, smiling in response. "Ava, Thomas, either of you want more too?"

"No, thanks," Ava said. Thomas just shook his head no.

As Lisette opened the refrigerator and pulled out the carton of milk, the doorbell chimed.

"Who could that be?" Ava asked, echoing Lisette's exact thought.

"I don't know," Lisette answered, setting the milk down on the counter. "But only one way to find out. Be right back." Tina was down in the basement doing laundry, so Lisette walked out of the kitchen, down the long hallway, through the foyer. The doorbell rang again just as she reached the grand front door, carved wood and glass. She opened it wide, and her heart skipped a beat and stuck in her chest, heavy like a rock. The beautiful woman before her had long, glossy black hair, a killer figure, and radiated attitude. "Vanessa."

"That's right." She smiled, but utterly without warmth. "Are you the maid?"

"No, I'm Lisette, the children's nanny," she said politely, knowing Charles's ex-wife probably didn't care one bit what her name was.

"Oh. Nice to meet you." Vanessa pointed to a pile of suitcases on the step beside her, three large ones and two smaller ones. "Those are mine." She walked into the house, brushing past Lisette. "If you'll see about having those brought inside, that'd be great."

Instant dislike flowed through Lisette's veins with a hot vengeance. She'd heard from Eileen how dismissive and condescending Vanessa had been with the staff when she was the lady of the house. But in person, it made Lisette's blood sizzle. "I'll see what I can do. Um . . . no one mentioned you were coming."

Vanessa turned back, arching a thin perfect brow at her.

"Why would anyone have to tell *you?*" she asked in a haughty tone.

Breathe. Just breathe. "Because I take care of the children, so if their activities were changed for any reason, I'd be notified."

"How efficient." Vanessa fixed her with a cold stare. "I'm their mother. I'm here now. While I'm visiting, your services won't be needed unless I ask for them."

Lisette swallowed hard, shoving her hands into her pockets to hide them as she clenched them into fists. "With all due respect, I don't work for you; I work for Charles. He'll be the one to tell me if my services are needed or not."

"Charles, huh? That should be 'Mr. Harrison' to you. Interesting." Vanessa's pale green eyes narrowed. "Is he here?"

"No. He's at work; he'll be back later this evening."

"Fine. Well, until then, consider yourself free. I'll be with my children." Vanessa turned her back and strolled down the hallway, calling, "Hello? Where are my kids?"

Lisette felt her skin flush from her chest to her hairline. Between the frustration, anger, and hurt from the fact that Charles hadn't told her his ex-wife was coming, Lisette's emotions were in a tailspin. Taking deep breaths, she walked down the hall, following Vanessa.

Ava came darting out of the kitchen. "Mommy?" The nine-year-old's voice and face relayed total shock.

"Oh, my beautiful princess," Vanessa cooed. "Look at you, you're so gorgeous! Come give Mommy a hug."

Ava stared for a second. Even from down the hall, Lisette could see her hesitation. Vanessa hadn't seen the kids in person since April, when she had taken them on a Disney cruise for a week. Ava slowly went to her mother and hugged her.

Thomas and Myles came out to the hallway, saw their mother, and rushed to hug her too. The saccharine voice Vanessa used to talk to them, as if she were Mother of the Year, made Lisette sick. Her stomach did a nauseous flip.

"I bet you're surprised to see me, huh?" Vanessa said.

"Totally!" Thomas said.

"Daddy didn't tell us you were coming," Myles said.

"Well, that's because he didn't know," Vanessa said, and a new burst of anger shot through Lisette's limbs. "I wanted to surprise you. And guess what? I'm going to stay for a few weeks, so we can all be together for Christmas. Won't that be great?"

"Yes! Yay!" the kids cried excitedly.

Lisette's heart sank to her roiling stomach. Charles would be furious.

"So, what are you guys doing right now?" Vanessa asked her children.

"Homework," Thomas ground out.

"Oh, you can finish that later," Vanessa said, tousling Myles's hair. "Let's go in the den, and we can hang out for a little while."

"I really don't think—" Lisette started to say, but the kids were all too happy to abandon their homework. They ran into the den.

Vanessa spared her a glance. "What?"

"They need to finish their homework," Lisette insisted.

"Right now," Vanessa said with blistering condescension, "what they need is their mother."

"They've always needed their mother," Lisette said quietly, but laced her words with steel. "Too bad."

"How dare you speak that way to me," Vanessa hissed.

"How dare you walk in here and disrupt their routine," Lisette replied. "I don't work for you. You can't just come in here and—"

"Those are *my* kids, honey," Vanessa snarled, hands on her hips, any pretense of pleasantry gone. "And when Charles gets home, I'm going to tell him how his employee spoke to the mother of his children."

"Go right ahead," Lisette said. She met Vanessa's glare

directly, not giving her an inch. Lisette knew damn well how Charles felt about Vanessa and wasn't the least bit concerned. But then it hit her. Vanessa's being here . . . If Vanessa found out about their affair, that Charles was involved with his kids' nanny, it would be exactly the kind of ugly mess Lisette and Charles had worked so hard to avoid. She drew a deep breath. "You want to spend time with your children? Enjoy it. I suppose you'll want to cook their dinner too, then. You must remember where the kitchen is. Have at it." This time, she was the one who turned her back on Vanessa, leaving the hallway to go to the stairs and straight up to her room.

As she locked the door, she realized her hands were shaking as much as her insides. God, she hated confrontation, but she wouldn't ever back down from a fight, especially with someone like Vanessa. Her father had taught her to stand up for herself, and for what was right, always. No matter what. And she always had.

She pulled her phone from her sweater pocket to text Charles and warn him what he was coming home to.

Chapter Twenty-Three

Charles glanced at the suitcases in the foyer with disdain. He turned to Bruck and said, "If you could get those in your trunk, I'd appreciate it."

"No problem, sir." Bruck grabbed the two biggest ones and took them out.

Swearing under his breath, Charles stalked down the hallway to the den, following the sounds of the kids and video games. He stopped in the doorway, and his jaw tightened. There was Vanessa, in a tight magenta sweater and black leggings, playing one of the *Just Dance* games with the kids. They were all dancing to "Baby Got Back." Charles would've laughed if the kids had been dancing to that song with anyone else, but with Vanessa, it seemed inappropriate and only fueled the fire of his already simmering rage. A muscle twitched under his eye.

"I'm back," he said, loud enough to be heard over the music.

"Daddy!" Myles ran to him, his face flushed and his hair stuck to his sweaty forehead. As he grabbed Charles in a hug, Myles said happily, "Mommy came to visit us!"

"So I see." He speared Vanessa with his iciest stare as the kids all gathered around to hug him.

"How was your trip, Daddy?" Ava asked.

"Fine, sweetie. A nice quick one. Told you I'd be back tonight, didn't I?" He kissed the top of her head. "Where's Lisette?"

"I don't know where she went," Thomas said. "She, like, disappeared."

"I think I have an idea about that too," Charles said coolly. "Hello, Vanessa."

"Hello, Charles. The house looks good. Haven't been here in so long . . ." She swept her long, straightened black hair back over her shoulders. "I thought I'd surprise the kids with a visit."

"Did you." His voice was flat. "How lovely." He looked down at the kids and said, "It's nine-thirty. That's bedtime on a Friday, and you all know that."

"But we were playing with Mommy," Myles said.

"And Lisette always puts us to bed, especially when you're not here, but she's missing," Thomas added.

"Can't we stay up a little longer?" Ava begged. "Pleeeeease?"

"No, you all need to go to bed now," Charles said. His tone brooked no room for debate. "You'll see your mother tomorrow. You can spend all day with her if you want. It'll be Saturday."

"Can we, Mommy, can we?" the kids asked her, all at the same time.

"Yes, of course," she smiled. "I'll be here when you wake up. Because I—"

"Apparently your mother has become an early riser," Charles said smoothly. "Because that means she'll be coming here from her hotel bright and early."

Vanessa blinked at him. "My hotel?" she echoed.

"Of course. I assume it's nearby." He met her stare with a ferocious one of his own, calling on all his reserves as the intimidating magnate that he was. He didn't move a muscle until she finally looked away.

"Go on up to bed, you guys," Vanessa said. "Come, give me hugs and kisses."

"Aren't you going to tuck us in?" Myles asked, looking up at her with his big blue eyes. "You're never here to tuck us in."

For once, Vanessa looked affected. She blinked, then slowly put her hand to his cheek. "Okay, cutie. I'll tuck you in."

"She'll tuck *all* of you in," Charles said. "After all, she hasn't gotten to in so long. She's going to do the bedtime juggle tonight."

She shot him a fierce glare.

"Go up and brush your teeth now," he said to the kids. "Your mommy will be up in just a minute."

They all looked from one parent to the other, sensing the tension, but left the room to do as they were told.

Charles and Vanessa stared each other down. "You should have told me you were coming to see them," he said gruffly.

"It was an impulse decision," she said, her hands on her hips. "Besides, you told me I could see them whenever I wanted."

"And you can. But some advance notice would be nice."

"Yeah, well, I'm not very nice," she said. "You told me that how many times?"

"Believe me, no one knows that better than I do." Still in his suit, he loosened the knot of his tie while never taking his eyes from her. "For the record, you don't walk into my home and start telling my staff what to do. You don't give orders. Am I clear?"

"Aww, did your mousy little nanny tell on me?" she said.

"Let's get a few things straight, right now." He took a step closer, spearing her with his angry gaze as his blood pulsed through his veins. "You want to see the kids, that's fine, but you have to tell me you're coming first. And you sure as hell don't have the right to walk in here and start issuing orders to my household staff. Especially when at this point in their lives, they know the kids much better than you do."

Vanessa sniffed, bored, and examined her nails.

"You *cannot* dismiss their nanny," Charles said in a low, lethal tone. "She's the one who's with them day in and day out. Her routines work for them. They've flourished under her care. If you ever speak to Lisette again with anything less than respect, I'll throw you out of here with my bare hands, in front of the kids."

Vanessa snorted out a laugh at that.

His nostrils flared. "Lisette happens to be incredible with the kids. *Your* kids. The ones you usually ignore." Charles cocked his head as he stared. "You should be kissing her damn feet for how good she is to them."

"She should be kissing my feet for letting her be with my kids."

"Letting her? *I* hired her, after the kids terrorized a few other nannies with their acting out. Because their mother fucking abandoned them."

"I didn't abandon them," Vanessa said curtly.

"Really? Where've you been, dear? Not here. Not even on this coast. You see them once or twice a year and think—you know what, you're not worth my breath. We both know what you are. Everyone does. Even those kids." Charles crossed the room, grabbed the remote, and turned off the flat-screen before tossing the remote back onto the couch. The sudden quiet seemed to add to the tension in the room. "Just so you know, you didn't chase Lisette off. She didn't scurry off because you told her to. After she informed me of the developments here, *I* gave her the rest of the night off. You wanted her gone? She is, for tonight. So pick up the slack. Go put your own three children to bed for once, *Mommy*."

High color spotted Vanessa's cheeks. Charles figured if

looks could kill, he'd be a dead man several times over. It didn't faze him one bit.

He walked past her to the doorway, saying over his shoulder, "When you're done putting them to bed, you'll leave the house. My driver has put your bags in the limo, and he'll drive you to whatever hotel you choose to stay at. Because you're sure as hell not staying here."

"My kids want me here with them," Vanessa said sharply, advancing on him.

He turned to look at her, fists in his pockets, and assumed the most bored look he could muster. "That's your fault for lying to them and getting their hopes up. But you've done that so many times, they're used to your letting them down. They've learned to live without you. I assure you they'll be fine if you don't have sleepovers this trip."

"But they want me to be here," she said, needling him. "You're really going to let them down like that?"

"Yup. Because you're not staying in my home. Period." Charles grabbed his tie and pulled it out of his collar, balling it up in his fist as he pinned her with a sharp glare. "This is *my* house. I don't know how long your visit will be, but remember what I said. While you're here, you'll defer to me, and to Lisette, on all things where the children are concerned. Or I'll personally escort you the fuck out of here and put you on a plane so fast your head will spin." The side of his mouth lifted in a hollow grin. His insides felt as cold as ice, and he was sure his gaze was too. "And, you speak to *all* members of my staff with courtesy and respect, or again, I'll throw you out without blinking an eye. Any other questions?"

"Yeah. When did you become such a prick?" Vanessa asked.

"When you decided you didn't want to be a mother. Just looking at you disgusts me." He turned his back on her and walked out. He felt eerily calm, considering the way his brain was churning, but he'd process this better later. For now, he had the enemy in his own home, and three children and a secret girlfriend he wanted to protect from her nastiness and manipulations. He strode down the hall, up the stairs, right to the bathroom the kids shared. Ava had gotten in her nightgown and was brushing her teeth slowly. "Where are the boys?"

"Already in their rooms," she said, her mouth full of toothpaste.

"Your mom will be right up," he said. He drew a deep breath as she spit her toothpaste into the sink. "She'll put you to bed tonight. Okay?"

Ava rinsed out her mouth, then met his eyes in the mirror. "You're not happy she's here."

He exhaled a deep breath. He wouldn't lie to her, to any of the kids. "No, I'm not. We don't get along, sweetheart. That's why we're not together anymore." *Among a hundred other reasons*, he thought. "Also, she didn't even tell me she was coming, and that's rude. You're supposed to ask people if it's okay to come for a visit."

"Maybe she didn't because she thought you'd say no," Ava said.

He sighed. "I'd never say no to her seeing you guys. But she isn't going to stay in the house while she's visiting. She misinformed you on that point."

"Daddy . . ." Ava faced him, her wide blue eyes somber. "Why is she here now?"

"I don't know," he said quietly. He leaned against the doorframe, feeling exhausted. "Does it bother you that she's here?"

"No," Ava said. "I just . . . wondered why. Because she's never just showed up for a visit like this before." She looked into his eyes. "What do you think she wants?"

The clear, level question hit him like a gut punch. He'd wondered the same thing. Vanessa didn't do anything without an agenda, unless there was something in it for her. But for his little girl to wonder that . . . Damn. Ava was only nine years old, but so wise beyond her years. Maybe too wise. "I think she wants to see the three of you, that's all. People get sentimental around the holidays. She probably missed you."

Ava considered that for a moment, then went to him and wrapped her arms around his waist. "I love you, Daddy," she said against his middle. "Don't be mad 'cause she's here. I don't want you mad."

"I'm fine, sweetheart. Don't you worry." He hugged her back tightly, sweeping his hand over her long hair. "And I love you too. More than anything in the world."

There was a soft knock on Lisette's door. She steeled herself, then went to answer it. It wasn't Vanessa, but Charles, leaning casually against the frame. The light glinted off his glasses for a second as he smiled at her. He wore royal blue and white-striped pajama bottoms and a blue top with two buttons open. She knew he'd just showered; she could smell the clean scent of soap off his skin, and his hair was even darker and wavier when it was damp. She wanted to wrap her arms around him, bury her face in his neck, and breathe him in, but she didn't. "Hi."

"Hi," he said softly. His brilliant blues lit as he gazed at her. "It's so good to see you."

"It's good to see you too," she murmured. "When did you get home?"

"About an hour ago. I helped Vanessa put the kids to bed, then took a shower."

Lisette only nodded. There were a million things she wanted to say, but she had no idea if she should say any of them, so she kept quiet.

"Can I come in?" he asked.

"You think that's wise?" she asked, darting a glance into the hallway beyond him.

"The kids are all asleep," he said, "and Vanessa is gone."

"Gone?" Lisette's brows lifted. "Really? She left?"

"Damn right. I made her leave." With that, he leaned in, slid a strong arm around Lisette's waist and yanked her to him, taking her mouth with his. He edged her into the room backwards, closing the door behind him with his foot and never breaking the kiss. His hand moved to the back of her head and pulled out the elastic, and he sifted his fingers through her hair, letting the long curtain of it shimmer down her back. "After this unwelcome homecoming, I need to hold you." He kissed her over and over.

"It's good to be held," she said against his mouth.

He eased her down onto the bed, still kissing her and holding tight. "You didn't really think she was going to stay here, did you?"

"Well, *she* certainly did. I didn't know—"

"Hell no. I can't believe she thought she could stay here. I made it very clear that wasn't going to be the case. For fuck's sake, the nerve of that woman . . ." He shook his head, new anger darkening his features.

"Shhhh." She wrapped herself around him, and they kissed until she felt the tension slowly ebb from his body. "Don't let her get to you."

He huffed out a breath, then nuzzled Lisette's neck, dropping tiny kisses and nibbles along her skin. "You're right."

"However you handle her while she's here, whatever you want, just tell me."

"I will." He lifted his head to look into her eyes. "I told her if she doesn't speak to you with respect, she's on a plane."

A little thrill burst in Lisette's chest, but she said, "I appreciate that, but we have to be careful. If we're going to keep our relationship a secret, and she's around us—"

"She'll pick up on it and pounce, I know." His gaze got steely, the determination obvious. "But there's no way I'm going to stay away from you." He brushed his lips against hers. "I couldn't if I tried."

Her heart fluttered at the soft, earnest words. She smiled and kissed him fully.

"She wants to spend all day with them tomorrow," he said. "So you'll have that time to yourself. I wish I could do something with you, but I want to keep an eye on her. She doesn't know the kids. I plan to either go along if they leave the house, or lurk if they stay here, whether she likes it or not."

"Good idea." She was so glad to hear him say that. She'd had similar thoughts and concerns for the kids. If he was going to be wherever they were, they'd be fine. "They must be happy to see her."

His jaw tightened. "The boys are. But Ava . . ." He rolled off Lisette onto his back, pulling her with him and curling her into his side. "She's glad to see her mother, but she's wary. How sad is that. Ava's nine, and already knows her mother is a fickle woman who must want something if she just showed up like this." His fingers absently played with Lisette's hair. "I don't know what's worse. Ava's astute intuition, or the boys' naïveté in thinking that their mommy loves them so much she had to come see them."

Lisette rested her head and one hand on his broad chest. His strong, solid heartbeat was comforting. "Both selections are kind of awful, actually."

"I know." He sighed and stroked her back in slow, tender sweeps. "Whatever. I'm not going to let Vanessa derail anything here. You and I will both keep an eye on the kids. She's visiting, and she'll leave soon."

I sure hope so, Lisette thought. She tilted her head to kiss Charles's jaw. "You smell really good."

He smiled. "Yeah?"

"Mm hmm." She pressed herself closer into his side and

snaked her arms around his waist. "How about we just lie here and hold each other for a while? I think you need that."

He looked at her, appreciation and affection clear in his gaze. "How do you always correctly sense what I need?"

She gave a tiny shrug. "I don't know. I guess I'm just . . . tuned in to you."

"Thank God for that," he murmured. With great tenderness, he kissed her forehead, then her mouth. He kissed her once more, long and sweet, then snuggled her tight. "Let me hold you. I missed the feel of you."

They lay together quietly for a few minutes, savoring the closeness, the intimacy, their bubble away from the world.

"I was thinking, on the plane back today . . ." He grazed his fingertips along her cheek. "You know about the huge gala Tess throws every December for the Harrison Foundation, right?"

"Sure," Lisette said. "It's one of Manhattan's biggest social events of the year."

"Yes. Well, it's on the eighteenth."

"Okay . . ." She waited.

"I want you to come with me," he said.

She pulled back a bit to look at him. "I thought kids weren't allowed there?"

His mouth pulled up in a half smile bemused by her confusion. "They're not. I don't mean for you to come as their nanny. I mean for you to come as my date."

"What?" She pulled out of his embrace altogether, sat up, and gaped at him. "You've got to be kidding."

"No, I'm not."

"What happened to our taking it slow, keeping it secret?" She stared at him, lying there so casually. "All of a sudden, you want to out us to the world?"

"I don't care about the world. I just want my girlfriend with me." He reached for her hand.

She wondered if he'd lost his mind. "I thought once we decided we were ready, we'd tell the kids first, *then* the world."

"Right. And we can tell the kids soon. Before the ball, for sure."

"That's less than a week away."

"Plenty of time."

"Didn't we *just* say how we don't want Vanessa to get wind of this?" Lisette stared at him in total confusion.

"Yes, but . . ." he said, "I just thought of something else. She can't hurt you if we out ourselves before she finds out about us."

Lisette shook her head vehemently. "No. You're . . . you don't get it."

His eyes held hers. "If we tell the kids first, no one can hurt them. If we tell the world first, no one can hurt you."

"That's a lovely thought, but that's not how this works!" she said, alarm flooding her. "Remember when I called you obtuse? This is beyond obtuse; it's being willfully ignorant. Arrogant. You want what you want, so you're willing to throw caution to the wind. But the truth is, if this all blows up, you're the only one who will escape unscathed."

"How can you say that? I'm just as invested in this as you are," he asserted.

She shook her head and swept her hair back from her face. Anxiety made her heart pound and her throat suddenly dry. "You're . . . being selfish, Charles. You're not thinking clearly. You're not really thinking this through. It's unlike you."

"Whoa." He stared hard, lines gathering in his forehead and around his eyes. He sat up too, facing her. "That's a little harsh."

"I'm sorry, but it's true."

"I'm selfish because I want my new girlfriend with me at a social event?"

"Yes."

A muscle twitched under his eye.

"You're jumping into this," she said, "without any forethought about the kids or me. I'm touched that you want me with you, but it's not worth hurting them over."

"How would it hurt them," Charles said, "to know that their father is happier than he's been in a very long time? Because of you, someone they care about?"

"They're little." She sighed. "They're not going to go from accepting me as their nanny to accepting me as your girlfriend overnight, just because you want them to."

"How do you know?" he asked. "Kids are very accepting, and they love you. For all you know, they'll be thrilled. I think they will be."

"Because you want to believe that, and you're used to getting your way. But . . ." She stared at him. She wasn't getting through to him. The anxiety and accompanying adrenaline had already made her hands tingle, and now they worked their way through the rest of her. She drew a long, deep breath and got up from the bed.

"Where are you going?" He frowned at her. "Come back, we're not done talking."

She didn't move away from the bed, but she didn't retake her spot beside him. "Thank you for the invite, but I'm not going to the ball with you," she said quietly. Her arms folded around her middle. "Now there's no reason to tell them so soon."

He rose from the bed, jaw tight and eyes flashing. "You're afraid to tell them."

"Of course I am!" she cried. "We—this—it's still so new! I don't want to hurt them!"

"No, that's not it." His stare pinned her. "You're afraid to tell them because it'll make this totally real. Something you can't pretend isn't happening. You're scared of it."

Her mouth fell open. "Is that what you think?"

He nodded.

"You need to leave now," she whispered.

His eyes flashed, and his lips flattened into a thin line. "No. Not until we finish this conversation."

"We're talking in circles. You don't want to hear me. It's pointless."

"I'm in love with you," he said fiercely. "So this isn't pointless. This is important for us to figure out, together, no matter how hard it may be."

Her heart skipped a beat, then took off like a racehorse. "Wh-what?"

He grasped her shoulders, bending a bit to look right into her eyes. "I was away for all of thirty-six hours, and I missed you so much it ached." He spoke softly, but wouldn't let her look away. "When I found out Vanessa was awful to you, I was so furious that someone would treat you that way I wanted to throw things." He reached up and smoothed back a lock of her hair, tucking it behind her ear. "I watch you with my kids, and it's so genuine. It's not just you doing your job, though you're damn good at it. It's more. You love them, and they love you. And . . . now I love you too." He brushed the pad of his thumb over her lips. "That's not going to change. It's only going to get deeper and stronger every day. So yes, I thought, why wait? I know how I feel."

"Oh, Charles," she whispered, wishing her heart didn't feel stuck in her chest.

"I don't mean to sound selfish, or obtuse, or arrogant," he said. "But you're right about one thing: I want what I want, and what I want is you." He brushed his lips against hers tenderly. "Forgive me for sounding so self-consumed. I'm sorry. I'm just frustrated, about ten different things, and I wish this situation were simpler."

"Me too." She slipped her arms around his waist and held tight. The sound of his heartbeat beneath her ear, strong and sure, was comforting, while her heart felt as if it were doing a jitterbug in her chest. "Yes, I'm afraid of our telling the kids, and their not accepting it, or being confused and angry . . . or rejecting me. I admit it."

"I really don't think that would happen," he said, his hands sweeping up and down her back in long, slow caresses. "And I admit that . . . with Vanessa here, it just feels as though we might need to do some things faster than we initially planned. Like telling the kids. Because I want it to come from us, not from her."

She nodded against his chest. "I get that. It just feels too soon. We haven't been together for that long . . ."

He sighed and let his chin rest on the top of her head. "I know. But that doesn't make it any less real. I know I love you. That's got to count for something."

"It counts for a lot." Her voice felt thick in her throat.

He pulled back enough to look at her, lift her chin with a fingertip. "So . . . how do you feel? Just curious."

A staccato laugh burst from her. "I can't believe you don't know."

His brow furrowed as he waited.

"I've been in love with you for a while already," she admitted. "I thought it was so obvious."

"Well," he said, grinning, "as you've pointed out on more than one occasion, I'm a little obtuse."

She giggled and shook her head. "Sometimes. It's okay. I love you anyway."

His smile widened, his eyes sparkled, and he lowered his mouth to hers to kiss her long and hard. "Do you really?"

"Yes."

"You're not saying it because . . . you know. Because you have to, because you're afraid for your job?"

"No! God, no."

"You're not saying it because you think it's what I want to hear, and I want what I want?" He said that facetiously, but she saw the serious glint in his eyes.

She nodded, overcome by emotion. "Charles, I love you

so much. I love you, and yes, I love your children too. So much it scares me. That's why I desperately want this to work."

"Me too." He let his lips sip from hers, lingering, savoring. "We'll make it work." He smiled and kissed her again before holding her tight. "So . . . we'll tell the kids in a few days . . . and then you'll come to the ball with me. Please. Have faith in me."

Her head was spinning. *He loved her*. He was in love with her, and he wanted her enough to tell the world about it. Would the kids be okay with this? Would they think it strange, or be angry at her for being with their dad? They'd always had him to themselves. And with Vanessa around for now . . . she hoped they weren't rushing things because she'd forced their hand . . .

She'd overthink it all tomorrow. For now, she just wanted to be held by him and listen to the sound of his heartbeat beneath her cheek. She pulled him to the bed, and they lay on it together. "Just hold me," she whispered.

Chapter Twenty-Four

When Lisette got down to the kitchen in the morning, Eileen was already at the stove, scrambling eggs. "Good morning."

"Ah, good morning, dearie!" Eileen said cheerfully. Lisette didn't know how Eileen was always so upbeat in the morning without coffee. Eileen had sworn off caffeine a decade before and said she'd never felt better. Lisette, on the other hand, went straight to the coffee pot. The morning fog in her head wasn't going to clear by itself.

"Thank you for making this," she said as she poured herself a cup of dark ambrosia.

"Of course."

"The kids downstairs in the playroom?"

"Yes. I gave them apples and bananas so they wouldn't bounce off the walls, and I'm making them a real breakfast now."

"Sounds right. Is Charles up yet?"

"He is, but he left early." Eileen reached for a small cup and added some cubed ham to the eggs. "Said he had some errands to run and would be back around ten-thirty or eleven o'clock."

"Good to know. Thanks." Lisette went to the refrigerator to find the flavored coffee creamers, chose the hazelnut, and added some to her coffee. Her stomach rumbled. At least she wasn't nauseous, but she was starving. She grabbed a banana from the large wooden fruit bowl.

Eileen pushed the eggs around with the spatula, then gestured for Lisette to come closer. "So the witch is back, eh?" she murmured.

Lisette nodded as she swallowed her bite. "And witchy as can be. I'll never understand how she roped Charles in," Lisette murmured.

"Won't you?" Eileen asked, her brows lifting.

"Because she's stunningly beautiful?"

"Nah, try again." Eileen winked. "Charles was never the sucker for a pretty face like his brothers used to be."

"Then I really don't know." Lisette took a sip of coffee. "It mystifies me, frankly."

"There's no mystery, sweetie," Eileen said. "She was a bad, bad girl. Plain and simple. Charles's father told him what to do his whole life. This was the one time Charles tried to buck the restraints and be naughty, you know?"

Lisette couldn't believe it was something that simple. "You think so?"

"I know so. It's textbook, really." Eileen moved to put the mound of eggs onto a huge platter. "There's no bigger pleasure than doing what you're not supposed to, you know what I mean? But when everything became familiar and he realized what life with her would really be like? Well, by then, it was too late; he'd already had a child with her, and he was stuck with her." Eileen shook her head in disdain. "He's so honorable, he would've stayed with it forever, simply because he'd made an oath. *She's* the one who left. She got bored. Yes, she broke his heart . . . but good riddance. Her leaving was the best thing that ever happened to him. She did him a huge favor."

Lisette's stomach did a wobbly roll as she considered what Eileen had said. That the forbidden is more enticing than anything . . . That certainly applied to their secret relationship, didn't it? Was that really why Charles wanted her so much? Not because he wanted *her*, but because he wasn't supposed to be with her? Doubt crept through her, nipping at her. He was unhappy with his regular life, sick of having his choices dictated to him . . . What better way to rebel and not hurt the company or his career than by having a fling with someone he shouldn't? Oh, God . . .

"I'm going to check on the kids," she said. "It's too quiet."

"Well, like I said, they're down in the playroom," Eileen said. "Could you tell them that breakfast is on the table?"

"Sure." Lisette set down her mug on the counter and left the kitchen.

The entire furnished basement was a playroom. The tremendous space had been split in half: one half was for the kids; the other half had a bar, a pool table, and three vintage arcade games—an adult playroom for Charles. As she made her way down the stairs, she could hear the children talking and the TV volume blaring. At the bottom of the stairs, while she was still in the hallway, her cell phone rang in her pocket. She pulled it out and glanced at the caller ID. The doctor's office. And it wasn't even nine o'clock yet. Her heart fell to the pit of her stomach. "Hello?"

"Hi, is this Lisette Gardner?" said a male voice.

"Yes, it is."

"Ah, hi, Lisette. It's Dr. Gilbert."

"You're calling awfully early," she said, her heart suddenly pounding. "And on a Saturday. Now I'm nervous."

"Well," he said, "we got some of the blood results back, and I wanted to speak to you right away."

A wave of panic flooded her, and she leaned against the wall for support. She *was* sick; oh, God, something was wrong with her. "Go ahead."

"The good news is, it definitely explains all the symptoms

you described to me," Dr. Gilbert said. "Lisette, you're pregnant."

Her head went all wavy, and she could barely breathe. "B-but that's impossible. I can't be pregnant."

"I'll admit, when looking over your files, I was surprised too. But according to the blood work, there's no question. You're pregnant."

Her legs gave out, and she slid down the wall. The roaring of blood in her ears almost knocked her out. She finally sputtered, "There has to be a mistake. I was told I'd never get pregnant. The scarring, the damage—there's no way—"

"Lisette. Take a deep breath," Dr. Gilbert instructed. "I'm sure you're shocked. But can you come in this morning? We'll do an ultrasound and see what's going on. We'll run more tests. How soon can you get here?"

She swallowed hard, her mind unable to process. This was impossible. The doctors had made it very clear . . .

Then again, she hadn't even had sex with anyone again— even once—after Brandon, so the doctors' opinions had never been tested. There'd been no sex until Charles.

Oh, God. Charles. What a mess. But . . .

New waves of mixed panic and excitement crested and battered her. She struggled to breathe. Could it really be possible? A baby of her *own*? The tiniest spark of hope ignited deep in her soul, in a place she'd locked up and snuffed out years ago . . .

"Lisette?" Dr. Gilbert said loudly. "Are you there?"

"Y-yeah," she whispered. "I'm here. Sorry. Just overwhelmed."

"I bet. Let's run more tests," he said. "Come to the office. All right?"

Eyes still closed, heart pounding, mind racing, hope fighting to rise to the top despite it all, she drew a shaky breath and said, "I'll be there in an hour."

* * *

Four hours later, Lisette entered the mansion in a total daze. Nothing felt real. So many emotions had gripped and slammed her that day that she was now drained. All she wanted was to climb into her bed and sleep until tomorrow.

She had so many decisions to make. Her life had just changed, massively and irrevocably, and she could barely process any of it. But there was one emotion reigning over all the rest: joy. She really *was* pregnant. The ultrasound, blood, and urine tests had all left no room for doubt. She was already approximately nine weeks along.

The doctor had told her it would likely be considered a high-risk pregnancy just because of her history, aside from her being a few months away from turning thirty-five, and he had given her a referral for an obstetrician in the same building. She'd gone straight there, and even heard her baby's heartbeat, strong and sure. The sound had been such a shock, such an unbelievable gift, that she'd burst into tears.

There were so many things to consider; she was completely overwhelmed. She needed time to think, to figure out how to tell Charles that he'd gotten her pregnant.

He'd trusted and believed her when she told him her story. What if he thought she had tricked him into getting her pregnant to take some of his substantial fortune? What if Charles wasn't happy about the news? He already had three children and was forty years old; maybe he didn't want the responsibility of another one.

She swayed in the foyer at that horrible thought. Her hand protectively went to her belly. She had no idea what would happen to her now, or what the reactions around her would be, but she knew one thing with every fiber of her being: she wouldn't let anything happen to this baby. Not for anything in the world.

Lisette looked around at the opulent mansion as she shuffled slowly inside. The expensive and tasteful furnishings were tangible proof of the billionaire lifestyle of the home's owner. Hell, the artwork on the walls? Any of those pieces likely cost more than she made in a year. Charles Roger Harrison III was a wealthy, powerful man from a long line with a storied history. Who the hell was she in comparison? She was nobody. An army brat with no roots, no family, no prestigious connections or money or anything substantial. She had nothing but her job and herself.

She passed the living room and caught a glimpse of the Christmas tree, majestic and beautiful. *A baby.* She was actually going to have a baby of her own. She'd have more than a job; she'd have someone in her life who would stay. Her eyes went to the holiday decorations adorning the house, sparkling and festive. It was almost like a Christmas miracle . . .

Excitement, anguish, and disbelief slammed her at the same time, the flood of feelings almost bringing her to her knees.

Bed. She needed her bed. Swallowing hard, she went to the stairs.

"Hey, there you are!" Charles's ebullient voice rang out from down the hall.

She'd made it to the bottom step. Lisette froze, and she felt the blood drain from her face. She wasn't ready to face him yet. "Hi," she choked out, heart thumping against her ribs.

"I was wondering where you were." Smiling brightly, he went to her, standing close but not touching her. "The kids went out with Vanessa for ice cream. We were here all morning, and she seemed okay with them, so I let her take them out on her own. A trial run, so to speak." He winked conspiratorially. "We're mostly alone; Eileen's in the kitchen, and Maisie and Felicia are cleaning the upstairs right now . . ."

He peered closely at her. "Where'd you disappear to? Didn't you get my texts?"

Of course she had. But she'd been otherwise occupied, crying and trembling from shock in a doctor's office. "Sorry. I was busy . . ."

His expression changed; staring, he frowned hard. "What's wrong?" He finally reached out to touch her, tipping her chin up with his fingers. "I'm rambling, and something happened; it's all over your face."

Her eyes shut again, as if that would shield her from his scrutiny. "I'm wiped out, and I need to lie down, that's all." She opened her eyes and added, "I'm fine."

"No, you're not." He edged closer, concern in his bright blue eyes. "Tell me what's going on."

Damn, he knew her too well already. Her mind raced, trying to think of an excuse that would sound plausible. "I . . . I ran some errands, but then I . . . had a doctor's appointment. Couldn't answer texts during my exam."

"You went, like I asked? Great." His hands gently gripped her arms. "And?"

"And they ran a bunch of tests . . . blood work and all . . . I'll hear back in a few days." She tried to smile as her eyes darted around the room. "I'm okay."

"What do they think it might be?" Charles asked. "Based on your symptoms?"

They think a miracle has happened, and you're going to be a father again in July. "Not sure. They didn't want to scare me with speculations. They'll call when they know something, if there's anything. Said I should eat better and sleep more, stay away from caffeine, etcetera, etcetera." At least that last part was true.

He held her face with both hands, forcing her to meet his eyes. "Why won't you look at me?"

Oh, God, oh, God, she wouldn't be able to keep this from him for long. And he had the right to know. But she had to figure out what her plans would be, prepare herself for every possible scenario. "I'm just really tired. I . . . threw up again on the way home from the doctor," she lied. "Probably from nerves, but I'm trying not to breathe puke breath in your face, and I just want to crawl into bed, you know?"

"My poor sweetheart. Come with me," he murmured firmly and led her upstairs, down the long corridor to his bedroom.

"There are people in the house," she whispered, looking over her shoulder. "We can't—"

"I'm locking us in here. No one will know." Charles ushered her into his room, immediately locking the door behind them. An arm around her waist, he brought her to his massive bed, covered with the multi-hued blue comforter and several throw pillows. He yanked back the covers and shot her a sweet grin. "Get in. Nap time."

Tears stung her eyes. The kinder he was, the more attentive and caring he was, the more it was going to kill her. "I should just go to my room."

"No." He frowned and rubbed the back of his neck. "I'm selfish. I want some time alone with you. Even if it's just holding you while you sleep."

"But when Vanessa comes back with the kids—"

"This will be the one room they won't look for you in, right? So you can sleep, uninterrupted. You do look a little tired." He smiled softly and caressed her face. "Lisette. You always take care of everyone else. For an hour at least, let someone take care of you. Me. The guy who loves you."

"Oh, Charles . . ." The tears welled and spilled over onto her cheeks.

"Hey." His thumbs tenderly wiped the tears away. "Shhh, you're going to be fine. The doctors will figure out what's going on, and we'll deal with it, and you'll be fine."

"*We'll* deal with it?" she echoed, sniffling.

"Yes. We're together, aren't we?" He lowered his head

and gently kissed her forehead, lingering sweetly for a moment before his eyes pinned hers. "I love you. That means whatever is going on with you, I'm here for you. You're not alone anymore, sweetheart. Neither of us is. We have each other now, right?"

Sobbing, she grasped at him, clinging to him as if for her life. She wished she knew what the future held. How was it possible to be so elated and so terrified at the same time? The sobs ripped from her throat, and she buried her face in his chest.

"Whoa. Shhhh." He held her tight and rubbed her back, kissing her forehead, her temple, trying to soothe her. "I'm here, sweetheart. Please try not to worry. I'm sure you're okay. Everything's going to be all right."

She cried for a few minutes, the tsunami of emotion finally sweeping her away. So many decisions to make, so much was going to change . . . She thought about telling him then, but she wasn't ready. She wanted to fully absorb this incredible news herself before she shared it with anyone else, even him. She'd tell him soon; of course she'd have to. But not today.

When she could finally draw some deep breaths, he released her and went to the bathroom, returning with a box of tissues. She thanked him in a hoarse whisper and mopped up her face.

"You soaked through my shirt," he said, trying to coax a smile out of her. "I guess I'll have to be half-naked while I hold you. Think you can stand that?"

She hiccupped out a watery giggle and nodded. "I'd love that, actually."

Grinning, he pulled the charcoal gray Henley over his head and dropped it to the floor, then kicked off his shoes. As he stood there in only his glasses and jeans, even in the depths of her turmoil, Lisette couldn't help but admire him.

"You're so beautiful," she whispered. "Inside and out."

He smiled warmly as he reached for her hands. "Thank you." He brought her mouth to his, kissing her tenderly. "C'mon. Nap time for you, missy." He nudged her to sit on the bed, then pulled off her knee-high black leather boots, then moved her up the mattress and placed her in the middle of his bed. He climbed in beside her, pulled up the covers over them, and curled his arms around her until they were in a delicious cocoon.

"Thank you for all this," she whispered against his chest, kissing his skin. "I'm too exhausted to be embarrassed or to fight you on this. So just thank you."

"Take a deep breath," he said. She did as she was told. "Another." She did so.

"I love you," she said softly, her eyes closing of their own volition. "So much."

"I love you too," he said, kissing her forehead. "Sleep as long as you need to." His hands swept over her hair and back in long, tender strokes. "You have the rest of this weekend off, you hear me? Catching up on rest is what you need."

She fell into a blissfully deep sleep, glad to be in his embrace and to escape everything for even a short while.

Chapter Twenty-Five

Lisette spent the rest of the weekend in her room or out of the house, which was understandable, given Vanessa's presence. But Monday morning, Lisette was 100 percent back in action, getting the kids up and off to school. All week, Charles didn't know what Vanessa did with her time while the kids were at school, and he didn't care. But she was more than happy to let Lisette pick them all up and go through their homework with them, coming to the house around five o'clock every day for the fun parts and staying until bedtime.

As much as it pained Charles to admit it, the kids were happy. Having both women around, bathing in the affection and attention being showered on them, their collective change in mood and attitude was palpable. It hurt his heart, because he knew damn well that come December twenty-sixth, Vanessa would be gone again, and who knew when the kids would see her next?

On Wednesday night, by the time Charles got home from work, Lisette was upstairs overseeing the kids while they showered. He found Vanessa in the main living room, looking at framed photos on the mantel above the fireplace.

"Are you staying to put the kids to bed?" he asked curtly.

"Oh!" Vanessa jumped, startled. "I didn't hear you come in. Long day at the office, dear?"

"Yes, actually, it was." He took off his glasses, pulled a microfiber cloth from the inside pocket of his jacket, and wiped the lenses clean. "So my patience for you is thinner than usual."

Her eyes slid over him. "Always dressed like a gentleman, even at home. Do you wear your suit and tie right up until you go to bed?" she teased. "Or do you sleep in them too? You must; probably helps keep the stick up your ass firmly in place."

He shot her a withering look, then crossed the room. The small wet bar was half-hidden by the enormous Christmas tree. He reached for the scotch and poured himself a dram. "So I hear you're planning to be here for Christmas morning? Were you going to discuss that with me, since you invited yourself to my house?"

"About that . . ." She turned and walked slowly toward him. "Yes, I'd like to be here for that. I know you don't want me here, and I've been staying at the hotel every night like you demanded. But yes, I'd really like to be here on Christmas Eve and stay over, so I can wake up with the kids on Christmas morning." She bit down on her lip and added, "I haven't had that with them in a long time."

"Your own doing," he said. His tone conveyed no sympathy or tolerance.

"I know that." She shifted her weight from one foot to the other. "When I spoke to them on Thanksgiving, they all sounded so different . . . They're getting bigger. They're growing up. And I'm missing it all."

"Again, your choice."

"I know that! Just get off your high horse for two minutes and let me speak, okay?" Her pale green eyes flashed as she brushed her sleek black hair back over her shoulders. "I came here only because I missed them. You don't have to take shots at me every chance you get, Charles. I know I'm a shitty mother."

"A shitty mother?" He smirked with cool disdain. "You'd have to actually *be* a mother to even qualify as a shitty one." Raising the heavy glass to his lips, he took a swallow of scotch. She glared at him, obviously wanting to snap back, but holding her tongue. *Wow, she must really want whatever she's about to ask me for*. "What do you want, Vanessa? Just say it."

She drew a deep breath. "I'd like to sleep here on Christmas Eve, and stay for Christmas Day with the kids. And sleep over again that night. Then I'll leave on the twenty-sixth, like I said I would."

"Where are you off to then?" he asked. "Must have plans, or you wouldn't be so amenable to keeping your word."

"Saint Tropez," she admitted quietly.

"Ah! That sounds more like you." He took another sip, then loosened the knot of his tie. "I'll allow you to come here and stay over on Christmas Eve. Not for you, but for the children, because they'd love to have you here. I don't think Myles even remembers ever sharing a Christmas with you."

Color darkened her face. "I know."

He studied her, his head cocking to the side. "What's this really about, Vanessa? I feel as if I'm waiting for the other shoe to drop. Just cut to the chase, and maybe we can work out whatever it is you're really pushing for here."

She met his eyes. "I have no agenda, Charles."

"I don't believe that for a second," he ground out.

"My kids don't know me!" she cried. "That's my fault, yes. And I'm not saying I'm going to sue you for partial custody, or that I'm even moving back to New York. I'm not. I just want to see them more. That's all."

He set his glass down on the bar and walked to her, his eyes never leaving her face. "Why do you suddenly care about the kids? You never have before."

"That's not true," she whispered. "I've always loved them. I care. I just . . . wanted to do other things. Staying here with them when they were little . . . I was bored out of my mind, Charles." She crossed her arms over her chest. "You were at work all the time, sucking up to your father, getting ready to inherit the crown. I was here, with two and then three babies, going insane. I'm not . . ." She scowled, shifted her weight. "I'm not the 'mommy' type. I'm not good with babies. I'm better with bigger kids, where you can actually talk to them, you know?"

"No. I don't know. Your kids are your kids." He hoped he sounded lethal, but some things she said resonated more than he wanted to admit. She sounded an awful lot like his mother, thirty years before. He'd heard the arguments between his parents. He was the oldest; when his parents divorced and Laura was basically banished from her kids' lives, Charles had already been fourteen. He'd heard her say eerily similar things to his father, on more than one occasion. It made his stomach churn. "You can stay for Christmas Eve and Christmas Day. I host Christmas Eve, so we'll all be here, and you'll have to deal with the rest of my family. Christmas morning, you can be here with the kids. But we go to dinner at my father's, around three o'clock. You really want to see *all* the Harrisons, by all means join us."

She visibly shuddered. "Think I'll take a pass on that. I can have dinner here by myself. Then I can see the kids after they get home from your father's, since I'll be leaving the next day."

"Do what you want." He strode back to the bar, grabbed his glass, and knocked back the rest. "It's been a long day, Vanessa. Help Lisette put the kids to bed, then leave." He started to walk out of the living room.

"Charles," Vanessa said.

He turned to look at her, an eyebrow arched, waiting.

"Thank you," she said.

She actually seemed sincere. It didn't matter if she was or not. He was being magnanimous for the kids, not for her. "Good night, Vanessa."

He left the living room, turned, and almost smacked right into Lisette. "Hey, hi."

"Hi," she said softly. "I wasn't eavesdropping. I came down to tell Vanessa the kids are ready for bed, but I couldn't find her."

With a flick of his chin, he gestured back over his shoulder. "She's in there."

"I figured, when I heard your voices."

"Any news back from the doctor yet?" he asked, dropping his voice so Vanessa couldn't hear. "The test results?"

She shook her head, but a hint of color bloomed on her cheeks. "Nope. Still waiting."

Her blushes were her tell. Was she holding out on him? He had a gut feeling she wasn't telling him something, and his gut rarely steered him wrong.

"I got a dress today," she whispered. "It's . . . extravagant."

"For the gala?" He couldn't hold back his smile. "Can't wait to see it. I bet it's gorgeous, and you'll be stunning."

"If I'm not hyperventilating," she said. "I'm so nervous about going . . . You know I hate crowds, much less something like this."

"Don't be nervous. I'll be right there with you. It's going to be great."

She gazed at him. "You're really ready to tell the world about us?"

"Hell yes." He reached up to grab the end of her long braid and curled the end around his finger. Leaning in closer, he whispered in her ear, "I'll text you when I know Vanessa has left the house. So you can come to my room."

She grinned and bit down on her lip. "Sounds good."

* * *

The night before the ball, Charles made Vanessa wait alone in the den and took the kids up to his bedroom. "I need to talk to you guys," he told them. "It's important, and it's kind of private. You guys can keep a secret for tonight, right?"

"Sure we can!" Myles yelped, excitement in his eyes.

"You can't keep a secret to save your life," Thomas sniffed.

"I can too!" Myles insisted as they got to the top of the second staircase.

"No, you can't," Thomas retorted.

"Don't fight," Charles said calmly.

"Is everything okay, Daddy?" Ava asked.

He glanced at her. She looked apprehensive. "Yes, sweetie, everything's fine. I promise. Come on." He ushered the three kids down the hall, into his room, and closed the door behind them. Lisette stood in the middle of the room, twisting her hands. He tossed her a wink, meant to reassure. He could almost see the waves of nervousness coming off of her.

"What's going on?" Ava asked.

"Sit down, you guys," Charles said, nudging them toward the wide loveseat beside the window. He pulled the chair from the corner over so Lisette could sit facing them, and sat on the arm of the chair. "Everyone comfortable?"

"Are we in trouble for something?" Thomas asked, looking from one adult to the other.

"Is this about Mom?" Ava asked.

"No, and no," Charles said firmly. "Everything's fine. It's really good, actually." He took a deep breath, gazing at his three kids. *Please God, let this go well.* "Lisette and I just wanted to tell you something."

"The thing is," Lisette said, her voice a little higher and more breathless than usual, "we have some news, and we wanted you guys to be the first ones to know."

"Awesome!" Myles chirped.

"You don't even know what it is," Thomas said, rolling his eyes at his little brother.

"But we're the first!" Myles said. "I like that."

Ava sat silently, her eyes filled with worry.

"So . . . about two months ago," Charles began, "Um . . . Lisette and I started spending a little time together. In a way that was different than usual. Because we . . . started becoming friends. I really like her, and she likes me. We get along well, and—"

"Are you like boyfriend-girlfriend now?" Ava cried, eyes wide.

Lisette laughed softly, even as she blushed. She looked to Charles.

He nodded as he grinned at the kids. "Well, yes, actually. We are. And I know that may be a little confusing, since Lisette is your nanny. But we . . . we're going to be together, but we wanted you three to know first."

"This . . . is weird," Thomas said, looking from one to the other.

"I think it's romantic," Ava said, a smile tugging at the corners of her mouth.

"What do you know about romance, young lady?" Charles demanded jokingly.

"I know things," Ava said. She stared at them. "I . . . I like this. If you two are happy, then I'm happy."

Lisette's breath caught, and she looked up at Charles in wonder.

"Sometimes," Charles marveled at his daughter, "you seem like you're nineteen instead of nine, I swear."

"I'm not confused at all," Myles proclaimed with a big smile. "I get two mommies now."

Charles and Lisette were both dumbstruck. Before they could say anything, Myles hopped up from the loveseat and flung himself at Lisette, hugging her. "I already love you, so this is great!"

Lisette's eyes closed as her arms wrapped around the boy. Tears slid down her cheeks. "I love you too," she whispered against his ear.

Charles was so moved, he didn't think he could speak.

"I don't need a replacement mom. Is that what this is going to be like?" Thomas said.

"What?" Charles blinked. "No. We're not getting married or anything; we only just started dating seriously a few weeks ago."

"You've been dating for weeks," Thomas said, "and you're only telling us now?"

"Because we wanted to wait," Charles said, "to make sure this was going to work. Going to be something serious enough to share with others. Do you understand?"

"No, and I don't care." Thomas stood up and headed for the door. "Can I go now?"

"No," Charles said to his son, springing up. "Wait, please."

"Why?" Thomas scowled. "You're together, okay, fine. Why does it have to be a big secret?"

"Well, it doesn't, really," Charles hedged, "now that you three know. But, um . . ."

"Thomas." Lisette released Myles, brushed away her tears quickly, and went to him. "There are some people who might think this situation is as weird as you do. And they may not be very nice about it."

"Like who?" Thomas asked.

Like my father, Charles thought. *Like the snotty moms of your friends at school. Like maybe even some of your friends*. This was what Lisette had been worrying about. Why hadn't that fully hit him before now? Why hadn't he listened?

"Like people who think a man as busy as your father," Lisette said, "shouldn't be making time for someone like me."

"What does that mean?" Thomas said, his growing frustration obvious.

"It means snobby people," Ava said. "I've seen movies and TV shows. Even when the girl from the streets gets the prince, people are mean to her about it."

"Well, I'm not from the streets," Lisette said, slightly amused. "And I can handle it if people are mean to me. I don't want them to say things that might hurt *you guys*, though. That's what worries me."

Ava shrugged. "I'll ignore them. I don't like mean people."

"And I'll beat 'em up!" Myles said, flying into his best ninja moves.

Lisette looked at Thomas. "Honey . . ." She knelt before him. "You look angry. Are you?"

"A little bit," he said, looking at the floor.

"Can you tell me why?"

He shrugged.

"Tell me," Lisette coaxed gently. "Go ahead."

"Our mom left because she didn't want to be our mom," he grumbled. "If you become our mom, and we're bad, are you going to want to leave too?"

"Why would you think that?" Lisette asked, her tone still gentle and calm. She placed her hand on the boy's shoulder.

"Well, if you're our nanny, you have to stay because Daddy pays you to," Thomas said. "But if you become our new mom, you don't have to stay if you don't want to. Our real mom didn't. Why would you?"

Charles swallowed hard, the lump in his throat lodged so tightly he could barely breathe. His eyes stung. But he managed to say, "Your mom didn't leave because of anything you kids did, Thomas. She, uh . . ." He cleared his throat. "She and I weren't right for each other. And she . . .

was overwhelmed, so she thought it would be better for you kids if she wasn't around. She was doing it *for* you."

Thomas's eyes welled with tears. "I don't believe you."

"She's downstairs," Lisette said quietly. "Why don't we go talk with her? I think if you said some of these things you've been thinking, and hear some answers from her, it might make you feel a lot better."

Thomas's eyes flew wide, and he shook his head. "No, I don't want to upset her. She'll leave again, and next week is Christmas. We haven't had a Christmas with her since . . . well, I don't remember."

"She won't leave before Christmas," Charles said gruffly. "I promise."

Thomas looked at Lisette. "Everything was fine the way it was. Why does it have to change?"

"Sweetheart," Lisette said, almost in a whisper. "I love you kids. More than you can imagine. All I can promise you is *that* will never change."

"Even if you and Daddy break up?" Thomas challenged.

"Even then," Charles said. "That hopefully won't happen, but even if it doesn't work out between us, she will still be your nanny, and still be in your lives. I promise. Okay?"

Thomas looked at his father, then back at Lisette. "This is weird," he whispered.

"I know. But maybe a little bit good weird?" Lisette said hopefully.

A long pause . . . then Thomas nodded. "Maybe."

"Can I hug you?" she asked him.

He nodded again. She wrapped him in her embrace and hugged.

Myles ran and jumped into Charles's arms, and Charles gave a little laugh as he did. He looked over to his daughter. "Ava? Are you okay?"

"I'm fine," she said, rising from the loveseat. "I think it's awesome. Lisette's already like part of the family. Now she really can be, right?"

"Come here, you." Charles held out an arm to Ava, who went to him and nestled into his side.

Thomas untangled himself from Lisette's embrace. "Does Mommy know about your being boyfriend-girlfriend? Or is that why you want us to keep it a secret for tonight?"

"Kind of," Charles admitted. "But you know what? If you feel you want to talk about it with her, go ahead."

"Nah," Thomas shrugged. "She already doesn't like Lisette. I'm not going to make her any madder."

Charles heaved a hard sigh. "Okay then." He looked over the kids' heads to Lisette, who was wiping tears from her face. He shot her a small smile. She only stared back at him, glassy-eyed and flushed, unreadable.

"I'm going to go lie down for a while," Lisette said to them all. "I know your mom's waiting downstairs; maybe I'll take a little nap while you hang out with her."

The kids, seemingly fine, left Charles's room and went back down to Vanessa. Charles closed the door as Lisette headed for it, gripping her shoulders. "Talk to me."

"I'm on overload," she whispered. "I need to lie down; I wasn't kidding."

"My bed's right there," he said, flicking his chin in its direction.

She looked over at it, then back up at him. Her eyes filled with fresh tears. "Too much too soon," she said, sniffling. "I need to process the things they said. I mean . . . God, Charles, did you hear him?"

"I thought I'd burst into tears there for a minute," he admitted roughly.

"I couldn't hold mine in," she whispered. "That poor, sweet boy."

He pulled her in, holding her close. "He's been thinking

those things, hurting that badly, all this time, and I had no idea what was in his head. Jesus, Lisette, I'm a terrible father."

"No, you're not," she said, letting her arms circle his waist. "But do you realize what you promised them? Even if we don't work out, you promised I'd always stay. We can't promise them that."

"I said what you did."

"No, no, you didn't. I promised them I'd always love them, because that's a promise I can keep." She pulled back. "People do leave, Charles."

"You're not leaving," he whispered fiercely.

"You say that now . . ." She shook her head, a new wave of exhaustion almost making her sway. "I need to lie down right now. I'm not kidding."

He slid an arm around her and walked her to his bed. "Here. I'll make sure no one bothers you."

Too tired to argue, she lay down. "Go be with them," she said. "In case Vanessa says or does anything, you need to be there."

"You're right." He stared down at her and shoved his hands into his pockets. "Are you okay?"

"I'll be fine."

"Are we okay?"

"We'll be fine." Her eyes slipped closed.

He sighed. "That wasn't as bad as it could've been . . . Ava is happy about it, and Myles is excited."

"They're all precious." The corners of Lisette's mouth curved up. "He has to understand I'm not another mom, but he is so adorable."

Charles watched over her. Within sixty seconds, her breathing grew slower and deeper, and he knew she was asleep. She hadn't been kidding; she'd fallen asleep so fast . . . Feeling weighed down by the world, he flopped onto the loveseat. He watched Lisette sleep as his children's words echoed in his head, and hoped to God he'd done right by them, and by her. Because if he had moved too soon, out of what he thought was optimism but was actually arrogance and willfulness, and someone ended up hurt, he'd never forgive himself.

Chapter Twenty-Six

Lisette stared out the window of the limousine at the frenetic scene as they pulled up in front of the Waldorf Astoria. There were so many people, all dressed up. Flashbulbs went off, and paparazzi called to some of the more famous party-goers as they entered the iconic, magnificent hotel.

So many people. Too many. Glitzy, powerful people. Ugh, she didn't belong here. How the hell had she let Charles talk her into this?

"Exciting?" he murmured in her ear. "Or overwhelming?"

"Both," she admitted. She cleared her dry throat and tried to smile.

"Shit, you look terrified." His arm slid around her shoulders to pull her into his side, and he kissed her temple. "We can go home right now if you want."

"No, you have to be here. It's your family's event."

"I can do whatever I want. If I want to leave, I leave."

"Tess is counting on your being here," Lisette pointed out.

At that, he paused. "That's true."

"You're not going to let her down because I'm a scaredy-cat."

He smiled and kissed Lisette's cheek, mindful of not

ruining her lipstick. "I'll be right by your side the whole time, scaredy-cat. Your hand in mine. All right?"

She nodded and gazed at him. Few men could wear an Armani tux like Charles did. He was breathtakingly handsome. No glasses tonight, he wore his contacts, and his blue eyes were sparkling with anticipation. She reached up to touch the few silver glints in his dark wavy hair, peppered around his ears. He disliked them; she adored them. She drew a shaky breath. "This is crazy."

"Hey. Any time you feel like a fish out of water tonight," he said, "please remember that I love you." He drew her in for a hug.

She closed her eyes and drank in his affection. *Will you still feel the same when I tell you about the baby?* She wanted to believe he would, but she was anxious. Her nerves felt like jangling live wires tonight.

"Come on," he said. "Let's get this party started."

Charles exited the limo, extending his hand down to Lisette to help her out. She emerged like a vision, a movie star. The dark green chiffon gown she wore was simple, elegant, and striking—just like her. Small cap sleeves, scoop neckline, an A-line cut that flattered her figure, swirling around her ankles with feminine grace . . . He'd never seen her look more beautiful. At the house, when she'd come down the stairs, ready to leave for the ball, he had not been able to stop staring.

Now, Charles grasped Lisette's hand in his as they walked into the Waldorf. Flashes went off, and he ignored them, only focusing on her. He wanted to make sure her jitters didn't get the best of her. He was used to this kind of thing, but it was all new to her, and she didn't like crowds under normal conditions, much less a circus like this. He squeezed her hand protectively. "You okay?" he asked her as they walked through the grandiose lobby.

"So far so good," she said, squeezing his hand back as she looked around.

He reached up to touch her hair, down and loose in flowing curls, then stroked her soft cheek. "I have a surprise for you later, by the way."

Her eyes danced as she insisted, "Give me a hint."

"Then it wouldn't be a surprise."

"Does it involve sweets? You know how I love sweet things . . ."

He kissed her cheek, then whispered in her ear, "You're the only sweet thing I intend to devour tonight."

She shivered and her breath caught. "Oh, my."

Grinning wickedly, he pulled back and took her hand once more. "Come on."

They followed the din to make their way to the tremendous ballroom. The lively buzz of more than five hundred guests talking filled the huge, magnificent hall. Charles scoured the room as they entered. It was already almost filled with guests, dressed to kill in their finest. Near the entrance stood Tess, Dane, and Julia. Dane was in a tux, Julia in a deep sapphire dress that hugged her voluptuous curves, and Tess, in a silver gown, stood and sparkled like the elegant, graceful hostess she was.

"Ah, the welcoming riffraff, I see," Charles said as he and Lisette approached them. He watched the split second of surprise that washed across all of their faces. Then Tess, God bless her, moved forward to grasp both of Lisette's hands with a dazzling smile on her face. "You look stunning. I almost didn't recognize you! Welcome."

"Thank you," Lisette murmured as Tess kissed her cheeks.

"'Stunning' understates it," Dane said, charming as ever. He flashed his famous smile and lifted Lisette's hand to his lips. "Belle of the ball, that's you. Well, you and my wife. And my sister. It's a tough call."

Lisette blushed and thanked him.

"That dress is goooorgeous," Julia gushed after she kissed Charles hello. She stood back to look Lisette over from head to toe. "It's perfect on you. And that color! It's like this steely green, not hunter, not olive, with a silvery cast . . . I love it. Where'd you find it?"

"Um, Nordstrom, actually," Lisette said. Charles could see she was both slightly uncomfortable and flattered at the same time. It was adorable.

"You win. You totally win." Julia turned her sharp gaze to Charles. "No, *you* win. You're a lucky man."

"I know it," Charles agreed. He glanced down at Lisette, who'd visibly relaxed at his siblings' warm welcome. "Where are Pierce and Abby? Are they here yet?"

"They're here somewhere," Tess said. "Getting a drink or something."

He moved forward to hug his sister. Standing more than six feet tall in her Louboutin stilettos, shimmering in her sparkly dress, Tess was more than stunning herself. "This is a major triumph you pulled off here. Congratulations on your success."

"Thank you so much." She pulled back and smiled brightly. "Gotta admit, I am feeling like a queen tonight."

"You should," Charles said. "Tonight, you *are* the queen. Relish it."

"Really outdid yourself this year, Tesstastic," Dane said.

"Thanks." Tess beamed at their praise. "I worked my ass off."

"Any totals yet?" Charles asked her, referring to the charitable donations for the function.

"Already looks like we topped last year," Tess pronounced. "By at least 2 million. I'll know exact figures tomorrow."

"Got my check, right?" Charles inquired.

"Of course. You didn't have to do that, you know." Tess shook her head at him, but her eyes lit like starshine. "Very, very generous."

"More than I sent?" Dane teased. He mock sneered at his brother. "Goddamn COO, throwing your weight around."

"Not my weight," Charles joked. "My funds. If not for charity, then what for?"

"Thank you both," Tess said to her brothers. "Neither of you ever have to contribute, and you always do. I appreciate it. The foundation appreciates it."

A waiter floated by, holding a tray of crystal flutes filled with champagne. They each took a glass; Charles took two, handing one to Lisette. She eyed it strangely, but he raised his glass and said, "A toast. To another fabulous Harrison Foundation success, masterminded by the unique, brilliant, amazing Tess Alexandra."

"Hear hear!" Dane cried jovially, and they all clinked glasses.

Charles noticed that Lisette took such a tiny sip, it was as if no champagne even passed her lips. But before he could say anything, Julia asked him, "Charles? Dane doesn't think Pierce and Abby are going to Christmas dinner at your father's. Do you know for sure?"

"Oh, they're not," Tess confirmed. "They'll be with Abby's family for the day."

"Does that surprise anyone?" Charles asked. "But they'll be at my house for Christmas Eve. He promised. He wants to see everyone, but he's already splitting his time with Abby's family."

"I've never seen him this happy," Tess gushed. "It's wonderful, isn't it?"

"Long overdue," Dane said. "And Abby's fantastic."

"She's always been very sweet to me," Lisette chimed in. "Pierce too, really. I'm happy for them. They make a fantastic couple."

Charles leaned in and kissed her forehead.

"Speaking of happy," Dane ventured, "you two look pretty smitten. So . . . you're here, out in public. Just fess up. Totally together?"

Lisette blushed and looked up to Charles. He met her gaze, smiled softly, then turned to the others. "She's the best thing that's happened to me in a long time. We told the kids last night. So, now it's time to let the world know that I'm a lucky man, and she's all mine."

Lisette blushed, but she couldn't hide the brightness of her smile.

Tess grasped her by the hand and said, "You make my brother happy. You don't know what that means to me." She kissed Lisette on the cheek. "I'm happy for you both. Glad that you found each other. You're both lovely, and I wish you luck."

"Thank you so much," Lisette murmured, visibly moved. "He makes me happy too."

Charles saw the glimmer in her deep brown eyes, and it warmed him right down to his toes. Then something occurred to him; he leaned over to Dane and whispered, "Where's Dad?"

"Around here somewhere." Dane subtly pulled him aside. "He's gonna flip the fuck out about you and Lisette. We all know that."

"I don't care," Charles said. "I just don't want a repeat of what he did to Pierce and Abby at your party last year. I don't think he'd dare, but I want to keep her away from him tonight just in case."

"Good idea." Dane squeezed his shoulder. "I've got your back. And hers. No worries."

No worries. When it came to their father, Charles knew better.

* * *

The evening was going much better than Lisette had thought it would. Charles introduced her to everyone he saw with such pride and affection in his voice, it made her heart squeeze each and every time. The four Harrison siblings were working the room, pressing the flesh with guests and being the famous host family that they were. While they did, Lisette got to eat unbelievably delicious food and chat with Abby. When Charles returned to her, he immediately pulled her into his arms and dropped a light kiss on her lips. He greeted Abby, then offered Lisette an apologetic smile. "Sorry I was gone for so long."

"Don't be," she said. "Abby has been wonderful company."

His smile grew as he nodded at them. "I'm sure she has. Excuse us a moment, though, Abby?" He put an arm around Lisette's waist and pulled her off to the side, behind a tremendous vase that overflowed with flowers in all shades of red. "How are you?" he asked. "Enjoying this at all?"

"I am, actually," she said, surprising both of them. "I mean, it's a wonderful party. Obviously, I've never been to anything like this in my life. The grandeur of it . . . I love looking at all the dresses, the people . . . I feel like I'm at the Oscars or something."

He chuckled and kissed her forehead. "I'm glad you're having a good time."

"I'm glad too." Her fingertips played along the silver glints in his hair, then curved around his ear before she pressed her mouth to his. "But when can we go home?"

"We're not going home tonight," he said.

She blinked at him. "What?"

"The surprise I mentioned earlier?" His blues sparkled as he grinned. "I reserved a room for us. We're staying here tonight." His hand lifted to caress her cheek. "You mentioned you'd never been here before, and I promised you we'd make up for lost time and for your not having any hot hotel sex, so I took the liberty . . ."

"Charles." He was being sweet, and maybe she was being oversensitive, but she suddenly felt she needed to set him straight. "You don't have to keep taking me to fancy places, getting me gifts . . ." She held his face and stared into his eyes, those stunning blue eyes she adored. "Listen to me. This is important."

"You have my undivided attention." He nodded solemnly.

She brushed her lips against his. "I love you for *you*. I don't care about your money. If you lost it all tomorrow, I wouldn't care. I know full well you're used to extravagance, but I'm not. So you don't have to keep doing things for me, getting me things, taking me places . . . I really need to know that you know that."

"I *do* know that," he said, low and somber. Both his arms banded around her waist. "But that's one of the reasons doing these things is so fun. I know you appreciate it." He kissed her long and sweet, sipping from her lips. "I have to go check in with my father, just show my face. Then maybe we'll get out of here. Okay?"

"Sure. Why don't you go do that," Lisette suggested, "and I'll take a little walk. I want to look around this palace of a place more anyway."

"That's not a bad idea." He lowered his head and kissed her softly. "Meet you back here in half an hour? I mean, it might take me ten minutes just to get through this crowd and reach him."

She watched him go, making his way through the sea of partygoers. She'd only verbalized out loud what he hadn't said and hadn't wanted to say: that he needed to see his father without her at his side. He'd been fine, even happy, to out their relationship to his siblings, but apparently wasn't ready to tell his father. Part of her was relieved, because she was sure when Charles's father found out about them, he'd be livid. But now that they'd told the kids, part of her couldn't help but wonder if Charles was still keeping her a secret for another reason, other than just sparing her a snob's wrath.

She watched Charles, midway through the crowd, shake hands and chat with a refined looking couple, a tuxedoed older man and a glamorous woman in a sparkling gown. Charles was dashing and self-assured, the very picture of sophistication, wealth, and power, completely in his element. This was his world. Lisette felt very much out of her element, and hoped she'd done a good job of hiding that. Despite her fancy dress and Charles's sweet words, nothing would ever make her feel as if she fit in with these people.

And she had to wonder if maybe, seeing her in his world tonight, outside the escapist privacy of the mansion . . . Charles knew that too.

She'd been telling the truth when she told Charles she wanted to see more of the hotel. It was such a beautiful place, and she was eager to explore the opulent décor, the exquisite architecture, the grandeur of the famous building. Her mood shifted again to a lighter, better one.

Before meeting Charles again, she ducked into the ladies' room closest to the ballroom. It was probably the most beautiful bathroom she'd ever been in. As she exited a stall and went to wash her hands, she couldn't help but overhear two women talking in the sitting room nearby.

"I mean, it's just so disappointing," the first woman said in a snarky, nasal tone.

"I know," the second woman agreed, her tone equally haughty. "One of the most eligible bachelors in the country, and he's taken up with *her?*"

Lisette froze where she stood. They couldn't possibly be talking about Charles and her, could they? No, she was just being paranoid. She reached for a thick paper towel to dry her hands.

"I guess he has a thing for exotic brunettes," the first woman quipped. "Remember his ex-wife? She was a bitch on wheels, but one of the most beautiful women I've ever seen."

"Well, when you've got a pretty young thing right there under your roof," the second woman said, "why wouldn't you take advantage?"

"Another one falls prey to the nanny," the first one said, disdain dripping from her words. "It's such a cliché, it's painful."

A wave of coldness swept over Lisette, and her stomach rolled nauseously. Jesus, they *were* talking about her and Charles. Oh, God. What to do? She stood motionless.

"To think I busted my ass in law school," the first one said. "I should've just been a nanny like the rest of these women; they're obviously smarter than me. Fuck your boss; take the money and run."

The second woman laughed, a brittle, hollow sound. "Really. When we hired our nanny, I made sure she was old and ugly. I wasn't taking any chances."

"Well, Charles isn't married, so he can do whatever he wants," the first woman pointed out. "It's just a shame. A man like him, wasted on some nobody. He's still so handsome, don't you think?"

"Oh my God, yes. He's aging like a fine wine. But men like that always do."

Lisette closed her eyes and braced her icy, tingling hands on the marble sink.

"I heard she's worked there for two years already," the first woman said. "Took her time, but damn, she's clever. Ingratiating herself with the children . . ."

"That's what I hate—when they pretend to care about the kids!" the second woman exclaimed. "It's shameful, how these nannies pretend to care, just to get close to a rich man. Charles is such a smart man, how does he not see that?"

"Well, he didn't with his ex-wife either. For a smart man,

he's dumb about women." The first woman exhaled a dramatic sigh. "Hell, she'll probably get more by spreading for him than I'll make this whole decade. Come on, you ready to go back?"

Lisette stood, trembling, waiting for the sound of silence for a full thirty seconds before venturing to the sitting room, empty now. In a daze she sank down on one of the three couches. The room was elegant and beautiful, like everything and everyone in the hotel. So beautiful . . . Her chest was tight, her heart was pounding, and she couldn't catch her breath.

She had known there would be gossip about her and Charles being together once they went public. She had just never thought she'd actually hear it firsthand, or this soon. Closing her eyes, she tried to draw deep breaths.

This would never work.

She'd been fooling herself, wanting to believe the dreamy tale Charles spun of their having a future together. Being with him wasn't only bad for her; it was bad for him. Her being with Charles would make him the target of snarky gossip amongst his colleagues and friends . . . She couldn't do that to him. And honestly, she didn't know if she had it in her to hear that kind of poison, or be put in a defensive position, on a regular basis. Pretending to care about the kids? She loved them as much as if they were hers. If anyone ever cast doubt on that and made the kids think even for a second that her affection for them wasn't genuine . . . She felt sick.

The awful truth hit her like a physical blow. If people thought this of her *now*, what would they think and say when they found out she was pregnant? What kind of backlash would Charles have to deal with? How long before his forbidden girlfriend wasn't so fun to be naughty with anymore, and was more of a serious burden to deal with?

Tears stung her eyes, and she sniffed them back.

The only thing that made sense now was the plan she'd formulated when she and Charles had first started seeing each other. She had to leave the mansion, find her own home, establish herself separately from Charles and the children. It was the only way she could keep her job, and him, and prove that she wasn't in this for money or power. She also had to tell Charles about the baby. They had a lot of serious talking to do, and she had a bad feeling about how that would go.

Chapter Twenty-Seven

"There you are!" Charles greeted Lisette with a wide smile and a kiss on the cheek. "I was starting to wonder if you'd blown me off," he added jokingly.

She didn't crack a smile. "Charles . . . we need to talk."

He stared down at her, his blood seeming to slow in his veins. "Well, that's never good," he said. "Not when it's said like that." He peered harder at her. She didn't look right. His gut hummed with dread. "What's wrong?"

"We just really need to talk," she repeated. "Privately."

He took her by the hand. "Come on. The room is ours whenever we want it. No time like the present."

"Don't you need to say good-bye to Tess?" Lisette asked. "Or your brothers?"

"I'll call them later. Let's go."

Ten minutes later, Charles opened the door to the luxurious suite he'd reserved for the night. Lisette walked in slowly, taking in her surroundings in quiet awe. The sitting room was lovely, with the bedroom just beyond. "It's gorgeous," she murmured.

"I wanted nothing but the best for you," he said quietly.

She eyed the two small suitcases against the wall. Charles had told her that he'd had bags packed for them, clothes to change into tomorrow. He'd thought of everything, and he thought she'd be glad. But from the middle of the sitting room, she turned to face him. Her wringing hands were another giveaway: something was wrong.

"Talk to me," he urged. He stuffed his hands in the pockets of his slacks and tried to seem at ease, despite the uneasy churning of his stomach.

"I . . . need to tell you some things," she said. She drew a shaky breath, then her chin lifted a notch. "I'm going to move out of the mansion."

He blinked. "What? Why?"

"Because I think I should have my own space," she said. Her voice was calm and even, which unnerved him even more. "I'm not quitting my job. But I need not to live under your roof. Not with the way things are now. I'll find a place nearby, so I can be at the house early and stay all day, until they're asleep—"

"No. Just no. This is ridiculous," he said, feeling a muscle twitch under his eye. "You'll do no such thing. Where the hell is this coming from?"

"Please let me finish," she said quietly. Her face was flushed, but the look in her eyes was pure determination. "There's more."

Charles's heart started thumping in heavier beats. "Go on."

"I, um . . ." Her eyes slipped closed for the briefest second, then focused again. "I think we should stop seeing each other."

"Lisette," he said gruffly, "what the hell is going on?"

"Reality set in," she murmured.

"Bullshit," he spat. "Something happened tonight, and you're not telling me. I can't fix it if I don't know what happened."

"You can't fix this one," she said. "And I wasn't even done yet."

"Yes, you are. I won't hear any more of this." He crossed

the space between them in three long strides and gripped her shoulders. "I love you. And you said you love me. Whatever happened, we'll deal with it together. Don't shut me out."

Her eyes widened, and spots of high color bloomed on her cheeks, but she shook her head in resignation. "You need to let me do this. I'm not quitting the job."

"But you're quitting *us*," he said. "You expect me to just go along with that?"

"You have to." Her eyes fell away.

"Why, goddammit?" He wanted to shake her. "*I love you. And I love having you in my home. I don't want you to leave.*"

"I have to. So I can prove to you," she ground out, "and everyone else, that I do my job because I love it, and that I'm not beholden to you for anything other than the job. That I'm not some . . . hired in-house whore."

He gaped at her in confusion. "What. Happened. Tonight?"

"I've been thinking about this for a while."

"You've never mentioned it, never even hinted at anything like this. So, again," he growled, losing patience. "Why?"

"I'm pregnant," she said.

He stilled, hands still on her shoulders. His eyes locked with hers.

She licked her lips and met his searing gaze. "I went to the doctor, like I promised. Turns out I'm not sick or dying. I'm pregnant."

Charles didn't move. "You . . ." His head cocked slightly. "I thought you said you couldn't get pregnant. That you couldn't have children."

"Because that's what I thought," she said. "That's what all the doctors told me. But . . ." She swallowed again, trying to dislodge the lump that felt like a rock in her throat. "I went to the doctor last week and, as it turns out, I'm pregnant."

"You've known for days and didn't tell me?"

The note of disbelief in his voice made her wince. "I wanted to, Charles. I just needed to really process it for myself first. I was going to tell you later tonight."

He continued to stare. She could practically hear all the thoughts and questions bouncing around in his brain. "It's mine, of course," he finally said.

She nodded. It was hard to breathe.

"How far along are you?" he asked.

"Nine weeks," she whispered.

His eyes widened. "That first time . . . ?"

She nodded again.

He rubbed his jaw slowly, absorbing the news. Then his eyes softened, and his hands lifted to cup her face. "Are you all right?" he asked gently. "You're healthy? And the baby too?"

Hot tears sprang to her eyes, and her throat thickened so she couldn't speak. She nodded yet again.

"You must have been more shocked than I am," he said, his voice like velvet.

A sob burst from her mouth, and she clapped her hand over it. Tears rolled down her cheeks, and she nodded vehemently.

He pulled her into his arms and nudged her head to rest on his chest. She cried and clung to him as if she were falling over a cliff and he was her lifeline. "I thought it had to be a mistake," she said between sobs. "I was convinced I was sick, like my mother . . . I mean, what else could it be? When he said I was pregnant, I didn't believe it and went back for more tests." Sniffling, she pulled back enough to look into Charles's eyes. "But there it was, on the ultrasound. A baby. I heard its heartbeat, Charles. And that just . . ." She dissolved into more sobs.

"Oh, honey." He wiped her tears away with gentle hands. "Shhhh. Everything's going to be all right."

She gaped at him as she tried to calm herself. "You're not angry?"

"Angry?" He looked at her as if she were crazy. "I'm stunned, I'm in shock, but why would I be angry?"

She couldn't process his reaction. He wasn't angry. But what did he think of her? "I didn't lie to you, Charles," she said, sniffing back the tears. "I didn't think I could get pregnant. I didn't trick you. You have to believe me."

"What? Of course I believe you!" he said. "Wait a minute. Is *that* why you didn't tell me right away?"

She nodded sheepishly. "Partly. And I . . . well, like I said, I was in shock."

"That's understandable." He wiped her damp face again. "This . . . wow. It's incredible. Sweetheart, you must be so happy. Are you happy?"

"Yes, of course!" she said. "The doctors were so sure I'd never have children! It just doesn't make sense that this baby even exists."

"It was meant to be," Charles murmured. His gentle smile melted her heart. "When are you due?" he asked.

"July. July thirteenth."

"Another summer baby. Okay then." He grinned. "Thomas's birthday is at the end of July, and Ava's is in August. I'm a pro at summer birthdays. No sweat."

She pulled back, wiping her wet face. "You're really okay with this?"

"Lisette." He tried to smile, but there was hesitation, and she sensed it. "Right now, my main concern is making sure you and the baby are both healthy. With your history . . . I'm going to find specialists first thing tomorrow, if that's all right with you."

"Sure, if you want," she said. She looked around the room; a box of tissues was on the elaborate cherrywood desk. He waited as she wiped her face, blew her nose, and took some deep breaths.

"Now," he ventured, "about your moving out. I don't understand why you think you have to leave. Especially if you're pregnant . . . I want you closer than ever, so I can keep an eye on you and the baby."

The nasty conversation between the two women resounded in her head. "I don't think it's a good idea for me to stay there. It's bad enough that you're sleeping with your nanny, but when it gets out that I'm pregnant, too? Charles . . ."

"That's crap. That's not it," he said tersely, then pinned her with a forceful look. "When I find out who said or did something to upset you tonight," he said in a low, lethal tone, "I'm going to make them regret they ever even looked your way. And honey, I *will* find out."

A chill ran over her skin. *That* was the Charles Harrison III the rest of the world saw, and it was both striking and intimidating.

"As for us not seeing each other anymore," he continued, "if you're pregnant, why the hell would we stop seeing each other? That makes absolutely no sense. Make me understand."

Her breath caught and stuck in her chest. "I . . ." The now-familiar hormone-induced exhaustion after a good cry was taking over her system. "Can we talk about that more later? I honestly need to lie down. I feel like I could fall down. It hits me hard lately."

She could feel the frustration bubbling underneath his cool surface. But he held a hand out in the direction of the bedroom. "Please, go ahead."

She walked into the bedroom and gasped softly. Low light reflected off the cream-colored walls, and a king-sized bed covered in a luxurious duvet and ornate throw pillows called to her. "What a beautiful room."

He leaned against the doorframe, his eyes canvassing the space before going back to her. "Lisette. This conversation is far from over. You know that, right?"

She nodded. "I just get so tired lately; when it hits like this, I can't even think."

"Okay." He scratched his head as he said slowly, "You know . . . a lot of little things make sense now," he said.

"What do you mean?" She slipped off her shoes and went to the bed. Running her hand over the soft bedding, she could feel the high quality in the threads.

"Your falling asleep, repeatedly, at strange hours. The look on your face when I handed you the champagne tonight." His mouth quirked. "You looked at it like I'd handed you a glass of toxic waste."

She couldn't help but giggle. "Yeah, I can't drink for a while."

"And in Aspen . . ." He watched her climb onto the mattress and lie down. "When you threw up. That wasn't low blood pressure, you little liar. Was it?"

"No," she admitted. "But at that point, I didn't know what was going on. And you looked worried, and I didn't want you to worry."

"That's you. You're always thinking of the other person." He walked to the bed and stood at the foot of it, gazing down at her. "But right now, even if you think you're doing right somehow by trying to end what we have? It's the first selfish move you've made, my dear."

Her stomach did a wavy little roll. "No, it's not. I'm not being selfish. I'm . . . God, I don't know how to get through to you, how to explain what I'm trying to do here so you'll understand. Sometimes you're so set on what you want that you don't listen. And I . . ." She yawned.

"You look drained. I'm not going to push you tonight." His jaw set as he held her eyes. "But tomorrow, you're going to tell me what happened here tonight, because I know something did."

Her eyes closed. She didn't have it in her to argue with him, and she didn't want to. He knew the truth about the baby now, and that was what mattered most. She'd figure out the rest as she went.

* * *

When she opened her eyes again, the room was dark, and she was disoriented. It took her a few seconds to remember where she was . . . and to realize Charles was asleep in the bed beside her. He'd stripped down to his boxer briefs and was sleeping soundly. She slipped out of the bed to remove her gown; she couldn't believe she'd fallen asleep in it. After laying it out on the loveseat across the room, she went to the window to peek outside. It must have been two or three in the morning; the streets were quiet, barely any cars or people, which was a strange sight in Manhattan. The lights of nearby buildings twinkled in the darkness.

She turned back to stare at the handsome man in the bed. He looked peaceful now. He'd taken the news well, but he also knew her well, knew something had spurred her to leave, and was frustrated and upset. She knew he wouldn't stop until he understood why.

For the first time in a long time, she wasn't looking forward to tomorrow. She was dreading it. She knew what she had to do, for his sake, for hers, and for the baby's. Charles was strong . . . but dammit, so was she. Her mother had fought cancer like a warrior, and her father had been a real-life warrior. She didn't call on that inner strength often, but when she did, she could be just as formidable as any of the Harrisons.

She crossed back to the bed and slipped beneath the covers, careful not to wake him, but snuggling close. This could be the last time they shared a bed. With his warm nearness, her body betrayed her. Lust sparked low in her belly, the heat of it shooting through her blood. She knew it wasn't right, considering she was going to end their relationship the next day, but she wanted to be with him one last time. Her fingers lifted to his face, tracing the outline of his gorgeous mouth before trailing down, as she savored the feel of his skin, his broad chest, his belly, over his ass and up his smooth back.

He stirred, his eyes fluttering open halfway. Before he could say a word, she pressed her mouth to his in a sweet, sumptuous kiss. Their arms slid around each other as he deepened the kiss, pulling her tighter against him.

No words were spoken as they kissed, touched, sighed, caressed, stroked, moaned, moved together . . . They made love as if the world were at stake. And they both knew, somehow, that it was.

Chapter Twenty-Eight

The ride from Manhattan back to Long Island was a tense one. The only thing they agreed on was that they shouldn't tell anyone about her pregnancy until she made it safely past the first trimester. But again, Charles pushed for her not to move out, and again, Lisette held her ground that she would. He didn't want them to stop seeing each other; she insisted that until things were settled, it was the best way. They argued carefully, a heated chess match of push and pull that left them both exasperated by the time the limo pulled up to the mansion.

He stopped her at the front door, looking down at her as he murmured fiercely, "This isn't finished. Far from it."

"I know," she said.

"But for now, the kids come first. We act happy, like everything's fine. Because I'm confident that it will be. And then we'll talk tonight, after they're asleep."

Something in her bristled. She knew damn well the kids came first. As for the rest of it . . . she felt like he was telling her how things would be, whether she liked it or not. That was *not* okay. But she only met his demanding gaze and nodded.

As soon as they got inside, the kids ran to them, loud and happy and hugging them both.

"You're back!" Ava cried. She looked up at Lisette. "I want to hear all about the ball. The dresses, tell me about the dresses!"

Lisette laughed and smoothed Ava's hair back. "Some of them were stunning. You wouldn't have believed it."

"I wish I could've seen them!" Ava pouted.

"Maybe we can look online later," Lisette offered.

"What are you guys up to?" Charles asked the boys.

Lisette snuck a glance at him. He seemed fine, but now that she knew him as well as she did, she caught the tightness around his eyes. Her heart gave a tiny squeeze.

"We're playing video games in the playroom," Myles said, bouncing happily. "Wanna play with us?"

"I thought your mother was spending the day with you?" Charles asked.

"She said she's coming later," Thomas said, a slight scowl on his face.

Charles looked from one child to the other. "What's up?"

"Mom's mad," Thomas grumbled.

"At you?" Charles asked with surprise.

Thomas shook his head and stared at the ground, suddenly finding his sneakers fascinating.

"Last night, she was here to be with us while you two were at the ball," Ava said. "Myles told her about your being boyfriend-girlfriend . . . and she got mad."

Lisette looked to Charles and watched that telltale muscle twitch under his eye.

"Did she say something that upset you kids?" he asked calmly.

"Not really," Ava said. "But she spent, like, most of the time on her phone, talking to her friends or something . . . about you two."

"It wasn't nice things," Myles mumbled. For the first time, he looked upset. "She used a lot of the bad words. You know . . . curse words."

Charles straightened and drew a long, slow breath. "I see. Well, I'm going to talk to her and set things straight, all right?"

"What he means is"—Lisette jumped in—"please don't be upset, and don't worry that she's mad. She's not mad at you; she's mad at us."

"No duh," Thomas said under his breath.

"Hey," Charles said sharply. "Watch yourself, young man."

Thomas glared at his father. "She was happy to be with us here, and now she's all mad. You guys will fight, and it'll be awful. Christmas will be ruined. You messed up everything!" Thomas whirled away and ran up the stairs. The sound of his bedroom door slamming echoed throughout the mansion.

Lisette's heart pounded in her chest, and her hands felt ice-cold. "Should I—?"

"No. I will." Charles crouched down to look at Myles and Ava at eye level. "I'm going to go talk to your brother. Then, I'm going to come down to the playroom, and we're going to play together for the rest of the day. Your mom and I won't fight when she gets here. Everything's going to be okay, all right?"

"Okay, Daddy," Myles said, clasping his little arms around Charles's neck for a hug. Ava nodded, looking up at Lisette, then back to her father.

Charles hugged his daughter too before straightening to his full height. "Why don't you guys go to the playroom for a while, okay?"

"Go on," Lisette said, snapping into Nanny Mode. "Do you guys want a snack? I'll make something and bring it down to you."

"Can we have popcorn?" Ava asked.

Lisette shrugged and grinned. "Sure, I don't see why not."

"Cookies too?" Myles asked with what he hoped was a persuasive smile.

She ruffled his dark hair. "Maybe. Go on down."

"Oh my God," Charles said under his breath, watching his children go. "I'm going to kill her."

"Don't. Orange isn't your color," Lisette joked. "She's not worth going to jail over. So don't kill her, okay?"

"No promises," Charles muttered. He looked toward the stairs. "Dammit."

"Charles," she began, trying to soothe.

"Not now, please," he said gruffly. "I need to focus on Thomas right now." He turned away from her and went to the grand staircase.

Lisette felt vaguely nauseous. She knew how upset Charles was, on top of their tense morning . . . Well, things had gone to hell fast, hadn't they? Exhaling a shaky breath, she went to the kitchen, willfully distracting herself with tasks. She microwaved popcorn, grabbed some oatmeal raisin cookies and mini water bottles, and brought them down to the kids. She stayed for a few minutes to chat with them, to make sure they were okay.

As she made her way back up the stairs from the playroom to the main level, the doorbell chimed. "I have it," she called out. She went to the door and opened it to see Charles Harrison II standing there, a malicious glint in his eyes.

Her heart sank to her stomach, and a chill prickled over her skin. "Hello, Mr. Harrison."

"Good," he said. His cold gray gaze raked over her, and a hint of a sneer lifted his thin lips. "You're the one I'm looking for."

The chill turned into a wave of anxiety as he pushed past her into the foyer. "Why do you want to see me?" she asked, closing the door behind him as he stalked further into the house. Her heart felt like a jackhammer in her chest, and waves of unease rolled over her. Charles was still upstairs with Thomas; he probably hadn't even heard the doorbell ring. She drew a deep breath, straining to remain calm as she followed Charles II into the living room.

He turned on her and appraised her for a long beat. He was six feet tall, the same height as his eldest son, and also had a lean build. That was where the similarities ended. Charles II's hair was lighter, and his eyes were not that sparkling blue but a flat, steely gray. His mouth wasn't full and sensuous like Charles's was, but a thin slash with a hint of cruelty. It twisted now as he gazed at her and began to speak.

"I know you've been a good nanny to my grandchildren," he said amiably. His sudden pleasantness alarmed her more than if he'd started out by shouting. "And your services have been appreciated. But I think it's in all our best interests for you to take your leave now."

She blinked in disbelief. "Excuse me?"

"You're leaving this position."

"I . . ." She gaped at him, confused. "You're suggesting I leave?"

"No, I'm *telling* you to leave," he said in a low sneer. "So you will."

"No, I won't," she said, her breath stuck in her lungs. "I work for Charles; he's the one who decides if I work here or not."

"His judgment is obviously in the crapper right now. Apparently he's been blinded while he's been sleeping with you," Charles II spat. A new chill rolled over her skin as her heart raced. Charles II looked her over as if she were yesterday's trash. "No wonder he never introduced me to his date last night. When I found out who he'd brought . . . Whatever. So. How much?" He pulled his checkbook from his back pocket and walked to the small desk along the far wall. Grasping a pen, he opened the checkbook and looked at her again. "How much?" he repeated impatiently.

"How much what?" she asked, clueless as to what he meant and still in shock.

"How much do I have to pay you to make you disappear? Get up to speed, dear."

Her stomach did a nauseating flip. "You're trying to pay me to leave?" she stammered.

"Jesus. You're pretty, but apparently not very smart." Charles II shook his head at her disdainfully. "Yes. I'm willing to give you a million dollars to leave this job, this house, and vanish into thin air."

Choking out a horrified laugh, she managed, "I don't—"

"Two million, then." He huffed out an impatient breath, obviously annoyed. "Take it and go."

"No," she said, with steel this time.

His eyes narrowed, and he threw down the pen. "You *will* leave," he ranted, pointing a finger at her. "I won't let you wreck Charles's life the way that other slut did. He has no judgment when it comes to women, apparently." Charles II drew a calming breath, then locked his hateful gaze on her. "I'll make it very much worth your while to accept my offer."

"Go to hell," she whispered.

Charles II grabbed the pen again and glared at her. "Two million, and an apartment somewhere faraway. You want to go back home? Back to France? I'll buy you an apartment in Paris; how's that?"

Her insides shook, not from fear, but from rage. "Maybe you didn't hear me. Go. To. Hell."

Charles II's face darkened, and he advanced on her. "You listen to me, you little gold-digging whore—"

She turned and fled from the living room, heading for the

stairs. Thoughts whirled in her head like storms, fierce and out of control. All she wanted was escape. Charles stood at the top of the landing. "Charles," she said urgently, "you need to deal with your father. And I need to get out of here."

"What?" he asked. "What's going on?"

Charles II burst from the living room, into the hallway, yelling after her, "Don't you walk away from me when I'm talking to you, you little tramp!"

"How *dare* you." Without missing a beat, Charles descended the stairs, his blues blazing daggers of ice and fire at his father. "How dare you come to my house and speak to her this way. Who the hell do you think you are?"

"I'm Charles Roger Harrison II, goddammit!" his father roared, his control snapping like a twig. "And I won't have another sneaky slut take you and your assets—the *family's* assets—to the cleaners."

Charles looked to Lisette. "You should go now. I'll handle this."

Without hesitation, she went down the hallway, intending to stay with Ava and Myles in the playroom.

Charles and his father sized each other up as Charles growled, "What the fuck is going on?"

"I told you the first time," Charles II said, "that Vanessa was fine to fuck, but you'd regret it if you married her. You wouldn't listen! You married her just to stick it to me. And guess what? I was right. She was your worst mistake." He pointed to where Lisette had gone. "And I find out now this little ragamuffin is your new lay? The *nanny?* How stupid are you? Deplorable. You think I'm just going to stand by and let it happen again?"

"I think you better shut your mouth," Charles said as he

returned his father's enraged glare. "Who I date is not your business. Get out of my house. Right now."

"I gave you everything!" Charles II roared. "I've put you first your entire life! Made sure you had every privilege, every benefit. Don't you tell me to get out of your house, you ungrateful little prick."

"I wasn't your son; I was your prize," Charles shot back, adrenaline racing through his veins. "You treated me like a piece of property. A fucking trophy. You have since the day I was born. I'm so tired of it. I don't owe you a word of explanation about who I date, you hear me? I don't owe you anything."

"You owe me everything!" Charles II yelled.

"I owe you nothing!" Charles yelled back, finally losing control. "I run the company now; I have for years. Harrison Enterprises is more successful than ever because of what *I've* done, because of *my* accomplishments, *my* constant work—to the point where I was ignoring my kids and had no life." He got right up in his father's face, and ground out, "I run the whole show, and I'm damn good at it. If anything, *you're* the one who now owes *me*."

"I can't believe you'd turn on me like this," Charles II said, face flushed. "And for what? A piece of ass? A woman you barely know?"

"I know her. And I love her," Charles added, just to see the flare of shock in his father's eyes. "And it's about a lot more than just her." His fists clenched, and he shoved them into his pockets. "Tell you what, Dad. I have no judgment? I owe you everything? Fine. You can take it all back and go fuck yourself with it. I quit. I'm done."

"That's pure crap," Charles II said.

"No, it's not," Charles retorted calmly. "I'm leaving Harrison Enterprises. You can run it your damn self. Find another puppet. I want nothing to do with you or any of it anymore. It's way past time I had my own life. I quit. You'll have my letter of resignation on your desk first thing tomorrow."

Charles II went still, and the color drained from his weathered face. "You don't mean that."

"I sure as hell do," Charles replied. He crossed his arms over his chest and widened his stance. "I'm done being your pawn. You've told me what to do my whole life, and made me think I should be grateful for the privilege. When I was younger, I didn't know any better. But I'm done. I don't want to end up like you." His blood zipped through his veins, the years of pent-up anger flowing furiously and making words fly from his mouth. His hands itched to throw something, and he raked them through his hair. "I won't do this anymore. It's a fucking nightmare, and I'm out."

"You can't . . ." Charles II rubbed his chest and coughed. "You can't just quit the family."

"I'm not quitting the family," Charles said. "But in case you haven't noticed, they've all quit *you*."

Charles II rubbed his chest again, then gripped his upper left arm.

"The poison, the resentment, the nastiness," Charles said. "It stops here. It ends now. At least, for me. I'm quitting the company, and I'm going to spend time with my children and have a better life. Fuck Harrison Enterprises, and fuck you too."

Charles II fell to his knees, eyes bulging, seizing his chest and gasping for air. "It hurts . . ."

"Dad?" Panic slammed Charles, and he rushed to his father, grabbing his father's shoulders and looking into his widened eyes. "Jesus Christ, Dad, if this is a joke, it's not funny."

Charles II fell to the floor, clutching his chest and wincing. His face was white now, but he was sweating. "Tripp . . ."

"Holy shit." With shaking hands, Charles wrenched his cell phone out of his pocket and called 911, holding his father's head in his lap. "Hold on, Dad. Just hold on."

Chapter Twenty-Nine

Charles rode with his unconscious father in the ambulance, terror and guilt choking him. He'd caused his father to have a heart attack. The self-loathing was all consuming.

The past half hour was a blur. He'd yelled for help, and Eileen had come running from the kitchen. Only now did he realize Lisette had likely kept the kids downstairs, away from the chaos, away from the chilling sight of their powerful grandfather lying on the floor, from the jolt of seeing an ambulance roaring up the drive and strange men wheeling in a stretcher . . .

Watching as the EMTs worked on his father, he called his brothers and sister with the news. The ambulance got to Northwell Hospital quickly, and his father was rushed into the ER. By the time Charles had sat down in a private waiting room, Tess burst through the doors. She flew at him, almost tackling him with her hug. Then she grasped his face in her hands and looked into his eyes. "Listen to me, Charles. This is not your fault."

Charles felt sick to his stomach. "Yes, it is, Tess. I told you. We fought; I quit the company—"

"He had that coming," Tess said. "But the heart attack is *not* your fault."

"You say that now," Charles said gruffly. "What if he dies?"

"He's not going to die," Tess said. "He's the toughest, most ornery man on the planet. Like Pierce always says, the mean ones live the longest."

"Well, he looked very frail on the floor of my foyer," Charles murmured. He pulled away, but took her hand and brought her to sit with him on one of the couches. "Pierce is on his way. Dane's coming from the city, so who knows when he'll get here, but he's coming."

"Okay, good." She dropped her head on Charles's shoulder. "Wow, Pierce is coming. I'm shocked."

"I think he's doing it to support us, not for Dad," Charles said. "I don't care. Just glad he'll be here."

They sat quietly for a few minutes, holding hands and trying not to worry.

"Hey . . ." Tess lifted her head and shifted so she could look at him better. "What were you and Dad fighting about? What started it?"

Charles blew out a huff of air and shook his head. "Not now. Please."

"Yes, now. Tell me."

He scrubbed a hand over his face, feeling the stubble there. He hadn't shaved that morning . . . His morning at the Waldorf with Lisette seemed like weeks ago now.

"Tell me," Tess insisted.

"He came to the house to confront Lisette." Charles snorted out a laugh at the horrified expression on his sister's face. "He found out she was my date last night, and I think he tried to make her leave."

Tess's mouth dropped open. "Please be kidding."

"Nope. He wanted her away from me before she could steal my fortune and mess with my life." He scratched his head absently. "Needless to say, I lost my shit. Big time. He did too. We went at it, and it got ugly."

"I don't know what's happened to him these past few years," Tess lamented. "He's just gotten so . . ."

"Sociopathic?" Charles offered. "Bitter? Twisted? Controlling?"

"Well, he was always controlling," Tess said.

Charles chuckled. "Well played." He rose from the couch and crossed the room to the water cooler. "Want some?"

"Sure, thanks." Tess waited until he came back with the cups of water and sat down before she ventured, "How'd Lisette handle him?"

"She looked mad as hell, and also freaked out. She's with the kids now. I didn't even get to talk to her about it." Charles sighed. It'd been one hit after another . . .

The doors swung open, and Pierce entered the waiting room. He kissed Tess on the top of her head, then sat on the couch opposite them and crossed his long legs. His eyes swept over his brother in a quick surveillance. "You okay?"

"No," Charles said.

"You will be," Pierce said. "It'll all be all right."

"Thank you for coming," Tess said.

"I came for *you*," Pierce said. He crossed his arms over his broad chest. "Just the three of you."

"We know," she said with a warm smile.

Dane arrived half an hour later. "Sorry, guys. Traffic was a bitch. Any news?"

"Not yet," Tess murmured.

Dane dropped into a chair and looked at Charles. "Hey. Chuckles. Snap out of it. This isn't your fault."

"I already tried," Tess said. "He's beating himself up too much to listen."

"I said some terrible things, and he dropped at my feet." Charles looked around at them. "How is this not my fault?"

"Because," Pierce said, "despite how Dad has always acted, you're not God."

All of them grinned in spite of themselves.

"And," Pierce continued, "knowing the players here? He probably deserved whatever you said. You've rarely given him shit, much less fought hard with him, so it was long overdue if you ask me."

"Agreed," Dane said. "Every word."

"Was it about Lisette?" Pierce asked.

"Initially, yes." Charles said. "Then it turned into everything I've been holding in for the last, ohhh, forty years. I really snapped."

"I would've paid good money to see that," Pierce quipped.

Tess took Charles's hands and squeezed. He sighed deeply. "My brain must be on overload, because at the moment, I just feel kind of numb."

"Chuckles. Listen to me." Dane leaned in on his elbows and held his brother's gaze. "Dad's going to make it and be fine. Everything's going to be fine."

"I hope so," Charles murmured.

"It will be," Tess said, smiling. "Listen to Dane; he's right." She kissed her brother's cheek.

"Whatever happens," Dane said, "we support you. We're here for you, man."

"Absolutely," Pierce chimed in.

Charles looked around at his siblings. He was so lucky to have them, and he knew it. "Thank you all. Really. It means a lot."

The doors opened, and two doctors still in green scrubs entered. "Mr. Harrison?"

All three brothers stood up.

"We're all his children," Charles explained. "Is he . . . ?"

"He's alive," the first doctor said. "But he's critical. He's had a massive heart attack, and he needs surgery as soon as possible. We're just getting him stabilized first."

"What kind of surgery?" Tess asked, rising to stand with her brothers.

"Triple bypass. Are any of you authorized to sign off on that for him?"

"I am," Charles said quietly. "How ironic is that."

The doctors discussed the risks with the four of them, but they all agreed it was the necessary course of action. As soon as Charles II was stable enough, the doctors would do the surgery. He'd remain in ICU until that happened, hopefully within a few hours.

"I'm staying," Tess said when the doctors left. "I'll camp out right here on this couch and stay the night if it comes to that. But I'm not going home until he's stable and has gotten through the surgery."

"I'll stay with you, then," Dane said. "Let me just call Julia and let her know, and check in at work." Removing his phone from his jacket pocket, he went to the far side of the room to make some calls.

"I'll call Abby," Pierce said quietly. "And order us a pizza, if we're stuck here. Because if you're all staying, I am too."

Charles squeezed Pierce's shoulder, then took out his phone. He tried Lisette twice, but she didn't pick up. Unwilling to wait for a response to a text, he called the main line at the house, and Eileen answered. "Mr. Harrison!" she exclaimed. "How's your father? Is he all right?"

"Still alive. He's critical and going into surgery in a few hours. Thank you for asking." Charles sighed. "They're trying to stabilize him so he can have an emergency triple bypass."

"Oh, dear Lord. I'll pray for him, sir."

"Thank you." He leaned against the wall, glancing around at his siblings in brief amusement at how all four of them were in different corners, all on their cell phones. "Listen, I wanted to let you know, and thank you again for everything you did at the house. But I need to talk to Lisette, please. She didn't pick up her cell. I thought maybe she's busy with the kids? I need her to know I'm going to be staying here at the hospital until my father is stable. If that means I'm here overnight, so be it. But I—"

"Mr. Harrison . . ." Eileen cut him off, sounding hesitant. "Lisette's not here."

"What's up?" Charles frowned, and an intuitive hum of alarm flamed in his core.

"Well, Vanessa's here now, and she's with the children. I am too, sir, and I'll stay tonight for as long as you need me to."

His body tensed. "Where's Lisette?"

"I don't know, sir," Eileen said. "She left an hour ago. With suitcases. Said she's taking some of the vacation time she's never used. Don't worry, she didn't leave without making sure the children were cared for. I'll be here, and so will Tina, in the morning. And, um . . . when Vanessa arrived, she and Lisette . . . had a brief argument. So Lisette said Vanessa could finally mother her children without interference from her."

Charles wanted to punch the wall. "Are you fucking kidding me?"

"The children are fine, sir," Eileen said hurriedly. "Lisette made sure of that before she left. She'd never shirk her responsibilities to them. But she's gone."

Charles could barely breathe and wondered if he'd have a heart attack himself. How had everything gotten so out of control in such a short time? "Where did she go, do you know?"

"She didn't tell me that, sir. And she took a cab when she left." Eileen sighed again, heavily this time. "She said goodbyes to the children. Told them she'd be spending the holiday with some of her family this year, and she'd be back some time after Christmas." Eileen cleared her throat. "And she left a letter for you."

"A letter?!?" Charles felt as if the world had gone insane. "I—I have no idea when I'll be home . . . Listen, I'm going to have Bruck bring me the letter. Give it to him when he comes for it, all right?"

He made a few more calls: to Bruck, asking him to deliver the letter to him; to his assistant, apprising her of the situation and providing instructions; and then to Lisette. He hung up on her voice mail, not even knowing what to say just then. Then he called Vanessa's cell.

"Hello," she said. "I'm sorry to hear about your father."

"Give me one reason I shouldn't throw you out of my house," Charles seethed, "and put you on a goddamn plane myself."

"Because your precious nanny girlfriend took off," Vanessa shot back, "so *I'm* taking care of my kids, and you need me here."

"I don't need you there. I have a full staff; they'd never notice your absence. They're used to it, remember?" Charles pushed a hand through his hair. "And if you want a medal for having to take care of your own kids, you won't find it on me."

"I know you must—"

"Shut up," he snapped. "Listen to me. I don't know what happened between you and Lisette after we left, but you're going to answer for it, and for the other crap you pulled in front of the kids last night. You can be sure of that." His heart was beating furiously, matching his emotions. "But, yes, you're in charge of the kids for now. I'm at the hospital, waiting to see if my father lives or dies. So be a responsible adult for once in your fucking life and stay with the kids until I get back. If you don't, if you pawn them off on the staff and disappear, I'll make sure you're not allowed to see them ever again." He clicked off the call and hurled his phone, sending it sailing to land on the nearby sofa.

His three siblings all stared at him in stunned silence.

"I miss being able to slam down the phone when you hung up on someone," Charles growled.

Chapter Thirty

Charles returned home the next afternoon in a daze. He was working on about five hours' sleep, caught on a couch in the private waiting room. His father was stable, had gotten through the surgery, and was expected to make a full recovery. As soon as Charles had heard that, he'd left the hospital. He had a crisis in his own home to manage now.

"Oh, you poor dear." Eileen started fussing over him as soon as he walked in. "You need a shower, a good meal, and some sleep in your own bed."

"Kids are still at school?" He followed her into the kitchen.

"Yes, but Tina just left to go pick them up."

"Okay. You two have been wonderful about picking up Lisette's slack," he said. "I can't tell you how much I appreciate it. It'll reflect in your Christmas bonuses; you can count on that."

"With all due respect, sir," Eileen said, "I know you're upset with Lisette for leaving so suddenly. But she made sure the children would be well cared for before she left. She did. She'd never abandon them."

But she abandoned me. He grunted and stalked across the kitchen to grab a bottle of water from the refrigerator.

"I'll stop now." Eileen went to the stove. "It's not my place. I'm sorry, sir."

"No, don't do that," he said. "You have nothing to apologize for. You care about her, and about me, and about the kids. I know that. I'm grateful for that." He swallowed some water, welcoming the cold flow down his throat. "I just . . . God, it's all too much. Too many things in too short a time. I can't even think straight. I'm wrung out."

"You need some decent sleep."

"I do. But that's not happening right now."

"Can I make you something to eat?" Eileen asked.

"Yes, please." He sat at the table in the nook of the kitchen. "I don't have much of an appetite, but I don't need to keel over either."

"How about some beef stew?" she asked. "Just made a big pot of it not an hour ago. It'll be good for you."

"Sounds fine. Thank you." He dropped his head into his hands. Lisette was gone. She loved his kids; she was pregnant with their child; they were supposed to love each other . . . and she'd left. His heart ached so much, it actually squeezed in his chest, a dull pressure. What he wouldn't have given to come home to her today, to be held by her . . . Devastation seeped through him.

He pulled the letter from his inside jacket pocket, adjusted his glasses, and read it for what must have been the tenth time.

Dear Charles,

I'm writing you this letter to explain why I've left. And, to force you to let me say what I need to without interruptions, rebuttals, or demands.

I love you. I've loved you for much longer than you've loved me, Charles, even though you didn't know it. And being with you has been like a dream. But dreams aren't reality, and our reality is a harsh one. There are just too many differences for this to truly work, and I know that now.

I want to believe in you, and in us . . . but whenever I voice my doubts and worries to you, you always dismiss them. Maybe in your mind, you're just trying to assuage my fears, but that's not how it has come across. It's frustrating for me. So, again, this letter.

You thought something had happened at the ball. I'll admit it now, you were right. While in the ladies' room, I overheard two women gossiping about us. I won't get into details, but they basically said the kinds of things I was afraid someone would. They think I insinuated myself into your life and pretended to love the kids to get closer to you. If the kids ever heard that, and wondered if it was true, that would kill me. And of course, they're looking down on you. I realized that most people in your circles are going to think, feel, and say similar things. And I don't want that for you, and the children. Also, truthfully, I don't want it for myself, and certainly not for the innocent baby we're going to bring into the world.

You once said I'm always thinking about the other person. You were so right. It's who I am; it's my nature to care for others. And I care for you more than anyone in the world. So before this beautiful thing we started building becomes tainted, before you become resentful, before I get hurt, before the kids get hurt, I'm taking myself out of the mix.

I'm so sorry I'm hurting you. I really hate that. I need you to know that.

You promised the kids that I'd stay, that I'd always be around. I told you that might come back to bite us, but I want to fulfill that promise. So I'm not leaving permanently, as I tried to tell you. I'll just

*move into an apartment close by, and go to work
every day, like most people do. I won't let the kids
down.*

*Charles, every time I've tried to talk to you about
these things, you just brushed them aside and
barreled on, blind to the realities of our being a
couple. We can't pretend those things don't matter.*

*Maybe I'm a hormonal mess right now (hell,
probably—I think I've cried more in the past month
than in my entire life), and maybe I'll regret this
later. But right now, I need space, and I need you to
HEAR what I'm telling you for once.*

*I know Vanessa is leaving on the 26th. I'll come
back on the 27th to take care of the kids. That's my
job, and I love my job. We can work out the details
when I return. I hope to keep my position as their
nanny; of course, that's up to you. We also have a lot
to figure out about the baby, too. But I don't see how
we can be together anymore.*

*I love you. I'll always love you. That will never
change. But you need to find someone who fits into
your world, and someone whose backlash won't hurt
the kids. I'm so sorry, but that's not me.*

Lisette

Charles folded the letter and put it back in his pocket,
then dropped his head into his hands. He'd never meant to
make her feel dismissed or that her concerns weren't valid
or being heard. He'd just wanted to assure her, make her
believe as he did . . . and all he'd done was push her away.
His goddamn pride, his ego, and yes, he was used to having
things his way. He had his whole life; it wasn't totally his
fault . . . Ah hell, yes, it was.

But she didn't have the option of just ending their relationship without hearing him out, dammit. Maybe, after she

had some space, he could talk to her, apologize, make her feel his respect and affection by really listening to her and then working things out together . . . He wasn't willing to let her go. He understood her concerns about gossip affecting the kids. Yes, she was selfless, and yes, she always put others' needs ahead of her own. But there'd been a pearl of another, simpler truth in that letter: she didn't want that negativity aimed at her. She didn't want the scrutiny, and she was afraid of getting hurt. He understood that. Did she really think he wouldn't?

And she wouldn't be there for Christmas. That really stung. He'd so been looking forward to spending Christmas with her. He loved her, dammit. This wasn't how things were supposed to be, especially if she still loved him too. Misery surged through him. What a mess. And where the hell had she gone?

The click-clack of feminine heels sounded across the tile floor. He raised his head to see his ex-wife walk into the kitchen. His eyes narrowed on her, and she stopped cold.

"I have no energy for you right now," he said wearily. "Do me a favor, just once, and leave me alone."

Eileen set down a steaming ceramic bowl in front of him and handed him a spoon and napkin. "Here you go, sir. Eat up, now."

"Thank you, Eileen." Without so much as another glance at Vanessa, he turned his tired eyes to his stew and took a spoonful.

Vanessa pulled out the chair across from him and sat down, folding one manicured hand on top of the other. He groaned and shook his head.

"How's your father?" she asked.

He snorted at her. "What do you care?"

"I don't care about him; you're right." She swept her long,

glossy black hair back. "But he's my kids' grandfather, their only grandfather. I care if they get upset."

"He's alive," was all Charles gave her before spooning stew into his mouth.

Eyeing the couple, Eileen wiped her hands on a dish towel. "Tina should be home with the kids in a few minutes."

"Excellent. Thank you." Charles took another spoonful of stew. "This is wonderful. I feel a little better already."

"See that you eat all of it," she said.

"You know your brogue gets stronger when you tell me what to do?" he said, grinning.

"Oh, now!" She laughed and left the kitchen.

He and Vanessa looked at each other across the table.

"You got your wish," he said. "Lisette left. She's gone." He spooned more stew into his mouth.

"I didn't want her to leave," Vanessa said.

He chortled at that. "Riiiight. Pull this leg while you're at it. It plays 'Jingle Bells.'"

"I'm serious," she insisted. "I mean . . . Okay, fine, I admit it. She's great with the kids. Better with them than I am. That's one of the reasons why I resent her so much. I'm . . . jealous."

Charles almost dropped his spoon. "Wow."

"Shut up." Vanessa gestured at the bowl. "Eat more. I'll talk; you listen."

He stared at her for a long beat, then took another bite.

"I'm jealous of her," she admitted. "She's nicer than me, younger than me, and everyone likes her. Everyone hates me."

His eyebrows shot up in shock at her candor.

"She also has you, and my children, wrapped around her finger. You all adore her. It's so obvious." Vanessa examined her nails. "I didn't expect to find what I walked into here . . ."

"And what's that, exactly?" he asked.

"A family." She met his eyes. "You're all a family, and you don't even know it."

Something in his chest tightened. He put down the spoon.

"She's good to you, Charles. Better than I ever was. She's kind and sweet, and she loves the kids, and she's amazing with them. Everything I never was." Vanessa shifted and crossed her legs beneath the table. "I always knew I was too selfish to be a good mother. I tried to tell you that, but you didn't listen. I'm impulsive, quick tempered, self-absorbed. I knew I'd probably be a shitty mom, because mine was to me, and my mom was all those things."

"I remember," he murmured. He couldn't believe how real, how *human* Vanessa was being. A flicker of the woman he'd once known shone through. There was still some decency in there after all.

"I honestly thought I'd see the kids a few times a year, but that in general . . . the truth is . . ." Vanessa drew a deep breath, then exhaled it slowly. "I knew, as a mother, I'd likely do more harm than good. That they were better off without me on a day-to-day basis. That's why I've stayed away."

"That's not the only reason," he said, picking up the spoon again. "You enjoy your life, the travel, the freedom of not being tied down."

"That's all true. I'm not going to deny it." Vanessa met his gaze dead on. "But what I just admitted is my main reason for not being around."

He stared and said, "And now?"

"I told you, I'm not good with babies, but I'm better with bigger kids. They're people; they talk; I have more patience for that. So, yes, I'd like to see them more. I *should* see them more. But the thing is, they don't need me. They have Lisette."

"She's not their mother," he asserted. "You are."

"Not in the way that counts. That's the truth, and we both

know it." Vanessa gnawed on her pouty bottom lip. "When you found her. You found a diamond. She's perfect for them. She's the mother those kids deserve to have."

A strange chill prickled over his skin. He swallowed hard, trying to dislodge the lump that suddenly clogged his throat.

"And she's also perfect for you," Vanessa added. "I knew as soon as I got here that you were crushing on each other. It was so obvious! I just had no idea you were having a real relationship. *That* surprised me."

He only nodded. "We've been keeping it a secret for the kids' sake. We didn't want to confuse them."

"Ah. Okay, now I get it." Vanessa reached for his water bottle and helped herself to a few sips. "That you're in love with her doesn't surprise me. She's gorgeous, yes. She's bright. She loves your kids. She's extremely capable, not a spoiled diva like me."

He had to laugh at that. "I've never heard you cop to that."

"Oh, please. I know what I am." She shrugged. "The thing is, I don't really care. I have a great life. I do what I want, when I want. But I can because someone like Lisette is here, taking good care of my kids."

"That, and the millions you wrangled out of me," he said.

"Yeah, that too." She grinned. "You and I . . . Charles, the sex was fantastic. And I loved some of the perks. But we were never right for each other. Lisette is everything you need. She's warm and sweet and loving and kind and all those good, good things you never got."

Hearing it stated so flatly made his heart wrench. "I have to agree with you."

"You agree with me on something? Oh my God!" Vanessa cried. She gripped the edge of the table in white-knuckled mock horror. "The world might end!!"

He laughed, full and free. "Too late. I think today, my world came close to ending. But I'm still here."

"That's right," Vanessa said. "You are. And you've never indulged in self-pity, so don't start now. But you *do* hold a grudge. No one knows that better than me."

He snorted and took another bite of stew.

"Charles. I know you're probably hurt and angry because Lisette left. But don't hold a grudge with her. She's too important to you. Swallow your pride, hunt her down, and beg her to come back here for Christmas. If you don't, you're a fool."

He gaped at her. He couldn't have been any more shocked by her advice.

"My kids love her," Vanessa said simply. "They want her; they need her. And so do you. You finally found the right woman for you, Charles. It wasn't me. It was never me. But you were so disappointed, so angry for so long, you couldn't just accept that."

"You made it easy to stay angry," he pointed out.

"You're right; I did. I'm no saint, that's for damn sure." She grinned ruefully. "But if you're happy, my kids will be happy. Then I have a clear conscience to go off and do my thing." She reached for his hand and grabbed it. "Lisette makes you happy. She makes all of you happy. And she loves you. Go find her and drag her back here."

"If she wanted to be here," he murmured, "she would be."

"I saw her before she left."

"I heard you argued."

"We did. Know why?" Vanessa snorted. "Because your sweet little nanny turned into a spitfire. When I got here, she came right at me, furious that I'd let the kids overhear the nasty things I was saying about you. So I got defensive . . . because she was right. She was absolutely right; I shouldn't have let the kids hear any of that. That's shitty parenting, and I felt shitty about it."

Charles could only stare.

"So since I felt stupid, put in my place, and I saw she was on the edge, upset . . . I turned it around, and I flung it in her face. I'm not very nice, remember?"

He sneered and shook his head.

"I told her to suck it up and do her job. That she was supposed to be the nanny first, and she could fall apart later. But something was really wrong, I could see it in her face." Vanessa played with a lock of her hair. "She was . . . weary. Like she couldn't take anymore, and she's pretty tough for all her quiet and gentle stuff. She had tears in her eyes. And suddenly . . . I felt bad. I did. So, I took it down a bit and told her to take a break. That I'd watch my own kids, and maybe she should take a short breather, go away for a few days to get her head together."

Charles's head reeled as he put the pieces together. So two people, in a very short time, had told an already emotional Lisette that she should leave. Jesus . . . he leaned in and speared Vanessa with a fierce look. "You told her to leave? On whose authority? This is *my* house!"

"I didn't tell her to quit!" Vanessa cried. "I told her to take a *breather* since I was here to watch the kids. When I saw her leaving, I figured she had taken my advice. I had no idea she'd left for parts unknown until I overheard you talking with Eileen."

He muttered a low curse. "You were right. She was already on the edge. Your argument likely pushed her over. But it's not all your fault. It's . . . mostly mine." He took a deep breath and took another bite of stew. What a disaster. A perfect storm. "I need to finish this food," he said. "Then I need a shower. Then some sleep. And in the morning, I'll be able to deal with all this a lot better. Right now, I must be really out of it. Because everything you've said has made sense. Like you actually give a shit, like you're trying to help."

"Surprise," Vanessa said softly. She grabbed the water bottle again. "Charles . . . just find her and talk to her."

"I don't even know where she is."

"Oh, please. You're Charles Harrison III," she reminded him. "You have ways."

"True." He nodded, finished chewing, and said, "Thank you, Vanessa. You've been . . . really decent. Almost helpful."

"You know me," she said with a wink. "Always full of surprises."

After his meal, Charles took a long shower and fell into bed, asking not to be disturbed unless the hospital called with urgent news. He slept like the dead for six hours. When he woke, his room had darkened, and the clock showed it was after 10 P.M. With a groan, he got out of bed. Events had so thoroughly scrambled his brain and his schedule, he didn't know whether he was coming or going. Scrubbing his hands over his face hard to wake himself up, he immediately thought of Lisette. His heart felt heavy as he pulled on a fresh pair of pajamas.

Lisette had told the kids she'd be spending Christmas with her family. But she didn't have any family. Where would she have gone? Would she get as far away as she could? Paris? No, she wouldn't fly out of the country and away from doctors just yet. Doctors . . . Maybe she'd stay hidden in plain sight. Be right there in Manhattan, so she could still see her doctors, take care of the baby. It was possible. She wouldn't go to her father; in her mind, he was pretty much already dead and gone. Goddammit . . .

Karen. She'd go to Karen, her best friend, her only true touchstone left in the world. As far as Lisette was concerned, Karen was family. God, it was so obvious, why hadn't he thought of it sooner?

He didn't know her last name, but he knew she lived upstate, near Rochester, and that she and Lisette had gone to college together. It was a start.

He grabbed his cell and scrolled through his contacts, finding one listed only as "Rexford." Charles made the call to the private investigator he trusted the most. "Hi, it's Charles Harrison. How've you been? Oh, good. Yeah. What can you do for me? Find someone. As fast as you can."

Chapter Thirty-One

The snow fell lightly onto the ground, the porch, the driveway, and the naked trees along the quiet street. Lisette used to love watching snow fall, those beautiful magic crystals that blanketed everything in purest white. When she and her parents had moved to warmer states, she had missed the snow in the winter. But as an adult, snow made her think of that one long winter, recuperating at Karen's parents' house after her accident. After her miscarriage. After her fiancé dumped her. After her life fell apart.

She'd come so far since then. She'd rebuilt her life, into something completely different than she'd once envisioned, but something decent. And it made her happy. For someone who'd felt anchorless, without roots, for her entire life, being so enmeshed with someone else's family gave her something of an anchor. She took care of herself, and she got to take care of children who needed her nurturing and affection. The first family she worked for moved to Hong Kong, and she had found a new job: working for Charles Harrison III, international power player, magnate, and single father who had three children he rarely saw because he worked so much.

Accepting that job had changed her life. She'd fallen in love with his family, and with him. And now, she was carrying his child. And he wanted her, and the baby, and everything they could be and have together.

And what had she done now? Freaked out. So when Vanessa had suggested she take a break, Lisette had decided to leave altogether. Charles would never be free of his obligations, both to his family and his career . . . If his father was involved, there would always be angst, a simmering poison. The people who would talk about them, like those vipers at the Waldorf had, would always have something to say, and the thought of it was exhausting. Plus, Vanessa was back and wanted to be a mother to her kids again—and she didn't want Lisette around; that was clear.

Lisette just didn't have the energy to fight all of it at once. She was already so tired . . . She'd convinced herself she was doing the right thing by retreating, protecting not only Charles and the baby, but herself.

What a load of bullshit, her conscience whispered. *You're running scared. That's all there is to it. Wouldn't your father be proud?*

She squeezed her eyes shut as she drew some deep breaths. When she was done berating herself, she went to the kitchen to make some decaffeinated tea.

Karen and her family lived in a big old house in a rural neighborhood about twenty miles from Rochester, New York. Her husband, Jeff, was some kind of computer-programming whiz and worked in downtown Rochester. Karen was a pediatrician's assistant; she'd found a great job in this sleepy town, which was why they'd moved there, leaving the city for suburban life. Lisette moved about the kitchen in content silence. Jeff and Karen were at work, and their precious four-year-old daughter was at preschool. Hallie was a joy, a sweet little wisp of a thing whose size belied her ebullient personality. Lisette loved her goddaughter very much, and it'd been too long since she'd come to visit.

When Lisette had showed up on Karen's doorstep two

days ago, with her suitcases and obviously distraught, Karen had simply opened her arms. Lisette had crumpled into her hug, grateful for the bond they shared, as she cried her eyes out.

Karen and her family had been in the middle of dinner. Karen had set a place for Lisette. Jeff made sure she was warm and comfortable, and little Hallie chattered excitedly through the whole meal, bombarding her with questions and cuteness. "This is the best surprise ever! Are you staying for Christmas? Did you get the Christmas card I made for you? Can we play Candy Land after dinner?"

Lisette and Karen had sat in the living room that night and talked for hours. After Karen was fully caught up on everything that had happened from the beginning, her pale blue eyes set on the woman she thought of as a sister, and she pronounced, "Lisette, my darling, my dearest friend in the world . . . you're an idiot."

"Well, thanks," Lisette had mumbled. "I needed to come all this way for you to tell me that?"

"Apparently so," Karen had said. "That man loves you. He's shown you that in so many ways. But you are so afraid he'll leave you one day that you took off instead. You're not protecting him; you're protecting yourself."

Lisette had fidgeted with the edge of the multicolored quilt on her lap. "You really think that's what I'm doing?"

"Yup. And deep down, you know I'm right." Karen had shifted on the sofa, tucking her legs beneath her. "I know there's a ton of crap going on around you guys, so you feel as if you're on shaky ground. Okay, he wasn't great at listening sometimes. But you're the one who was afraid to believe; you're the one who hightailed it out of there."

The shrill whistle from the teakettle startled Lisette from her reverie.

You hightailed it out of there. Oh, God, that was exactly what she'd done. The hormones were partly to blame, and they were certainly doing a number on her. But mostly it was fear, pure and simple. She'd gotten scared and overwhelmed. Scared to entrust her heart to Charles in the first place, then the shock of finding out she was pregnant, then by Vanessa's showing up, then the big gala with too many people all looking at her and wondering about her—and those bitches in the ladies' room, and then Charles II raging at her . . . Lisette had bent from the pressure. She wasn't proud of herself for that.

But there was more. From the start, deep down she had been afraid she wasn't enough for Charles. *That* was at the heart of it. He'd told her over and over that he didn't care about their differences, that he loved her for her; he'd shown it in numerous ways . . . and she hadn't fully believed in him. That was on her.

She'd loved Brandon and had been so very wrong about him. Now she was afraid of getting hurt again. But Karen was right. Running away had been unfair. Lisette wasn't asking the big questions, because she was afraid of the answers.

The worn old grandfather clock in the hallway struck two. Karen would pick up Hallie from preschool at three, and they'd be home for the rest of the day. Lisette had baked brownies earlier; she took one now, along with her cup of tea, and went to lie on the sofa in the living room and let herself drown in her thoughts.

The Christmas tree was in there, and Lisette loved the way the smell of pine filled the room. The tree was covered in sparkly tinsel and delicate ornaments, and the strings of white lights around it blinked randomly. She took her phone out of her pocket and made herself comfortable under the quilt. Scrolling through, she looked at all of Charles's texts again. They varied between pleasant, then angry, then sad, then pleading. The last one pierced her heart. He'd sent it early that morning: I won't let you go without a fight. I love you too much.

God, she missed him. The heartache filled her with long-ing and regret. Tears sprang to her eyes. She loved her job, those kids, that house, that man. Dammit, she didn't want a life without Charles in it, by her side, especially once the baby came. What had she done?

Tomorrow. She'd call him tomorrow. She had no idea what to say, but . . .

With a heavy yawn, she found the holiday music station on Pandora. She set the phone down beside her as she nib-bled the brownie, sipped her tea, and watched the snow fall. U2's version of "Christmas (Baby Please Come Home)" played, and Lisette teared up, her eyes stinging as she lis-tened to the lyrics. She'd so been looking forward to her first Christmas with Charles, and now . . . Sniffling, she hit the FORWARD button to hear a different song. Bing Crosby crooning "White Christmas". She let that play as she watched the snow and thought of Charles . . .

The doorbell rang, jolting Lisette awake. Disoriented, she looked around and realized she must have dozed off. She glanced at the phone, which was now playing the Hall & Oates version of "Jingle Bell Rock", and saw it was 2:40. The doorbell rang again.

"Coming," she called out, throwing the quilt back and rising from the couch. She glanced down at herself: purple plaid flannel pajama pants, an old white sweater over a purple long-sleeved T-shirt, and her sheep slippers. Her hair was mussed now in its ponytail thanks to her impromptu nap. She must've looked ragged, but whoever it was wouldn't care; he or she wasn't there to see her. "Coming," she called again, trying to fix her hair as she went to the door and opened it.

Charles stood before her, in a long black wool overcoat and jeans, snow falling lightly on his dark hair and shoulders.

Her heart stuttered in her chest, and her breath caught. A wave of shock washed over her as she gaped at him.

"Hi," he said softly, and with that one velvety word, everything in her screamed for him. She wanted to throw herself into his arms and never let go.

"Hi," she managed. "How did you find me?"

"Once I narrowed down the possibilities, it wasn't too hard. It's also good to have a first-class private investigator on speed dial." He wouldn't stop staring at her, the relief and adoration coming off him in palpable waves. "May I come in?"

"Oh! Good Lord, of course!" She moved aside to let him into the house, only then noticing the black town car parked in front of the house. Charles brushed snowflakes from his coat and looked around briefly, assessing his surroundings. His presence seemed to fill the room. She closed the front door behind him and watched him as her heart pounded and she tried to remember how to breathe.

"Anyone else home?" he asked.

"No, not yet. Soon, though. By three-thirty for sure." She cleared her suddenly dry throat. "Would you like some tea?"

"No, thank you."

"Brownies? I baked them this morning."

"No, thanks." He didn't even unbutton his coat, just kept gazing at her from across the room. The Christmas tree stood behind him, and the white lights around him made him seem otherworldly.

"Um . . ." She fidgeted with her ponytail. "Your father. Is he . . . ?"

"He's recovering," Charles said. "He had surgery, and he's expected to make a full recovery."

"Good. That's good." She swallowed hard, trying to grab a coherent thought from her shocked brain. His eyes didn't leave hers. "I don't know what to say," she admitted, his quiet stance making her feel as if she had to talk.

"That's okay," he said. "For now, I'm so happy to see you, I'll just stare."

Melting inside, she couldn't help but grin. "Well, I didn't know I'd have company. I'm a bit of a mess."

"A beautiful mess," he said, open reverence in his voice and his gaze.

That made her knees wobble. She cleared her throat. "Do you want to sit down?"

"What I want is to pull you into my arms and not let go." His voice was thick with emotion as he jammed his hands into his coat pockets. "What I want is to kiss you until you can't remember your name. But most of all, what I want is for you to tell me why you left. Not the bullshit excuses in that letter. The truth."

Her heart plummeted to her stomach. "I did tell you the truth."

"No. No, you didn't." His eyes narrowed, and he took a step toward her. "Because we talked about things. A lot. About how we were both willing to do whatever it took to be together." He took another step closer. "How we love each other, how incredible our connection is, how much we can do and have together." Another step. "And suddenly, you were gone." Another step, and his brows arched. "Wait, I take it back, not everything in that letter was bullshit. You made some valid points."

"Such as?"

"I do brush aside your concerns sometimes, and I want to apologize for that. But it was meant to soothe you, you know? To reassure you that we'd be fine, that I'd be there for you no matter what. I'm sorry I made you feel dismissed when I did that. But now I'm aware of it. So come back and let me show you I can be a better listener, okay?"

She released a shaky breath, every nerve in her body lit with awareness of him, his presence, his strength. "You want me to come back? Even after I took off?"

"Hell yes, I want you back. This is nothing we can't get

past, Lisette." He stopped in front of her. "But you have to trust me."

"I do!" she said.

"Then why'd you run?" he asked, his blue eyes pinning her, searching. "Dammit, tell me what you're afraid of."

"A lot of things," she whispered. She drew a deep breath . . . and took the leap of faith she knew she must. "But most of all, I'm afraid of how I feel about you. Because I love you so much, it's overwhelming," she finally said. "I want this with you so much it scares me. I don't want to lose it. But I'm so sick of swallowing my feelings. My desires. My dreams." Tears slipped out and rolled down her cheeks, but she met his gaze. "I want to believe you when you say you don't care what people say, but those women were vicious, Charles. Them, and your father, and Vanessa . . . and it threw me. I got scared again. I swallowed my feelings again. I mean . . . I've done that for so long, I don't know how else to be."

"Then just stop," he said gently. "If I did it, so can you." He reached out to touch her face. "The past is the past. Stop punishing yourself already."

"I thought I'd done that." Her voice cracked on a sob. "And instead it's made me feel like I'm in a freefall."

"I'll catch you," he murmured. His eyes held hers as he wiped her cheeks with his thumbs, then cradled her face. "I'll catch you, sweetheart. I promise."

Her lungs felt tight, and her heart pounded mercilessly. "I'm scared to death." She drew a shaky breath, looked down, and gently tugged at the loose thread at the bottom of her sweater. "But I've been so scared of getting hurt again that I haven't been living. I've been hiding. You . . . dragged me out into the light."

"You've done the same for me," he said, and tipped her chin up to make her look at him. "I was in a deep, dark hole.

You helped pull me out. I didn't even realize how deep it was until you came along."

"Oh, Charles . . ." She lifted her hands to his.

"We're so much stronger and happier together than apart," he said fervently. "We belong together. We're right for each other. I love you, Lisette. I love you, I want you, and I'll always stand by you. Do you hear me?"

She pressed her lips together to hold back a sob, but nodded.

"Please come home," he whispered. "It's Christmas. Our first one together. Come home with me." He caressed her cheek. "Come home *to* me. To all of us. We need you, sweetheart. We all love you."

"I love you all too." The tears seemed endless. "But . . . what about the baby?"

His brow furrowed. "What about it?"

"I know it's been a shock," she said quickly, making herself get the words out. "But do you really want another baby? Are you really okay with it?"

"Oh my God," he whispered. "Of course I'm okay with it; I'm more than okay with it. It's amazing! It's your little miracle. *Our* little miracle."

"Really?" she asked. "You're happy? You can love this child?"

"Of course!" He stroked loose tendrils of her hair back from her face. "I'm already so crazy in love with this baby's mother, it's ridiculous." He cracked a grin. "I'll have another child to love, and I'll do right by him or her from the start . . . It's a new chance for *both* of us, honey. I'm totally on board, and I don't know why you doubted it."

She flung herself against him, holding tight as she cried. "I'm so sorry."

His arms wrapped around her and pressed her close. "I am too. I kept trying to dismiss all your fears, your concerns . . .

but that didn't make them go away; it just made them fester. I'll work on that, I promise."

"I want a life with you more than anything," she said. "I was scared to admit it."

"How about now?"

"Now? I'll never let you go. My God, Charles, you tracked me down and showed up at the door. After I left like a thief in the night." She couldn't stop crying. "I'm assuming you flew up here?"

"Gotta love that private jet," he said with a crooked grin. "If I had driven, it would've taken me six hours or so, and I couldn't wait that long. As soon as I found out where you were, I couldn't get to you fast enough."

She shook her head in awe. "If you'd do all this, show up here, say these things, ask me to come back, I know you do love me as much as I love you." She looked up to meet his eyes. "I'm so sorry I hurt you . . . Oh, God, I really messed up."

"Shhh, it's okay. We all mess up. It's all right now." He rubbed her back and kissed her forehead, then wiped her wet face with the edge of his sleeve. "You're coming home. And it's going to be *our* home. I love how you love my kids. We're going to have a great life together and welcome a new baby into the mix. We'll be a new kind of family. Everything's going to work out."

"It's all my dreams come true," she said, choking on sobs as he pulled her into his arms.

"Then why are you still crying and sad?" he asked.

"I'm not sad anymore!" she croaked between sobs. "These are happy tears."

He laughed and squeezed her tighter. "Sorry, I couldn't tell the difference."

"Well, I've been crying so much lately," she blubbered, "it's understandable."

"Damn hormones," he teased.

"They're wrecking me," she said, laughing through her

tears. "I'm usually not like this, crying all the time, I swear. I think I'll get back to normal in a few weeks."

"I want to be with you every step of the way for this pregnancy," he said, leaning his forehead against hers and looking into her eyes. "I love you, Lisette."

"I love you too."

He lowered his mouth to hers, kissing her tenderly. As soon as his lips touched hers, it was as if a spark ignited. The kiss flamed hot, both of them consumed as they held each other.

"So we might have to find a new nanny." He interlocked his fingers at the small of her back, holding her close as his eyes twinkled. "Mine's knocked up. Know anyone good?"

She hiccupped out a watery laugh. "I can help out for a while," she joked, snaking her arms around his neck. "But actually, can we go back tomorrow? I really want you to meet Karen and her family. She'll be home any minute, with my goddaughter. Can we stay for dinner, at least?"

"Sure. I'd like that," he said. "I'm a little intimidated to meet the famous Karen, though. Think she'll approve of me?"

"I think she might. You can be pretty charming when you want to be," Lisette said, smiling so brightly her cheeks started to hurt. "And don't lie, mister—nobody intimidates you. You're Charles Harrison III."

He cupped her chin and looked into her eyes. "Lisette, I'm nobody without you."

Epilogue

Three months later

The clear turquoise waves of the Caribbean lapped onto the white sands of the beach. On the deck of their private villa, soft breezes caressed their skin as Charles held his girlfriend close and they watched the fiery sunset.

"I still can't believe you brought me here," Lisette said against his chest.

"Amateur," he scoffed. "I planned this a month ago."

"And I still can't believe Vanessa was willing to take the kids for the whole spring break," Lisette marveled. "How'd you swing that?"

"Believe it or not, I asked." A crooked grin spread on his face. "She said she wanted to see them more, so I gave her a chance to prove it."

"Amazing." Lisette inhaled a deep breath of beach air. "Speaking of amazing, this was an incredible surprise. You've outdone yourself. Thank you so much, honey."

"My pleasure," he said, taking her mouth with sultry kisses. They had eight days together at the Parrot Cay Resort, a sumptuous tropical paradise far away from their busy world. Crystal-clear waters, soft sands, a villa with a private pool and direct beach access . . . the five-star luxury resort had been the right choice. He was glad he'd found it, then kept the trip a secret.

"We're going to do nothing this week but relax and enjoy each other," he said, moving lower to kiss and nibble her neck. Her breath caught as her breasts, fuller from pregnancy and more sensitive, brushed against his chest. He smiled against her skin, reaching down to dig his fingers into her lush hips and press her closer. "You know . . ." He continued to devour her neck, knowing where she liked to be kissed and bitten. One hand lifted to thread his fingers through her hair. "This morning, you went out, and when you got back, you said you had a surprise for me tonight. But then I surprised you by putting you on a plane and bringing you here." He drew back to look into her eyes and flash a playful grin. "Well, it's tonight. I want my surprise now."

She laughed and said, "Okay, okay. You're in luck; I brought it with me. But it's nothing nearly as extravagant as a get-away to paradise."

"Please tell me you don't think I care."

"I know you don't. That's one of the many reasons I love you so much." She kissed him before pulling out of his embrace. "Be right back. Stay here."

Charles smiled as she disappeared into their private villa. He turned and watched the clear blue waves just beyond and thought about his life. He was the luckiest man in the world. He'd lost sight of that for a while, the years when he'd been depressed and lonely and overworked. But once Lisette had come into his life, it was as if the sun had started shining on him again. She showered him with her warmth and light, and he blossomed under her radiance. He loved her so much it astonished him.

Other aspects of his life had improved too. Vanessa was more involved with the kids, which was nice for them—but not too involved, which was nice for him. Business was booming. He'd stayed at the company; he'd realized he was born to run the Harrison empire, and when things were good, he really did love his work. He'd lessened the stress and the volume of his insane workload by assigning different projects to several of his very capable executive vice presidents, and so far, the new system was working well. His father was so grateful Charles had decided to stay on that he kept his grumblings to a minimum.

Charles II had softened a bit after the heart attack. Being suddenly frail had humbled him, and perhaps he'd had something of an epiphany himself, because he wasn't as nasty, domineering, or controlling as before. It'd only been three months since the heart attack, but so far, Charles II had behaved decently. All Charles could do was hope it was a permanent change.

As for him, Charles was wildly in love with Lisette, who glowed more from her pregnancy every day. After the first trimester had ended and she felt well again, they told everyone. The household staff had been surprisingly supportive—luckily, they all loved Lisette, so they were happy for her happiness. Tina and Eileen, of course, were like excited aunts, and Charles was grateful. His siblings were equally supportive and happy for them. His father had been livid, and Charles didn't care. And when they had told the children about their soon-to-be brother or sister, the children had been over the moon about the baby, and happy that Lisette was going to be an official part of the family.

Charles grinned to himself. He intended to make that permanent. Discreetly, his hand went to his pocket to feel for the small velvet box. Yup, still there, safe and sound.

"I'm back," Lisette said from behind him. "Close your eyes."

He did as she asked. "They're closed. Are you naked?"

"What?" She laughed hard. "You're incorrigible."

"Well, this is a private villa," he said. "No one can see us.

I thought maybe you were going to seduce me out here on the deck or something."

"No, that's not my surprise, but I can do that later."

A hot surge of lust rushed right to his groin. "Ohhh. Yes, please. Now, can I finally have my surprise?"

He felt her brush up beside him, felt her lean into him. "Okay," she said. "Open your eyes."

He opened them slowly. She was holding a picture of something in front of him. He peered at it closer, then felt his breath hitch. "Another ultrasound?"

"Mm hmm." She smiled, luminous and happy. "Charles . . . we're having a girl."

His eyes flew to hers. "It's a girl?"

"Yup." Her smile widened, the sweetness and joy in her expression enveloping his heart with love. "Surprise."

"Best surprise ever!" He pulled her into his arms, kissing her hard and holding her tight. "Another girl. I'm so excited!"

"I'm so glad you are," she said between kisses. "I hope Ava will be happy."

"Are you kidding? She'll be thrilled." Charles looked into Lisette's warm brown eyes. His sweet, beautiful Lisette. This woman had brought so much light and joy into his life. He only hoped he could give her half as much as she'd given him. He planned to spend the rest of their lives achieving that balance.

He reached into his pocket and palmed the velvet box. "Sweetheart, there was a reason I wanted to bring you to such a magnificent place. I have a surprise for you too."